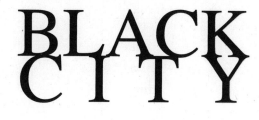

BLACK CITY

BLACK CITY

ELIZABETH RICHARDS

G. P. PUTNAM'S SONS
AN IMPRINT OF PENGUIN GROUP (USA) INC.

G. P. PUTNAM'S SONS
A division of Penguin Young Readers Group.
Published by The Penguin Group.
Penguin Group (USA) Inc., 375 Hudson Street, New York, NY 10014, U.S.A.
Penguin Group (Canada), 90 Eglinton Avenue East, Suite 700, Toronto, Ontario M4P 2Y3, Canada
(a division of Pearson Penguin Canada Inc.).
Penguin Books Ltd, 80 Strand, London WC2R 0RL, England.
Penguin Ireland, 25 St. Stephen's Green, Dublin 2, Ireland (a division of Penguin Books Ltd.).
Penguin Group (Australia), 250 Camberwell Road, Camberwell, Victoria 3124, Australia
(a division of Pearson Australia Group Pty Ltd).
Penguin Books India Pvt Ltd, 11 Community Centre, Panchsheel Park, New Delhi—110 017, India.
Penguin Group (NZ), 67 Apollo Drive, Rosedale, Auckland, 0632, New Zealand
(a division of Pearson New Zealand Ltd).
Penguin Books (South Africa) (Pty) Ltd, 24 Sturdee Avenue, Rosebank, Johannesburg 2196, South Africa.
Penguin Books Ltd, Registered Offices: 80 Strand, London WC2R 0RL, England.

Published simultaneously in Canada. Printed in the United States of America.
Design by Ryan Thomann. Text set in Sabon.

Library of Congress Cataloging-in-Publication Data
Richards, Elizabeth (Elizabeth Fleur), 1980– Black City / Elizabeth Richards. p. cm.
Summary: Ash, a sixteen-year-old twin-blood who sells his addictive venom, "Haze," to support
his dying mother, and Natalie, the daughter of a diplomat, discover their mysterious—and forbidden—
connection in the Black City, where humans and Darklings struggle to rebuild after a brutal war.
[1. Fantasy. 2. Race relations—Fiction. 3. Drugs—Fiction. 4. Social classes—Fiction. 5. War—Fiction.]
I. Title. PZ7.R37953Bl 2012 [Fic]—dc23 2011051631
ISBN 978-0-399-15943-5
1 3 5 7 9 10 8 6 4 2

For Mum and Pops

1
ASH

AN AIR-RAID SIREN wails in the distance, alerting Black City citizens to lock their doors and turn out the lights. They don't want to be out in the dark alone. They might meet something dangerous. Something like me.

I head under the canal bridge and wait for the girl, taking a packet of Sentry-regulation smokes from my back pocket and sparking up. The nicotine courses through my veins, making them throb with adrenaline; the sensation is almost like a pulse . . . *almost*.

Footsteps approach the bridge, and a short girl with straggly black hair appears from the shadows, dressed in men's work boots, tight black trousers and a tailcoat made from a patchwork of clashing fabrics. Her hazel eyes gaze up into mine. She's brave. Not many cherry-poppers have the courage to look me in the eyes. She hands me an old playing card with two hearts on it, one red, one black. It's my calling card. It seemed an appropriate choice; that's what I'm selling her after all, an illusion of love. I slip it into the pocket of my dark green military jacket.

"You're late," I say. "Last thing I need is to be caught out here after curfew by a Tracker. They're just begging for a reason to throw me in jail."

"Sorry, they've put up extra checkpoints, stopping everyone. There's tanks everywhere!" she babbles. "I guess they can't be too careful with the Sentry Emissary back in the city, what with the boundary negotiations with the Legion and—"

"You paid Beetle?" I interrupt.

The girl nods.

"Terms and conditions," I say. "No refunds. You don't enjoy it, you puke, you freak—not my problem, okay?"

She nods again.

"You pregnant?" She blushes furiously. "I'll take that as a no. It may cause drowsiness, so don't drive or operate any heavy machinery." She smiles at this, and I grin. They always like that. "And no repeats for at least two weeks, all right? I mean it."

"That all?"

"No kissing. Strictly business, okay?"

She seems a little disappointed by this, but I don't like to mix business with pleasure. She shyly unbuttons the collar of her coat, revealing her slim, pale neck. Hunger grips my stomach at the sight.

"What do I do?" she asks.

"Lean back," I say.

She obeys like a good girl. I place a hand against the wall and slip my other hand between her thighs, gently easing her legs apart. Touching her doesn't turn me on, but I groan like it does, knowing she'll enjoy that. They all do, even the guys—it's why they come to me instead of the Haze dens. I slide my body between her thighs so we're face-to-face. Her shallow breaths are warm against my cool skin.

"Relax, okay? It's more enjoyable if you relax."

"My heart's pounding a mile a minute." She gives a nervous laugh.

"Can't say I know how that feels," I admit.

She tentatively presses a hand against my chest, and her eyes widen. "So it's true, then? You don't have a heart?"

"I have a heart," I growl, shoving her hard against the wall. *It just doesn't beat.*

A small tear snakes down her cheek, her thin lips trembling.

"Sshhh, it's okay, sweetheart. I didn't mean to frighten you." I gently wipe her tear away. "Forgive me?"

She nods, then tilts her head to one side, exposing the smooth whiteness of her neck. The poison sacs behind my fangs swell with venom.

Focus, Ash. Don't blow your load.

I lean toward her, pressing my lips against the soft flesh on her neck, just below her ear. Her pulse flutters under my lips, and I nearly lose it. I begin to nibble on the flesh, tickling the tiny hairs on her neck with my tongue, making them wet with my saliva.

"Do it," she whispers.

So much for foreplay. I sink my fangs into her jugular. Hot blood spills over my tongue, making my taste buds burst with its sticky sweetness. Man, I love the newbies; they always taste the best. She sighs as my venom enters her bloodstream. I wait for the Haze to take effect before I start to drink from her. That's the bonus of Haze; my clients get high from me, and I get high from them by drinking their drugged blood. It's win-win.

A sour, bitter flavor suddenly floods my mouth, and I gag, leaping back.

"What the—" I spit up blood.

The girl stares at me with glazed eyes, blood trickling down from the two puncture wounds in her neck.

"Everything's sparkling," she says dreamily.

"Didn't Beetle tell you I don't take clients on meds?"

She lurches toward me, and I grab her before she falls into the water.

"I love you," she slurs, trying to kiss me.

I shove her, hard. She falls back against the wall and slides to the ground. Her eyes roll back into her head, and she begins to spasm, white foam bubbling out the corners of her mouth.

"No, no, no! Wake up." I kneel down and shake her, panic rushing through me.

The girl jerks, her boots leaving black scuff marks on the cobblestones. *Fragg!* This is why I don't take clients on meds. You can never tell how they're going to react to the Haze. I shrug off my jacket and place it under her head.

A Sentry tank rolls over the bridge, and I shut my eyes and wait for it to pass. Even though the war is officially over, I still get chills at that sound. Wherever they went, Death followed. I had a few close scrapes during the war. During those days, the fact that I was a legal citizen and half human didn't mean much to them. If you weren't 100 percent human, you were the enemy. Every day was a fight for survival. Not much has improved since then; I'm still the enemy in most people's eyes. All they can see is the Darkling in me. The tank turns down Bleak Street toward the Sentry Emissary's headquarters.

The girl groans. It's too dangerous here; I have to go. *I could just leave her* . . . No, that's not an option, but I can't take her to the hospital. I'd get in so much trouble.

Beetle!

I peer down the canal. A yellow barge is moored about one

hundred feet away. The lights are off. Where is he? He's meant to be my wingman; that's why I came to the bridge in the first place. *Can this get any wor—*

An explosion of pain bursts inside my chest, and I clutch a hand over my lifeless heart. I sense someone behind me and turn.

A girl stands by the entranceway, lit by the headlights of a passing truck. In the fleeting light, I catch a glimpse of cornflower-blue eyes flicking between me and the Hazer writhing on the ground.

Her gaze finally fixes on me.

I fall back, struck down, as the pain in my chest blooms again.

Shivers run through my body, rushing toward a single point in my chest. There's a spark of electricity and then:

A flutter.

2

NATALIE

"**I DIDN'T SEE ANYTHING,** okay? I'm not looking for trouble," I blurt out, fear spiking in me.

The boy clutches his chest, like he's in pain. He looks up at me with sparkling black eyes, and my heart stumbles and races to catch up with the beat. He blinks, shakes his head like he's trying to remember where he is, while my head spins as it dawns on me that I somehow *recognize* him. But how? Even in my panicked state, my brain's able to process the fact we haven't met before. I sure as hell would've remembered him. I don't need to see his fangs to know what he is: hair like black fire and glittering eyes are all the evidence I need. A twin-blood Darkling.

I should be running a mile—every instinct is screaming at me to leave, but my feet are glued to the ground, my body paralyzed, as memories I've repressed all year flood my mind: a pair of white fangs, my father's anguished face, blood spraying across the ceiling.

The drugged girl beside him moans, her dark hair falling away from her face. She looks just like my sister, Polly.

"Help me," she whispers.

I hesitate, uncertain. What if she were my sister? Would I leave Polly here with *him*?

My decision is made for me when a Sentry truck pulls up on the road overhead and the engine cuts out. I dart under the bridge and press my back against the mildewed wall, placing a finger to my lips. A moment later, a door opens and footsteps echo along the road above us. The Darkling boy tenses, glancing up at the sound.

"I'm sure I saw her," a voice says above us. *Sebastian.*

There's silence for a moment. I shut my eyes and pray he leaves.

A man snorts. "She's more bloody trouble than she's worth." The deep voice sounds like Kurt, one of Sebastian's troop leaders.

"I suggest you hold your tongue—unless you want me to cut it out?" Sebastian says.

"Sorry, chief," Kurt says quickly. "I didn't mean any disrespect."

"Let's try down Bleak Street," Sebastian suggests.

They head off on foot. I let out a long sigh, and so does the twin-blood Darkling boy. We warily eye each other for a few seconds. I doubt he'll attack me when there are Trackers so close by. He's a twin-blood, not one of those mindless Wraths, so he'd understand the risks to himself if he attempted it. This thought eases my mind a little.

"Thanks," I say to him.

"No worries, blondie. Any enemy of the Sentry is a friend of mine," he drawls.

A strange sensation pulls at my heart as I take a step toward him. I pause. *That's odd.* I take another step. It happens again, a definite tug this time, drawing me closer to him, despite the warning voice inside my head that's telling me to keep my distance.

I kneel down beside him and the Hazer girl, my black tulle skirt fanning around me.

"What happened?" I say, turning the girl's head, revealing the two puncture wounds. "Haze?"

He nods.

"She needs to go to the hospital," I say.

"That's not going to happen. She knew the risks."

"She could die."

He shrugs. "Not my problem. I'm not getting executed for her."

I glance down at the girl again and anxiously bite my lip, drawing blood. Big mistake. The Darkling boy's head snaps up, his nostrils flaring, and the air around us sparks with static. His gaze is like a thrilling darkness sliding over my body, cold like winter's frost, leaving a trail of goose pimples where his eyes have touched me.

The Sight.

It's a force Darklings use to mark their prey in order to ward off others of their kind. I've only been touched by the Sight once before, the night my father died. The Darkling boy slowly surveys me, his eyes drifting to the shiny red scar cutting across my skin over my heart, visible beneath the fine lace of my corset. I hurriedly cover the scar with my hand, and he drops his gaze, breaking the spell.

Footsteps approach the bridge, and my stomach leaps into my throat. Sebastian and Kurt have returned.

"Let's get back to headquarters," Sebastian says to Kurt as he climbs into the truck. "Natalie's probably gone home."

"She better have," Kurt mutters. "The Emissary will have my head if her daughter gets chomped by a rogue Darkling. Bloody nippers, I don't know how they keep getting over the wall."

The Darkling boy's eyes narrow. "You're the Emissary's daughter?"

Fear tiptoes down my spine. I gulp, realizing the danger I'm in.

"I don't want any trouble," I say.

"Too late for that, blondie." The corners of his mouth curl up to reveal his fangs.

I hurriedly edge away from him. My back slams into the cold stone wall. I'm trapped.

The Hazer girl groans.

"I think she's going to be okay. There's no need for anyone else to get involved," I say, panic rising in my voice.

We eye each other steadily, waiting to see what's going to happen next. There are only two options: he lets me go and trusts I won't report him. Or he kills me.

My heart bangs against my chest. I hold my breath, waiting.

He snarls. "Tell anyone about me, and you're dead."

He gets to his feet, and in a flash, he's gone.

3
ASH

THE BLACK COBBLED STREETS are deathly quiet as I head home, but that's normal at this time of night. You'd have to be suicidal or insane to be out here after curfew. I'm still deciding which one I am.

I hurry home, knowing it's unlikely I'll encounter any more trouble tonight but not wanting to push my luck. The soot-encrusted Cinderstone houses on either side of me smolder in the dark, still burning after last year's air raids that destroyed the city.

I can't resist running my fingers through the soft ash coating the walls of the houses, staining my skin black. *Black.* That's the color of my world here: black streets, black buildings, black skies. Black everything. I've almost forgotten what color looks like.

A memory of the Sentry girl's blue eyes flashes across my mind, and my chest tightens. What happened back under the bridge? I swear I felt my heart . . . what? Stir? I laugh. The idea's so stupid; my heart's never moved a millimeter in my whole life. It just sits lifelessly inside my chest. It must've just been the bad blood from that Hazer girl. That can mess you right up. *Yeah, that must've been it.* I can't allow myself to hope.

Above me, digital screens the size of billboards dominate the rooftops, looking out of place against the Gothic architecture of the centuries-old buildings. The screens broadcast continual footage from SBN, a government-owned network. It only shows propagandist messages, advertisements and news stories promoting the Sentry government.

A female voice booms out from the monitors. "And now a message from your government."

A pair of penetrating silver eyes appears on the screens.

I recognize them immediately. They belong to Purian Rose— the spiritual leader and head of the United Sentry States. A message rolls along the bottom of the screen: *His Mighty sees all sinners.*

Chills run through my body, and I quicken my pace. I instinctively head down City End and stop dead in my tracks. Why do I always end up here, even when I don't mean to? I stare up at the Boundary Wall, a stone wall over thirty feet high, covered with posters of Purian Rose urging citizens to vote for Rose's Law. The wall divides the city in two, segregating the humans from the Darklings. It would take you over a day to walk around the entire circumference of the wall, which encloses the Darkling ghetto known as the Legion, the largest of its kind anywhere in the United Sentry States. Every city in the USS's nine megastates has walled ghettos just like this one, keeping the humans and Darklings apart.

Behind the Boundary Wall is a second, smaller wall covered in spikes and barbed wire, and beyond that . . . *my family.* All my Darkling relatives live over there: my aunts, uncles, cousins. I turn away, not wanting to deal with this tonight, and take the longer route home to the Rise, the district in the northernmost part of the city where the poorest residents live.

There are five superdistricts in Black City: the Rise, the Park, the Chimney, the Legion and the Hub, where the Emissary's headquarters are located. There are nine Emissaries in total, one for each of the country's nine megastates, and our Emissary is the *worst*. It sucks she's back in the city; things were so much better when she was evacuated to Centrum during the air raids last year.

I duck under the flimsy wire fence that surrounds the Rise. The fence is a rather halfhearted attempt to keep out any Wraths that have escaped over the Boundary Wall. They're feral Darklings infected with the deadly C18-Virus, and they roam the streets hunting those foolish enough to still be outside after curfew. Idiots like me.

I sneak through the sleepy cobble streets, dimly lit by cast iron oil lamps, following my usual path home. The Rise earned its name because of the hundreds of high-rise apartment blocks that dominate the city borough. The Sentry government had to erect some tenements quickly after Black City was bombed, and they've never bothered to come back to finish the job. Several of the buildings are already falling down, threatening to topple at the slightest touch. Six months ago, one of the buildings collapsed and killed over a hundred people. It didn't even make SBN news. No one gives a fragg about us.

I approach two derelict high-rises, which lean against each other like sleeping giants. Nestled in the crevice between them is an old church, its gray stone walls strangled by ivy, the bell tower leaning slightly. *Home.* Outside the church are a dozen apple trees, bursting with deep red fruit, which Mom planted to make the graveyard look less gloomy. Mrs. Birt's ginger tabby cat sits on a nearby headstone and hisses at me as I pass. I growl back, and it scrams.

I take another pace, then pause. The hairs on the back of my neck prickle. I peer into the gloom, in search of movement, but see nothing. *Huh*. I must be imagining things. I reach the front door and scowl. Fresh graffiti is sprayed over the dark wood, just two words painted in large red letters: RACE TRAITOR. The letters are smudged where Dad's tried to scrub the words away. I sigh and go inside.

Dad's sitting in one of the church pews, waiting for me. He seems to have aged another year since I left the house this morning. His thick brown hair has gotten grayer around the temples, his beard more disheveled, his blue eyes duller. It's difficult to believe he's the same man who used to make Mom giggle like a schoolgirl just by smiling at her.

"Where have you been?" he asks.

"Out," I say.

"Where's your coat?"

"Lost it," I say, which isn't technically true. I know exactly where it is: under the Hazer girl's head. Maybe I'll swing by tomorrow and see if she left it. I loved that jacket, got it off a Darkling Legion Liberation Front freedom fighter during the war, just before he got captured by a Tracker.

I walk past Dad toward the pokey room at the back of the church. Propped against the padlocked door leading down to the crypt is a rusty old camp bed where Dad sometimes sleeps when he's not down in there, which isn't very often. I don't think he's seen daylight in weeks, not since *she* came back. I turn my back to the crypt door, not wanting to look at it, not wanting to think about what's behind it.

The rest of the room is taken up with a small table and a

few kitchen appliances. The room's filthy, with grime on the walls and dirty dishes piled high on every surface. On the floor are several crates filled with tinned food; donations from the locals to hand out on our next charity run. Around the kitchen table are three chairs: one for Dad, one for me, and one chair that hasn't been occupied in eight years. Slung over the back of it is a Lupine-fur coat, which Dad gave to Mom on their wedding day.

I pick up the coat and press my nose against the silvery fur. I almost believe I can smell Calder lilies on it, the scent of a much happier time. A familiar pain bunches up in my chest, and I carefully put the coat back on the chair.

On top of the cluttered table is a mountain of bills. I pick them up, and my mind wanders back to the Sentry girl. What had the guards called her? *Natalie*.

I dolefully sift through the bills, trying to focus my mind on other things, but my mood worsens with every red letter. I'll need to get some new clients to pay for all of this, and the idea sickens me. I hate getting the kids at my school hooked on Haze, but I have no choice. It's that or we're out on the streets. That's not good in a place like Black City.

"Are you going to tell me where you were?" Dad says as he enters the kitchen.

"Library. I was returning some books," I lie.

"You risked being caught outside after curfew to return some books?"

"What can I say? The library fines are astronomical."

"The library burned down last week."

Oh.

"Heavens, Ash, if anyone catches you out after curfew—"

"I *know*."

"You have to be more careful. Trackers are crawling all over the city now that the Emissary is back in town."

He doesn't need to remind me. After the Emissary was evacuated last year, only the general police force—the Sentry guard—was left behind to control the city. Now she's back to open negotiations with the Legion to extend their territory, and the city is swarming with Trackers, a specialist military unit dedicated to hunting one thing: Darklings.

I toss the bills on the table. "I was getting some money for us. Someone's got to pay for all these!"

Dad narrows his blue eyes at me. "What have you been doing?"

I rub the back of my neck.

"I told you not to deal Haze anymore!" Dad yells. "What if they catch you? Honestly, sometimes I think you're trying to get yourself killed."

My mouth twitches.

"Do you want to die?" Dad persists, on a rant now.

"I already *am* dead."

"Just because your heart doesn't beat doesn't mean you're not alive."

"You don't understand," I say quietly. "You have no idea what it's like to be a freak. How can you? You're human; you're nothing like me."

Dad has a heartbeat, and Mom even has two. Yet somehow I ended up with nothing but a stone-cold lump inside my chest. No matter how many times he tries to explain it—my heart doesn't beat because it doesn't need to, the symbiotic protozoa in my blood feeds oxygen to my organs instead; it's just one of the many weird and wonderful side-effects of mixing human and Darkling DNA—it doesn't make any difference. I'm still a monster.

"I don't want you going out at night anymore," he says.

I let out an irritated sigh.

"I'm serious, Ash. I don't want any Trackers sniffing around here asking questions."

"Okay, okay," I mumble.

Dad goes to a drawer and pulls out an envelope.

"This came through the mail," he says quietly.

Dad hands me the envelope. Inside are a pamphlet and a copper wristband. I scan the contents of the leaflet:

DARKLING REGISTRATION ACT

ON THE ORDERS OF PURIAN ROSE, head of the United Sentry States: Darkling citizens living in Sentry territory must wear Identification bracelets at all times. Failure to comply will result in death.

I examine the wristband. There's some text engraved on it: *Ash Fisher #000121 Property of Harold Fisher, Ivy Church, the Rise.*

I inhale sharply. "They can't be serious. I'm not a dog! I'm no one's property."

"I'm sorry, son," Dad says, unable to meet my eyes. "Just promise me you'll wear it. I don't want you getting into any trouble."

I swallow back my shame and slip on the wristband, not wanting to give Dad any more reasons to be worried about me.

I cover the band with my sleeve, but I still know it's there. It's humiliating. In the space of a few minutes, I've gone from being someone's son to being his pet.

"At least this way a Tracker won't mistake you for a rogue Darkling," Dad says, his voice strained.

"Yeah. Look, it's no big deal; it's just a wristband," I lie, whether to him or to myself, I'm not sure.

I glance at the padlocked door leading to the crypt.

"Has she eaten?" I say.

Dad shakes his head. "I was waiting for you."

I go to the fridge and take out a sachet of Synth-O-Blood, a synthetic form of O-positive blood. The Sentry engineered it shortly after war broke out eight years ago, in order to feed the thousands of Darkling citizens they'd forcibly relocated to the Legion ghetto, behind the newly constructed Boundary Wall. They were the luckier ones who managed to bribe, bargain and fight their way into the ghetto, knowing it was their best chance of survival. The rest were sent to "migration camps" in the Barren Lands. Now the only Darklings you'll find on this side of the wall are a few domesticated housemaids, some trespassers hiding out in Humans for Unity safe houses, rogue Wraths and *me*. The last twin-blood in Black City.

Dad moves the camp bed and unlocks the padlocked door. We walk down the stone steps in silence. The crypt stinks of death and decay. In the center of the room is a battered armchair, a discarded book on the armrest. I force myself to look beyond it toward the creature hunched in the corner of the room.

She stirs.

My grip tightens around the bag of blood.

"I've . . ." I clear my throat, which is dry like cotton. "I've brought you some dinner."

The creature growls, tugging at the chains holding her to the wall. I slide the sachet of blood across the floor, and it comes to a juddering halt in front of her. She rips into the sachet and slurps at the blood with her black tongue, splashing blood all over her partially rotted face, revealing the full length of her long, curved fangs.

I sit down on the armchair, watching from a safe distance. The Wrath virus isn't airborne, but I'm still at risk if she bites me. Tears prick the corners of my eyes, and I angrily wipe them away. Dad's right. We have to be careful with the Trackers back in town. I glance over at the creature.

They mustn't know about Mom.

4
NATALIE

I HURRY UP the gleaming white steps to the Sentry's regional HQ, my new home. One wing of the white marble building is still being reconstructed after it was blasted during the air raids, but otherwise it's come out relatively unscathed. Not like everywhere else in this city. It probably wasn't our forefathers' smartest idea to build Black City using cheap Cinderstone bricks, as once they start burning, they're impossible to put out. But it takes immense heat to start the reaction, and how would they know that, centuries later, our "great leader" Purian Rose would firebomb the city and everyone in it?

I miss the Sentry headquarters in Centrum, the state capital of the Dominion State, where we spent the past year after we were evacuated from Black City. It was much nicer than this one; simpler, less ornate. I've never liked Black City HQ, and neither did Father—he didn't think it was a safe place to raise a family, which is why he insisted we live in the manor house on the outskirts of the city when I was growing up. *He couldn't have been more wrong.* But now here I am, back in Black City, a place I never wanted to see again.

I pass several Sentry guards by the front doors, and they salute me. I swipe my identity card over the scanner and step inside the sterile entrance hall. Tucked under my arm is the twin-blood Darkling's coat. The Hazer girl gave it to me, saying she didn't want it, and just holding it sends shivers down my spine.

I should be grateful nothing seriously bad happened tonight; it was reckless of me to walk the city streets alone after dark, but I just wanted to get some souvenirs from my old house for my sister, Polly.

I never did make it to the mansion after bumping into that twin-blood boy. I still don't quite understand why he let me go. Maybe he just wanted to get out of there fast and leave me to deal with the Hazer girl? Another shudder ripples through me. *Tell anyone about me, and you're dead* . . . I'm not going to tell. There's no point—I'll never see him again.

Besides, I don't want to give my mother an excuse to increase my security. My bodyguard, Sebastian, is more than enough for me, thank you very much. At least I can wrap Sebastian around my little finger and occasionally get some freedom.

I head straight for the stairs, intending to find Polly, when the blond-haired receptionist raises her head and looks at me.

"Emissary Buchanan's expecting you. She's down in the laboratory."

"But I'm not allowed in the labs . . . ?"

She shrugs. "Emissary Buchanan was very clear that you're to meet her down there."

I don't have a chance to put the Darkling boy's jacket anywhere, so I take it with me as I walk to a glass elevator, confused as hell as to why I've been asked to go to the labs. Why's

Mother letting me down there now? The elevator doors start to close, but a hand darts through them, prying them back open. Furious green eyes glare down at me.

"I've been looking all over for you," Sebastian snaps, stepping into the elevator beside me.

"You didn't have to come running after me."

Sebastian clenches his jaw and punches the basement-floor button. The elevator slowly descends as we stand in silence, attempting to ignore the tension simmering between us. I can see his reflection in the glass, and my eyes trace the contours of his face: wide eyes, framed by brows that seem to be permanently knotted together; tanned skin newly darkened with day-old stubble; the small freckle on his lower lip that I've kissed a thousand times.

Never again.

My mind drifts to the boy under the bridge, and that tugging sensation I felt before pulls at my heart again. *Weird.*

"So?" Sebastian says.

"What?"

"Are you going to apologize for making me worry like that?" he says.

"Are *you* going to apologize for hunting me like some Darkling?"

"You're being dramatic."

"All I wanted was a few minutes alone, and you couldn't even let me have that. You're always following me."

"It's my job," he says impatiently. "Your mother *asked* me to guard you."

"I don't need a babysitter. And for your information, the only reason she gave you the job is because I stupidly asked her to." *Back when I still loved you.*

The elevator doors ping open. I push past Sebastian and walk out onto a metal platform overlooking a laboratory.

Sebastian grips my wrist. "Okay, fine, I admit it. I was following you, but so what? I care about you. Why can't you accept that?"

"Why can't you just accept the fact that we're over? We've been over for months."

"Because I can't. I love you."

I yank my arm free from his grip. "You don't love me. You just want to date me because you think it'll help your career."

His eyes darken. "Don't pretend it hasn't crossed your mind that we'd both benefit from the arrangement. I'd buy you anything you want; I'd keep you in the life you're accustomed to. I'm going places, Natalie. I'll be the next Purian Rose one day, and I want you by my side when that happens."

"As tempting as that 'arrangement' sounds," I say sarcastically, "I'd never be your girlfriend again, not after—"

Mother's voice rings up from the laboratory below.

"When will the new strain be ready, Craven?" she asks.

"A few weeks. I think we've singled out the gene that's causing the problem," Craven replies.

"You better have. I can't afford any more screwups," Mother says.

"Natalie's back," Sebastian calls down to them.

"Come down—it's time you saw this," she says.

We head down to the laboratory, a claustrophobic space of concrete and steel, and I'm excited to finally see what's down here. To our right are four doors leading into small cells.

"What's in there?" I ask Sebastian.

"The specimens, of course."

Specimens? I gasp when I glimpse them through the cell windows.

Darklings.

Dozens and dozens of them, crammed like cattle into each tiny cell. I'm too stunned to move at first, horrified by the sight in front of me. As frightened as I am of Darklings, seeing them cramped together like this is still shocking.

In the first cell is a pack of Shu'zin Darklings—the purple-eyed, claw-footed creatures commonly found in the Copper State—shackled to the walls with heavy silver chains. All their hair has been shaved off, so it's hard to tell which ones are male and which are female. They look back at me with glazed eyes, their expressions blank, like they're already dead.

Sebastian pulls my arm, urging me on, but I have to see for myself what's been kept hidden from me all these years. In the second cell, a small colony of Nordin Darklings hang upside down from the ceiling, their silky wings wrapped around their bodies. They're the rarest of all Darklings, from the now-uninhabited volcanic regions in the Mountain Wolf State, famed for their flame-colored eyes and ice-white hair. They're the only breed of Darkling with wings, and the one I fear the most. The Wrath that killed my father last year was a Nordin Darkling.

Sebastian taps the window on one of the cell doors, taunting the Darklings inside.

"We found whole families of them hiding in safe houses around the city," he says. "I don't know what goes on in their tiny brains. They know it's against the law to climb over the Boundary Wall, and yet they continue to do it anyway."

My father must be turning in his grave. He wanted to help the Darklings after he witnessed the horrors of the migration camps in the Barren Lands. He spent the last months of his life secretly working for them, and what did he get in return? A Wrath murdered him.

We carry on walking. I can't see what's inside the third cell with a silver marker above the door because the window is closed. Finally, I look into the last cell. A teenage boy sits on the floor, his head hunched over, his back to me. I can't see his face, but the dark hair and pale skin are familiar. *It's the twin-blood! They found him!*

The boy turns his head, sensing me. It's not the twin-blood boy at all, but an Eloka Darkling—the most common breed found in the majority of states across the country—his face half rotted away from the Wrath. Revulsion crawls through me.

Mother and Dr. Craven, Sebastian's father, stand beside a gurney in the center of the room, dressed in bloodied surgical scrubs. A Darkling is strapped to the gurney; at least I assume that's what it is. It's hard to tell when they get so ravaged by the Wrath, a plague that's been killing the Darklings. All that remains are bones and teeth, barely concealed beneath a jelly-like membrane.

My chest starts to tighten, and I take a deep breath, worried I'm going to have a panic attack if I don't get out of here soon. I feel like a fish in a shark tank, surrounded by all these monsters. If I'd known the lab would be filled with Darks, I wouldn't have come down here.

"Do you know what time it is?" Mother says.

I innocently glance down at the antique wristwatch that used to belong to my father. The bronze casing is tarnished and the numbers are faded, but the unusual ivory watch face still has a beautiful golden sheen to it, like it's been painted with a shimmering varnish.

"Well?" Mother presses.

"Sorry," I mumble.

"You're *sorry*? I had half the guard out looking for you. Do you know how dangerous it is out there? We have a curfew for a reason. What if you got attacked by a Darkling?"

An image of the twin-blood Darkling boy pops into my head. I bite my lip.

"I thought you'd grown out of this silly business of sneaking out at night. I wish I knew what you were thinking sometimes, Natalie," she says.

Then why don't you just ask? But she never does. Mother likes to do all my thinking for me. That way I can be the perfect, dutiful daughter she wants. Maybe if she left me alone once in a while, I wouldn't have this constant, yearning need to escape. Roaming the streets at night is the only time I feel free.

"I'm cutting off your allowance for one month," Mother says.

"But—"

"That's final. And no more nighttime jaunts, do you understand, young lady?"

"Yes, Mother."

The Darkling on the gurney lets out a pitiful moan and turns its yellow eyes on me. They're eerily empty, and I realize what's missing: hope. Rattled, I look away, not wanting to feel sorry for this creature, even though a part of me does.

Craven lowers his surgical mask and gives me a toothy smile. He's tall, like Sebastian, and they have the same green eyes. The only difference is his hair, which is bronze and wiry, while Sebastian's is blond and wavy. Craven's the head of the Anti-Darkling Science and Technologies Department, where they make weapons to defend us from the Darks.

"You've grown big since I saw you last," he says.

"It's been a year. I'm sixteen now."

"I hope my son took good care of you down in Centrum?" he asks.

"Of course I did," Sebastian replies.

A jumble of emotions twist in my stomach. At least Sebastian has the decency to look ashamed. He came to live with me, Mother and Polly when we were evacuated to Centrum, and Craven was ordered to stay behind in Black City to continue his work. Sebastian was assigned to me as my personal bodyguard, and it was a great setup until . . . *until the thing happened.* I hate thinking about it.

"What are you doing with that Darkling?" I ask Craven.

"Testing a new anti-Wrath spray," he says cheerfully, pointing to an aerosol on his workbench.

It has the words GO AWAY WRATH SPRAY! written on it in blocky red letters. *Another spray?* They seem to release a new one every month. I guess it's a lucrative market; everyone is terrified of being attacked by a Wrath. It's a dreadful way to die.

"It's just a prototype, but it's very effective. Watch." Craven picks up the aerosol and sprays a foul-smelling gas over the Darkling on the gurney. The creature instantly writhes in terrible pain.

Sebastian covers his nose from the rotten scent, while I put a hand over my mouth to mask my shock. *This isn't science, it's torture.*

"Wonderful work, Craven," Mother says.

I've seen enough.

"Can I please go?" I ask Mother.

"Don't be so sensitive. It's just an animal," Mother snaps. "You need to toughen up if you're going to work here."

"What do you mean?" I ask, confused.

"You've been accepted to the Fast-Track Science program," Craven says. "After you complete this year at school, you'll be my new intern. I thought you'd want to see where you'll be working for the next five years of your life. I promise I won't be a complete slave driver."

"Congratulations," Sebastian says.

My shoulders slump, thinking this must be some sort of joke. "I applied for the Political program."

"I didn't think a political career was right for you," Mother says.

"So you changed my application without even consulting me?"

"I know what's best for you. Not all of us are cut out to be politicians, Natalie," Mother says.

"But—"

"Don't be ungrateful. Very few people get on the Fast-Track, and Craven pulled a lot of strings to get you on the Science program."

Why didn't Mother "pull a few strings" to get me on the Political program like I wanted? The money and career prospects are so much better; not to mention, all my friends back in Centrum signed up for it. I don't want to be the only one not doing it. It's so embarrassing, especially since my mother is the Emissary.

"Cheer up, pumpkin. Working with me won't be so bad," Craven says.

I somehow doubt that. There's no way I want to be involved in his "science experiments." This must be evident on my face, because Mother lets out a tired, exasperated sigh—a sound I'm all too familiar with. My whole life has been one long disappointment to her. I'm sick of it.

So Mother wants me to toughen up? Fine! I make my expression as cold and steely as possible, determined to act like I'm not bothered by what's happening around me, when all I really want to do is run away.

Craven turns his attention back to the Darkling on the gurney. The creature lolls its head in my direction again, and my eyes are drawn to its chest, where two hearts pulse rhythmically underneath its transparent skin. One heart is considerably smaller than the other, but beats much faster.

Craven notices me looking.

"The bigger heart is the primary heart. And this is the dual heart," he says, pointing to the smaller one. "Typically they don't beat, but we have seen some instances, like this one, where it has activated, although we're not sure how or why. It's fascinating really, almost as intriguing as twin-blood physiology. What I wouldn't give to get my hands on one of them. A living creature with no heartbeat—"

Sebastian yawns loudly. He hates talking science.

Craven mutters under his breath as he picks up a syringe and sticks the needle in the Darkling's arm. Gooey blood quickly fills the green-capped phial, and the Darkling lets out a pitiful howl, spraying spittle everywhere. Some of it lands on my face, and I hurriedly wipe it off.

"I'm not going to catch the Wrath now, am I?" I panic, thinking about the contaminated gunk that was just on my face.

"No, pumpkin." Craven chuckles. "So far the virus has only affected Darklings, twin-bloods and a few isolated wild dogs, but they have to be bitten or drink infected blood to contract it."

I don't like the way he says "so far," like there's a chance it'll spread to humans.

He puts the blood sample on the sideboard, beside a row of sharp wooden stakes.

"So are you ready for your big day tomorrow?" he says.

I can't believe he wants to talk about school, here of all places. Then I remind myself I'm supposed to act like this doesn't bother me.

"Do I have to go? Why can't I just be homeschooled?" I say.

"Because Purian Rose demanded you go to the city school," Mother says, and a chill runs through me at the mention of his name.

"Why?" I ask.

A knowing look passes between Mother and Sebastian.

"Because Purian Rose said so. Those are his orders, so you'll do as you're told," Mother says.

"I'll have nothing in common with the other kids. They're all Workboots. They'll hate me," I say.

There's always been a tension between the proletarian class, known as Workboots because of the ugly leather ankle boots they all wear, and the Sentry—the ruling class. Only Sentries can work for the administration, which is why it's called the Sentry government; it's just a way to remind the Workboots of their place in society.

"It's not fair. I liked my *Sentry* school filled with my *Sentry* friends," I continue.

"Just do as you're told, Natalie," Mother snaps. "I don't want you making Purian Rose angry; you know what he's like. Do you want to put your sister at risk again?"

"No," I whisper, a thrill of fear rising in my throat.

Sebastian throws me a sympathetic look. He knows all about what happened to Polly. I confided in him when we were dating, and Mother told Craven, since he's the closest thing to a friend she has in Black City.

"Do you want me to stay with Natalie, make sure she gets settled in?" Sebastian asks.

"No! Mother, *please*. I don't need a bodyguard when I'm in school. It's perfectly safe," I say.

Ever since Polly got hurt, Mother's made sure I've had a bodyguard watching my every move. It's so smothering.

"He can drop me off in the mornings and pick me up every afternoon," I offer quickly. "Please. I don't want to be the only student with a bodyguard. It'll make me more of a target, if anything."

Mother considers this. She looks at Sebastian. "Make sure you bring her straight there and back each day, no dillydallying."

"Yes, Emissary."

"I'll call the Headmaster and arrange for one of the girls to keep her company," Mother replies.

"I don't need a rent-a-friend," I say.

Mother slaps me with a silencing look.

The creature on the gurney beside me stirs, and I force myself to ignore it.

Mother notices the Darkling boy's coat still slung over my arm. "Where did you get *that*?"

"I traded for it," I say quickly. "I thought I'd wear it to school, so I can fit in with the rest of the kids." Actually, that's not a bad idea!

"No daughter of mine is wearing Workboot clothes."

"It's going to be hard enough fitting in as it is. I need to look like them," I say.

She opens her mouth to protest.

"Oh, before I forget!" Craven says a little too brightly as he

takes a lab pass and a bottle of pills from a drawer and tosses
them to me. "There's enough medication there to last you for
the month. And I've had your lab pass activated; feel free to
pop down whenever you want and I can show you the ropes.
Welcome to the team."

I turn the bottle of heart medication over in my hand. I can't
stand having to be so reliant on these tiny white pills. *Just one
more thing controlling my life.*

The Darkling on the gurney suddenly wails in pain, making
the other Darklings in the cells around us howl in unison. Craven picks up a wooden stake from the sideboard and plunges
it twice into the creature's chest, penetrating its two hearts. It
thrashes for a few seconds, spraying blood and spittle everywhere, before collapsing lifeless onto the gurney.

"Was it really necessary to kill it when I was standing so
close?" Sebastian complains, wiping Darkling gunk off his red
jacket.

"It was the humane thing to do. It was in pain," Craven replies. "The acacia wood kills them instantly. Better this than to
die of the Wrath."

He glances at Mother, who returns a frosty look.

Craven opens a metal drawer, pulls out a pale green surgical
sheet and covers the Darkling's dead body with it. Blood soaks
through the material, reminding me of my father's blood seep-
ing through his clothes . . .

I have to get out of here right now.

I rush upstairs to Polly's room. She's the only person I want
to be around these days. She's sitting in a plain wooden chair in
front of the windows, staring at the drawn curtains, her hands
folded in her lap. She doesn't acknowledge me, but I don't expect her to—she barely speaks since the night Father died. The

doctors say it's post-traumatic stress. Sometimes she's totally lucid, and it's like I've got my old sister back, but most of the time she's trapped inside her own mind, not talking to anyone for days—sometimes weeks—on end.

Our housemaid, Martha, has already unpacked her clothes and belongings, not that my sister has much need for clothes, since she spends all day in her bathrobe and slippers. All around the room are pictures of Polly: photographs of her at ballet recitals and school plays; paparazzi shots taken of her at glitzy events; posed black-and-white portraits by the famous artist Kendra, which Mother paid through the teeth for. She's so exquisitely beautiful in all of them. It was always her dream to be a big-shot actress in Centrum, and now that's never going to happen. I don't know how she can stand having the photos all around her, reminding her of what she's lost.

Sebastian's in some of the photos. They were in the same year at school, and he was infatuated with her, the way I was obsessed with him. When she turned him down, he opted for second best: me. Not that I cared at the time, I was just thrilled that such a good-looking older boy would want to date me. I know I'm nothing in comparison to Polly. She's tall, with silky straight black hair and gorgeous silvery gray eyes, while I'm short, blue-eyed and have wild curly blond hair like my father's. You'd barely think we were related.

I place the twin-blood boy's green jacket on the floor by Polly's feet and open the curtains. The starlight illuminates her face, highlighting the patchwork of scars across her skin. One side of her face is almost unrecognizable, the shredded flesh contorting her once-beautiful features. It's weird, though. I hardly register the scars anymore; she still looks like my big sister to me.

Polly's silver eyes drift to the green jacket on the floor.

"I found it. Well, I didn't exactly *find* it." I tell her about meeting the twin-blood boy in the underpass. "It was insane— he could've killed me. If Mother found out, or Purian Rose . . ."

She glances up at me.

"I won't do anything silly like that again, I promise. I won't risk anyone hurting you."

She grips my wrist and pulls me close, the sudden movement surprising me. Her expression is intense.

"Don't be afraid to do what's right. Don't let Father's death be for nothing."

She releases me, and her eyes glaze over, lost in that dream world of hers again. Sometimes I envy her; it must be nice not having to live in this reality. I kiss her forehead, pick up the jacket and head to my bedroom, her words ringing around my head. *Don't be afraid to do what's right.* How can she still think that after everything that happened to her and Father? She was always braver than me.

I enter my room and kick aside the unopened cardboard boxes that clutter the plush white carpet. The balcony windows have been left open all day, and it's wintry cold in here, but that's how I like it. I drop the dark green jacket beside my pillow and chuck my pills into my battered satchel.

Martha is hanging up my new black and red school uniform in my wardrobe. She's the only Darkling I can tolerate being around these days, and that's only because I've known her my whole life. Besides, she's no threat. All domesticated Darklings are neutered when they start working for a Sentry family.

I sigh, flopping onto my king-size bed.

"Do you want me to unpack these boxes?" Martha asks.

"No, I'm never unpacking them. I'm not staying. As soon as

the boundary negotiations are over, I'm on the first train back to Centrum."

She gives me a sad smile. We both know we're never moving back to Centrum.

"Oh, before I forget. I have a gift for you." I rummage around one of the cardboard boxes until I find the small square box wrapped in fancy paper and pass it to Martha. She carefully unwraps it and opens the box to reveal a bangle made from twined strands of white and yellow gold.

"I've had it engraved," I say.

Martha reads the inscription: *Martha Zhao #00118 Property of Natalie Buchanan, Black City HQ, the Hub.*

"It's your new identity bracelet. Do you like it?" I ask.

Martha nods slightly, not saying anything. She must be overwhelmed; it's a very expensive gift. She slips it on.

There's a low hissing sound by the balcony windows, and my kitty, Truffles, leaps off the balustrade and pads into the room, his golden eyes fixed on Martha. Despite being a tiny speckled fur ball, he has the attitude of a cat ten times his size. He hisses again at my housekeeper.

"I should go before that cat attacks me," Martha says.

She leaves, and Truffles pounces onto my bed and sits on my lap. I scratch the back of his velvety pink ears.

"So where have you been, huh?" Truffles purrs and rubs his nose against my hand.

He climbs off my lap and sniffs the green jacket draped over my pillow, then lets out a questioning meow. I rummage around the pockets, curious to see what's inside. All I find is a handful of loose change, a packet of cigarettes and an old playing card. The design on the back swirls and weaves around itself, like it's alive, creating new designs every few seconds. I flip the card over and lightly trace my fingers over the two hearts: one red, one black.

I chuck the jacket on the floor and lie back, looking at the ceiling. When we were kids, Polly and I used to play a version of I Spy where we'd search for patterns in the textured plaster. *I spy a lion, a three-eared rabbit, a phoenix, the face of a Darkling boy . . .* My eyelids start to become heavy. I quickly slip into a deep, troubled sleep, my dreams filled with nightmarish visions.

I'm standing inside a dark, empty cave. The space is vast, terrifying, and instantly I know something is very, very wrong. The walls are strange. I stretch out my hand and touch the smooth stone, expecting it to be cold and hard, but instead it's warm and slick. I withdraw my hand. My fingers are sticky with blood.

Somewhere in the dark, something stirs. I'm not alone.

Fear rises up inside me. I remember I've stolen something, something precious, but I can't remember what it is. All I know is that they want it back. I have to get out of here before I'm discovered. I try to move, but my feet are stuck in the wet, spongy earth. I sense the Thing getting closer, searching for me. I try to remain calm, but then it happens. The cave starts to close around me. Panic boils over as the walls get closer and closer, until they're squeezing me. I can't breathe, I'm being suffocated, I—

I wake up with a start, my skin drenched with sweat, my heart pounding a mile a minute. I've been having the same nightmare ever since I was a little girl, and it still scares me. I take one of the pills Craven gave me earlier and pad over to the balcony to get some fresh air.

From up here, the buildings glow like embers. In the distance

I can just make out the dark line of the Boundary Wall. Centrum seems like a lifetime away. I hate being back here. My insides feel hollow. I have no one: my father is gone, my mother barely registers my existence, and my sister is like a zombie most of the time.

Truffles saunters outside to meet me, letting out a pointed yawn.

"Cats are supposed to be nocturnal, you know?" I say.

He meows at me and leaps onto the marble railing.

"At least I have you," I say.

His hackles rise, and he dashes back inside my bedroom.

I peer into the gloom, trying to see what it was that spooked him so much, but find nothing. *Crazy cat.*

Still, I'm unable to shake the unnerving feeling that someone was just watching me.

5
ASH

"GET UP, YOU LAZY ASS!"

I throw a stone at the yellow barge moored on the canal, close to where the Haze appointment was last night. The Hazer girl's not lying dead on the ground, so she's either alive or there's a zombie strolling around the city somewhere wearing my jacket. The stone bounces off the barge's rotting wooden wall, then plops into the water. There's no sign of life. *Right, you asked for it.* I push against the barge with all my might, rocking it until Beetle's pale face appears in one of the boat's dusty windows. He idly scratches his scruffy brown hair, then sticks his middle finger up at me. I laugh and jump onto the barge.

There's no polite way of putting it; Beetle's room is rank. There are stinking clothes heaped in piles on the floor, cigarette butts ground into the threadbare rug and several dinner plates with something green and furry growing over them. On the wall is an old Legion Liberation Front poster, featuring a stylized black-and-white photo of Sigur Marwick—the Darkling ambassador and former civil rights activist—looking defiantly into the distance, toward a "better tomorrow." Hatred boils inside me.

"Love what you've done with the place," I say.

This earns me another flip of the bird.

My eye catches sight of a small glass phial of Haze partially hidden under his bed.

"What in the hell are you doing with this?" I say, picking it up.

He scratches his tangled hair, not meeting my eyes.

"Did you get this from Linus?" I demand, referring to the punk-ass dealer who's been trying to steal my clients.

He gives a faint nod.

I toss the phial out the small cabin window, too furious to say anything. I've spent months trying to wean Beetle off Haze; now he goes and does *this*. Given his dilated pupils, it's a safe bet he's still high.

"You look like crap," I say.

His hair is all over the place, he's skinny as a worm, and I can smell him from here. It's not his fault; his aunt Roach isn't interested in raising a kid. All she cares about is Humans for Unity.

"You don't look so hot yourself," Beetle says.

He has a point. I've been up all night expecting the Sentry guards to bang down my door and arrest me, but they never showed. It could only mean one thing: that Sentry brat Natalie didn't tell anyone about me. *Good.* My threat must've gotten through her stupid blond head. I light up a cigarette and take a long drag. *Fragging Sentry.* The world would be a better place without them in it, but I can't see that happening any day soon.

"Ash?" Beetle's voice comes back into focus.

I blink. Has he asked me a question?

"How did it go last night?" he asks for a second time.

I flash him an angry look. "Where were you?"

He points to a bunch of freshly painted placards stacked up against the wall. "My aunt kept me at Humans for Unity all night painting those."

I tilt my head to read the upside-down words: ONE CITY UNITED! and NO BOUNDARIES! and SAY NO TO ROSE'S LAW!

Rose's Law. Just the thought of it makes my fangs pulse with venom. It's a law the Sentry government's trying to pass to keep Darklings and humans permanently segregated. The Emissaries of the nine megastates have been tasked with persuading the citizens of their respective states to vote for Rose's Law in the referendum later this month. If it gets a majority vote, it will become federal law. When you consider that every major city has a Darkling ghetto, just like the one we have here in Black City, the impact will be enormous. Darklings will never be free again.

Of course the Emissaries are making a show of acting like the Darklings have any say over their fates by holding boundary negotiations with them next week to discuss moving the wall and giving the Darklings more space. Anyone with two brain cells can see it's just a PR stunt to stop the Darklings from causing trouble in the lead-up to the ballot, in the desperate hope they might expand their territory. It's their last opportunity, and they know it.

I point to the placards. "I'm guessing these are for the boundary negotiations next week?"

"Right on, they are. Those Sentry bastards can't keep the Darklings stuck behind the Boundary Wall. It has to come down, period. If we tell Rose where to shove his segregation laws, maybe the other cities will rise up as well."

I grunt a response. I'm not interested in lost causes.

He stretches like a cat, and his blanket slips down below his waist.

"Are you allergic to clothes?" I say, looking away.

"It's how Mother Nature intended us to be, man."

I shake my head. "Come on, we're gonna be late."

He quickly pulls on his crumpled uniform, and we walk to school. Beetle doesn't say anything as I cut across Bleak Street, over the streetcar tracks, and turn down City End, even though it's going to add an extra five minutes to our journey. He understands. We stroll the length of the Boundary Wall, sneaking in another smoke before school. I hand him the roll-up and drag my fingers over the rough concrete wall, trying to picture what life's like on the other side. An unexpected bubble of hope rises in me at the thought that maybe, just maybe, the wall will come down one day, but it quickly bursts. I need to stop chasing dreams. I'm alone in this city—why can't I just accept that?

The digital screens on top of the buildings around us flicker as a new ad plays. It shows a beautiful woman with blue eyes and glossy red lips.

"Citizens! Need an ID bracelet for your Darkling domestic help? Then come to Smithers, Smythe and Sons, the best jewelers in town. Don't delay, they're selling out fast!"

Text across the bottom of the screen reads *Darklings found without an ID bracelet will be executed.*

"Can you believe it, bro?" Beetle says, shaking his head. "Before you know it, they'll be making every Darkling wear them, even you. It's disgusting."

I subconsciously rub the copper band around my wrist, hidden beneath my shirt.

"Yeah . . . it's terrible," I mutter.

I don't want to tell him about the bracelet. He'll just use it as another reason I should join their stupid protest next week.

I sense someone moving about on the Boundary Wall above me. A Legion guard stares down at me with sparkling, curious eyes. He's dressed head to toe in black robes, his pale face hidden behind black cloth to protect him from the sun. I know why he's looking. I'm quite the celebrity in the Darkling world, thanks to my mom.

A steam-powered streetcar rattles along the tracks beside us, billowing black smoke into the charcoal sky. Most vehicles these days are steam-powered or horse-drawn, because of gas shortages. Only the Sentry guard is allowed gas for their trucks and tanks. Workers are crammed into the streetcar like cattle, dressed in their simple gray overalls and leather work boots. They turn their dull, distrustful eyes on me.

One of the workers, a man with a shaved head and a rose tattoo above his left ear, smacks me with a murderous look. "Hey! Go back to where you belong, nipper!" He spits at me as the streetcar passes by. It splats on my boot.

"Fragg!" I mutter, wiping my boot against the dirt.

"Forget it. Those Purity types are pathetic," Beetle says.

Disciples of the Purity, the new religion that's sweeping the nation, led by Purian Rose, all shave their heads and get a rose tattoo above their ears to prove their love, faith and loyalty to him. As if it weren't enough for Purian Rose to be the leader of our country, he now has to be our messiah too. It's not the law to follow the faith *yet,* but I bet it'll be in the cards soon enough.

"Come on, we're late," I say irritably.

We round the bend. I smell them before I see them: three

dead figures hanging silently from the wall, their heads drooped against their chests, their bodies naked, their hands bound. They look like grotesque scarecrows, which is what they are: a warning to any Darkling or human who tries to get over either side of the wall. One of the scarecrows is a human; the words *race traitor* are carved into his flesh. The other two are Darklings, their skin yellowed and gangrenous, signs they had the Wrath just like Mom. I scrunch my nose as we pass, blocking out the worst of the smell.

"How's your mom?" Beetle asks quietly.

He's the only person I've told about her being back with us.

"I don't think she's got long left." My voice cracks as I speak.

He suddenly stops.

"What?" I say.

He points to a poster on the wall. There's a photo of a teenage boy on it, wearing horn-rimmed glasses. Above his photo are the words WANTED: TRAITOR.

"That's Tom," he whispers. "He went AWOL from Humans for Unity a few weeks ago. We think he left the city."

"It's probably best if he has." I wonder what he did to get on the Sentry government's Most Wanted list.

We walk the rest of the way to school in silence, both knowing Tom's probably already dead.

We slow down as we approach Black City's only surviving secondary school. Something isn't right. There are camera crews and Sentry guards everywhere—it's like a circus. But that isn't what's caught my attention. In the far corner of the plaza, a group of workmen are erecting three imposing wooden crosses.

"What are those for?" Beetle asks quietly.

I shrug, but it can't be good.

Near us, a red-haired reporter dressed in a corset-blouse and skintight patchwork leather pants argues with one of the Sentry guards, waving her press pass in his face. I recognize her as Juno Jones from Black City News.

"I'm allowed to be here. Since I last checked, I still have the right to free speech!"

The guard shoves her, and I catch her before she falls. Her eyes widen when she sees me, but she quickly composes herself.

"Thanks," she says. "Nice to know chivalry isn't completely dead in this city."

"What's going on?" I ask.

"The Emissary's making a big announcement."

"Move it along," the guard snaps.

Juno rushes off in a different direction before she can tell me any more about it, no doubt looking for a more sympathetic guard she can charm.

When Beetle's distracted, I show my ID bracelet to the Sentry guard, then we join the rest of the school in the town square, standing at attention in a sea of black and red uniforms. To the east and west of us are the skeletal remains of burned-out buildings. I stand in their jagged shadows, staying out of the direct sunlight, although my skin still prickles like red ants are crawling all over it. Flakes of ash peel off the buildings' scorched walls and rain down on us like black snow.

Just one soot-encrusted building remains to the north of the square, the old town hall that's been converted into the Black City Secondary School. It was only opened last year, after the war ended. *Shame it didn't burn down too.* Three Gothic spires twist out of the school's gray slate roof, the tallest of which contains a tarnished copper clock that chimes the hour with a low, melancholy sound.

I risk a look behind me at the Boundary Wall running along

the south side of the plaza, trying to imagine what the town square would look like if it weren't there. I can't picture it. The wall's been here too long; I barely remember a time without it.

In the center of the wall are the massive iron-armored gates, the only safe passage in and out of the Legion ghetto. Guarding the gates are dozens of Sentry guards, while on the wall itself stand rows of Legion guards. No one gets in or out without their permission, not that many people try. You need top-level clearance to move freely between the two sides of the wall, and only a handful of government workers and the Sentry guard have that sort of access. If you want to get over the wall, you have to climb it and just pray you don't get caught.

I think about the scarecrows hanging on the wall and shudder. I could've been hanging up there with them if the Sentry girl, Natalie, had told on me last night . . . My chest cramps, the sudden pain making me inhale sharply.

"You all right?" Beetle asks.

"Heartburn," I say, unable to think of another explanation.

"I didn't realize you got that. What with your heart not working . . ." He trails off when he sees my expression. "Must be that cheap Synth-O-Blood the Sentry's trying to pass off as food. The fascists probably engineered it that way."

"I don't think heartburn's at the top of their Agenda of Evil."

"I wouldn't put it past them. Phase One of their diabolical plans for world domination. When was the last time you had any real blood?"

"I had a drop last night from that Hazer girl, but I spat most of that up. Otherwise, it's been a while." You can only buy human blood from the black market traders in Chantilly Lane, but I don't have that sort of money to splash about. "Why? You offering?"

Beetle chuckles. "Only if you buy me dinner first."

There's a sharp *whip* against my leg.

"Ouch, mother—"

I turn to see Gregory Thompson, the head Prefect, sneering up at me, cane in hand. The Prefects are a group of students who have the authority to discipline the rest of us. He's short for his age, barely reaching my chest, but what he lacks in height he makes up for in arrogance. He flicks his lank hair out of his watery, deep-set eyes.

"Why aren't you wearing your beret, nipper?" he says in a nasally voice.

I take the crumpled scarlet beret out of my pocket and put it on. It immediately falls off. Hats and Darklings really don't mix. My hair's alive, always moving, searching the air around me for traces of blood. There's blood everywhere, if you're looking for it. A shaving cut on a girl's leg, a grazed knee, a split lip. It's overwhelming here.

Behind Gregory is his fraternal twin brother, Chris, who follows Gregory everywhere like a shadow . . . a very tall, sickeningly attractive shadow. When it comes to genes, Chris certainly got the lion's share. Gregory is small, mean and aloof, while Chris is athletic and approachable and always has a smile on his face—but that's probably because he's high as a kite most of the time. He's one of my best clients. The only similarity between Gregory and Chris is the bright hazel color of their eyes.

Chris languidly picks up my beret, passing it to me.

"Thanks," I mutter.

Chris gives me a nonchalant nod, thrusting his hands into his pockets.

Gregory eyes me angrily.

"What's your problem?" I ask.

"*You're* my problem, nipper." He jabs at me with his cane, and I grab it, pulling him toward me.

"Back off. You're not a Tracker yet." I snap the cane in half with a flick of my hand.

Gregory whips me across the face with the remaining half. "That just earned you a detention after school, mongrel."

My cheek stings where he hit me, but I refuse to let my pain show.

"Leave him alone, Greg," Chris sighs.

"They should never have allowed you to come here," Gregory says, ignoring his brother. "Things were better before they agreed to let your sort into our schools."

Before the war ended, I had to be homeschooled by Dad. Those were the days.

"Well, tough," Beetle interrupts. "Ash is a citizen, the same as you and me, so he's got to come to this stupid place like the rest of us. It's the *law*."

"Not for long. When Rose's Law passes, the first thing they'll do is make sure half-breeds like him in every city are sent to the ghettos with the rest of the nippers, where they belong," Gregory says, stomping off.

Chris rolls his eyes at me, mouthing "sorry" as he passes.

I touch my stinging cheek and turn back to face the school. A bookish-looking girl with caramel-colored skin, wearing wire-rimmed spectacles and a pristine red beret, walks up the school steps, her long dark hair swishing around her shoulders. She stands beside four empty chairs, her hands held awkwardly in front of her.

"What's Day doing up there?" Beetle asks.

I quirk an eyebrow. "Why do you care what she's doing up there?"

"No reason, just saying." The tips of his ears turn pink.

"Is it because you *love* her?"

"Shut up."

"You want to kiss her."

Beetle punches my arm. "Oww!" he says, shaking his bruised fist.

"Reinforced bones, my friend." I laugh. There are a few perks to being a twin-blood.

We stand at attention as the Headmaster steps up to the microphone beside Day. Behind him a Sentry flag flutters on the breeze. It has two horizontal stripes, one red, one black, and at its center is a rose emblem, a recent addition to the flag, symbolizing the Purity faith.

"Good morning, school!" the Headmaster's voice crackles across the town square. He raises his arm in the air, palm facing us, and we all follow suit.

The school begins to chant. "I vow to serve the savior of our great state, Purian Rose—"

I move my lips but don't say the words. Beetle's making up his own rude lyrics, and I try not to laugh. I remember Dad's warning: *act like them, don't stand out, keep your head down.* Yeah, easier said than done when you're a foot taller than everyone else and have a set of deadly-looking fangs. I'll never fit in.

"I pledge my eternal devotion to the United Sentry States, to uphold the mighty Human Power! To create one state, one race under His Mighty," the school continues, Gregory speaking loudest of all. "Long live the Sentry!"

The sound of hooves reverberates around the town square,

and a moment later, an ornate State carriage drawn by six Cremello horses enters the square from one of the side roads. It drives past the students, who crane their necks to see who the passengers are, although it's impossible to tell behind the curtained windows. TV cameras pan around to face the carriage, which comes to a halt beside the school entrance. I feel a strange tugging in my chest as I wait to see who's inside.

The Headmaster beams. "I am delighted to announce that we have some very special guests visiting today. Please give them a warm welcome."

A footman opens the carriage door, and five people get out. They walk up the school steps.

"I don't believe it," Beetle growls under his breath.

The first person is a waspish woman, whom I recognize immediately as Emissary Buchanan, flanked by two older men. They're dressed in long black robes with a red rose emblem on the chest—the uniform of the Sentry Council. The fourth is a teenage boy, a few years older than me, wearing a crimson military coatee, black trousers and boots—the uniform of the Trackers. On his sleeve are three black stripes indicating his high rank. The other visitor is a blond girl, her back to me, a familiar green jacket slung over her arm. She turns her head, nervously scanning the faces in the crowd, and her blue eyes snag on mine. Her mouth drops open into a perfect O, mirroring my own surprise.

It can't be her!

6
NATALIE

✺ *IT CAN'T BE HIM!*

A chilling coldness creeps over my skin as he stares at me across the plaza. What he's doing here, of all places? He didn't seem like the going-to-school type. His threat still lingers in my mind. *Tell anyone about me, and you're dead . . .* That odd, yanking sensation pulls at my heart again, like it did the last time I saw him.

"You okay?" Sebastian whispers to me.

I nod and plaster a fake smile on my lips, knowing my image is being broadcast to every TV in Black City right now. Slung over my arm is the twin-blood boy's jacket, and I wish more than anything I hadn't brought it now, but how was I to know he'd be here?

Across the square is the Boundary Wall. I shudder at the sight of the Darkling guards patrolling the top. *Why did Mother agree to let me come here?*

There's a movement to my right. The girl next to me forces a smile. She must be my new rent-a-friend. I turn back to the crowd and discover the twin-blood is still looking at me, his pale lips set in a grim line.

The Headmaster's metallic voice rings out over the crowd.

"I have the great honor of introducing you to Natalie Buchanan, the Emissary's daughter. She'll be joining us as a student today, so please make her feel welcome." The *or else* is implied.

My cheeks turn pink as the heat of everyone's gaze falls upon me, *his* being the most intense of them all. I hate people looking at me. I wish the ground would open up and swallow me whole.

The clapping dies down, and Mother moves to the microphone. Silence falls over the town square, until all I can hear is the faint static buzzing from the microphone. When Mother speaks, her words aren't just for the hundreds of students in front of us, but for everyone watching at home too.

"We have all faced difficult challenges as we've struggled to rebuild our great nation after the war ended almost one year ago, and no one has suffered more than the people of this city. The Sentry government understands this better than anyone, and we've allowed many misdeeds to go unpunished in our efforts to make this transition easier for you. However, the time for leniency is over."

My eyes find the twin-blood boy in the crowd again, and I'm surprised to see he's watching me, instead of my mother. He turns his head away. Mother continues her speech, and I pretend to be interested. We must keep up appearances for the press, right?

"You will notice the new addition to your town square." Everyone's eyes turn to look at the three crosses looming over them. "Purian Rose believes our compassion for you has allowed this city to be corrupted by sin, and it's time we purged it out.

From now on, any citizen caught guilty of committing a grievous crime against the United Sentry States will be executed."

There are hushed gasps from the crowd. Mother takes a moment to let her words sink in.

"That's outrageous!" Juno Jones yells from near the school steps. "What qualifies as a 'grievous crime against the state'? We all know where this is leading! Before you know it, no one will have the right to free speech. No freedom of the press. We'll be no better off than the Darklings."

Mother subtly waves her hand, and like magic, a handful of Sentry guards swoop in on the reporter and drag her down one of the side alleys. Her screams are swiftly muffled. No one else speaks out; no one else dares. Mother gives a smile that doesn't reach her eyes.

"Of course, in order to help purge the city of this sin, we will need *your* assistance," she says. "As such, I am lowering the minimum age to become a Tracker, and invite you all to take the test to see if you are eligible to join them."

This news is met with mixed responses from the students. Some cheer wildly, but the majority remain mute.

"The Trackers will come to your school next week to run the examination," she continues. "The test is mandatory for all children between the ages of fifteen and eighteen. Anyone found to have the V-gene will be automatically enlisted to the Trackers. Thank you."

It takes a moment for people to start clapping, as they're too stunned to respond. *An army of children?* What's Purian Rose thinking? Even during the war's darkest days, children were always kept safe from combat.

"I thought the war was over," I whisper to Sebastian. "Why does he need more Trackers?"

He doesn't say anything, but his silence speaks volumes. He knows something's going on and is keeping it from me.

The bell rings, and the students quietly file into the school, giving the three crosses a wide berth.

"I'll meet you here straight after school," Sebastian says, before escorting Mother back to the carriage.

The reporters hurriedly pack up their equipment, clearly shaken by what happened to Juno Jones when she was dragged away and beaten. A crisp wind cuts across the square, stirring up the thin layer of ash that's settled on the ground. I shiver and slip on the twin-blood boy's jacket and search for him in the crowd, but he's gone.

7
ASH

I ENTER THE SCHOOL behind the other students, Beetle by my side. My blood pulses at the thought of Natalie Buchanan. The Sentry has invaded every aspect of my life—now they're in my school? I thought her type were forbidden to mingle with us common people. So what is she doing here? And what's she doing with *my* coat, the thieving bitch?

I catch sight of her across the hallway as she's led through the crowd by Day. Students hurriedly get out of her path, letting her through like she's fragging royalty.

"Come on, let's go this way," I say to Beetle, heading in the opposite direction. Just because she's at my school doesn't mean I have to see her.

We head toward the main stairwell, following the stream of students going to their classrooms. We pass a few unfortunate ninth-graders who are getting punished by a group of Prefects, for Lord knows what reason. The Prefects make up any excuse to beat us; it's like a sport to them. My cheek still stings where Gregory hit me earlier.

"I can't believe the government's going to enroll school-children in the Trackers! I'll never join those fascists. No way, man," Beetle says as we climb the stairs. "And did you see those crosses?"

"They were hard to miss," I say.

"It's so obvious Purian Rose is sending Humans for Unity a message. He knows we're rallying support against Rose's Law, and he's bricking it. He doesn't want us uniting with the Dark-lings, so he's trying to scare us off."

I rub my brow. He's probably right. "Look, maybe you shouldn't go to the protest next week. It's not worth dying for—"

"You of all people should be out there with us. Honestly, are you willing to die for anything, bro?" Beetle replies.

I don't respond, rage and guilt silencing me. Why can't he just drop it? I'm not going to die for a pointless cause. Why can't he accept the wall's never coming down? I have.

We head up to our classroom on the fifth floor in bitter si-lence. The room is musty smelling, with rows of wooden desks, the types with slanted lids and decades of graffiti scrawled over them. Above the blackboard is a life-sized portrait of Purian Rose. There's something deeply disturbing about his face, with its unnaturally silver eyes and waxy skin so tight, it would tear if he ever smiled. It's probably lucky he never does.

My desk is in the darkest corner of the room, away from Gregory and, more important, away from the windows. Even though they're covered in wire mesh, I can't risk being exposed to the sun when it gets too bright. I can only just tolerate the dim morning light as it is.

Chris leans back in his chair, arms behind his head, chatting to two of the prettiest girls in the class. Gregory's slouched in the seat beside him, being ignored.

"Great party on Saturday," one of them coos. "Maybe we could go out again this weekend?"

"Sure thing, babe. Why don't we double date?" Chris replies.

The second girl looks at Gregory, who offers her a watery smile.

"I'm busy this weekend," she says, turning her back on them.

The smile slips from Gregory's lips. *Ha!*

"Look, I'm sorry," Beetle says to me as we cross the room.

"Whatever." That's the closest thing to an apology he'll get from me.

"Watch out! Dead man walking," Gregory says as I pass him on my way to my seat.

"Give it a rest, Greg," Chris mutters.

Heat rises up my neck. It's not my fault my heart doesn't beat—I never asked for this. I slump down in my seat. Beetle groans and rests his head on the desk, starting to come down from his Haze high.

"This is room 5B."

I jerk my head up at the sound of Day's voice. She stands by the doorway with Natalie. Something stirs in my chest, the motion as faint as a breath caught on a breeze, so slight I barely register it even happens.

So much for trying to avoid her!

Natalie tucks a blond curl behind her ear and quickly scans the room. She spots me in the corner and boldly holds my gaze. I glare back at her, refusing to break eye contact first. She eventually looks away.

"We come here in the morning and after lunch," Day says, leading Natalie to the two empty seats in front of me and Beetle.

Beetle looks up and the tips of his ears turn pink. He's still got it bad for her, and I sort of see why. She's attractive in a skinny, prim way. Her round glasses slip down her nose, and she irritably pushes them back into place.

"You're allowed in here if it's raining, but otherwise we're expected to stay outside during break," Day says to Natalie.

Natalie hesitates, clearly uncertain about sitting anywhere near me.

"Don't worry, he's not going to bite you," Day says.

"Not unless you ask *real* nice." I show a glimpse of fang.

"Grow up, Fisher," Day replies as they sit down.

"Aren't you going to introduce us?" Beetle asks Day.

She lets out an exasperated sigh. "Natalie, this freak of nature is Matthias."

"Beetle. No one calls me Matthias," he corrects her.

Day turns to me. "And this charmer is Ash."

"Nice coat," I say. "I had a jacket just like that, before some Sentry brat stole it."

"Maybe she didn't steal it? Maybe she found it under a bridge after some lowlife dreg left it behind?" Natalie replies. "Of course, she could just hand it to the Sentry guard. I'm sure they'd be *very* interested to find its real owner."

I narrow my eyes at her. *Just you dare.*

"Hey, isn't that your coat, bro?" Beetle says.

Day gives Natalie a quizzical look. "Do you know each other?"

"We had the displeasure of meeting last night," she says.

"I want my jacket back," I say.

"Tough. Finders keepers," she says.

I curl my fists under the desk.

Beetle lets out a moan and rubs his forehead. He's getting the Haze Headache, one of the unpleasant side effects of coming down from the drug. Day narrows her dark eyes at him.

"Are you *high*?" she spits.

Beetle's guilty look in my direction is all the answer she needs. She whips around on me.

"I don't believe you, Ash Fisher! It's not even nine in the morning, and you're already getting Beetle high?"

"I didn't!" I exclaim.

A shadow crosses our desks, cutting off our discussion.

Gregory stretches out a hand toward Natalie.

"I'm Gregory Thompson," he says. "My father works for the Department of Subspecies Management, sorts out the Synth-O-Blood shipments to the Legion, that sort of thing. Maybe you've heard of him?"

Natalie smiles politely. "The name doesn't ring a bell." I try not to laugh. Gregory's making it sound like his dad is somebody important in the ministry, when really he's just a foreman at the Synth-O-Blood factory.

He looks disappointed. "Well, it's an honor to have you here. I'll happily show you around the school—"

"Day's doing that, but thanks," she says dismissively.

"You don't want to be seen with *her* sort, she's one of the Rise kids," he says to Natalie. "I'll set you up with the right type of people to know."

Day's cheeks burn red.

"I can make up my own mind about who the 'right type of people' are," Natalie snaps. "I'm already getting a pretty good idea of who I want to avoid."

He pushes his lank hair away from his eyes. "Of course, my apologies. By the way, may I give you my heartfelt condolences about your father's death last year?"

"Thanks," she mutters.

I roll my eyes, and Gregory turns on me.

"Show some respect, nipper."

I dig my fingers into the edge of the desk, crushing the wood. "Why? All his death meant to me was one less Sentry in this world. That can only ever be a good thing."

Natalie flinches and quickly turns her back on me, but not before I've seen the tears glistening in her eyes.

"Just ignore him. He's a jerk," Day whispers to Natalie.

Gregory smirks at me and skulks back to his desk.

Natalie wipes her eyes, and guilt crawls through me. I immediately force that emotion aside. Why should I care if she's upset? She's just a fragging Sentry.

"I don't know how I'm going to get through the rest of the year with *her* here," I say to Beetle through gritted teeth.

"Just avoid her, man," Beetle says.

"I swear, we'll be lucky to make it to the end of the term without killing each other," I say.

I mean it as a joke, but part of me wonders if I'm right.

8
NATALIE

I HURRY OUT of the classroom with Day, eager to get away from Ash, still hurt by what he said about my father. Yet again I'm reminded why Father was wrong to defend the Darklings; they're rude and cruel and don't care about anyone's feelings but their own.

Ash exits the classroom and follows us down the corridor, hatred emanating off him. Rattled, I grab Day's arm and drag her into the girls' restroom. Ash shoots me a loathing look as the door swings shut.

"You okay?" Day asks.

I nod, but my hands are trembling. How am I going to survive being around Ash all year, when one glance from him turns my blood to ice?

"Is Ash such a jerk to everyone?" I say.

"Pretty much," she says. "Just avoid him. That's what I do."

I sigh. That sounds like a good plan. "What's up with that short guy?"

"Gregory Thompson?"

"Yeah. Could he be more of a suck-up?"

Day laughs. "He's a power-hungry troll. He thinks he's so special just because he's Head Prefect. Thanks for defending me earlier. He's really got it in for me."

"Why doesn't he like you?"

"Oh, let me see," she says, tapping her lip thoughtfully. "He hates girls, he particularly hates ones who are *much* smarter than he is, he hates the fact I live in the Rise, he—"

"Basically just hates everything?"

"Pretty much. So I heard you were living in Centrum this past year—is it as amazing as everyone says?" Day asks.

"It's even *better*. You wouldn't believe it, the place is huge. It must be twenty times bigger than Black City, and so cosmopolitan. Absolutely everyone wears the latest fashions, and there's so much to do."

"What about the buildings? Are they really as high as a mountain?"

"Not quite, but close enough."

"And are the streets really paved with gold coins?"

I laugh. "No, but the stones they use do have a metallic sheen to them, so when it's sunny, they sparkle and the whole city turns brilliant gold."

"It sounds wonderful; it's my dream to live there, but I'd never be able to afford it on a typical Workboot salary." Day pushes her glasses up her nose. "So I've applied for the Fast-Track Political program to work for the Sentry government. I really hope I get on it."

I feel a pinch of resentment at the fact I only got on the Science program.

"I'm sure you'll get on it," I lie. The truth is, very few Workboots ever get on the Fast-Track program. The only ones who do are the children of businessmen who've been able to scrape up enough money to bribe the application committee.

"Do you think it's safe to leave yet?" I ask.

She nods, and we head to first period. I'm relieved to see Ash is nowhere in sight. The day goes by in a blur, and by the end of last period, my head is swimming with all the new names and faces I have to remember.

Day walks me to the main entrance, her arms laden with books. I was disappointed to discover we only have four lessons together: art, drama, history and advanced combined science. She's in the advanced classes for all the other subjects, and I'm . . . well, not. I've always been an average student, except at science, which is the one subject I'm actually quite good at, although it's never interested me as a career, even less so now that I know what sort of "experiments" they do.

She chats to me about all the extracurricular activities she's doing to help her Fast-Track application, and I nod occasionally to show I'm listening while all the time keeping an eye out for Ash, making sure I don't bump into him again.

Just when I think I'm in the clear, my heart suddenly yanks. Nearby, Ash walks down the stairs with Beetle. His mouth goes tight when he sees me. For a moment, I can't breathe as we stare at each other.

I blink, breaking the connection.

"Let's get out of here," I say to Day.

Once outside, I immediately spot Sebastian at the bottom of the steps, ready to take me home, back to my prison. He's busy checking out a group of girls as they walk by, so he hasn't noticed me yet. I have a flash of inspiration.

"Can I come home with you and hang out for a while?" I ask Day.

She looks at me uncertainly. "I . . . I don't think—"

"I'll return the favor. I'll even introduce you to my mother. She can tell you all about being an Emissary."

I can see her mind whirring, trying to weigh her options. "You do know where I live?" she says.

I nod. The Rise is a slum and no place for an Emissary's daughter, but I don't want to go home. Not yet.

"You'll really introduce me to your mother?" she asks.

"I promise."

"All right," she says.

"We can't let Sebastian see us, okay?" I tuck my hair into my red school beret to hide my distinctive curls.

We do our best to blend in with the other students as we walk down the stairs, bowing our heads as we hurry past Sebastian. He scans the crowd but doesn't see us. He'll have a complete fit when he knows what's happened, but I'll worry about that later.

The walk to the Rise takes around thirty minutes, and I'm starting to regret wearing my delicate patent shoes, the ones Mother picked out for me. I stop for the umpteenth time to rub my feet, and Day huffs loudly, finally losing her patience.

"These books aren't getting any lighter, Natalie," she says to me, referring to the heavy pile of textbooks in her hands.

"Sorry," I mumble, taking a few from her, embarrassed that I've let her carry them for so long without offering to help. My servants normally do things like that for me.

The constant stops have been a blessing, though. Ash is up ahead, and it's kept us far enough back for him not to detect us. I can't help but notice how everyone else is in groups or pairs, but he walks alone.

The Rise is even more dilapidated and impoverished than I could have ever imagined. The buildings creak and groan under their own weight, and the cobbled streets are running with black water and even blacker rats. The only thing of beauty in the whole place is a rickety old church, covered in bright green ivy that adds a pop of color in an otherwise bleak palette. As we near it, I notice the words RACE TRAITOR have been crudely painted on the door, and I soon understand why, as Ash walks up the pathway and goes inside. Day notices me looking.

"His dad's a Minister of the Old Faith."

I can't hide my surprise at the knowledge that Ash is a *preacher's* son.

We walk a little farther down the street, and I get a few puzzled looks when people recognize me. But then they shake their heads, thinking they must be crazy—why would the Emissary's daughter be in their neck of the woods?

Day's house is a small, one-story Cinderstone building with a corrugated iron roof. She unlocks the door and invites me in.

Her house isn't anything like I expected. Sure, it's way too small—I couldn't possibly live in a place like this permanently—but it's warm and inviting, with bright handmade wallpaper and patchwork curtains that are obviously cheap but pretty nonetheless. I expected it to be much dirtier and drab, but there's actually some color here, and it's very clean, almost as clean as our house.

We're in a small room that seems to be serving as a kitchen–cum–dining room. The wooden furnishings are simple but functional, and on the table in the center of the room is a vase of wildflowers that smells of herbs.

A plump woman with light brown skin and a round, pretty face enters the kitchen from an adjoining room, her arms laden with clothes. She stops dead when she sees me. Her dark eyes flick from me to Day, then back to me again.

Her mouth drops open. "Oh, my—"

"This is Natalie Buchanan, the Emissary's daughter. Nat, this is my mother, Sumrina," Day says quickly.

"It's a pleasure to meet you," I say.

"Mama, can Natalie stay for dinner?" Day asks.

Sumrina nods her head slightly, still dumbstruck.

Day ushers me down a very short, tight corridor toward her room. The passageway is packed with old books from before the war. *Forbidden* books. I study their gorgeous covers, admiring the illustrations, the colors, reveling in the vibrancy of it. All books these days look the same, with Sentry regulation red and black covers. Fear crosses Day's eyes.

"It's all right. I have some contraband books myself," I say, and she relaxes. It's not the worst offense to be caught with forbidden books; it's certainly not considered a "grievous crime." All you'd get is a public flogging, but it still deters most people.

"They're my papa's," Day explains. "They've been here for so long, I don't even notice them anymore; they're just part of the furniture. I totally forgot they were there."

"So your father likes to read, then?" I say as we enter her cramped bedroom, dropping the textbooks on her desk.

"He's a teacher," she says.

She indicates for me to sit on the metal-framed bed, while she takes the hard wooden stool by the desk. The walls of her room are covered with photos of the Emissaries of the nine megastates that form the United Sentry States: the cosmopolitan Dominion State; the mining state of Black River, where Black City is found; the ice-capped Mountain Wolf; the wild and dangerous Barren Lands; the industrial Copper State; the tranquil waters of Golden Sands; the ancient Provinces; the farming Plantation State; and the forests of the Emerald State.

Most of the photos are of Emissary Bradshaw, a fat-cheeked, red-faced man who oversees the Dominion State, where Centrum is located. It's the most prestigious state and the best position for any Emissary to be given. We stayed with him last year when we were evacuated from Black City. He's one of the nicer Emissaries, as these things go. They're not all like my mother; some of them have compassion, such as Emissary Vincent from the Copper State. She recently made it illegal for children under twelve to work in factories.

"I take it you want to be the Emissary of the Dominion State?" I tease.

Day's cheeks turn rose red. "Well, I certainly don't want to be Emissary of the Barren Lands."

I laugh. That job's a poisoned chalice. All the Emissaries who have been sent to the Barren Lands have been killed within a year, either by Wraths or the outlaws who live there. It's a very wild place, and the citizens aren't much nicer. Emissaries only get sent there if they're being punished.

There's not much else in Day's room except a pile of books by her bed. A photo pokes out of one of the novels, and I take it out. The snapshot's of her when she was about eight years old. She's standing outside the church I saw earlier—Ash's home— with her arm looped over Beetle's shoulder.

"You were friends with Beetle?" I ask, taken aback.

"We were an item for a while. We all met at Minister Fisher's church."

"You're not with him now?" I ask.

She shakes her head. "I just use that old photo as a bookmark."

"What happened?" I ask.

"Ash happened," she says bitterly, then adds, "Beetle's parents were killed in the air raids last year. He was crushed, as you'd imagine. He went to live with his aunt, a Humans for Unity nut job, filling his mind with all their dangerous—never mind," she says, getting back on the subject. "Beetle spent a lot more time at Minister Fisher's church, searching for some answers, I guess. He was always on good terms with Ash, but they became best friends. There was no room for me anymore."

"So you don't speak to Beetle because he's close friends with a twin-blood Darkling?"

"No, I'm not friends with Beetle anymore because Ash got him hooked on Haze, and Beetle became a stranger to me. He used to be so ambitious, so smart. We had dreams of moving to Centrum," Day says, her eyes glistening. "But that all changed when he became an addict. He just didn't care about anything except getting high. He skipped school, lost interest in his appearance. He even cheated on me with some Hazer skank when he was tripping." She mutters the last bit.

"I'm so sorry," I say quietly. "Someone I cared about cheated on me too, so I know how it feels."

She gives me a small smile. "I was willing to forgive him if he promised never to do Haze again, but he told me to fragg off. He chose drugs over me. So that was that."

A door slams in the other room, and a deep voice bellows out to greet everyone.

"We're home!"

"That's Papa," Day says, beaming.

We go back into the kitchen, where Day's mother, Sumrina, has already started preparing dinner over the open fire in the hearth. She's changed out of her work uniform and has put on a pale blue, floor-length bustle dress, with intricate beadwork over the corset. The dress is clearly old, probably an heirloom, and somewhat over-the-top for a family dinner. Day's father places a fish wrapped in greaseproof paper on the table, then kisses his wife.

"You look beautiful," he says to her.

"Not now, Michael. We have a guest," she says, shooing him away.

Michael looks at me with inquisitive, bespectacled eyes. He doesn't seem particularly impressed that I'm here. He's quite handsome for a dad, with skin the color of the blackest Cinderstone, a broad nose and a warm smile. Sitting at the table behind him is a young boy, who looks a lot like his father, except his spine is all curved over, like an old man's. I think of Polly when I look at him. Why didn't Day tell me she had a brother? Then again, I haven't mentioned my sister.

Day wraps her arms around her brother and looks challengingly at me. It's the same expression I give people when they see Polly's scars, daring them to say anything. I go over to him and crouch down so we're eye height with each other. Everyone in the room goes silent.

"My name's Natalie. What's yours?" I ask.

He smiles. "Michael Junior Jefferson-Rajasingham."

I hold out my hand. "It's a pleasure to meet you."

He shakes my hand with surprising vigor. Day's father, Michael Senior, laughs heartily.

"Let her go, MJ, before you take her arm off."

MJ grins and lets me go.

Sumrina puts a pile of potatoes on the table.

"You lot peel those spuds."

They each grab a potato. I sit where I am.

Michael Senior looks at me. "We all help prepare the meals in this house, even the guests."

"Dada, you're embarrassing me," Day says through gritted teeth.

"It's okay." I pick up a knife and a potato, wanting to help, but quickly realize I don't know what to do. I've never so much as peeled an orange in my life; anytime I've wanted a snack, Martha gets it for me.

Day shows me how it's done. She occasionally chucks bits of vegetable at her brother, who sticks his tongue out at her. Everyone chats and laughs, and I sit back and watch them. So this is what a normal family feels like? It's nice.

MJ reaches out for another potato, then groans. Michael Senior is by his side in a flash. He soothingly rubs his son's bent back. Sumrina wrings a dishcloth between her hands.

"Did you get any painkillers at the market?" she asks.

Michael shakes his head. "I didn't have any coins left after I bought the fish."

"What's wrong with your brother?" I whisper to Day.

"He has kyphosis, curvature of the spine. He gets really bad back pain sometimes."

"I'll get you some painkillers," I say.

They all turn and look at me, dumbfounded. I bite my lip. Is it really such a surprise that a Sentry would offer to help them?

"I have access to a laboratory. We have lots of medicines; no one would miss a few painkillers," I explain.

"No, thank you. We don't want you getting into any trouble, not for us," Michael Senior says, when what he really means is "we don't want *your* charity."

"Michael," Sumrina whispers, glancing at their son.

He takes a deep breath, then resignedly nods. "Thank you,

Miss Buchanan. That would be very generous of you, if it wouldn't get you into any trouble."

"It won't."

"Thank you," Day says quietly. "Most people treat MJ like he's some sort of freak. But he's not—he's just special."

"I have a sister, Polly, and . . ." My voice cracks a little; it's always so tough talking about her. "She got hurt, and now she's not very well, and people can be really mean to her, so I know what it's like to have people be cruel to the person you love."

"Then you understand?" Day says, smiling a little.

I nod. "We have to protect them."

Michael Senior studies me with curiosity.

"Did you know Dayani's applied for the Fast-Track Political program?" Sumrina says to me, trying to lighten the mood.

"She mentioned something about that," I say.

"We're so proud of her. To think one day our little girl will be an Emissary living in Centrum!" she says.

"I haven't even been accepted yet, Mama," Day says.

Sumrina waves a hand. "A technicality. There's no one smarter or better qualified than you, sweetie."

Michael Senior wipes his spectacles, then puts them back on. "This country will be a better place with a Workboot for an Emissary. It's time we had someone who understands the needs of the working man."

"Not now, Michael," Sumrina snaps.

There's a knock at the front door, and a moment later it opens, bringing in a gust of icy air that makes the fire flicker in the hearth. My heart smashes against my chest as Ash Fisher walks into the room, followed by an older man dressed in a gray preacher's smock, who I presume is his father. They're both carrying crates of food.

The atmosphere in the kitchen drops by a few degrees when Ash spots me sitting at the table. Surprise registers on his face.

He's changed out of his school uniform and is now wearing dark trousers, leather work boots and a fitted black shirt that accentuates every inch of his powerful, muscular frame. He looks at me, *into* me, like he can see every secret I have, every rush of my blood. My pulse races with fear and a much more disturbing, unexpected emotion: *desire.*

I turn away, horrified at my body's reaction to him. It's sick and irrational. He's a *Darkling,* a predator that would gladly rip my throat out, given the slightest provocation. Then why are my cheeks burning so red?

I'm just hot from the fire, that's all.

"Ash!" MJ beams.

"Hey, MJ. I swear you've shot up another inch since I last saw you," Ash replies, ignoring the frosty look from Day. "You'll be almost as tall as me one day."

MJ laughs at this. I doubt anyone will be as tall as Ash. He has to hunch over to stop his head from hitting the low ceiling as he walks over to Michael, passing him a crate of canned goods. It all seems so absurd. Ash is a Darkling, not to mention a Haze dealer. He's a monster.

If that's true, then why is Ash giving Day's family all that food? my father's gentle voice whispers inside my head. *Is that the action of a monster?*

A Darkling murdered you! I angrily silence him.

Great, now I'm having arguments with my own imagination. That's how much Ash Fisher's unsettling me.

"Thanks, Ash," Michael says, inspecting the tinned food. "Look, Sumrina, peaches. Not had them in a while."

Sumrina takes the food, casting an anxious look in my

direction, like *I'm* the person she's most afraid of in this room, not Ash.

Day barely conceals her contempt for Ash as she helps her mother put the tins away. I don't blame her: if he'd got someone I cared about hooked on Haze, I'd hate him too. Haze is one of the worst drugs out there; it's so addictive and destroys lives.

He slides another look in my direction, and the air between us crackles with tension.

"Don't you have somewhere else to be, Ash? Like under the canal bridge?" Day says abruptly, referring to the place where he meets his clients.

Ash's lips tighten into a thin line.

"Well, it was lovely seeing you, Minister Fisher, Ash. I'm sure you've got plenty more homes to visit before curfew, so we won't keep you waiting," Sumrina says, rushing them out the door as fast as possible.

Minister Fisher glances at me, and his mouth twitches. He knows who I am.

"You're right, we should go. I hope to see you at my service on Sunday," he says, ushering Ash outside.

"That was rude. The Fishers are our friends," Michael says to his wife the instant she shuts the door.

A glimmer of fear crosses Sumrina's brown eyes. *She's really afraid of me.* I never thought of myself as threatening before, but when I think about it, I *am* the Emissary's daughter. I can get her family into a lot of trouble for mingling with "race traitors" if I want to, and crush any hope of Day getting onto the Fast-Track program.

Michael Senior watches me from the corner of the room. He's not scared of me; he's not ashamed of the fact he's friends with the Fishers or frightened to voice his opinions on the Sentry. In many ways, he reminds me a lot of my father.

The rest of dinner goes by smoothly, and I'm having such a nice time, I don't notice the night sky rolling in. The wail of the air-raid siren, signaling the start of curfew, surprises us all. I leap up, panicked. Mother's going to kill me!

"I have to go. Thanks for a lovely evening," I say.

"I'll walk you home," Michael Senior says, going to the cupboard to get a can of anti-Wrath spray, which every family owns, no matter how poor they are.

Day follows me to the door. "See you at school tomorrow?"

"I'll speak to Mother about inviting you over for dinner sometime," I say, remembering the deal we made earlier.

"That's okay. I didn't really expect you to do that."

"I want to," I say, and it's true.

I'm hoping Day and I can be good friends. I have a small spark of hope that maybe my life in Black City won't be so awful after all.

9
NATALIE

THE NEXT DAY at school isn't as nerve-racking as the first, mainly thanks to Day. She walks me to all my classes, even though she then has to run to get to her own lessons on time, which is no mean feat with so many books to carry. I don't know how she does it. It really reminds me of my first-ever day at school, and how Polly took care of me. The recollection makes me smile, and I make a mental note to buy Day a satchel the next time I go to the market.

The bell for lunch period rings. I shrug on Ash's jacket, which I've decided to keep because I actually like the way it looks on me—plus I guess I like how irritated he gets when he sees it— and follow the other students out into the corridors. I check my antique wristwatch as students jostle and bustle against me. I'm supposed to meet Day in a few minutes by the cafeteria. I think I remember where it is.

A boy from my homeroom, Chris Thompson, smiles warmly at me as we pass in the corridor, a cute dimple forming in his right cheek. Color floods *my* cheeks, just like last night when I saw Ash Fisher at Day's house. My skin tingles at the memory.

I rub my arms, forcing the sensation away. I don't want to remember the attraction I felt toward Ash, no matter how fleeting it was.

I manage to find the cafeteria, where Day's already waiting for me.

"I need to take my medicine before I eat," I say to her, then add in a lower voice, "I've got the drugs for MJ, but I don't want to give them to you here. I'll get in trouble if anyone catches me with them."

She nods, and we go to the girls' restroom.

"What are those for?" she asks as I wash some tablets down with tap water.

"I was born with a hole in my heart, and I needed a heart transplant when I was eight. I have to take these pills every day and try not to get 'overexcited' about things. It's no big deal." I put the medicine back in my satchel, and take out the painkillers. I pass them to Day.

"Thanks. You don't know how much this will help MJ—he's always in so much pain," she says quietly.

"That's what friends are for," I say.

She smiles. Her glasses slide down her nose, and she impatiently nudges them up again.

"You don't happen to have any new spectacles in that laboratory of yours?" she teases.

I laugh. "Nope, sorry. Hey, do you want to come over to my place tonight? I can't guarantee my mother will be there, but if she is, I'll introduce you. You can sleep over too, if you like."

"I'd love to," she says.

We exit the girls' restroom, stepping into the stream of students. I'm so busy chatting to Day that I don't spot Ash Fisher crossing our path and almost smack face-first into him.

I manage to flatten my back against the door just before we collide.

He glares down at me with sparkling black eyes—eyes that could be considered beautiful on anyone else but him. My heart wrenches, the feeling more intense than ever before. Why does it always do that when he's nearby?

We're standing so close, his cool breath spills over my skin, sending frissons of pleasure down my body until I'm tingling all over. Heat rises up my neck—I'm horrified by the way my body is reacting to him.

"Watch where you're going, blondie," Ash snarls.

That brings me crashing back to reality.

"You're the one who should watch it," I snap back. "It's not my fault your gigantic Darkling body gets in everyone's way. You should come with hazard lights or something."

He growls, flashing his fangs.

I recoil, my mind bursting with images from the night Father died: fangs dripping with venom, a pool of dark blood, my father's face contorted with pain.

I hear someone whimper and realize it's me.

Ash steps back, alarmed. "I wasn't going to bite you."

I nod, unable to speak. Day puts a comforting arm around my shoulder.

"I think you've frightened Natalie enough for one day, don't you?" Day says to Ash.

He takes the hint and leaves, muttering curses under his breath.

Day leads me to the cafeteria and gets me some food, although I don't have much of an appetite. The sensation of Ash's breath against my skin still lingers in my mind.

"You all right, Nat? You look a little flushed," Day says.

"I'm fine, just flustered about what happened with Ash. He scared me pretty good," I say, telling a half-truth.

"You don't need to be afraid of Ash. His bark's worse than his bite, no pun intended," Day says, tucking into her meager lunch. "He may be a Haze dealer and a total jerk, but he's never attacked a person, even when they've been beating the living daylights out of him."

"Do people attack him often?" I ask.

She shrugs. "Not so much now that he's bigger, but when he was younger? Sure."

I find it hard to understand why Ash wouldn't defend himself when he's being attacked. He can't possibly care about injuring a human, can he? He's a Darkling. Since when did they care about hurting humans?

After lunch, we head to our next period: history with Mr. Lewis.

"Hey, where are we going?" I ask as Day leads me outside.

"To the library. We have to enter via the fire exit, since the normal entrance got blasted during the raids last year. Twelve people died. It was horrible."

"I'm sorry," I mumble, like it's my fault. But in a way it is: guilty by proxy. The raids were a "desperate move by a desperate man," at least that's what Craven told me once. The Darkling rebellion—the Legion Liberation Front—was gaining control of Black City. They were winning the war, and the Sentry was about to lose one of their most important strategic strongholds. If Black City fell, the next stop would be Centrum, and then all would be lost. Something drastic had to be done. So Purian Rose ordered an airstrike on the city. It didn't matter whom he killed—men, women, children—just as long as the Legion Liberation Front was crushed and the Darklings surrendered, which they did. Rose's plan worked, but at what cost? Black City and everyone in it were in ruins.

I pull Ash's oversized jacket tighter around myself. Across the town square, several Darkling guards watch us from the Boundary Wall. I shudder.

We're running a bit late by the time we get to the library. The room is enormous, crammed to the rafters with Sentry-regulation books. Above each shelf is a sign indicating what type of books they are. It's the only way to tell the difference, as all the covers are the same, black and red.

There are only two available seats left: one next to Beetle, the other beside Ash. His jaw tightens as he spots me.

"You've got to be kidding me," Day mutters.

She drags her heels across the room and reluctantly sits next to Beetle. I groan, scanning the library for an alternative place to sit. Lacking any other options, I sit beside Ash. He looks around the room, at the floor, the ceiling, everywhere but me. I take out a packet of mints from my satchel and pop one in my mouth. I roll it around, letting it clank against my teeth.

"Could you stop that?" Ash hisses, finally acknowledging my existence. "It's annoying."

I bite down on the mint and munch it loudly. He mutters a curse under his breath.

The Thompson twins, Gregory and Chris, sit at the table next to us. Chris leans toward Day, his wavy brown hair falling over his gorgeous hazel eyes.

"Hey, babes, do you have a pen I can borrow?" he says.

She flushes, fumbling around her pencil case for a pen and handing it over. Beetle rolls his eyes. It seems no girl is immune to Chris's charms.

Chris then turns to Ash, his voice low. I try not to eavesdrop, but it's hard when Ash is sitting next to me.

"Hey, have you heard about this new Golden Haze doing the rounds?" Chris asks.

Ash shakes his head. "That's a new one on me, but I'm not really interested in the crap the dens are dealing. Why are *you* so interested in it?"

Chris looks sheepish. "I just heard it was meant to give you a really pure high, with no Haze Headaches afterward. I thought you might've heard of it."

"I only deal Haze straight from the fang. You can't trust those street blends; they could've been mixed with anything. You shouldn't touch that stuff with a barge pole," Ash says.

Chris nods, sitting back. "Yeah . . . yeah, you're probably right."

Gregory turns his liquid hazel eyes on Ash, hatred burning in them.

At that moment, Mr. Lewis—a mousy man with a big bushy mustache—enters the library, a projector wheel under his arm. He sets it up at the front of the class.

I shrug off Ash's jacket and sling it over the back of my seat. Ash leans toward me, his lips right next to my ear. My heartbeat quickens.

"I want my jacket back, blondie," he says quietly.

"Tough luck."

"I'm warning you, give it back or—"

"What? You'll kill me? You know that threat's really starting to wear thin."

He shakes his head. "Keep it, I don't care. It reeks of you now anyway."

"There's nothing wrong with the way I smell," I say.

He cocks an eyebrow, saying nothing.

I don't know why this upsets me. Why should I care what he thinks about me?

Mr. Lewis turns off the lights, and everyone in the room giggles and goes *ooh* as we're plunged into darkness. I can see Ash's eyes sparkling from the corner of my vision. I try and concentrate on the lesson, the origins of the Blood Wars, but I'm finding it hard with Ash so indecently close, his knee almost touching mine.

Ash picks up a pen and taps it against the desk—*tap tap tap*—watching the screen at the front of the class, his face somber.

Click: a photo of the city prewar, the filthy streets lit by neon lights.

"The United Sentry States was drowning in corruption," Mr. Lewis says. "Drug and crime rates were at their highest since records began, and overcrowding was fast becoming an issue as more Darklings migrated to the cities in search of work and food."

Mr. Lewis looks around the class. "Does anybody know what the biggest killer of humans was during this troubled time?"

Day's hand shoots up. "Haze addiction."

Mr. Lewis nods. "Over seventy percent of the human population of the United Sentry States was hooked on this highly addictive drug. It was a very dark period of our history."

Gregory scowls at Ash.

Click: a partially built concrete wall.

"Purian Rose, as the newly elected head of the United Sentry States, realized the nation's best chance of rehabilitation and recovery was to segregate the Darkling population from the humans, and in every city across all nine megastates, he ordered that Darklings be relocated into walled ghettos."

Click: thousands of Darklings being led at gunpoint by Sentry guards into a ghetto.

"Relocation was successful, with minimal casualties to the Darkling population, although some rebel factions refused to leave their homes—mainly those who had cohabited with humans and borne twin-blood children," Mr. Lewis says.

Ash stares at the screen, his face set like stone.

"Purian Rose graciously allowed the twin-bloods to stay with their human parents," Mr. Lewis continues. "However, a law was passed shortly after this that prohibited relationships between Darklings and humans, to prevent any further twin-blood offspring being born. Anyone found violating these terms was sentenced to death."

Click: a Sentry General with blond hair and piercing blue eyes.

Grief spills over me in waves.

Father.

"However, even with segregation, overpopulation was still a massive burden on the state, so General Jonathan Buchanan put forward the Voluntary Migration Scheme, which saw over five million Darklings relocated to migration camps in the Barren Lands—"

"That's not true," Ash says.

Everyone turns to look at him.

"Would you like to teach the class?" Mr. Lewis says, his voice dripping with sarcasm.

"If you're offering," Ash replies.

"You're treading on thin ice, Fisher."

"Why? If you're going to teach us 'history,' at least you

should get your facts straight. There weren't any migration camps in the Barren Lands."

Mr. Lewis's mustache twitches irritably. "So I suppose all those Darklings just vanished into thin air?"

"No," Ash says.

"Then where did they all go?"

Ash looks directly at me. I swallow hard, my world spinning. *He knows.* The truth is they weren't migration camps; they were concentration camps. Purian Rose sent those Darklings to the Barren Lands to die, cut off from any blood supply.

If he'd had his way, he would've sent all the Darklings to the Barren Lands, but politically that would've been disastrous. People wouldn't have been able to ignore the migration of the *entire* Darkling population. Father once told me it was like boiling a frog. If you drop it in boiling water, it'll hop straight out of the pan. If you put it in cold water and very slowly turn up the heat, the frog will happily swim around the pot until it boils to death. Purian Rose was slowly turning up the heat on our society, making sure the humans came around to his way of thinking without ever realizing they were doing it.

The first stage of his plan was the ghettos, which were just a means to dupe the liberals into believing things weren't really "that bad" and that the other Darklings who were being sent to the Barren Lands were going there out of choice. The government made it sound like the camp in the Barren Lands was a holiday resort, and people were willing to believe it, because it's much easier to believe a lie than face a terrible truth. Purian Rose committed genocide right under their noses, and they didn't even blink.

Then one by one, the Darkling survivors in the Barren Lands got sick with a strange new virus, the Wrath. Now the only

Darklings left in the Barren Lands are mindless monsters infected with the virus. I know all this because my father witnessed it firsthand; he was in charge of the relocation program. That experience changed everything; that was the reason he turned sides and tore our family apart.

"Well?" Mr. Lewis demands.

The rest of the class turns to look at me, curious. My heart hammers in my chest. *Don't say anything, please, please, please.* I don't want the whole class knowing what my father did to those Darklings. They may not understand. All that's left of my father is his reputation. I have to protect it.

Uncertainty passes quickly over Ash's face.

"They all flew to the moon," he says.

I exhale.

"Very amusing, Mr. Fisher." Mr. Lewis turns on the light. "Being that the first anniversary of Armistice Day is coming up a week from Saturday, I want you all to write an essay on the Blood Riots and the events leading up to disarmament. Oh, and before I forget, I need you all to get your parents to sign these permission slips for our class trip to the Black City Museum." He taps a pile of papers on his desk.

There are a few groans from around the room. We open our books and read in silence for ten minutes, although I can't take in any of the words. I'm still rattled by what just happened. Beetle's doodling on his notebook, the words *one city united* repeatedly scrawled across his work. He peers up at me with unfriendly eyes.

"I take it you don't support Rose's Law, then?" I say.

He snorts. "Course not, it's—"

"Leave it," Ash growls under his breath.

"No, I won't leave it. I'm not afraid of telling it like it is," Beetle replies.

"Here we go again." Day rolls her eyes.

"The Boundary Wall needs to come down. End of story," Beetle says.

"I agree, but it should be negotiated through political discourse, not through threats and terrorism, which seem to be Humans for Unity's way of dealing with things," Day replies.

The tips of Beetle's ears turn pink. "You're so naive, Day. Things won't change unless we force the government's hand."

"I disagree," she says stiffly. "The best way to influence a government is from the *inside*. When I'm an Emissary—"

"Oh, please. That's not going to happen. They'd never let a Workboot onto the Fast-Track program," Beetle replies.

Day looks at me, and I give her a weak smile. Gregory Thompson turns his attention to us, listening in.

"Purian Rose won't let the wall come down," Ash says quietly. "He's fought too hard to keep us all segregated."

"He won't have much choice if we all rise up and vote against him," Beetle continues.

"Don't you get it? Rose always gets his way. You're wasting your time if you think he's ever going to allow that to happen," Ash replies.

"Bringing the wall down won't benefit anyone. Who wants those nippers back, roaming our streets?" Gregory chimes in with his whiny voice.

"It might benefit me," Ash snaps, silencing Gregory. "I'd like to see my family. But I don't suppose that matters to the Sentry government?" He aims the last part at me.

Hostility simmers between us as we turn our attention back to our books. We continue reading in silence. The quiet is broken by Ash banging his pen against the table. *Tap tap tap, tap tap tap.*

"Will you stop that?" I pretend to be irritated to get him back for earlier.

Ash continues to tap his pen, deliberately this time. *Two can play at that game.* I roll another mint around my mouth, clanging it against my teeth.

Ash slams his pen against the desk. It rolls off the side and both of us lean down to retrieve it at the same time. Our heads bump. Sharp pain shoots through my head and, bizarrely, my chest as well. Ash gasps and flinches, almost falling off his seat as he clamps a hand over his chest, which rises and falls rapidly like he's struggling to breathe. He staggers to his feet and rushes out the fire exit.

"What's up with him? He's being more of a freak than normal," Day says.

"Heartburn," Beetle mutters, getting up to go check on him.

I rub the bump on my forehead and stare at the empty space where Ash had just been. It didn't look like heartburn to me.

10
ASH

I STUMBLE OUT the fire exit into the town square, my feet slipping on the uneven ground. I don't get more than ten feet before my legs buckle beneath me and I crash to the floor, panting, trembling as a terrible heat blazes through my body, melting the ice in my blood. *What's happening to me?* My stomach turns over, my veins explode with pain. I dig my nails into the cobbles, trying to cling to reality as my body violently shakes. It's like my insides are being turned inside out.

Shivers of electricity shoot through my fingers and toes, rushing up my limbs to a single point: my heart. There's an excruciating explosion of pain in my chest, and my body jerks, almost snapping my spine like a wishbone. All I can think is *I'm dying, I'm dying, I'm dying.* I let out a desperate howl, and then the pain evaporates as swiftly as it came.

I lie on the ground, sweat dripping down my face, my chest heaving, as my fingers press against the blazing-hot skin covering my rib cage and feel something that's not meant to be there:

A slow, steady heartbeat.

I let out a startled cry, somewhere between joy and terror.

Footsteps slap against the cobbled street, and I loll my head to one side to see Beetle's bashed-up boots next to me. He grips my shirt and drags me out of the direct sunlight before hauling me up into a sitting position.

"You all right, bro?" he asks.

I shut my eyes and just listen to the rhythmic thrum of my heart. *My heart* . . . I can't believe it's really beating! After a whole lifetime of silence, it's the most amazing sound I've ever heard. For the first time in my existence, I feel truly alive and not like a zombie walking around with a reanimated body.

Beetle squeezes my shoulder, bringing me back to reality.

"What happened?" he asks.

I take his hand and press it against my chest.

"Whoa!" He takes his hand back. "How?" he finally says.

"I don't know. I think . . ." I shake my head. "You're going to think this is nuts."

"Tell me."

"I think Natalie did it." I tell him about our first meeting under the bridge, how I thought my heart had fluttered. "And when we bumped heads just now, my heart started beating. It can't be a coincidence."

Beetle scratches his head, like he's trying to put the pieces of the puzzle together. "But how did touching Natalie actually kick-start your heart? Is the girl electric or something?"

"I don't know."

"Have you ever heard of a twin-blood's heart activating like that before?" he asks.

"No."

"Do you think it's permanent?"

"Fragg, why all the questions? Can't you just be happy for

me?" A sudden terror grips me. What if this is only temporary? I've wanted a heartbeat my whole life. All I've ever wanted was to be *normal,* to fit in, to be left alone. That's impossible when you're the only boy in the city with no heartbeat; it tends to single you out. I don't want to go back to being a freak.

My thoughts are cut off midstream when the town square erupts to life. A platoon of Sentry guards marches into the square, followed by hundreds of citizens. Many of the laborers are still dressed in their regulation gray work uniforms, as if they've just dropped what they've been doing to come here. Nearby, a group of ladies in long bustle dresses cool themselves with lace fans, gossiping excitedly with each other as their husbands ignore them. A moment later, the library doors burst open, and our history class rushes out of the building to join everyone else in the square.

Natalie exits the library with Day, Gregory and Chris. She looks in my direction, and my heart hammers against my rib cage so hard, I think it's going to burst out of my chest— *ba-boom ba-boom ba-boom!* If there was any doubt my newfound heartbeat wasn't somehow connected to Natalie, that's just cleared it.

"What's going on?" Beetle asks.

I tear my eyes from Natalie. "I don't know. Let's get a better look."

He helps me to my feet, and we push our way through the crowd toward the stage. People shove and jostle against one another as they try to get closer to the three crosses by the Boundary Wall. A reverend douses the crosses with acacia solution, and Sentry guards hastily erect a platform in front of them. A group of guys with shaved heads goad the Legion guards on the wall.

"Hey, isn't that your aunt Roach?" I point to a woman with wild dreadlocks down to her waist and a thin, freckled face, standing by the stage.

We go over to her, and she briefly hugs Beetle. It's like a mosh pit around us, with everyone pushing each other to get a better view. The Sentry guards throw a few punches, trying to keep people in order.

"Why's everyone here?" Beetle asks.

"It's Tom Shreve—they've found him," Roach says, referring to Beetle's friend who went missing a few weeks back.

All the blood drains out of Beetle's face.

Ba-boom! My heart suddenly clenches, and somehow I know it's because Natalie's nearby. I turn and see her being led in our direction by Gregory.

"Come on, I want to get a better view!" Gregory says.

They head closer to the stage, and Natalie's arm brushes against mine as she walks by. Darts of electricity shoot through my biceps, and I instinctively grip my arm, trying to push the pain away. Weirdly, Natalie mirrors the action with her own arm, like she felt it too. She furrows her brow, a questioning look in her eyes.

A hush falls over the square as a tall Darkling in long purple robes and a gold face mask appears at the top of the Boundary Wall. *Sigur Marwick.* The one thing I hate more than the Sentry is *him.* He's followed by a girl in a blue hooded robe, her face shrouded in shadows so all you can see of her is the sparkle of black eyes.

An excited whisper spreads through the town square as three people, their heads covered in sacks, are led onto the platform in front of the crosses, followed by the tall, blond-haired Tracker who was with Natalie on her first day at school.

"This is awesome. I can't believe they're actually going to crucify someone," Gregory says to Natalie. "I've always wanted to see one; I heard they happen all the time in the Plantation State. Isn't this exciting?"

She looks at him in horror. "No, it's revolting. Someone should stop it."

Day lightly touches Natalie's arm. "You okay? You look pale."

"I can't stand seeing people get hurt, not after watching my father die," she says.

The Sentry guards line up the prisoners below the crosses. My blood turns to ice, looking at the chilling sight. How can something so seemingly innocuous—a plain wooden cross—strike so much fear in me? *It's not what it is, but what it represents. Pain. Suffering. Death.* I can't think of a worse way to die. The prisoner's hoods are removed. One of the prisoners is a boy wearing horn-rimmed glasses. *Tom.* Beetle wails and rushes forward, but his aunt holds him back.

"Don't do anything," Roach urges in his ear.

The second prisoner is an elderly man who looks a lot like the boy. He's sobbing, begging for mercy. I stare in horror at the third prisoner. She's a teenage girl wearing a yellow dress, with long white hair and eyes as orange as the setting sun. *A Nordin!* She must've snuck over the wall.

The Tracker tears off the girl's dress and exposes her naked body to the crowd. The Legion guards howl. A pair of iridescent wings unfolds behind her, spanning eight feet in length. They flutter, catching the light and creating small rainbows around her. The crowd oohs like they're watching a fireworks display.

The blond-haired Tracker snaps back the Nordin's head and

removes her fangs with a pair of pliers. She lets out an unearthly howl, and I flinch. *Neutered.* The final humiliation for
any Darkling. He throws her teeth into the crowd. A dozen
people scrabble for the souvenirs. I cover my mouth, my fangs
throbbing just at the thought of being neutered. I'm surprised
to see Natalie is doing the exact same gesture as me. She lowers
her hand, a puzzled expression on her face again.

The Tracker draws his sword and, with two swift movements, cleaves off the Nordin girl's wings. She screeches as
dark blood spills down her body. He picks up the wings and
tosses them into the air. They spin like blades over the crowd,
and people frantically reach for them. They'll fetch a fortune
on the black market. Many cultures believe Darkling wings
have aphrodisiac properties, but because their governments
are more tolerant toward Darklings and have granted them
civil rights, they have to illegally import them from the United
Sentry States. The girl's wings will soon be ground down to
make love potions for rich humans.

"We have to help Tom," Beetle says to me and Roach.

Roach discreetly takes a small envelope from her pocket. She
shakes out a red capsule into my upturned hand. Natalie slides
a look at us, then turns her attention back to the stage, but I get
the impression she's listening to our conversation.

"Cyanide," Roach explains. "We hoped to slip it to Tom before he got taken up on the stage, but there wasn't time."

"What about Tom's granddad and the Darkling girl?" I ask,
wondering why there's only one pill.

"We didn't know Frank had been captured, and cyanide
doesn't work on Darklings," Roach explains.

I glance at the stage. If we're going to help Tom, we have to
act fast; he's being undressed and nailed to the cross, surrounded

by a group of armed Sentry guards. It's going to be hard reaching him. We've only got one shot at this.

Roach clamps a hand on my shoulder. "Ash, you're fast, you should do it. You're our best chance."

"What if I get caught?" I say.

"Come on, bro, you have to help," Beetle urges.

Should I do it? I study the red pill. Is helping Tom really worth the risk of being arrested? Before I can make a decision, the pill is snatched from me.

"Hey!" I cry out as Natalie pushes through the crowd away from us, the stolen pill in her hand.

Fury rages through me as I chase after her, determined to get the pill back before she can give it to her Tracker friend. The crowd starts to close around us; there's not much time. She slips between two people, and I roughly shove them out of the way. My fingers grasp the edge of her satchel, but she twists out of my reach and climbs onto the stage.

Fragg!

"What are you doing?" The blond-haired Tracker narrows his green eyes at her.

"I want to look that race traitor in the eye, if that's all right with you, Sebastian," she says.

Sebastian. So that's his name.

He stands aside, and she leans over Tom.

"Your kind makes me sick," she says, and slaps Tom across the face, managing to slip the pill into his mouth as she does so. The sleight of hand is so good, no one would've noticed unless they were looking real close. Tom's eyes widen for a fraction of a second before understanding crosses his face.

She helped him. She bloody well helped him! I struggle to process this thought as Beetle and Roach join me.

The crowd starts to jeer, getting bored.

"Kill the race traitors! Kill them! Kill them! Kill them!" they chant.

Sebastian clears his throat, steps forward and reads aloud from a scroll.

"For the crime of racial defilement, for having indecent relations with a Darkling, I sentence Thomas Shreve to death by crucifixion."

There are cheers from the crowd.

"For the crime of racial defilement, for having indecent relations with a human, I sentence Jana Marwick to death by crucifixion."

There are angry howls from the Legion guards, the sound like baying wolves. Sigur raises a hand, silencing them immediately.

Jana Marwick? Is she related to Sigur? I didn't realize he had any family left. I thought they'd all been executed at the start of the war.

"For the crime of harboring two fugitives of the United Sentry States, I sentence Frank Shreve to death by crucifixion."

Movement on the wall draws my attention. There's a shift in the atmosphere, a sudden stillness in the air as scores of Legion guards in black flowing robes appear on the wall, their dark eyes glittering in the dusky sunlight, capturing everyone's attention. One by one, the Legion guards turn their backs to us.

"What are they doing?" Beetle whispers.

"I think it's a protest. They're refusing to watch the execution," I say. Purian Rose may have the power to execute us, but he doesn't have the power to make us watch. That's the one small freedom we've got left.

The three crosses are winched upright and screams fill the air. Tom's grandfather is mercifully already unconscious from shock, but the other two are still alert as they stare out across the crowd. Blood seeps down Tom's body from the nails in his wrists, while Jana's sensitive flesh begins to crackle and sizzle as she finally succumbs to the toxic effects of the acacia wood. Flames start to lick out of her broken skin, crawling up her legs.

"Demon!" someone yells at her. I think it might be Gregory.

I can't imagine being on that cross, staring out at a sea of sneering faces as you slowly suffocate, all alone . . .

The fire rapidly spreads up Jana's body, but she doesn't scream, she doesn't make a sound. She simply turns to look at Tom as her body is consumed by flames. He holds her gaze for as long as he can before swallowing the pill. It's not a moment too soon, as the fire spreads to his cross and sets him ablaze.

The crowds cheer as the lovers burn.

"One race under His Mighty!" they chant.

From across the stage, Natalie's eyes meet mine as red flames and black smoke billow behind her.

Sebastian leads Natalie off the stage and hands her over to another guard, a brawny black man who has a broken nose and three savage claw marks down his neck. She's ushered down City End away from the mob. Day chases after Natalie.

Roach turns to us. "Get out of here, kids."

We don't need to be told twice—we slip through the crowd and out onto City End. I immediately spark up a cigarette and pass it to Beetle.

"I'm sorry about Tom," I say.

Beetle takes a puff of the cigarette. There's a fierce look in his eyes that I only see when he's off on one of his rants. "All Purian Rose has done is given us a martyr. Tom's death won't be in vain."

"You can't be serious. He was your friend."

"He was a freedom fighter; he'd want to die for the cause if it helped us, which it will."

I rake a weary hand through my hair. Now's not the time to argue with him. We turn the bend and come face-to-face with Natalie and Day, several Sentry guards and a Tracker—the black man with claw marks down his neck. The guards draw their swords and point them at me.

"Where's your ID bracelet, nipper?" Claw Neck says.

Beetle stands in front of me. "He doesn't have to wear—"

I roll my sleeve up to show the guard my copper wristband, my blood boiling with anger and humiliation.

Beetle's eyes widen.

"Lower your weapons. I know these people," Natalie orders.

They look at Claw Neck, who also orders them to lower their swords.

"You can go, Kurt," she says to Claw Neck.

"You know I can't do that, miss, I have strict orders—"

She rolls her eyes. "Fine. Will you at least walk down the road a little way, so I can have some privacy?"

Claw Neck waves his men on, mumbling under his breath.

"I'm so sorry about your friend," Natalie says to us. "That's no way to die."

I give a gruff laugh. "Look, thanks for your help, blondie, but if it weren't for your kind, he wouldn't have been up there in the first place."

"*My* kind? Honestly, Ash, you're such an ass." Natalie heads toward Bleak Street with Day. She doesn't look back.

My heart's slowing down now that Natalie is walking away.

"Why did it have to be *her*? Why is my heart beating now?" I mumble.

Beetle shrugs. "Karma's a bitch sometimes."

"But what does it *mean*?"

"It doesn't mean anything. She's a Sentry, end of story," he says.

"But—"

"Forget it, Ash. I'm all for Darklings and humans getting along, and Natalie did help Tom, so that does go in her favor, but she's still a *Sentry*. That's wrong on epic levels, bro. That's like collaborating with the devil!"

"I know! Do you think I wanted this to happen?" I kick the wall.

"Why didn't you tell me about your ID band?" Beetle asks.

I let out an irritated sigh. "Because I knew what you'd say, and I don't want to join Humans for Unity."

"Well, maybe this is a sign you should reconsider."

"What's the point? Nothing's ever going to change. Fragg, I hate it here!" I yell.

A shadow falls over us as a Legion guard patrols the Boundary Wall. He moves on, leaving the wall unprotected. I wonder how hard it would be to climb up. *Thirty feet.* I'm sure I could do it before getting caught; other Darklings have managed it before when they've snuck over the wall from the Legion side. The wall's guarded twenty-four hours a day by Sentry guards trying to keep Darklings from getting out of the ghetto, and by Legion guards trying to prevent humans from getting in. Even so, they can't protect every inch of the wall at all times, it's just too vast. So it is possible to get over if your timing is right. This is my chance.

"Uh-oh, I recognize that look," Beetle says. "Don't even think about it, man."

"I just want to see what's on the other side," I say, now consumed by my desire to see the other Darklings. They might have some answers about what's happening to me.

"Don't be stupid." There's a note of panic in his voice. "It's too high; you'll fall."

"No I won't."

I step up to the wall and dig my fingers into the tiny grooves in the concrete. Taking a deep breath, I pull myself up the wall, one hand over the other.

Twenty-five feet to go.

Twenty.

Fifteen.

I'm going to make it!

"Ash! Get down!" Beetle calls.

His voice attracts the attention of the Legion guard farther down the wall. The guard starts to run in my direction. I don't know whether he plans to stop me or help me over so I can finally meet my family, but I don't want to chance it being the former option.

Crap!

My fingers scrape against the concrete, pulling out chunks of stone in my desperation to get up.

Ten feet.

So close!

Five.

I'm almost there.

Four.

The guard's just steps away.

Three.

My brethren. I'm going to see my family.

Two.

My hand slips, and I'm falling before I know what's happened. My feet kick at thin air, my fingers drag against the concrete. I smash into the pavement.

Beetle rushes over. "Are you still alive?"

I groan. "Just."

The Legion guard stares down at me, shakes his head, then turns away.

I stand up, more embarrassed than hurt. "Let's get out of here."

11

NATALIE

"**WATCH THE GARBAGE BIN**—it's full of medical waste," I say.

Day makes an "eww" noise, giving the overflowing garbage bin a wide berth as we walk down Bleak Street toward the Sentry HQ's kitchen entrance, Kurt and the other guards following a short distance behind.

"Why are we taking the back entrance?" she says as I punch in the security code and enter the kitchen.

"Habit, I guess," I say.

I worked out pretty quickly that there's less security on this entrance, which means there are fewer people watching my comings and goings. I hate the fact I'm always being monitored.

I dismiss Kurt and his troop, and they head upstairs.

"Let's hang out in my room until dinner," I say to Day when they've gone.

"Can't we take a tour of the house first? I've always wanted to see inside this place," Day asks.

I sigh. "Sure."

What I hope will be a five-minute tour takes nearly an hour, as Day stops to examine every room, even the staff restroom, asking me countless questions about the history of the place, as if I know! Polly and I grew up at our mansion in the Park.

I don't usually spend much time outside of my room when I'm in the building, and the unfamiliar labyrinth of corridors on the way back to the living quarters starts to look the same to me.

"Er . . . I think it's this way," I say, leading her down a long hallway and immediately realizing we've gone the wrong way when we stumble upon a massive steel door manned by several heavily armed guards.

"What's through there?" she asks.

"The interrogation rooms."

Day raises a brow. "They do that here?"

"How do you think the Trackers get their intel?"

"I thought they just felt stuff," she says, referring to the V-gene that all Trackers are born with that helps them sense Darklings.

I laugh. "They may have the V-gene, but they're not *psychic*. They still need to do police work, interrogate dregs to get leads on new Darkling nests or Haze dens around the city, that sort of thing."

"Are there many Darkling nests in the city?" she says.

"Enough to keep Sebastian and the other Trackers in work," I reply.

"How are the Darklings even getting over the wall?"

I shrug. "The wall can't be guarded all the time, and Darklings are good climbers."

"I always wondered why the Nordin Darklings don't just fly over the wall," Day says.

"There are automated gun pods all around the city to shoot down any Nordins if they attempt that."

At that moment, the steel door opens and three guys are escorted out, being released. Their skin is sallow and laced with black veins, which are characteristic of long-term Haze abuse. Day hides behind me. One of the Hazers—a teenage boy with bright purple dreadlocks—gives me a hard stare as he passes. A guard nudges the boy with the end of his gun and leads him away.

"Come on, I think we need to go this way," I say to Day.

We find our way back to the living quarters and head upstairs. The door to Sebastian's room yanks open as we walk by. Sebastian scowls at me.

"I need to talk to you," he says to me.

I quickly introduce him to Day.

"I'll meet you in my room. Last door on the left," I tell her.

"Nice to have met you, Day. I'm sure we'll see each other again at the Tracker trials next week," Sebastian says, referring to the test that will determine which kids at school have the V-gene. "I hope you'll be joining my squad."

She forces a smile and leaves.

As soon as she's turned the corner, he pulls me into his bedroom, which is big and luxurious, with exotic animal skulls mounted on the burgundy walls, a Lupine-fur rug by the marble fireplace and a mahogany four-poster bed covered in black silk sheets. It all screams power and sex: the two things Sebastian loves most. On his dressing table beside me is a brand-new copy of the Book of Creation—the Purity holy text. *When did Sebastian start reading that nonsense?*

"Why did you do it?" he demands.

"I don't know what you're—"

"Cut the crap. I saw you give that race traitor the cyanide pill."

"You did?" I say, stunned. I thought I'd been so careful. "The boy was in so much pain. No one deserves to die like that."

"He was a race traitor, a Darkling lover. He deserved everything he got," Sebastian says.

"You're one to talk."

Sebastian's fist clenches, and I know I've overstepped the line.

"That's different," he says.

"How?"

"No one will ever find out. Will they?" he says.

"Your secret's safe with me," I reply, not that he deserves my loyalty. But I don't want to get him into trouble, no matter how badly he hurt me, and he knows it.

He takes a deep breath, calming himself.

"You're lucky it was me up on that stage and not Kurt or one of the other Trackers," he says. "They wouldn't think twice about reporting you to Purian Rose."

My heart leaps into my mouth. "You're not going to tell on me, are you?"

"Of course not. I'd never let anyone hurt you," he says. "But you have to be careful, Natalie. Don't give Purian Rose another excuse to hurt you or Polly."

Sebastian tenderly strokes my cheek, and for a moment I let him, remembering the reason I used to love him. He was so kind and gentle with me after my father died; it was exactly what I needed. Then I recall the reason we broke up and slap his hand away, ignoring his wounded look.

I pick up the Book of Creation from his dresser. "What are you doing with this?"

"I thought I'd read it and see what all the fuss is about."

"You know it's a load of insane, rambling bullcrap written by Purian Rose, so why bother?" I say.

He shrugs. "It might improve my chances of getting a promotion if I follow the faith. I don't have to actually believe in it. I just need to have read it."

Everything he does always has to benefit his career somehow, including dating me. I toss the book on his dresser and head to my room, checking on Polly along the way. She's sound asleep. The medication they put her on makes her drowsy, so she sleeps a lot.

In my room, Day's lying on my bed next to my cat, Truffles, reading the latest issue of *Sentry Youth Monthly*. Truffles softly meows at me. I'm struck by the sight of Day with her feet kicked up in the air, ankles crossed, flicking through the fashion section of the magazine, just the way Polly used to do. It's like a flashback from my past. I swallow hard.

Day sits up. "You okay, Nat?"

"You just reminded me of my sister for a second. The way she was before she got hurt."

I press Truffles close to my face. I love the way he smells; it's so warm and comforting. He lets me hold him for a minute before wriggling free and making a beeline for the rug.

"What happened to your sister?" Day asks.

"She got tortured."

Day's eyes widen. "By whom?"

Something warns me not to tell her the whole truth.

"An enemy of my father," I say. "He ordered Polly's torture to punish my father and made us all watch. It was horrible. It was my fault she got hurt."

"I don't believe that for a second."

"It's what my mother thinks, and she never lets me forget

it. Mother loved Polly so much more than me; she thinks I'm a waste of space."

"I'm sure she doesn't feel that way."

I don't say anything. Day has no idea how my mother treats me, how she has to make every decision for me because she thinks I'm incapable of doing anything on my own.

"How's MJ doing?" I ask her, to get the focus off me.

She shrugs. "He has his good days and his bad ones. Thanks for the painkillers—they'll really help."

I lightly touch her hand. "I'll get you some more whenever you need them. Okay?"

She nods, her chocolate-brown eyes watering.

"Let's change the subject to something more cheerful. We're supposed to be having fun," I say.

Day smiles awkwardly. "So . . . erm . . . what do we do at a sleepover, exactly?"

"Have you never been to a slumber party?"

Day pushes her glasses up her nose. "I don't really have time for them. I'm always studying."

She doesn't look at me, and I wonder if the real reason she's never been to a sleepover is that she doesn't have any friends other than me. I open up my bedside cabinet and pull out my makeup kit and secret stash of candy.

"Well, it's obligatory that we paint our nails, eat candy and talk about boys," I say.

I choose a pretty coral pink nail varnish from my makeup bag and begin painting Day's nails.

"Sebastian's quite attractive," Day says, getting into the spirit of things.

"I suppose. We dated for a while, but we split up a few months ago."

"Why?" she asks.

"I walked in on him having sex with another girl."

"That's awful!" she says.

"You don't know the half of it," I mutter.

"Why would he sleep with another girl, when he had *you*?"

I blush. "Well, I'm a . . . we didn't . . ."

"You're a virgin, aren't you?"

"Day!"

"Sorry, wasn't I supposed to ask that?"

I laugh. "It's a *little* blunt. Yes, I'm a virgin, but that was no excuse for him to cheat on me."

"No, of course not. He's a total jerk."

She lies against the pillow, blowing on her nails.

"Are you a virgin?" I ask.

She blushes furiously. "No."

My mouth drops. I didn't expect that.

"What was your first time like?" I ask.

She sighs. "Sort of crap, really. It wasn't romantic like in the books. It was uncomfortable and squelchy, and neither of us knew what to do. Plus it was super embarrassing being naked in front of Beet—" She cuts herself short, but the damage is already done.

"You slept with Beetle?" I say.

"Yeah," she whispers. "On my fifteenth birthday. It was a complete mess. We thought we were in love. Then his parents were killed, he started hanging out with Ash and doing Haze, and that was it. I wasn't important to him anymore; all he cared about was getting high and helping out with the 'Darkling cause.' I hate Ash Fisher. He took Beetle away from me—he ruined my life."

"I'm sorry."

"It doesn't matter. I'm so over him."

"No you're not."

"Maybe not, but what's the point in loving him anymore? We just can't agree on anything. You heard us earlier in history class. How can two people who are so opposite to each other ever be happy?"

"I don't know," I say quietly. An image of sparkling black eyes crosses my mind. *What is going on with me?*

After we eat dinner in my room, I put on an old movie, but we're both too tired to watch it after such an eventful day and agree to call it a night. I lend Day one of my nightshirts, and we get ready for bed.

"Sorry I didn't get a chance to introduce you to my mother," I say, unrolling my sleeping bag. "She works such long hours . . ."

"That's fine. I didn't agree to stay over tonight so I could meet her; I wanted to hang out with you."

I beam. My friends in Centrum only visited when my mother was around. None of them have called me since I came back to Black City.

"I'm having a fun time. Maybe we could do it again?" I say.

"I'd like that." Day climbs into my bed.

It doesn't take long for Day to drop off, but I lie awake, tossing and turning in my sleeping bag on the hard floor. I look at the stars through my open window. They glimmer back at me, reminding me of Ash's eyes. Why do I keep thinking about them? Why am I thinking about him at all? He's a twin-blood, for His Mighty's sake. I roll over so I can't see the stars anymore.

Truffles pounces off the bed, landing on me.

"Ouch! You little pest," I say, picking him up. "You want to go out?"

He meows in response.

I get up and open the balcony window as quietly as possible. Truffles slips from my hands and climbs onto the balustrade. I tickle him under his chin and go back to my sleeping bag, leaving the window open to let in some cool air. Within seconds, I'm asleep and dreaming.

I'm inside the cave again. I don't know why I'm here, but I get a sense I've done something very wrong. I've stolen something, but what? I have to find it, they want it back. Panicked, I search for the object inside the cave, but it's empty. There's nothing here but those sticky, warm, pulsing walls and . . .

A whimper.

Fear rises in my throat.

In the center of the cave is a small child. The child is naked except for the green sheet modestly wrapped around its waist. I can't see its face. All I see is a shaved head. A boy? Who is he? Somehow, I feel I know him.

The walls start to contract. I know what's about to happen. I have to get out of here. I try to move, but my feet are stuck in the spongy earth. The cave starts to close around me. Panic boils over as the walls get closer and closer, until they're squeezing me. I can't breathe, I'm being suffocated—

Screams fill my mind, so loud they're deafening me. But they're not my screams. They're coming from someone else. Somewhere else. Day!

I start awake, fear ripping through me. Day stands on the bed, yelling her lungs out as she points toward an object dangling from the light above me. Something warm and sticky drips on my cheek. I glance up. At first I don't know what I'm looking at, then I start to make sense of the mangled shape above me: patches of white fur, a paw, an ear.

Before I scream, I'm able to notice one thing:

Truffles's heart is missing.

12

NATALIE

AFTER TRUFFLES'S MURDER a few days ago, Mother decided the best way for me to get over his death was to spend my Saturday shopping with our housemaid Martha and Sebastian. She even gave me thirty coins, since I didn't have any cash after she cut off my allowance. That's her answer to everything. Why deal with my feelings when she can just fob me off with money?

"I bet it was a member of Humans for Unity," Sebastian says as we walk down Bleak Street toward the station. "It's the kind of despicable thing they'd do."

I sigh, tired of having the same discussion with him. Yesterday he was certain it was the Legion Liberation Front. The day before that, he thought it might be some psycho stalker. I had a few of those when we were living in Centrum; it just comes with the territory when you're the Emissary's daughter. None of the options makes me feel any better about the fact that a cat murderer broke into my bedroom. How did they even get in, when my room's on the top floor?

"But why kill Truffles? He was just an innocent kitty. Why did they have to rip his heart out?" I say.

"They were probably sending your mother a message, letting her know what could happen if she doesn't listen to their demands and bring down the Boundary Wall," Sebastian replies. "Just be grateful it was your cat and not you."

I can't get the image of Truffles's twisted, battered body out of my head. *All that blood, just like the night Father died . . .* My chest starts to tighten with panic. I take a deep breath, trying to remain calm. Martha gives my hand a gentle squeeze, and I'm grateful for the small act of kindness.

The city streets are buzzing with activity. The boundary negotiations started today between Mother and the Darkling ambassador, Sigur Marwick, so protesters have swarmed into the city, either to support the government or to rally against them. If Humans for Unity really did kill my cat, all they've done is shoot themselves in the foot. Mother doesn't respond to threats. If anything, it strengthens her resolve.

Footage of the opening of boundary negotiations is being broadcast on the giant screens on the rooftops around us. The news report shows Humans for Unity protesting outside the Boundary Gates as my mother is greeted by Sigur. They both enter the Legion ghetto.

A female voice booms out of the screens. "And now a message from your government."

The story cuts to a still picture of Tom Shreve and Jana Marwick, their charred bodies bound to the crosses. All the citizens stop and gaze up at the screen. Text scrolls below the image: *To sin with a Darkling is to sin against His Mighty.*

I shiver.

The steam-powered streetcar pulls up at the Bleak Street station, and we hop on. It's crammed with commuters, and we barely manage to squeeze on, pushing through the jungle of bodies to find somewhere to stand. I regret wearing Ash's heavy coat, but I don't own many Workboot clothes, and I don't want to draw attention to myself as we trade for supplies in the market. Thankfully, I managed to persuade Sebastian to wear his civilian clothes, so it will be easier for us to blend in.

The tram slowly rattles through the city, spewing white clouds of steam into the air. Every few minutes, we pass an armed checkpoint or a Sentry tank rumbling down a road, and I lose count of the number of Sentry guards patrolling the streets. Civilians hurry past them, heads bowed, and scurry inside as quickly as they can. Down one alley I see the burned-out shell of a Sentry truck and several smashed windows. Violence is already spreading through the city, and it's only the first day of negotiations. It's like the war never ended.

"Maybe this wasn't the best idea. Let's go back to HQ," Sebastian says.

"No. I really need to get out of that house," I reply. "I keep seeing Truffles's little body all ripped apart . . ."

Sebastian lets out an impatient sound. "Fine."

"Hey! What's that nipper doing on here?" an elderly man calls out when he spots Martha beside me. Everyone turns. One woman in a black taffeta bustle dress screeches dramatically, and her husband comforts her.

"She belongs to me," I say, pointing to Martha's ID bracelet.

"She has no right to travel the steams with us, little girl," he says.

Sebastian points a finger at him. "Don't talk to her like that, *old man*. Do you know who she—"

I shake my head at Sebastian, silencing him. We're meant to be incognito.

"Let's walk. I could use the exercise," I say.

We get off at the next stop and walk the final mile to Chantilly Lane Market, the oldest and largest marketplace in the city, taking it slow, as Martha's clawed feet struggle with the cobbled sidewalks.

Chantilly Lane Market is brimming with life. Music spills out of the nearby taverns, and all around me, colorful flags flutter in the wind, announcing what each stall trades: fish, meat, vegetables, medicine, weapons, clothes, and accessories.

Ladies dressed in garish corseted gowns gossip with each other as they trade at the stalls, taking care that their long skirts don't drag through the dirt. They smile at a troop of Sentry guards as they march by.

A small crowd has gathered around a man standing on a crate. He's got a shaved head and a rose tattoo on his face—the symbol of the Purity. He raises his hands in the air, like he's praying to His Mighty.

"And we shall rid the Darkling plague from His Mighty's green earth, for they are demons sent to tempt us with their opiates and their bodies and their sinful ways. But they are Damned creatures! And anyone who lies with a Darkling is Damned as well, cursed to spend eternity in the burning depths of hell."

The people in the crowd all murmur, "So sayeth His Mighty."

Sebastian listens, enraptured.

"Don't tell me you're starting to believe this crap," I whisper to him.

"I've been reading the Book of Creation, and it actually makes a lot of sense to me."

Sebastian continues to listen to the preacher, occasionally

chiming in with "So sayeth His Mighty" with the rest of the crowd.

A shiver runs down my spine at the sight. I thought Sebastian was too smart to be suckered into the Purity faith.

I tug on his arm. "I didn't come here to listen to some preacher. I want to go shopping and cheer myself up. That's why we're here."

Sebastian looks at me impatiently, then back at the preacher. I can tell he wants to stay.

"Can Martha and I at least go? We'll just be over there." I point to some nearby clothes stalls.

He hesitates.

"No one will recognize me dressed like this. I'm perfectly safe. Please?" I touch his arm.

He looks down at my hand where I'm touching him. Hope sparkles in his green eyes, and in that moment, I hate myself for stooping to such low, manipulative measures. It's something my mother would do.

"As long as you stay with Martha, and don't wander off too far . . . ," he says.

"Great, see you later!" I say, before he can change his mind.

We wander over to the stalls closest to Sebastian. Outside all of them are mannequins modeling the "Latest Fashions, All the Way from Centrum!"—although really they're just hideous knock-offs. I doubt anyone here has ever been to Centrum, as it's two states away and you have to cross the Barren Lands to get there. I've only been through the Barren Lands twice in my life, once when we moved to Centrum and the second time when we left. It's a wild, desolate place, with scorched red earth as far as the eye can see. I don't know how people can live there, it's so deadly.

Martha waits patiently as I try on a few outfits, eventually settling on a pair of tight knee-length trousers, some cheap scarves, and a gaudy Gypsy dress covered in tiny coins.

"We should probably go back to Sebastian, dear," Martha says after I've paid for the clothes.

"I want to get my friend a satchel," I say, thinking about Day carrying all those books.

"That stall's in the center of the market," Martha replies.

Sebastian's still entranced by the preacher. I doubt he'll notice if we're gone for a few more minutes.

"We'll be quick," I say.

The light dims as we navigate the narrow alleys, walking deeper into the market. The bag stall is nestled between a bookstall and a metal shack with a wooden sign hanging over its doorway, reading MOLLIE MCGEE'S TAVERN. The place stinks of Shine—the cheap alcohol that most Workboots drink. I inspect a few of the satchels, trying to decide which one Day might like.

A few people look in our direction and whisper to each other.

"We really should leave," Martha says anxiously.

"I'm almost done," I say, selecting a tan leather bag from the pile.

At that moment, the door to Mollie McGee's bursts open and three rough-looking men stagger out, drunk on Shine. They all have the black and red rose Purity symbol tattooed on the side of their faces. One of them spots Martha and points her out to the other men.

"Rogue!" he calls out.

"She's not a rogue. She belongs to me," I say, but they're not listening.

One of the men grabs a metal rod from a nearby ironmonger

and twirls it in his hand as he walks toward us, a sinister grin on his face.

Oh, heck! I grab Martha's hand, and we dart down one of the alleyways as the drunken men lumber after us. I drag her into a jewelry stall and hold my breath as the men near us. Why did I go so far away from Sebastian? It was stupid of me.

The stall owner, an overweight middle-aged woman wearing gaudy makeup, tries to shoo us out of her shop.

"I want no trouble here," she says.

"I'll buy something expensive if you hide us," I whisper back.

This satisfies her, and she ushers us farther into the stall.

"Here, nipper, nipper, nipper. Come out wherever you are," the man with the rod says.

He bangs the metal poles holding up the stalls, making a terrible clanging noise, trying to scare us out. We shrink deeper into the shadows, and the men walk by, not seeing us. We wait in the stall for a few minutes, until I'm certain the men are gone.

I buy an overpriced gold ring, as promised, and leave.

"Are you all right?" I say to Martha when we're outside.

"I'm fine, dear. It happens all the time."

"Really? I had no idea," I say, stunned.

"We should find Sebastian before those men come back," Martha says.

We head through the maze of alleyways, getting turned around a few times until I'm not certain where we are. As we approach a butcher's stall, I stop dead. Between the waving flags, I catch a glimpse of pale skin, rippling black hair and sparkling black eyes. My heart yanks. *Ash.*

He looks up, sensing me watching him.

"What are you doing here? Aren't the designer stores in Centrum more your scene?" he says as we approach him.

"How would you know what my scene is? You know nothing about me," I reply.

"I know enough," he says, glancing at the ID bracelet around Martha's wrist.

She covers it with her clawed hand, like she's ashamed.

I furrow my brow. Is Martha embarrassed to be working for me?

"Do you know the way out of here, dear? We've got terribly lost," she asks him.

His expression softens. "I'll walk you out after I've got my blood."

I curl my lip at the sight of the butcher's stall. Pig carcasses, strings of sausages and legs of lamb hang from hooks above the counter, all swarming with flies. The ruddy-cheeked butcher swats at them with a bloodied rag. They disperse for a second, then return.

Ash places a copper coin on the counter of the butcher's stall. "One bag of Synth-O-Blood."

The butcher chuckles. "Not for that price, sonny. It's two coppers a bag now, or hadn't you heard? The government's started putting taxes on Synth-O-Blood. Can I do you a deal on some pig's blood?"

I laugh. "That's apt. I always thought you were a total pig."
Ash clenches his jaw.

When did I turn into such a brat? I'd never let Martha eat pig's blood; it's not fit for anyone. I pass the butcher some coins.

"Here, I'll pay for it."

"I don't want your charity," he snaps.

"Well, what are you going to eat, then? You can hardly eat human food. Or can you?" I never thought to ask this about twin-bloods.

"No, it'd be like you eating grass. I can't digest it," he admits.

The sudden clang of metal on metal behind us makes me jump. I turn, fear rippling through me. The three Purity guys who were chasing us earlier sneer back at us. They've blocked the alleyway.

"Found you," the man with the iron rod says to Martha.

"Don't you dare touch her," I warn.

The men just laugh.

"One race under His Mighty!" Iron Rod says, raising the weapon.

The men charge at us.

It all happens so fast, I barely have time to react. Ash pushes me to one side and runs in front of Martha, who falls over as she tries to back away from the men. Ash roughly grabs Iron Rod by the throat and tosses him into the butcher's stall, sending blood and meat everywhere. A leg of lamb lands at my feet.

"Watch out!" I cry as a second man rushes toward Ash.

I grab the leg of lamb by my feet and swing it like a club, hitting the man on the head. He staggers back one, two, three steps, before fleeing. His two friends quickly follow before Ash and I can do any more damage.

We sit Martha down on a wooden crate. Her gray hair has come loose from her headscarf; her clawed hands are trembling. I drop the meat and briefly hug her.

"Are you injured?" Ash asks her.

Martha holds out her hand. It's bleeding.

"I'm such a silly old crone. I cut it as I fell," she says, attempting a gap-toothed smile.

Ash cringes, looking at the holes where her fangs should be.

"We need to bandage her hand," I say, passing him one of the scarves I bought earlier.

He tenderly wraps it around Martha's hand. I barely recognize the boy in front of me. His face is usually so hard and angry, but now it's gentle and full of concern. His eyes briefly flick up, sensing me studying him. I flush.

"Thank you, dear," Martha says, patting his cheek when he's done.

"Yeah. Thank you, Ash," I say quietly. "I don't know what would have happened if you hadn't been here."

He rubs the back of his neck and stands up. "Anytime."

Martha studies him with interest as he helps her up. "Your name's Ash? As in Ash Fisher?"

"Yeah. Why?"

She smiles. "I know your family. Before the war, I regularly attended your father's services, and we grew quite close. I even used to babysit you."

Ash takes a moment to think about it, then a wide smile spreads across his face. "You're the lady with the blood-candy!"

She smiles. "That's right. My, haven't you grown? The last time I saw you, it was just before the war broke out. You were eight years old and chasing my granddaughter Lillian around the graveyard, trying to put spiders down her top."

I laugh at this image, and Ash laughs too, a deep throaty chuckle. I've never heard him laugh before. The sound suits him. I quickly look away, my emotions in a jumble.

"How is Lillian?" he asks.

"She was sent to the Barren Lands during the war with my daughter and her husband. I haven't heard from them since."

"I'm so sorry," Ash replies. "I heard rumors about what was happening in the Barren Lands. My mom used to hold her Legion Liberation Front meetings at the church, just before she was sent to the ghetto, and they discussed it a lot."

So that's how Ash knew about the execution camps during Mr. Lewis's history lesson? Guilt and shame crawl through me. We all know my father was responsible for sending Martha's family there. I don't know how she can stand being around me or my mother, but I suppose she doesn't have a choice—she's our servant. I recall how she covered her ID bracelet in front of Ash, and it finally hits me why she'd be ashamed of it. *She's not our servant. She's our slave.* My stomach churns. How could I have been so blind to this?

"How about Annora? Did she make it through the war?" Martha asks him.

A shadow crosses his features.

"I'm sorry, dear. I didn't mean to intrude . . ."

"Mom and Dad split up years ago. It's just me and Dad now."

"I am sorry to hear that. Your parents were such a lovely couple," Martha says.

"It was inevitable. Humans and Darklings just aren't meant to be together." He flashes me a look.

"Natalie! There you are. I was worried sick," Sebastian's voice sounds behind me.

His blond hair is ruffled from running, and his cheeks are flushed. He looks relieved to see me. Then he catches sight of Ash.

"Get away from her, nipper," he says, storming over to us.

"It's all right. I know him," I say, getting between them.

The two boys size each other up, their fists clenched, a hostile look in their eyes. Ash towers over Sebastian, but if push came to shove, Sebastian's years of Tracker training could give him the edge in a fight.

"Leave him alone, Seb. He just saved us from some thugs," I admit.

Sebastian's mouth twitches. He's itching for a fight; I can see it written all over his face.

"I want to go," I say, lightly touching Sebastian's arm.

He glares at Ash for another second, then nods.

"I knew coming here was a bad idea," Sebastian mutters as we walk away.

"Ash is such a nice young man," Martha whispers to me.

I look over my shoulder at Ash. Our eyes lock for a lingering moment before he heads off in the opposite direction.

"Yeah. He is," I reply.

13

NATALIE

I CATCH UP WITH DAY at school on Monday and tell her all about the fight in the market.

"I can't believe Ash helped you. It seems so unlike him," Day says as we head to the gym hall for Tracker trials.

"I know. It surprised me as well. Maybe we've misjudged him?"

Day laughs. "Let's not get carried away. One random act of kindness doesn't make him a saint."

"I never said he was a saint. I just meant maybe he's not a *complete* jerk? Besides, it wasn't one act of kindness. He does charity work too, as you know—"

Day whips around on me. "Oh, my heavens. You like him."

"No I don't!" I say.

"Then why have you gone bright red?" she says.

"I'm hot, that's all."

"Need I remind you he's a twin-blood Darkling?"

"I don't like him," I say.

"And a low-life Haze dealer, who got his best friend hooked on drugs," she continues.

"Day! For the last time, I don't like Ash Fisher. Okay? I would never, ever allow myself to fall for a Darkling after one of them murdered my father."

"Mmm," she says, unconvinced.

I'm not surprised she doesn't believe me. I didn't convince myself.

We carry on walking to the gym hall in silence. There's no way I can tell her about the *other* thoughts I'd been having about Ash all night, such as the funny way my heart reacts whenever I'm near him, the memory of him as he tenderly bandaged Martha's hand, that lingering look between us as we left the market.

Something flutters in my stomach, and I realize it's nerves. Am I actually excited at the thought of seeing Ash? No! Day's right—nothing's changed. I can't fall for someone like him.

"I'm really sorry about Truffles. Do they have any leads yet?" Day says.

I tell her about Sebastian's theory that Humans for Unity were involved.

"Would Humans for Unity do that?" I ask.

"Some of the members are pretty extreme, and they've always preferred violence over diplomacy," she says. "It's one of the things Beetle and I always argued about; I just couldn't support his decision to be a member of that group. Their obsession with the Darkling cause is dangerous. They're going to get Beetle killed one day."

"Should we ask Beetle if he knows anything about it?" I say.

"He's hardly going to admit they did it."

"I guess," I mumble as we enter the hall.

The noise is unbelievable as students chat excitedly about their chances of having the V-gene. Sebastian is already at the front of the hall setting up the equipment with Kurt. Sebastian's getting a lot of attention from the girls in my year, which he's lapping up, smiling flirtatiously at them. Urgh. Whatever.

My heart yanks, and I search for Ash in the crowd, knowing that he must be nearby. Sure enough, he's leaning against the wall, Beetle beside him. Ash rakes his fingers through his rippling black hair, and for a second, I wonder what it would feel like to have his fingers running through *my* hair . . . I glance away, mortified. *Why is he having this effect on me?* If anyone knew what I was feeling right now, they'd lock me up and throw away the key.

I take Day's hand and casually join the line close to where Ash and Beetle are standing. Ash catches my eye, and my pulse quickens. Blushing, I pretend to check the time on my father's watch, which shimmers gold in the overhead lights.

"You're looking surprisingly 'hot' again," Day whispers to me. "It wouldn't have anything to do with a certain twin-blood boy?"

"Sshhh!" I say, glancing at Ash.

He looks at me, cocking his head slightly. Oh, Lord, did he hear that? *Don't be paranoid, Natalie.* Darkling hearing isn't *that* good.

Beetle murmurs something to Ash. I edge closer to them, curious to know what they're talking about and secretly hoping to hear my name. I catch snatches of their conversation.

"How's she doing?" Beetle says.

A pained look crosses Ash's face. "Worse. It could be any day now."

"I'm so sorry, bro. How's your dad holding up?"

"He's a mess. He won't leave her side. I don't know how he does it; I can't stand looking at her."

I wonder who they're talking about.

Sebastian claps his hands, getting everyone's attention. The room falls silent.

"Purian Rose has given you all a very special opportunity today, a chance to join the Trackers and make this world a better, safer place for the mighty human race," he says, pacing around the room. "There are fifty squads like mine across the United Sentry States, from Mountain Wolf all the way to the Emerald State. Today's test will determine if you have the V-gene and have what it takes to join my squad—"

"The best fragging squad in the whole Black River State!" Kurt roars.

The line starts to move forward. The first victim is ushered up to the machine—a short girl with cropped brown hair. Kurt rolls up her sleeves and places her arm inside the machine.

"Don't worry, you'll only feel a little prick," Sebastian says.

"I bet he's said that to a lot of girls," Day mutters.

I stifle a laugh.

The brown-haired girl winces as her sample is taken.

Kurt shakes his head. "Next."

Day starts to turn a sickly shade of green as she looks at the needle.

The next student goes up and takes the test. It's another fail. It goes on like this for thirty minutes: negative, negative, negative, positive, negative, negative, negative. By the time it gets to Gregory Thompson, only three students have been picked. He haughtily strides up to the machine, rolls up his own sleeve and confidently inserts his arm.

"Pass!" Kurt says.

Gregory punches the air and joins the other Trackers, who all pat him on the back. His twin brother, Chris, saunters up to the machine next.

"Fail."

Gregory can't contain his glee at his brother's failure, a wide smirk crossing his lips. Chris mumbles something under his breath and stalks over to the rest of the rejects.

"Looks like I'm next," Day says, the color draining from her face. "At least if I get on the troop, it might help with my Fast-Track application."

She nervously sits down and screws her eyes shut as the needle sinks into her arm.

"Fail," Kurt says a moment later, leading her away.

She seems relieved. I'm next. I feel the heat of Ash's gaze on me as I walk to the front of the hall.

"Let's get this over with," I mutter to Sebastian, placing my arm in the machine.

Beetle chats quietly to Ash, but he's not paying attention. His focus is solely on me.

The needle sinks into my flesh, making me wince. Lights blink on the machine as my DNA is tested. I roll my eyes. This is so dumb.

"Pass," Kurt says.

"What? Are you sure?" I say.

Sebastian grins at me. "Congratulations!"

Disappointment surges through me, which is odd. Why should I care if I'm a Tracker—isn't this something I should want? Ash holds my gaze for one lingering heartbeat as I'm bundled toward the rest of the Tracker cadets.

Beetle's ushered up to the machine, and Sebastian barely looks at the result before he announces, "Fail."

Beetle grins, giving Ash the thumbs-up, and saunters over to the rest of the rejects. Ash is next. He doesn't even attempt to take the test and instead walks toward the rejects.

"Where are you going, nipper?" Sebastian sneers.

I furrow my brow. He can't be serious.

"Everyone needs to take the test, including you," he says.

They coolly eye each other, the tension palpable between them.

"I'm waiting," Sebastian drawls.

Ash mutters a curse and walks up to the machine. Kurt punches the button, bringing the needle down on Ash's arm. Lights blink and flash as his DNA is analyzed, and a moment later, Kurt checks his results. He frowns and reads the results again before turning to face Ash, his expression curious.

"Positive," he says. "Welcome to the Trackers, Mr. Fisher."

Ash Fisher is the topic of conversation on everyone's lips for the rest of the morning. How can a twin-blood Darkling be a Tracker?

"He'll never hunt his own kind," I say to Day as we walk to art class, my least favorite subject, since I have all the artistic skill of a rabid squirrel.

"He doesn't have a choice," she replies.

"It's such a sadistic thing to make Ash do."

Day doesn't say anything. She doesn't need to. It's not exactly the first time a Darkling has been forced to hunt its own kind; it was common practice during the war for less moralistic Darklings to collaborate with Trackers in return for food and protection.

Ash is already outside the art room with Beetle; they're talking quietly to each other. He looks up at me as we approach.

"I'm sorry." I can't think of anything else to say.

He gives me a sad smile.

The art class door opens, and Mrs. James, a frumpy woman

with wild brown hair, ushers us inside. The room is spacious and bright, with colorful paintings on the walls and wonky-looking clay sculptures spread along the shelves. My stomach sinks when I see the circle of easels surrounding a plinth in the center of the room.

Day rushes to an easel, and I drop my bag next to the one beside her, watching Ash out of the corner of my eye to see where he's going to sit, half of me wanting him to sit near me, the other half wanting him not to. I furiously push the first thought out of my head. What's gotten into me?

He heads to an easel on the opposite side of the circle, and Beetle takes the seat next to him.

"Hey, babes, is this seat taken?"

Chris Thompson smiles down at me, his dark brown hair falling into his hazel eyes. There's a faraway look in them, like he's not quite on this planet. His brother, Gregory, hovers behind him, all pinched and mean looking.

"Er, no," I say.

Ash's head turns ever so slightly in our direction.

Chris sits next to me, while Gregory grumpily takes the easel beside Day, turning his narrow nose up at her as he sits down.

"Swap seats with me," Day hisses under her breath.

I imagine an hour of Gregory waxing lyrical about my mother and how he hopes to "follow in his father's footsteps and work for the government." Gag.

"Sorry," I mouth.

Day huffs loudly.

Mrs. James claps her hands to get our attention. "Right, class, who wants to be our victim?"

I shrink down in my seat. I hate people looking at me,

especially at my surgery scar over my heart. Mother always has it airbrushed out of photos, and I don't blame her; it's so ugly.

"Day, why don't you model for us?" Mrs. James says a little desperately.

Day reluctantly takes her place on top of the plinth. Her glasses unceremoniously slip off her face and fall on the floor. Gregory laughs. Chris leans across me and punches his brother in the arm.

"Don't be a dick," he says.

Beetle hurries out of his seat and hands Day's glasses back to her. She gives him a grateful smile, and his ears go pink, the way they always do around Day. Ash teasingly rolls his eyes at Beetle when he sits down.

I stick my brush in some paint and splash it on the canvas, not taking much care over it. A familiar chill creeps over my skin, and I look up. Ash is watching me from across the room. His eyes dart away.

"Congratulations on making the squad," Chris says to me.

"Oh . . . yeah. Thanks."

"Don't tell my bro, but I'm glad I didn't make the squad," Chris says quietly. "I don't want to hunt Darks for a living."

"Same here," I admit.

"It's crazy about Ash, isn't it? Poor guy, that's gotta suck. Fragging Sen—" He catches himself when he remembers who he's speaking to. "Sorry."

"No problem," I mumble.

I focus on my painting, feeling guilty even though it's not my fault Ash has been enlisted to the Trackers. A few minutes later, I sigh and inspect my masterpiece. It's a hideous mess of brown and gray. Oh, well. If Mrs. James asks, I'll tell her it's impressionistic.

Ash stands up all of a sudden, drawing my attention. He shrugs off his jacket, exposing the lean muscles of his toned arms. The tiny red pinprick is still visible on his left forearm.

"Looking good," Chris says, making me jump.

"What?" I ask, my mind still on Ash.

Chris points to my painting. "You've got a real eye for it."

I make a really unladylike snort-laugh sound that grabs everyone's attention. I cringe, sinking lower in my chair.

"You're joking, right?" I say to Chris.

"Okay, I admit it's not the best I've ever seen."

I inspect his painting. It's not bad; it actually looks a little like Day.

"So," Chris says, running a hand along his chiseled jaw, "I was wondering, if you're not doing anything after the museum trip tomorrow, maybe we could hang out or something?"

"Erm . . ." I glance at Ash.

"Or we could go to the Armistice Day celebrations on Saturday?" Chris adds.

Ash continues to paint, seemingly oblivious, although his ear twitches slightly like he's listening in.

"I've got a boyfriend." The lie falls out of my mouth before I know what I'm saying. "Sebastian, the Head Tracker? He's really protective of me." All of which is true, apart from the boyfriend bit.

Ash turns to face me, a dark emotion blazing across his face.

"Too bad," Chris says.

I turn back to my painting, my heart not in it.

Chris gets up and strides over to Ash, who quickly covers his painting, looking like he's been caught with his hand in the cookie jar. What's he hiding? Surely his painting can't be worse than mine. Chris doesn't seem to notice as they talk quietly, their faces serious. Ash nods and passes something to Chris—a playing card! I think back to the two of hearts playing card in my jacket pocket. Ash must give them out to all his Haze clients. The thought disappoints me slightly; I don't like being reminded that Ash is a dealer. I'd much prefer to think of him as the boy in the market. I don't completely hate that version of Ash.

Gregory chucks a piece of scrunched-up paper at me to get my attention.

"What?" I say irritably.

"I'm really excited about our first training session with the squad on Thursday, aren't you? It's just a shame we have to share our lesson with that nipper," he says, looking at Ash.

Anger boils up in me at the use of the word *nipper*. Weird. I've not had an issue with people saying it before. My friends in Centrum used it all the time.

I turn back to my painting, ignoring him. The rest of the lesson passes quickly. I soon give up on my painting, knowing it's a lost cause, and spend the rest of my time daydreaming about being back at the market in Chantilly Lane, reliving the lingering look between me and Ash. The bell finally rings, and everyone packs up. Ash scrunches his painting into a ball and tosses it into the bin. He pauses by my easel, and my heart tugs in that strange way it does whenever he's close by.

"How's Martha doing?" he asks.

"Fine. It's amazing how quickly she's recovered; her hand is as good as new."

He shrugs. "Darklings heal fast. It's one of our skills."

What other skills does he have? Heat rises up my neck.

He opens his mouth to say something else, then seems to change his mind and moves on. The door swings shut behind him.

Day takes a tour of the room, inspecting everyone's pictures of her.

"I look hideous in all of them! Am I really that ugly?"

"No, don't be silly. We're just *really* bad painters," I reply.

She finds Ash's balled-up painting in the bin and curiously opens it. Her mouth drops open in surprise.

"Is it really awful?" I say.

She shakes her head and ushers me over, handing me the painting. I expect to see a portrait of Day, but that's not who he's painted at all. What's really there takes my breath away. The painting is *alive,* the vibrant colors constantly changing as they swirl into each other, so it looks like the portrait is moving. Darklings are gifted artists, able to capture the pure essence of their emotions in the painting. I trace a finger along the contours of the portrait's face, not recognizing the girl staring back at me. Her eyes shine the brightest blue, and her hair's like spun gold, tumbling around her shoulders. Then I register who the girl is.

It's me!

Down the center of my chest is my scar, but it's not the eyesore I always thought it to be. Somehow it makes me look beautiful, powerful, like I'm a mighty warrior. I sit down, unable to take it all in. Is this how Ash really sees me?

I stare at the portrait, dumbfounded. And I swear, the more I study it, the more the painting seems to throb like the beat of an untamed heart.

14
ASH

THE MOON IS HIGH above the city as I lie on the roof of Beetle's barge, arms behind my head. The boat rocks as he climbs onto the roof and sparks up a cigarette. He passes it to me, but the nicotine doesn't give me the same kick as it did before. Nothing feels as good as the heart beating inside my chest.

"How's your mom doing?" he asks.

I shut my eyes, forcing out the grief balling up inside me. I don't want to deal with this right now.

"I wish she'd go back to the Legion," I say eventually, opening my eyes.

"You don't mean that, bro."

"It was selfish of her to come home. All it's done is upset Dad. What really sucks is she only returned because her boyfriend kicked her out when she got sick."

"You don't know that," he replies.

"Why else would she have come back? Certainly not for me or Dad. She doesn't give a fragg about us; otherwise, she wouldn't have left in the first place." I hand the cigarette to Beetle. "Let's talk about something else. I'm getting bummed out."

"I'm thinking of having a small get-together for my birth-day," he says.

"Yeah? Sounds good. Who are you inviting?"

"Well, you."

"That's not a gathering. That's a date."

Beetle chuckles. "You wish. Maybe I'll invite Day as well."

"I thought you two were over."

He shrugs. "The heart wants what the heart wants."

Yeah, he doesn't need to tell me twice.

"Do you think she'll come?" he asks quietly.

"Maybe, but why are you wasting your time on her? You can do better."

"No I can't, bro. She's intelligent, loving, and she really pushes my buttons," he says.

Natalie certainly pushes my buttons. She isn't afraid to stand up to me, and she's not like any other Sentry I know. She helped Tom, even though she put herself at risk. She's brave and kind.

"Plus, Day's got these amazing . . ." He cups his hands in front of his chest.

"Well, that changes everything," I say. "So, are you inviting any other girls?"

My heart speeds up, thinking about Natalie.

"I wasn't planning on it," he says.

"Cool, whatever." I try and hide the disappointment in my voice.

Fragg! Why should I care if Natalie's coming or not? She's the Emissary's daughter. Getting involved with her is the worst thing I can do. Her parents were responsible for the deaths of millions of Darklings. *But Natalie didn't kill them. She's not to blame.*

I press a hand over my chest and feel the steady thrum of my heart under my fingertips.

Dad used to tell me everything in life comes with a price, and boy, was he right. I got the thing I desired the most, a heartbeat, but at what cost? I'm indebted to a Sentry girl. That was never part of the agreement. I wish I understood what was going on between us. Does she have feelings for me? Sometimes I think she does. I've caught her looking at me a few times, but I can't be certain. It might just be in my head.

"Oh, before I forget!" Beetle pulls out a slip of paper from his pocket and flattens it against the roof.

It's the permission slip our parents need to sign to let us go on the museum tour tomorrow. Beetle scrawls his aunt's signature on his form. I rummage around in my pockets, find my form and pass it to him. He's better at forging my dad's signature than I am. I could just ask Dad to sign my form, but I've gotten so used to Beetle faking his signature on all my bad school reports, it's become habit.

"We'll show our faces for a few minutes, then skip out," Beetle says.

It's a risk, playing hooky, but I'd rather have three lashes than spend an entire day at the Black City snoreseum. He passes my slip back to me.

"I could try forging a letter from your dad to get you out of Tracker training, if you'd like. It might be worth a shot," he offers.

"Somehow I don't think a pissy letter from my 'dad' is going to change their mind."

He sits up. "So you're just going to train with them?"

"I don't have a choice. It's not worth getting crucified over."

Beetle grinds the cigarette out on the wood, muttering to himself.

"If you've got something to say, just say it," I snap.

"Is there anything you're willing to die for? Humans for Unity are out there every day, risking their lives to free the Darklings, and what are you doing? Nothing!"

I stand up. "Why should I do anything? I'm not a Darkling. I'm not a human. I'm nothing, so why should I care what you do? It's not my war."

I leap off the barge onto the canal pathway and head toward the bridge where I first saw Natalie.

"That's right, run off like always!" Beetle yells after me.

I flip him my middle finger. *What does he know about anything?*

The air-raid siren wails across the city, letting us know curfew has started. I walk under the canal bridge and run my hand over the rough brick wall, remembering the last time I was here. This is where it all began; this is where my heart came to life.

It has to mean *something*. There's only one way to know for sure. I have to ask her.

15
NATALIE

🌠 **A TWENTY-FOOT STATUE** of Purian Rose looms over us in the foyer of the Black City Museum, his wolfish eyes glowering down on us all.

Sebastian whistles, impressed. "One day there will be an even bigger statue of me in this museum."

I roll my eyes, wishing Sebastian weren't here with me today, but there's no way Mother would have allowed me to come on this school trip without my bodyguard. To make things worse, Sebastian's wearing his Tracker uniform—a bright red military coatee and black trousers, with a gleaming silver sword strapped around his hip—making him stand out like a sore thumb. Everyone stares at me as I approach the base of the statue where my history class is waiting.

Ash is resting against the sculpture. He's so striking in contrast to everyone else—tall, pale and darkly beautiful. He raises his sparkling eyes and studies me for a fraction too long, making my body temperature rise by a hundred degrees.

Since I saw his painting of me, I haven't been able to stop

thinking about him. Does he really think I'm beautiful? Now that there's the possibility he might, I've found myself fantasizing about what it would be like if it weren't illegal for us to date. Would we be together? I can't believe I'm even considering it! He's a twin-blood and yet . . .

Sebastian catches me staring at Ash. His jaw clenches.

"Please don't make a scene," I say to him.

"Don't give me a reason to," he replies.

I bite my lip. He can't possibly know what I was thinking about Ash. Could he? No. I'm being paranoid.

I walk over to Day. Nearby, Chris and Gregory are having a heated discussion under their breaths.

"I'll tell Mom and Dad on you one of these days," Gregory snips in his whiny voice.

"No you won't. You love me too much, bro," Chris replies, ruffling his brother's limp hair.

Gregory slaps Chris's hand away. "I'm just looking out for you. Do you really want to be a Hazer for the rest of your life?"

Chris shrugs, his face hardening. "My life, my business."

Sebastian goes over to Mr. Lewis to talk about my security procedures, giving me a brief moment alone with Day.

She nudges me, pointing toward someone in the foyer. "Hey, isn't that the Hazer who was being interrogated at your house the other week?"

Sure enough, it's the purple-haired guy we bumped into outside the interrogation rooms. He's with a skinny tattooed girl and a tough-looking guy. They're tipping over trash cans and harassing visitors as they walk through the door. A security guard yells at them, and they stalk down one of the corridors leading to the main exhibition, laughing like hyenas. We're not the only ones to have noticed the purple-haired boy—Ash has seen him too, and he's furious.

"What's Linus doing here?" I overhear Beetle saying to Ash.

"Guess he's forgotten whose turf this is," Ash replies.

"Should we go speak to them?"

Ash considers this, then shakes his head. "Not here. Later."

Beetle nods.

Chris casually strolls over to Ash, hands thrust into his pockets. Gregory watches his brother, his eyes burning with fury.

"Hey, you still on for our appointment on Thursday?" Chris asks.

Ash groans. "No, sorry. It's Beetle's birthday. We're doing a thing. Can we arrange it for Friday?"

A hint of desperation enters Chris's voice. "I really wanted it on Thursday; my parents are out that night."

Ash shrugs. "Sorry, mate. You understand?"

"Thanks for nothing," Chris mutters as he leaves.

Beetle nervously rakes a hand through his tangled brown hair. Ash nudges him.

"Ask her," he whispers.

"Do you want to come to my birthday party?" Beetle blurts out to Day.

"What?" Day stammers.

"Forget it, nothing, don't worry," he says.

"Were you being serious?"

He nods, not looking at her. "It just won't be the same without you there."

She thinks about it for a moment. "All right. I'll come, on the condition there are no drugs—"

"There won't be, I promise. I'm getting clean," he says.

"And Ash isn't there," she continues.

"He's my best friend. He's coming," Beetle challenges her. "You can't keep avoiding me just because you don't like Ash. I don't like your friend, but I'd be willing to hang out with her."

"I'm so honored," I mutter.

"Please come," Beetle says to her.

Day sighs. "Only if Natalie comes too."

Beetle nods.

"That's enough out of you kids! Get a move on—I haven't got all day," Mr. Lewis scolds as he leads us through the ticket office and into the exhibitions.

"Ladies first," Beetle says to Day, letting her through the turnstile.

She rolls her eyes, but a slight smile plays across her lips. Beetle goes next. At the exact same time, Ash and I move to the turnstile and clumsily bump arms, sending electric shocks shivering right down to my fingertips. Ash inhales sharply, like he felt them too. There's an awkward moment, then Ash steps back.

"After you," he says softly.

As Ash follows me through the turnstile, a dark thrill caresses my body, and I know he's watching me. Sebastian catches up with me a moment later and takes my hand, dragging me away from Ash.

"I don't want you anywhere near that nipper, all right?" he says to me.

My heart skips a beat. Maybe I wasn't being paranoid earlier. Does Sebastian suspect I have feelings for Ash? "Fine," I snap back.

Day hurries after us.

The first room we're dragged around is a new exhibition on

Purian Rose. I occasionally scribble down a few notes, in case Mr. Lewis tests us on it later.

"Isn't it fascinating?" Sebastian says as we walk past the waxworks of Purian Rose.

The exhibit charts his meteoric rise to power, from his early days as an unassuming government official, to his inauguration as president, right through to the present day, where he is the head of church and state. Somehow in the middle of that, he managed to find the time to write the Book of Creation and start a war against the Darklings. That waxwork frightens me the most, as he's standing on top of a pile of dead Darklings, the victor in the "war against corruption."

"He's a true inspiration," Sebastian continues. "I hope to achieve as much one day."

"How can you admire him when you know what he did to my family?" I say.

Day looks at me with curiosity. I never told her the full story of why Polly was tortured and my father killed.

"He who walks on the path of sin will suffer the wrath of His Mighty," Sebastian says, quoting the Book of Creation.

I'm too flabbergasted to speak at first. Is he insinuating Polly and my father got what they deserved?

"Who *are* you?" I say.

"I've just had my eyes opened to the corruption around me, Natalie," he says.

We carry on with the tour. I cross my arms, silently seething at Sebastian. How can he be so callous? He cared for Polly, once upon a time. Walking nearby are Chris and Gregory. Chris looks agitated and bored as his brother stops to inspect every exhibition.

We enter a dimly lit, semicircular room filled with stuffed dead animals and fossilized skeletons. There's a Lupine—a giant wolflike creature with beautiful soft gray fur, a winged Nordin Darkling skeleton, the skull of a catlike creature with long saber teeth, and a waxwork of a Wrath, which sends tremors down my spine.

"What's that?" Day asks, looking at the skull of the catlike creature.

"That's a Bastet," Sebastian says.

I read the information placard beside the skull.

BASTET—Origin: Emerald State. Lifespan: Unknown. Diet: Darklings.

These rare creatures were once falsely worshipped as gods. They grow to six feet in height, and live in prides of up to two hundred. Bastet venom is highly toxic to Darklings and has been found to contain traces of the flesh-eating bacteria Vibrio necrosis.

"Gross," I mutter.

"Look, this is pretty cool," Sebastian says, pressing the cat's saber teeth. They retract into the skull cavity. "They do that to prevent their fangs from getting damaged."

"Its teeth are shimmering," Day says.

"That's what makes Bastet ivory so valuable; it's imbued with the venom. People used to make ornaments and jewelry from them. Obviously Bastets are very rare these days; the poachers took most of them."

I inspect the other animal exhibits as Sebastian and Day chat. The animals' dead eyes stare at me as we walk by, making me feel uneasy. I can't shake the feeling that I'm being watched . . .

A flash of blue catches my eye from the display to my left. I peer into the shadows. *Huh, there's nothing there. Stop spooking yourself, Buchanan!*

Sebastian stops talking. His hand curls around the hilt of his sword.

"Is everything all right?" I say to him.

He nods, although he's clearly distracted by something.

There's movement to my right, making me start, but it's just Chris Thompson sneaking off to one of the other rooms when Gregory's back is turned, followed by the drug dealer Linus.

"Stay close," Sebastian says to me.

"What's wrong?" Day asks.

"My V-gene is triggering. I can sense a Darkling nearby," Sebastian replies.

Day looks at me, worried.

"Just keep moving," Sebastian says.

We round the bend, and my heart wrenches as I spot Ash having a smoke with Beetle. Wisps of smoke spill from Ash's parted lips, and for a fleeting moment, I wonder what it would be like to run my tongue over those lips, taste the smokiness of his mouth.

Sebastian lets out a sigh. "False alarm. I was just sensing that nipper."

"Stop calling him that," I say.

A sensation like molten lead suddenly leaks into my stomach and scorches my insides as darkness spills over my skin. *The Sight.* Ash looks in my direction, alarmed. He's by my side in a heartbeat, Beetle soon behind.

Sebastian draws his sword, pointing it at Ash.

"A Darkling's hunting her. I can sense him using the Sight," Ash says to him.

"Where is it?" I ask Ash, terrified.

"I don't know," he says, surveying the room.

"I'll go look for it," Sebastian says.

"No! Don't leave me." Images of Truffles's bloodied body pop into my head.

"We have to get rid of it," Sebastian says.

"I have an idea. Do you trust me?" Ash asks me.

I look up at his beautiful, earnest face. My heart contracts.

"Yes," I whisper.

"Look into my eyes," he says quietly.

I obey. He holds my gaze, staring at me, *into* me. His black eyes sparkle like stars in the dusky light . . . they're so pretty . . . all glittery . . . they're making me sleepy. Soon I'm lost in them, sinking, falling, until there is nothing left but him and me. Suddenly the darkness that has enveloped me starts to lift as Ash shifts the power of the Sight from the other Darkling over to him.

Mine . . . mine . . . mine, he's telling them. *Leave her, she belongs to me.*

The darkness evaporates.

Ash blinks, breaking the spell.

I let out a shaky sigh. "Is it gone?"

"I can't sense it anymore," Ash says.

"I'm going to check the perimeter. Wait here," Sebastian says to me, flashing Ash a bitter look. "You lay one fang on her, I'll slice your head off. Understand?"

Ash's fist clenches, but he says nothing as Sebastian stalks away.

Day hugs me. "Do you think that's what—"

"Killed Truffles?" I finish for her. "Yeah. I think I'm being hunted, but why?"

"You're a prime target for the Legion Liberation Front," Beetle says, referring to the Darkling militia group that fought the Sentry during the war.

I turn to Ash. "Thanks for protecting me."

"No problem. I just didn't want to get blamed if you got attacked."

Anger flares up in me. "Don't put yourself out for me! Next time, just let the damn thing eat me."

I stomp away, furious at myself for ever thinking that Ash Fisher had a heart. He catches up with me a moment later beside the Bastet skull.

"Hey, blondie, why are you mad at me?" he asks.

"Just leave me alone," I say.

"Not until you tell me why you're so pissed."

I let out a frustrated scream. "By His Mighty's Name, you are *so* annoying!"

"Okay, so we've established I annoy you. Anything else?" he asks, a small smile playing on his lips.

Yearning unfurls inside me. I remind myself I'm meant to be mad at him.

"Yes! You don't care about anyone but yourself. You only help others if it helps *you* somehow," I say.

"Ouch." He looks genuinely offended.

"Well, it's true."

"No it's not. I helped you because . . ."

"What?"

"I didn't want you to get hurt."

"Oh. Then why did you say otherwise?"

He shrugs. "Because I shouldn't care what happens to you."

"But you do?"

He doesn't say anything. Instead he turns his attention to the exhibition. I nervously look around me to make sure no one is watching us, my heart pounding a mile a minute, aware that I'm crossing over some invisible line by talking to him. Sebastian's checking the perimeter, Day's chatting with Beetle, and the rest of the class is in the next room. We're alone.

Ash turns to me, a determined look in his eyes. "Natalie, there's something I've wanted to talk to you about."

I raise an eyebrow. "Really? What?"

He takes a deep breath. "I don't really know how to say it, so I'm just going to come out with it. You'll probably think I'm insane."

"Okay . . . ," I say, wondering where this is going.

"The other day, when we were in our history lesson, we bumped heads and—"

"What do we have here, then?" a boy's voice says behind us.

The boy with the purple hair—Linus—saunters by with his two goons. The tattooed girl gives me a hard look, daring me to make eye contact. I don't.

"Since I last checked, this was still my neighborhood," Ash says.

Linus smirks, his hand closing around a glass phial sticking out of his jacket pocket. It's filled with a milky liquid that shimmers with a golden hue when the light catches it.

"Not anymore, nipper. This is Mr. Tubs's ground now," Linus drawls.

Ash grabs Linus by the collar, and the boy flinches. His goons close in.

"This is my turf," Ash says.

"People are watching," I warn him.

He releases Linus and indicates some nearby doors. "The exit's that way. I suggest you use it."

"Make me."

Ash's jaw tightens. He can't do anything, not here.

"Sebastian will be really interested in hearing you were here, Linus. He might even call you in for questioning. *Again*," I say.

He turns his attention to me. "What makes you think he don't already know I'm here, sweet cheeks?"

What does he mean by that?

The tattooed girl loops an arm over Linus's shoulder and presses herself provocatively against him.

"Let's go test out the merchandise," she murmurs.

Linus shrugs her off him and smooths his collar. They head down the corridor toward one of the other exhibitions.

"What was in that tube?" I ask Ash.

"Darkling venom, Haze," he explains.

"I thought Haze was white. That stuff had a golden shimmer to it."

"It's probably that Golden Haze that's been doing the rounds."

I'm about to carry on our conversation about what happened when we bumped heads in history lesson, when Sebastian enters the room. I step away from Ash, not wanting to give Sebastian any reason to cause a scene.

"Did you find anything?" I ask him.

"No, the nipper's long gone," he replies, sheathing his sword.

I let out a relieved sigh.

A scream from the next room startles us all, and a moment later, the tattooed girl sprints out of the room, tears spilling down her face. She pushes past us, heading for the exit. Without thinking, I rush into the next room, wondering what all the drama's about, and instantly wish I hadn't. Sprawled on the floor are the bodies of Linus and the shaven-headed guy, their dead eyes staring up at the ceiling. Their faces are contorted in a mask of pain, their lips as black as coal.

Clutched in Linus's dead hand is the open phial of Golden Haze.

16.
ASH

"THE FIRST RULE of surviving a Darkling attack is to run," Sebastian says to the group.

All the Tracker cadets sit in a circle in the center of the hall, dressed in our sparkling new uniforms. Sebastian's second-in-command, the brawny black man with claw marks down his neck, gives me a cold, hard look from across the room. I tug at the collar of my jacket, trying to get some air between it and my skin, feeling claustrophobic in the expensive cotton. One of the other Trackers—a girl with wavy brown hair—flashes me an appreciative look. *Whoa!* Since I put on this uniform, everyone at school's been treating me differently, like I'm one of them at last. It feels good to be respected, but it's a bittersweet emotion. I shouldn't have to go to these extremes to get respect.

Natalie's sitting close by. She tucks a golden curl behind her ear, revealing a small freckle just above her collar. I wonder what it would be like to place my lips over that freckle, to sink my fangs into her neck . . . She turns and catches me looking. A small smile flits across her lips, and in that instant, my fate is sealed.

I want her.

Someone kicks my foot. *Sebastian.*

He gives me a warning look.

"What do you mean, we're supposed to *run*?" Gregory whines, referring to Sebastian's earlier comment. "I thought we were here to learn to fight."

Sebastian nods at Claw Neck, who unbuttons the top two buttons of his jacket, revealing his upper body. The claw marks go all the way down his chest, and there's a huge chunk of flesh missing where a Darkling's taken a bite out of him. It has the desired effect—everyone's paying attention now.

"Darklings are taller, stronger and faster than us. If you take one on without the odds being in your favor, which they rarely are, then they'll kill you before you can blink," Sebastian says. "If you want to survive, *run*. There's no shame in coming back to HQ alive."

"We hunt in packs," Claw Neck continues. "That's how we put the odds in *our* favor. Your unit is your family now. Your life is in their hands. It's vital that you learn to move as one, anticipate one another's movements and protect one another. This way, we're unstoppable."

"We have an added benefit, of course. The V-gene," Sebastian says. "With training, it allows you to sense Darklings, giving you an edge over the enemy. Learning to hone this sense can mean the difference between life and death. But first, the essentials. Sword fighting. Get into pairs."

I grab a sword from the rack and turn it over in my hand. It doesn't feel right. There's no way I'm going to risk stabbing another Darkling. I put the blade back.

"What are you doing?" Claw Neck growls at me.

"I don't need a sword. I have my own weapons," I say, flashing my fangs.

Natalie takes one of the smaller swords, giving me a shy smile. My heart pounds inside my chest, *ba-boom ba-boom ba-boom.* I can't believe I nearly told her about my heart when we were in the museum. What was I thinking? She'll say I'm crazy, a freak; she'll never want to talk to me again. I can't risk that, when I still don't know how or why she's doing this to me.

Gregory bumps into me.

"Get out of the way, mongrel," he says.

"Sorry," I say sarcastically. "I didn't see you down there."

Gregory's nostrils flare. He takes the biggest sword on the rack.

"You know what they say about boys with big toys?" I say.

Natalie giggles, and Gregory narrows his eyes at me. Everyone pairs up, leaving just me and Natalie.

"I'll try not to hurt you too much," she says

Sebastian strolls over to Natalie, lightly touching her shoulder. Just that small familiar gesture makes my fangs hurt.

"Maybe you should sit this one out. I don't want you putting too much strain on your heart," he says.

Her cheeks flush crimson. "I need to practice, don't I? Otherwise what's the point of being here?"

"I'm just looking out for you—"

She lifts her sword threateningly at him. "I'm perfectly fine. My heart's fine. Stop treating me like I'm a child!"

I stifle a grin.

Sebastian squares up to me, giving me attitude. "You hurt her, I'll hurt you, got it?"

"Loud and clear," I growl back.

"Sorry about Sebastian," Natalie says when he's gone.

"Your boyfriend's a dick," I say.

"Seb's not my boyfriend." She laughs. "I only told Chris that so he'd stop hitting on me."

Hope flickers like a flame inside me, making me glow.

We run through a few basic strikes and parries, and it's pretty clear Natalie's done this before. Her movements are swift and precise, but even so, she doesn't manage to strike me once.

"No fair. You keep moving!" she teases as I dart out of the way of another one of her attacks.

"That's sort of the idea, isn't it? A Darkling isn't going to just stand there and take it."

She beams that beautiful startling smile of hers, and I falter. She thrusts again and this time catches me on the arm, making a small rip in my jacket. I rub my arm dramatically.

"Wimp," she says.

"You've done this before."

"My father taught me," she says. A shadow briefly crosses her features, and I wonder what dark memory she's revisiting.

"How have you been since we found Linus?" I ask gently. It's been two days since we discovered his dead body in the museum.

She shrugs. "I keep having nightmares about it. There was a short article about it in the paper. Did you see it?"

I nod. It was just a paragraph lost in the sea of news stories. They'd chalked his death up to a Haze overdose—and that was that. A whole life summed up in a few short lines. It's not much. Would I get even that much coverage if someone found me dead?

"You've got your frowny face on," Natalie says.

"Huh?"

She pulls a very serious face, mimicking me.

"Sorry, I was just thinking about Linus. That was a tough way to go," I say.

"I can think of worse," she mutters. "What do you think was in that Golden Haze? It must've been strong to kill Linus and his friend so quickly."

"I'm not sure. Dealers often mix it with naturally occurring hallucinogens, so maybe something like that?" I reply.

We continue to sword fight, although her mind isn't on it anymore.

"Ash, what were you going to talk to me about at the museum? Something about us bumping heads . . . ?" she says.

My stomach flips. Damn. I'd hoped she'd forgotten about that.

"I just wanted to make sure you weren't hurt. I've got a pretty thick skull," I say, tapping my head.

She narrows her eyes suspiciously at me. "I lost a few brain cells, but there's no permanent damage. Is that really what you wanted to ask me?"

"Mmm-mmm. So, you looking forward to Beetle's party tonight?" I ask to change the subject.

She grimaces. "Not really. Beetle hates me."

"And Day hates me."

"It's going to be a fun night," she says. "Anyone else coming?"

I laugh. "Nope. Beetle's not exactly popular around here."

Natalie bites her lip shyly. "So it'll just be the four of us? Like a double date?"

I hadn't thought of it like that, but . . . oh, fragg, are we going on a date?

"Uh-huh" is all I manage to say.

"Everybody circle up," Sebastian calls out.

We gather back in our group, and I sit as close to Natalie as possible without being too obvious.

"Well, to say your sword-fighting skills are appalling would be a gross understatement," Sebastian says. "Peter Gibb, you have to keep your eyes *open* when you strike. Gregory, you fight like you're trying to hack your way through a jungle. Natalie . . . good work."

She blushes slightly, and my fangs throb again.

"When are we going to learn how to control our V-gene powers?" Gregory says.

"You need a Darkling to learn how to do that, and you pathetic excuses for soldiers are in no position to be in a room with a Darkling."

"What about Ash?" Gregory suggests.

"No way!" I reply.

Sebastian scratches his chin as he weighs this up. "All right, let's give it a go. You're all so awful at fighting, it might be your only chance of survival, and you'll need to learn this before you go on your first hunt next week."

"We're going on a hunt? Awesome," Gregory says.

"I'm not going to be anyone's guinea pig," I say, but no one's listening to me.

Natalie stands up and gives me a weak smile.

Sebastian turns off the light, plunging the hall into darkness, and there are a few startled exclamations from the cadets. His voice drifts out from the gloom, moving around the room as he walks easily between us, even though he must not be able to see a thing. That's one big advantage I have over him: I can see in the dark.

"Spread out around the room. I want you all to focus on

Ash. Picture him in your mind's eye. You should experience a faint electric shock when you sense him—this is your V-gene triggering. The sensation won't be as strong with a half-blood, but you'll still be able to detect him. I can."

With a swift, deft movement Sebastian swings his sword and slices off some of my hair.

"What the fragg!" I say, leaping back. "You could've chopped my head off."

He just laughs in response.

"Seb, we can't run around a dark room swinging swords at each other. Someone will get hurt," Natalie says.

"Fair enough. Everybody, place your weapons on the ground. When you find the nipper, just tap him on the shoulder and say, 'Tag, you're dead.'"

My fangs flood with venom, enraged at being called a nipper. *Right, you asked for it. This is war.*

There's a clatter of metal as everyone puts the swords on the ground, then the cadets start to move around the room, their arms outstretched, searching for me like they're playing a game of Blind Man's Bluff. Only Natalie and Gregory remain still, both of them trying to channel their V-gene.

"Over here," I whisper.

A number of cadets lurch toward me, but I deftly move out of the way, and they crash into each other. *This is going to be fun!* I silently patrol the room, occasionally knocking the wall beside one of the cadets to draw their attention away from the group. I tag three out within a minute.

I tap another unsuspecting cadet on the shoulder. "Tag, you're dead."

The cadet grumbles and sits out.

"Don't underestimate your opponent," Claw Neck says in

the gloom. "Darklings will often try and lure you away from the pack so you're easier to take down."

Is that what I've been doing? I hadn't realized—it was just instinct.

There's movement from the center of the room, and Gregory starts walking roughly in my direction, slowly, deliberately.

"Come out, come out, wherever you are, nipper," he says.

He veers off to the right, clearly not sensing me at all. Natalie, on the other hand, heads straight for me. I'm too stunned to move at first, and she's almost upon me before I gather my wits and sidestep out of her way. She immediately turns and comes for me again. I see her smiling in the dark.

"There's no point running, Ash. I can feel you," she whispers.

She almost gets me again. Bloody hell! She really *can* sense me!

Well, there's no way I'm letting her get the better of me. I'll never live it down. I pounce at Natalie, knocking her off her feet and pinning her against the wall.

"Tag, you're dead," I whisper mockingly in her ear.

Somewhere in the dark, Sebastian and the cadets move about the room, closing in.

I release Natalie's arms and expect her to walk away, but instead her hand moves up to my face and she lightly traces her fingers over my lips, brushing across my fangs, making them throb with venom. My breath catches in my throat at her forbidden touch. What's she doing? *If they catch her doing this to me . . .*

"You can run, but you can't hide," Gregory taunts somewhere to my right.

Shame squirms inside my gut, loathing how my body's responding to her. A million reasons run through my head why I should push her away, but I don't. Instead, I do the one thing I shouldn't: I reach out my hand and gently touch her face. She lets out a soft, breathy moan as my fingertips explore the contours of her face. In a weird way, this is the first time I've truly "seen" her; my fingertips chart a map of her features, committing every tiny detail to memory. Desire and guilt wage a war inside me, and I'm torn between wanting her and my loyalty to my species. *She's a Sentry. This is so wrong!* And yet I'm unable to control myself. My fingers brush over her smooth skin, running past the dimple on her left cheek before finding the soft fullness of her lips.

"Ash," she sighs, tilting her head up.

Her lips touch mine. They barely make contact, but a force like a lightning bolt shoots through them and straight into my heart. An explosion of pain erupts inside my chest. Natalie stumbles back, and I know she's as stunned as I am because that's when I feel it:

A second heartbeat pounding inside my chest.

"Natalie . . ."

Rough hands grab me in the dark, and Gregory whoops victoriously. "Tag, you're dead, nipper."

The lights flick on, and I quickly step away from Natalie. She studies me through thick lashes. Something's wrong. Her lips are pale, and she's struggling to breathe.

"What did you do to her, mongrel?" Sebastian demands as he rushes over to her.

She opens her mouth, but no words form. Instead she turns on her heel and runs out of the hall, slamming the doors behind her. As soon as she's gone, the pain in my chest fades, until I almost believe it never happened. Did I imagine it? Then why did she react like that?

Did she feel it too?

17
NATALIE

SEBASTIAN TAKES ME HOME, fussing over me the whole way back. As soon as we step inside the door, I head to Craven's lab, pretending to need some more heart medicine. My lips still tingle from my almost kiss with Ash, my heart racing at my reckless behavior. What possessed me to caress him like that, in front of everyone? He must think I'm mad! *Except . . . he touched me back.*

Something really strange happened between us in that hall. Did I really feel Ash's heart beating inside me? How is that even possible? Twin-bloods' hearts don't beat! I need to speak to Craven. Maybe he's heard about this happening before.

He's alone in the laboratory, hunched over a microscope, his half-moon spectacles perched on the end of his long nose. On the workbench beside him are beakers filled with a rainbow of pretty, colorful liquids: reds, golds, greens, whites and blues.

I pass the door with the silver marker above it on my way to Craven. *What's inside there?*

"Hello, young lady. What can I do for you?" he says.

I can't look directly at him—I'm terrified he might see the

guilt written all over my face. No one must ever know what I did with Ash.

"I have a science question. We're covering genetics in biology, and my teacher said that twin-blood hearts don't beat. Is that right?"

Craven wipes his glasses. "That's correct."

"A boy in my class said he knew of a twin-blood who had a heartbeat, but is that even possible? Has it ever happened?"

"I don't think so. Half-breeds' hearts don't beat, because there's simply no need for them to."

"Why's that?"

"Well, the official line is that twin-bloods are Damned souls forced to live between the realms of the living and the dead." Craven raises a skeptical brow. He collects a blood sample from the fridge and places the slide under the microscope. I peer through the lens. Tiny microscopic creatures wriggle around in the blood plasma.

"What are they?"

"*Trypanosoma vampirum.* They're what keep twin-bloods alive. They feed oxygen to their organs—"

"So their hearts don't have to do it?"

"Exactly. So it becomes dormant. It's just one of the many quirks of mixing Darkling and human DNA."

"Can their hearts ever become . . . er . . . *un*dormant?"

"I've never heard of it happening."

My shoulders slump. I must've been imagining things. I mean, I kissed Ash . . . sort of. That's going to make any girl's heart pop, right? That's clearly all it was.

I go upstairs, more confused than ever. I have to talk to him about it tonight at Beetle's party, but what will I say? I don't know how I feel about our near kiss. Mother would never forgive me if she found out I was attracted to a Darkling, and I can't simply forget the fact a Wrath killed my father. *But didn't he want Darklings and humans to be together, as equals? Would he really mind?*

I rub my temples, feeling a headache coming on. There's no point getting my head in a spin until I know how Ash feels about what happened. First things first. I need to ditch Sebastian somehow, as there's no way I'm letting him follow me to Beetle's barge and ruin everything. My best bet is getting a new guard to look after me; I'll work out how to ditch them when I get to Beetle's place.

I go to Mother's room. She's sitting on the edge of her bed, staring at the pearl bracelet in her hand. She's dressed in a long blue gown, cinched in at the waist to accentuate her fashionably skinny frame, and her glossy black hair is tied up in a bun, giving her gaunt face a stretched look. If I hugged her, I'm sure she'd shatter like glass. I guess it's lucky she never wants me to touch her.

"Everything okay?" I ask.

"I can't do up the clasp."

I clip the bracelet around her slim wrist.

"I'm presuming this wasn't a social call. What do you want?" Mother says.

"I want a new bodyguard."

"This again?"

"Yes, this again. You know Sebastian and I aren't dating anymore. It's getting awkward having him around all the time." I don't add that I've got a date with a twin-blood tonight and don't want Sebastian finding out.

"Fine," Mother says wearily.

"Thanks!" Wow, that was easier than I expected.

"But only in the evenings and weekends. Sebastian will continue to take you to and from school."

I knew I'd gotten away with that too easily. "Why?"

"Because I said so," she says.

It's better than nothing.

I hurry to my bedroom and instantly start searching for the perfect outfit to wear tonight, pulling off my clothes at the same time. I catch a glimpse of my reflection in the full-length mirror and pause, my eyes resting on the raised scar scratched down my heart. It was so silly of me to think I'd felt Ash's heart beating inside me. Like Craven said, it's not possible. Besides, even if twin-bloods did have a heartbeat, that wouldn't explain what I felt inside my own chest. The only rational explanation is my heart was overexerted from the sword fighting and I had a funny turn, that's all. *Then why don't I believe that?*

Half an hour later, I'm dressed and ready, wearing black cropped pants tucked into over-knee boots, a bustier top and Ash's jacket. I open my bedroom door, and Sebastian's waiting for me in the hallway.

"You *replaced* me?" he says.

I push past him, checking Father's watch on my wrist. The crystal is cracked, but I can still just make out the time underneath it: six fifty. I'm going to be late! Sebastian chases after me.

"Get a clue!" I yell at him. "I don't want you around me anymore, all right?"

"I won't let you ditch me like this," he says.

"Get out of my way before I get my new guard to escort you out of the building."

Sebastian's jaw clenches, but he steps aside.

My new guard, Malcolm, is waiting for me by the front door.

He's around forty years old, with slicked-back brown hair and eyes that are constantly searching his surroundings.

"Any chance you won't come?" I say.

He shakes his head, and I roll my eyes.

We go outside. The air feels rinsed after the rain, and I anxiously pat down my hair, trying to tame the frizz. All around us, colorful flags have been strung across the streets in preparation for the Armistice Day celebrations this Saturday. I wonder if Ash still wants to see me tonight. After my running out on him earlier today, I'm probably the last person he wants to see. But maybe (I'm clutching at straws here) he wants to talk about what happened? I mean, I felt his heart beating inside me! I *think*. Oh, I don't know! It sounds so crazy, but *something* happened.

I'm so busy thinking about Ash that I don't immediately notice the air temperature around me dropping a few degrees. A sudden electric shock crosses my skin, making my flesh goose pimple, just the way it did during Tracker training when my V-gene triggered. Malcolm stops. He's sensed it too.

"What?" I whisper.

He surveys our surroundings, checking the shadows for signs of movement.

"Do you see anything?" I ask, my heart hammering. "Is it a rogue Wrath?"

Wraths have been getting over the wall more often these days, mainly because there are so many of them as the disease continues to spread through the Legion ghetto. The Wraths don't have any fear of being caught by Trackers; that part of their brain has turned off. All they want is to hunt.

"No," he says quietly. "You can smell those a mile off . . ."

He waits another moment, then signals for me to carry on.

His hand doesn't leave his sword the entire way to Beetle's boat. I keep close, worrying that the Darkling we sensed was the same one who killed Truffles and followed me to the museum. I can't feel it anymore, though; perhaps seeing Malcolm scared it off?

"Wait here," I say to Malcolm when we get to the embankment.

He scowls at me.

"For His Mighty's sake! I'm going to be on the *barge* with my *friends*. No one's going to hurt me, and you'll know exactly where I am. We'll only be going a short way down the canal."

He makes a gruff noise that I interpret as "okay."

The yellow barge is lit with strings of glass lanterns, the kaleidoscope of colored light reminding me of Winterfest. Beetle and Day are already on the deck, drinking Shine from coffee mugs and flirting with each other. Beetle's normally unruly hair is clean and brushed, and he's wearing a smart shirt and black pants, while Day is wearing a simple but pretty blue dress. Beetle sees me first and mutters something, which I know isn't a compliment, given the punch on the arm he receives from Day.

Beetle spots Malcolm watching from the embankment. "Is he coming with us?"

"No. I told him to stay put."

Day offers me a drink, and I take it, looking past her shoulder for any signs of Ash. My stomach sinks when I can't see him.

"If it's just going to be us three, I can go and leave you two alone," I say.

"Ash is joining us in a minute; he's waiting under the bridge. I figured you'd bring a guard, so we thought it best he hang back," Beetle says.

Beetle starts the engine, and a minute later, we're cruising down the waterway, the chilly air brushing against my skin, the stars sparkling overhead. I wrap my arms around myself, my breath a ghostly mist as it spills out of my parted lips. It's going to snow soon.

We approach the bridge, and Beetle eases up on the throttle, slowing the boat. There's a heavy thud as the boat rocks to one side. Ash appears a second later. He's still dressed in his Tracker uniform from training earlier today and looks oh so gorgeous in the red coatee and black trousers. His black eyes meet mine, and my knees feel weak.

"What are you wearing, bro? It's not a costume party," Beetle says.

"It's just easier walking around the city wearing this. People respect Trackers," Ash replies.

"That's not respect—it's fear, and you of all people should know that. How can you?" Beetle says.

Ash grabs a drink and knocks it back in one hit. "Leave it alone. I don't see what the big deal is. It's just a uniform."

"That's bull, and you know it," Beetle replies.

"Fragg off. What do you know about anything?" Ash says. "Do you have any idea what it's like being a twin-blood in this city? I'm not going to apologize for wanting an easy life for once."

He takes off the red coatee and tosses it on the bench.

"Look, I'm sorry," Beetle says to Ash. "We still buddies?"

"Yeah, we're buddies," Ash replies.

"Let's get this party started!" Day says, pouring me another cup of Shine.

Beetle puts on some music and tops off our drinks. I try and focus on what Beetle and Day are saying, but the subconscious part of my mind is fixed on Ash, acutely aware of his presence all around me, my body aching to be touched by him again.

I take a risk and look at him full on, holding his gaze for a second longer than necessary. The air between us crackles, and a thrilling darkness slides over my skin. The Sight. He's marking me as his prey. *Mine,* he's silently warning others. I tremble slightly, afraid of the thought of him biting me, but liking the fact that he wants me. It's so messed up. My head's telling me he's dangerous and to run away, but my heart is keeping me here.

Beetle grabs Day and swings her around to the music.

"I've missed you," Beetle whispers to her.

"I've missed you too. But we can't do this."

"Why not? Don't you love me anymore?" he says.

"Of course I do. I never stopped loving you. But nothing's changed. I told you it was either the Haze or me, and you chose Haze."

"I made a mistake." He kisses her, hard.

They're so caught up with each other, they won't notice if I slip away with Ash for a while. We climb onto the barge's flat roof and lie down, looking at the stars, our arms pressed against each other. Even through our layers of clothing, crackles of electricity shoot down my arm where we're touching. We're so close, I can see the tiny silver flecks in his black eyes.

In the distance is a strange, eerie music. Often you can hear Darklings singing to each other inside the Legion ghetto; songs of woe, songs of celebration. Tonight, the song is beautiful and joyous.

"What are they singing?" I whisper.

"The Blood Vow," Ash explains.

"What's that?"

"When a Darkling finds a Blood Mate, they sing the vow to consummate their union, like wedding vows. It roughly translates as 'So begins my heart, so begins our life, everlasting.' They then feed on each other to seal the bond."

"That's both beautiful and utterly gross," I say, half jokingly.

Ash stands up, making the boat rock slightly. Tilting his head up to the sky, he lets out a long, low howl. Somewhere from the Legion ghetto, another Darkling howls back at him. Then he sits down.

"What did you say to them?" I ask.

"It's hard to translate—it's more an expression of an emotion. I was telling them 'love.'"

"It must be hard for you, being so close to them and not being able to see them."

He sighs. "I'm used to it."

"I'm sorry," I say.

"What for? It's not your fault."

I prop myself up on my elbow. "Do you miss your Darkling family?"

"I've never met them. I'm not even sure they're alive."

"Maybe the wall will come down one day and you'll get to meet them," I say.

"I doubt it. Besides, even if it did, I'm not sure they'd want to see me. My mom's family didn't approve of me."

"Because you're a twin-blood?" I say.

He nods. "A lot of them turned their back on Mom when she married my dad."

"It must've been tough growing up in a mixed-race family."

"Actually, it wasn't so bad. Our neighbors were mostly tolerant of us, and we had a lot of friends. My dad was one of the few ministers in the city who did both human and Darkling sermons, so my parents were very active in both communities. Obviously that all changed when segregation started."

He doesn't need to say any more. Even though I was only a child when segregation began, I remember how quickly friends turned on each other just because they weren't of the same race.

"You mentioned your parents split up?" I say, remembering his conversation with Martha at the market.

"Yep," he says, not meeting my eye.

I anxiously play with my watch strap, worried I've said the wrong thing.

"Isn't that a man's watch?" he asks.

I nod. "My father's."

"I'm sorry about your loss," he says sincerely. "It must've been hard for you."

"I guess." It doesn't feel right talking about my grief to Ash, when my father was involved in sending the Darklings to the Barren Lands to die during the war. He was a faithful follower of Purian Rose until he saw the horrors of the concentration camps. That was the turning point for my father. That's when he flipped sides.

"I remember hearing about it on the news. It was a Darkling attack, wasn't it?" he continues.

"Yes," I say, although that's not the whole story. My voice is raw with pain, even after all this time. "Some would call it poetic justice, I suppose."

"I suppose. How come you're so nice to me, then?"

"What do you mean?"

"Well . . . I'm half Darkling . . ."

"I hadn't noticed," I joke, but it falls flat.

Ash puts an arm behind his head, revealing the copper band around his wrist. Shame spills over me, remembering how I gave Martha something similar when we moved here. He covers the bracelet with his sleeve.

We're silent for a minute, just listening to the Darklings sing. Suddenly he tilts his face toward me and the mood between us shifts. The air becomes still. The time has come to discuss what's really on our minds. We don't talk immediately; we just wait for the other to speak first.

"I'm sorry I ran off earlier," I say.

"Why did you leave?"

"I was startled."

"Why?" he asks.

I'm suddenly afraid to tell him, in case he thinks I'm crazy, that what I felt wasn't real.

He props himself up on his elbow. "I felt something."

"What?" Excitement bubbles up in me.

"I think you know."

"I thought maybe it was just me."

"What did you feel?"

"Another heartbeat," I say, realizing the words sound ridiculous as soon as they escape my lips. What if he's referring to something else?

But he doesn't laugh. Instead he lies back down and runs a hand over his face.

"That's what I felt too."

"But how? You don't . . . I mean, twin-bloods . . ." I don't know how to put this delicately.

"Don't have a heartbeat?" he finishes.

"Yeah."

"I don't know."

In the distance the two Darklings continue to sing their beautiful Blood Vow duet, and we quietly listen, enjoying the music. It's so heartwarming to know they've found someone to love. But then Ash sits bolt upright.

"I can't believe I've been so dense!" he says.

"What? What is it?"

"Have you ever heard of the story of Aegus and Zanthina?" he says.

"No," I say.

Ash points up at the full moon. "According to Darkling legend, the moon goddess Lune and sun god Solis fell in love with each other, but because she was the Night and he was the Day, they weren't able to have children. So to please his wife, Solis sculpted a boy—Aegus—from the stars." He points to a constellation made from six stars. I squint, trying to find a pattern in it. "Lune loved Aegus so much, she carved a second heart for her son to make sure he lived forever."

I smile, although I'm not sure where this is going.

"Aegus was happy at first, but as he got older, he became very lonely. He didn't want to live forever if it meant wandering alone in the dark, so he tore out his second heart and cast it down to Earth."

I watch Ash's mouth as he speaks, mesmerized by the gentle curve of his lips. *Concentrate, Natalie!*

"As Aegus wept, his tears fell upon the Earth, forming the first oceans. He watched in amazement as a beautiful female slowly rose from the sea, his abandoned heart beating inside her chest. He named her Zanthina, 'my eternal love.' Overjoyed, they danced across the stars, their movements forming the galaxies. From that point on, Aegus and Zanthina ensured that every Darkling was born with a dual heart, which triggered whenever they met their Blood Mate as a reminder of their love."

My eyes open wide. "That's why a Darkling's second heart activates? That's so beautiful. I had no idea."

Ash cups my face and lightly runs his thumb over my lips. "There's a reason why I want you to know that story."

"Why?" I whisper, barely able to concentrate on anything other than his fingers against my skin.

"You're my Blood Mate."

The beat of his heart pulses through my veins, and I know it's true.

"Does it freak you out?" he asks.

I bite my lip. It *is* a lot to take in. When I woke up this morning, I wasn't even sure Ash liked me and now he's telling me we're Blood Mates. Things are moving so fast, any normal girl would be running for the hills, but the truth is I'm not scared or even that surprised. Being with Ash is as instinctive to me as breathing.

I lace my fingers through his. I've been trying to fight my feelings for Ash since we met under the bridge, but there's no need to pretend anymore. I'm his Blood Mate. That explains the strange way my heart tugs whenever he's around and the reason I can't get him out of my head. It's a relief in many ways, to know what I'm feeling for Ash is more than just a crush, that it's something beautiful, that we're destined to be together. Even so, I can't entirely shift the guilt I feel about being attracted to a Darkling. The notion that humans and Darklings shouldn't be together has been ingrained in me for years; that's not going to change overnight. But change has to begin somewhere. At least that's what my father told me once.

"No, it doesn't freak me out. Does it bother you?" I ask.

He shakes his head. "It seems—"

"Natural?"

He nods.

"But how is it even possible? I'm human," I say.

"I'm not sure. Maybe because I'm half human, it works differently for me?"

"I don't suppose it really matters how. I'm just glad it's happened."

He beams. "You swear?"

"I swear," I say.

"So where do we go from here? Nothing's changed. I'm still a twin-blood—"

"And I'm the Emissary's daughter."

"And it's illegal," he gently reminds me.

I know we're playing a dangerous game. If we're caught, we'll be executed just like Tom and Jana. Is it worth the risk? Ash strokes my cheek, and my whole body tingles, awakened, alive.

Yes.

"I want to be with you. We just need to be careful," I say.

"If anyone finds out—"

"They won't." I gaze up at him.

His eyes burn with black fire, his lips parting slightly as he leans closer, his breath cool against my cheek. It's like I'm on the top of a roller coaster, ready to tip over at any second, the anticipation building. Almost . . . almost . . .

Our lips meet. I sigh against his mouth, melting into him as he kisses me hungrily. His heartbeat pounds in my ears; his hands stroke my face, my back. He pulls me toward him, and we both gasp as a powerful jolt sparks between our hearts, opening an invisible channel between us, allowing all his emotions to flow into me: his pleasure, his love, his joy. They flood into my heart until I think it might burst.

The sensation's too much, and I pull away, my chest heaving. "What was that?"

His lips turn up into a perfect smile. "We were Soul Sharing."

I throw my arms around his neck and press my lips against his again.

"What the hell's going on here?"

The sound of Day's voice pulls us apart. Day and Beetle glower at us from the deck.

"It's not what it looks like," I say instinctively, although I know it's a dumb thing to say when we've been caught red-handed.

Ash helps me to my feet, and we climb down the stairs.

"It looks like you two were sucking face," Day says to me.

"So? You don't get to dictate to me who I kiss," I say. "Who the hell do you think you are? Purian Rose?"

"He's a drug dealer; he ruins people's lives," Day says.

"It's not Ash's fault Beetle would rather be high than be with you," I snap back.

Day flinches.

"If you're a true friend, you'll be happy for me," I say to her.

"If you were a true friend, you wouldn't even consider being with Ash," Day zings back.

Ash steps toward Day. "I'm not taking Natalie away from you, if that's what you're worried about."

"Like you did with Beetle, you mean?" she says.

I roll my eyes. "There's room in my life for both of you. There's no need to be jealous."

She bristles. "I am *not* jealous—"

"You're certainly acting that way," I reply.

"Ash Fisher is a bad influence, a Haze dealer and a jerk,"

Day says. "If you go out with him, then we can't be friends any-more. So who's it going to be?"

I laugh. "Are you seriously making me choose between you?"

"Yes," she says.

"Fine. I pick Ash," I say.

Hurt flashes across her face. I'd feel sorry for her, but I'm just too angry. How dare she give me an ultimatum?

Beetle takes her hand and stares daggers at Ash. "Bro, what are you doing? She's the Emissary's daughter!"

"Yeah, so what?" Ash says.

"What's happened to you, man? First you become a Tracker, and now you're hooking up with Sentry girls? You know what they called people like you during the war? Collaborators."

Ash lunges for Beetle. The two of them fall to the deck and wrestle, throwing wild punches at each other. Ash lands a well-aimed blow at Beetle's face, causing blood to pour out of his nose. He draws his fist back again.

"Ash, stop it!" I plead.

Ash immediately releases Beetle. "Don't ever fragging call me a collaborator again," he yells.

Day rushes over to Beetle and tries to stem the bleeding. She glares at me, and I return the hostile look.

"Are you okay?" I ask Ash.

"Yeah, I'm—"

CRASH!

The boat judders wildly. Ash dashes to the tiller, which has been left unmanned during the fight, and steers the boat back on course. When it's steady, I check the side of the boat for dam-age. The paintwork's scuffed, and a few lanterns are smashed, but thankfully, there's no real harm done.

Beetle takes charge of the tiller, and the rest of us sit in angry silence, not looking at one another. I wish the barge were a steamboat so we could be home already. The sooner I'm off this stupid barge and away from Day, the better. I thought we were true friends, but if she can't be happy for me and Ash, then clearly I was wrong. The boat finally approaches the mooring, and Beetle turns off the engine. Ash puts on his Tracker jacket, and I'm about to disembark when he grabs my arm, stopping me.

"Something's wrong. I can sense blood," he says, his hair stirring.

"Malcolm!" I yell.

I jump off the boat and rush over to the embankment, fear clogging my throat with every step. A figure is slumped on the grass. There's so much blood . . . just like Truffles . . . just like Father. Malcolm's clothes have been torn open to reveal a gruesome cavity in his chest. I stifle a scream.

His heart's been torn out.

A pair of headlights illuminates the road beside us, heading in our direction. It looks like the Sentry guard has already been called to the scene.

"Go. It's not safe here," I say to Ash.

Ash takes one last lingering look at me, then disappears into the shadows.

Back in my bedroom, Martha wraps a blanket around my shoulders and hugs me tight. She's so soft and plump, it's like cuddling a pillow.

"It's my fault. I told him to wait there. If I hadn't . . ." My sentence is cut off by more tears.

She strokes my hair, saying soothing things in my ear. Part of me can't help but resent my mother for not being here with me.

She even delegates her motherly duties to the staff. That's all I am to her, another chore to be dealt with.

"What's worse is I'm almost relieved," I admit. "That could've been Sebastian. Is that terrible of me?"

She shakes her head. "You care for him, no matter what's gone on between you both."

There's a knock at the door and Sebastian strides in, worry etched over his handsome face. Martha moves aside as he pulls me into a tight embrace and kisses my forehead.

"I've spoken to your mother. It was a mistake to let Malcolm guard you tonight; we've agreed that I'll be the only person protecting you from now on," he says.

I expected as much, and to be honest, I'm grateful. The thought of that Darkling still out there, hunting me, is terrifying. I know Sebastian will never let it hurt me.

I sit up, remembering something. "Someone was following us earlier."

"Are you sure?" Sebastian asks.

"Yes, Malcolm sensed it. I'm certain now it's the same one who killed Truffles and stalked me at the museum."

I burst into fresh tears. Why did I go out tonight? I should've turned back the instant Malcolm sensed something was wrong. I don't understand what's happening. Why is that Darkling after me? And why is it ripping out its victims' hearts?

"I want to be alone," I say.

The instant they're gone, I grab Ash's jacket off the floor and wrap myself in it, letting the tears fall freely, wishing more than anything he were here with me. I breathe in the scent of his jacket and my heart flutters.

Blood Mate. I'm his Blood Mate.

The door opens, and Polly slips into the room. She lies down beside me and strokes my hair. The zigzags of scars down her face look stark in the moonlight. More tears spill down my cheeks, remembering how she used to comfort me like this back in the old days, before she got hurt.

"I've met a boy," I confide in her. "But he's a Darkling. I don't know what to do. Mother would kill me if she found out, and after what happened with Father . . . I just feel like I'm betraying him by wanting to be with Ash."

"You're not betraying Father—you're honoring him. He wanted Darklings and humans to live as equals. It's what he died for," she whispers back.

"But they're so dangerous," I reply.

"Is this boy dangerous?" she asks.

"He's my Blood Mate. He'd never hurt me." I tell her about Ash's heart and how I activated it. "He's not like those other Darklings. He's kind and generous, and he cares about me."

"It sounds like you know what you want to do," she replies.

"I'm scared," I admit.

Polly squeezes my hand. "Don't live your life in fear. If you want to be with him, then do it. Be brave, little sister."

Her words ring around my head. *Be brave.* I'll do my best. I want to be with Ash, and I'll fight for him, but deep down, I worry we'll never get our happily ever after. Polly wraps her arm around me, and I'm soon asleep.

I'm inside the red cave. The walls around me pulse, and I finally understand why they feel so warm and sticky to the touch. This cave isn't made of stone; it's made of flesh. Terror rips through me. Where am I?

The shaved-haired child stands in the center of the cave wearing nothing but a green sheet around his waist. Lying by

his feet are the corpses of Malcolm and Truffles. Blood continu-
ously seeps out of their bodies, filling the room until it sloshes
around my ankles.

"What is it you want?" I yell.

The boy brings his hands up to his face and starts crying, a
horrific, chilling sound. He slowly turns, his hands still obscur-
ing his face. Something is terribly wrong.

I scream when I realize what it is.

There's a hole in his chest where his heart is meant to be.

18
ASH

THE NEXT DAY IS TENSE. I didn't pick Beetle up on the way to school like normal, and he enters class just after the morning bell rings, looking more of a mess than usual, his nose still swollen from our fight last night.

He walks over to Day's desk.

"What are you doing?" she spits.

"Sitting down?" he says.

"Not next to me," she replies.

His brow furrows. "But . . . last night, we kis—"

"Sshhh," she says, placing a finger to her lips. "Nothing's changed. I can't be with you. Go away."

There go Beetle's ears again, turning bright pink. He scans the classroom for another place to sit. There are only two other spaces available: one at the table beside me, next to a girl named Annabelle, who looks at him like she'd rather vomit than have him sit next to her, and one next to me.

He opts for me. I don't say hello; I'm still mad at him for calling me a collaborator. What the hell does he know about anything?

I overhear Annabelle chatting to two girls in front of her.

"I can get my hands on some of that Golden Haze for the party," she says quietly. "You can buy it from this guy, Mr. Tubs."

My fangs throb at the mention of Mr. Tubs's name. He runs a Haze den in Chantilly Lane, and Linus used to work for him. I'm surprised anyone would buy Golden Haze after Linus died, but then again, Hazers don't really care about the risk; they just want to get high. Besides, it's not like everyone who takes the drug dies. Otherwise, it wouldn't have become so popular with the Hazers. Linus was just unlucky.

At that moment, Sebastian enters the classroom, followed by Natalie. My heart somersaults. Her lips flicker into a smile, but she quickly hides it. Sebastian leads her toward Day's desk.

"Not there," she says, and sits next to Annabelle instead.

"I'll be waiting for you by the steps after school. Don't be late," he says to her.

She nods, but doesn't look at him as he leaves.

We have a study period now, so we all get out our textbooks to catch up on the week's homework. Natalie glances over at me, just for a few seconds, but so much meaning passes between us in that look. I need to talk to her; I have to find out where we stand. I tear off a corner of paper from my notebook and scribble a note:

I can't stop thinking about you.

I screw it up into a tiny ball and wait until Annabelle gets up to sharpen her pencil before tossing it onto Natalie's desk. She furtively looks around her, checking no one is watching, before unfolding the note. Smiling, she quickly writes a separate reply.

Picking up some pencils, she walks over to Annabelle,

dropping the note on my desk as she passes by, the sleight of hand so good, no one except Beetle notices. He flashes me a disapproving look, but he can go fragg himself. This is none of his business.

I open the message:

Me too. So what now? I'm willing to take the risk, are you?

The memory of Tom Shreve and Jana Marwick being executed comes into my mind. Can I really do this? Dare I risk it? Natalie sits back down and flicks a look at me with those beautiful cornflower-blue eyes of hers, waiting for my response. My blood suddenly feels red hot in my veins.

I nod.

She shyly smiles.

Natalie tucks the note I wrote to her into her satchel. I pop hers in my pocket. I can't believe we're really going to do this, but at the same time it feels inevitable that we would. The instant we met, our fates were sealed; we were destined to be together.

Next to me, Beetle takes a ragged breath. He's holding back the tears as he stares forlornly at Day.

"I'm sorry, mate. She doesn't know what she's missing," I say before I can help myself.

He wipes his eyes and shrugs. "Whatever."

I mutter a curse under my breath. Why am I being nice to him after what he called me last night? Fury wells up inside me.

"I'm not a collaborator," I whisper, so we can't be overheard. "I'm not one of those Darklings who hooked up with Trackers during the war. She's my Blood Mate. Do you understand what that means?"

He looks at me with wide eyes. "I didn't know."

"Do you really think we'd risk everything if this weren't

serious? Honestly, I thought you of all people would be happy for me. You're such a hypocrite."

"She's the Emissary's daughter. The Sentry government bombed this city and killed my parents. I can't just forget that," he replies.

"No one's asking you to forget," I say. "Just put the blame where it belongs. Natalie had nothing to do with those air raids. She can't help who her parents are; it doesn't automatically make her a bad person."

"I know. I'm sorry I was such an ass, bro."

"You really were."

"We okay?" he asks.

I shrug. "I'll think about it."

The rest of the day goes better than normal, and it's all because of one thing: Natalie. We make sure we're not seen together very often, and when we are, we keep our distance so people don't suspect anything. But even so, we pass secret smiles and more notes between us. Her heart beats inside mine, and it's like I'm carrying a little piece of her with me wherever I go.

At some point during the day, it begins to snow, and by the time it gets to last period, the city is covered in a blanket of white. I head to drama with Beetle. Natalie and Day are already in the dark auditorium, although they're not sitting together. I steal a look at Natalie, and my heart somersaults. I can't believe we're together. Beetle slumps down in his seat and shuts his eyes. He's looking sweaty and pale. He's either getting sick, or he's going into Haze withdrawal again. I suspect the latter. I'm not going to give him any Haze, unless I can't avoid it. The longer he goes between hits, the less he'll need it.

Our drama teacher, Mr. Kimble, a slender man wearing a

velvet patchwork suit, walks onto the stage and runs us through the day's assignment: acting out a scene from Elward's play *Demetrius and Helene*. All the boys in the auditorium groan, while the girls giggle. Mr. Kimble assigns us all our roles. Of course, the two most popular students in the group get the lead parts.

"Who would like to help with the props and lighting?" Mr. Kimble asks.

Natalie and I shoot our arms up in the air.

There are more mumblings from the boys as we head backstage. Natalie and I search for props to decorate the stage sets, while the cast gets props for their outfits.

"I'm going to find a sword," Beetle mumbles, heading into the depths of the prop store.

Day ponders what costume to wear, while everyone else just grabs what's nearest. Natalie strolls over to me, and we pretend to look through a wooden box of clothes. Our hands slide under the material, and I lace my fingers through hers. Her cheeks flush.

Day shoots us a bitter look.

"I take it Day's still mad at us?" I whisper to Natalie.

"She can be as mad as she wants. It's her fault we're not friends anymore," she replies.

"Maybe we should cut her some slack?"

Natalie raises a brow at me.

"I just feel bad for her. She's all alone," I say.

"She has only herself to blame. If she apologizes, then I'm willing to forgive her, but until then, she's on her own," Natalie says.

"Everybody back onstage in one minute," Mr. Kimble says.

Natalie takes a handful of props up to the auditorium while I look for Beetle. He's tucked away in a corner of the room, wedged between two rails of costumes. In his hand is a phial of Haze, which shimmers gold, just like the stuff Linus had.

I grab it from him and smash it under my boot.

"What do you think you're doing? You're supposed to be quitting," I say, keeping my voice low.

"I can't do it, bro. I'm not strong enough."

"Yes you are."

He lowers his eyes. "I just need a small hit to tide me over."

His skin has a ghostly pallor, and his hands are shaking. He looks really sick. I've known users to die from Haze withdrawal.

I sigh. "This is the last time."

He tilts his head to one side, revealing two old puncture wounds. Guilt squirms through me, but he needs this. I sink my fangs into his neck. Hot blood splashes over my tongue, and for a second, the predator in me hungers to just drink him dry. I only release a small amount of venom into his system before—

"What are you doing?" a shrill voice says nearby.

I turn to see Day, her hands laden with props. She drops the items on the floor and rushes out of the room.

"Day, I'm sorry," Beetle says, staggering after her.

I wipe the blood from my lips, hating myself.

I head to the auditorium to meet Natalie. We climb up to the rafters above the stage and check the lighting rig while the other students run through their lines. Even from up here, the tension between Day and Beetle is palpable as she shouts her lines at him during a comedic scene while he just silently sways. I only gave him a drop of Haze, but even so, he's probably feeling pretty spaced out.

"That was a very *interesting* direction to take the scene," Mr. Kimble says. "But perhaps next time do it with a little more . . . er . . . humor?"

Day stomps off stage, Beetle walking unsteadily after her.

"What was that all about?" Natalie whispers.

I don't like reminding her I'm a Haze dealer, but I can't lie either, so I tell her the truth, including the fact I'm trying to wean Beetle off the drug.

"I feel like such a jerk giving my best friend Haze," I admit.

"You're trying to help him," she says.

We sit down on the rafter, our legs dangling over the edge, as we watch the play.

"Ash, why do you deal Haze?" Natalie asks.

"My dad and I need the money," I say.

"Does he know you deal?"

I nod. "He's terrified I'll get arrested, but we don't have much choice. If there were any other way for me to earn money, I'd take it, but there are no opportunities for me in this city."

Natalie looks at the copper band around my wrist. "People like my mother have made sure of that."

"Does it bother you that I deal Haze?" I ask, covering the wristband.

"Yes," she admits. "But I accept you for what you are, the good and the bad, the same way you've accepted me, despite my family."

I slide my hand along the rafter until our fingertips touch. It's a small gesture, but I can't risk holding her hand in case anyone looks up at us.

The lesson ends and the students hurry outside to play in the snow. The air is crisp and cold, and the city feels at peace for the first time in weeks. Students laugh and run around the town square, throwing snowballs at each other and hiding behind the three crosses. The snow on the crosses has turned pink as it soaks up the dried blood stained into the wood. It's chilling watching students play beside the crosses, but that's life in Black City. Everywhere you turn you're reminded of death, but you have to block it out, otherwise you couldn't carry on living.

A snowball smacks me in the face.

Beetle grins sheepishly at me. He's clearly feeling much better. I lob a snowball at him, and he staggers back like he's been shot. Natalie giggles. I grab some snow and toss it playfully at her.

"You're in big trouble, Fisher," she warns, scooping up some more snow.

We break out in a full-on snowball fight and are drenched in icy cold water within minutes, but none of us cares. Day walks out of the school, her arms laden with library books, and rolls her eyes at us. Beetle chucks a snowball at her, hitting her on the cheek with more force than I know he meant. She stumbles back into Natalie, knocking them both to the ground. Day's library books fall everywhere while the contents of Natalie's bag spill over the snow. Other students have stopped their own games to watch.

Beetle rushes over to help Day.

"Leave me alone!" she yells, her cheek red and raw where the snow has stung her.

"I'm sorry . . . I . . . It was a mistake," he babbles.

She scoops up her books, glowering at me. "I bet *you* put Beetle up to this, Fisher. You're such a bad influence on everyone."

"Hey!" I object.

"Don't you dare say that about Ash," Beetle snaps.

We've never heard him tell Day off before, and it surprises all of us.

"Ash is my best friend and a decent guy. He's not a bad influence," he says.

Day sniffs haughtily. "Really? He got you addicted to Haze."

"No, he didn't." He looks up at Day with shame-filled eyes. "Linus got me hooked on Haze. Ash has spent the past year trying to wean me off it. That's what we were doing in the prop room. He was *helping* me."

Day inhales sharply, then looks at me, her brow furrowed.

"I think you owe Ash an apology," Natalie says to Day.

Day's mouth tightens. She'll never say sorry to me.

"Forget about it," I mumble.

Day swishes her ebony hair over her shoulder and strides away.

"She really should've said sorry," Natalie says as I help gather the books and pencils that fell out of her satchel.

A shadow falls over us. Sebastian is silhouetted against the stormy sky, flakes of snow melting in his blond hair.

"Get away from her, nipper," he says.

I stand up, my heart pounding. Sebastian notices the chunks of snow on my clothes, the dusting of white powder on Natalie's.

"He was helping me pick up my books, Sebastian," Natalie says quickly. "Someone hit me with a snowball, and I fell over. It was so silly."

It's clear he's trying to decide if he believes her or not. Thankfully, he bends down and starts picking up the remainder of her schoolbooks.

And that's when I see it.

A piece of torn paper fluttering on the snow beside Sebastian's foot.

My heart jackhammers against my chest. Cold sweat breaks out on my brow. Natalie looks alarmed; she's seen it too. *Don't let him notice it, don't let him notice it, don't let him notice it.* Sebastian shoves all the books back into Natalie's satchel and hands it to her. I exhale.

"Thanks," she says.

"Let's go," he orders.

He moves his foot, and that's when he sees the scrap of paper by his boot.

The world stops.

Sebastian picks up the note, quickly scanning it.

I swallow.

Natalie's hands are drawn into tight fists, trying to stop them from shaking.

He looks slowly up at her, his green eyes burning. *"I can't stop thinking about you?"*

Oh, fragg.

She licks her lips, and I know she doesn't mean to, but she gives me a fleeting look. Sebastian turns and studies me. His fist clenches around the note.

"It's from this boy, Chris Thompson," Natalie says. "He asked me out, I said no, but he keeps sending me messages. It's embarrassing."

Sebastian holds my gaze for a beat too long. I can't breathe.

"Sebastian, we really should go. It's getting dark," Natalie says.

He throws the note back in the snow and roughly takes Natalie's arm. They walk through the town square. I start breathing again the instant they're gone.

The sky fades to white as a blizzard rolls across the city, making the buildings look like snowcapped mountains. I trudge toward Chris's house, my stomach grumbling, hoping he's still in need of a Haze fix after I blew off yesterday's appointment. I need some Synth-O-Blood; I haven't eaten in ages. At the back of my mind, it registers that he wasn't at school today. Neither was

Gregory, which is odd—Gregory would never miss a day of school. Maybe they're both sick? I hope not; at least not Chris.

My heart's still pounding a mile a minute after my run-in with Sebastian. I think Natalie managed to convince him with her cover story. I can't believe what a close call that was. We've only been together for a few hours, and already we've nearly been caught.

I walk down City End, following my usual path along the Boundary Wall. The Darkling guards peer down at me with judgmental eyes, and I swear they're whispering at me as I pass by—*traitor, turncoat, collaborator*—but they can't possibly know I'm dating Natalie. It must be in my head. Even so, I quicken my pace, eager to get away from them.

I cross through the security gates leading into the Chimney, the factory district, and find Chris and Gregory's house amid the bustling refineries and warehouses spewing clouds of choking smoke and toxins into the air. High above the twisting spires of the factories are giant screens, which play the same grainy film footage of Purian Rose on a loop. He smiles benevolently down at us, saying a bunch of stupid slogans like "work sets you free" or "love work, love your country." I make a rude gesture at the screens as I pass.

The hairs on the back of my neck suddenly prickle. Someone's watching me. I stop walking and scan the buildings. There's nothing there. I must be a little jumpy from the run-in with Sebastian.

I knock on the green door of the Thompson twins' house. There's a long pause before footsteps shuffle toward the door. A middle-aged woman answers, her brown hair tangled around her freckled face. Her eyes are red and moist.

"Can I help you?" she says, her voice cracking with emotion.

"I was wondering if Chris—"

The woman's eyes widen when she registers what I am. "Mark!"

"What is it, Anne?" The door swings open, and a tough-looking man glares down at me.

Just be calm. I clear my throat. "Sorry to bother you—"

The man grabs my shirt. "What did you do to my son?"

"Get off me!" I reply, struggling free from the man's grip. It was a mistake to come here. What was I thinking?

"Who is it, Dad?" Gregory says, rushing to the door.

He stops dead when he sees me. A look of burning hatred crosses his narrow, pinched face.

"You killed my brother!" he screams, rushing toward me.

"I didn't!" I say, confused and suddenly terrified. *Chris is dead?*

Gregory picks up a loose brick from the low wall running down the length of the path. I back away, but my feet slip in the slushy snow, and I crash to the ground. Gregory's on top of me in seconds.

"I'll kill you for what you did!" he yells, lifting the brick over his head.

"I'm calling the Sentry guard!" Gregory's mom darts back into the house.

"You've made a mistake," I say.

Gregory smashes the brick against my temple, and red spots explode before my eyes. Then the world turns black.

19

ASH

I WAKE UP to a blinding light. *Is this paradise?* My dad always described his vision of heaven as a bright white light. No. My kind don't go to that place, we go to the Elsewhere. Darts of pain shoot through my skull where I've been hit. *Definitely not in paradise.* I blink twice and try to adjust my eyes. At first I think I'm outside, the light is so piercing. Then things begin to come into focus: a door, UV strip lights, polished metal walls.

I howl as another white-hot pain strikes me, like a thousand hands ripping me apart. My body has been stripped naked, and it's red raw and blistered where the UV rays from the lights overhead have scorched my skin.

I try to move and realize I can't; my left foot is bound to the wall by a heavy silver chain. *Oh fragg, oh fragg, oh fragg . . .* I yank on the chain, which sizzles into my palms and ankle, but it doesn't budge an inch.

The metal door clanks open, and Natalie's mom, the Emissary, appears at the threshold. Her pale hands are clasped in front of her sickeningly thin body, her breastbone clearly visible beneath her stretched skin. There's nothing of Natalie's warmth and softness about her; there's no resemblance at all, except the cornflower blue of her eyes. In the corridor behind her, Martha— the Darkling housemaid I rescued at the market—is mopping a stain off the floor. A worried look flits across her face when she sees me. The Emissary impatiently shoos her away.

Emissary Buchanan enters my cell, and the guards shut the door. She holds a sachet of Synth-O-Blood in one hand, while the other is closed around a small object I can't see.

"I didn't kill Chris," I say through cracked lips. "I didn't even know he was dead."

She contemplates me for a long moment, then opens her hand to show a two of hearts playing card. My calling card! I'd given it to Chris earlier this week.

"Does this look familiar to you?" she says.

"You can't keep me here. I have rights."

"You don't have any rights, twin-blood. You're not *human*."

I pull against my restraints, a low growl escaping my lips.

She steps back warily. "I recommend you control yourself."

"I didn't kill Chris," I say again, desperation creeping into my voice.

"Chris Thompson died of a Haze overdose. You're the only twin-blood registered in the city, and he had your playing card, which I've been informed you give to your 'clients.' That's all the evidence we need."

A cannonball drops in my stomach. I can't believe this is happening! I'm going to get executed for a crime I didn't even commit.

"Just confess to the crime, and this will all be over," she says icily.

"I didn't do it!"

She makes a signal with her hand, and a second later the UV lights turn up to full power. I howl again as my skin explodes with pain. She waves a hand, and the lights lower. I curl up into a ball, my body shaking. I urgently need blood to heal myself. In the faint recesses of my mind, I wonder why she's the one questioning me and not one of her goons.

The Emissary dangles the Synth-O-Blood in front of me. "Is this what you're after, half-breed?"

I refuse to look at it. I'm not going to beg for food like a dog.

She takes out a hairpin and pierces the bag. Blood drips onto the floor beside me, just within my reach. My nostrils flare, and my fangs drip with venom.

"This can be yours," she says softly. "All you have to do is confess that you killed Chris."

"Never."

She squeezes the bag, and more blood spills onto the floor. I shut my eyes.

"Just confess—"

"No."

"Confess!"

My stomach coils and cramps. The smell of blood is intoxicating, so sweet and delicious and—

I crouch over and lap up the spilled blood, humiliated and disgusted with myself. But I can't stop, it tastes so good . . . *All you have to do is confess, and the rest is yours.* My skin immediately begins to heal as my blood is replenished, the red flesh turning to pink, then pearl white.

Loud voices sound outside the cell, and a second later, the steel door bangs open and a tall Darkling sweeps into the room, his face covered by a gilded mask.

Sigur!

The Darkling ambassador tears off the mask, revealing his furious face. Blackened claw marks scar his cheeks and cut across one of his huge orange eyes. His good eye flicks from my chained leg and bloodstained lips to the bag of Synth-O-Blood in the Emissary's hand. He knows what's been going on.

"Untie him immediately!" he orders.

"I don't think so," the Emissary says. "He's a suspect in a murder—"

"There was no crime. A boy died of a drug overdose. It was foolish, but it wasn't murder."

"I'll be the judge of that," the Emissary replies. "And how dare you barge in here, making demands of *me*? Your diplomatic privileges do not give you the right to come into my place of business without prior arrangement."

Sigur's top lip curls, but he composes himself. He graciously bows, and the Emissary gives a satisfied smile.

"Emissary," he says politely, though I can tell every word is a struggle, "there has been a misunderstanding. This boy is innocent. It would be a step toward reconciliation between our two species if you let him go."

The Emissary narrows her eyes, clearly weighing up her options. If Sigur Marwick has personally come here to demand my release, he means business. Is it really worth risking another conflict between our species, over me?

"Let him go," Emissary Buchanan finally says.

The guards bring in my clothes and unchain me. I dress hurriedly and follow Sigur through the maze of corridors to the entrance hall. The elevator doors ping open, and Natalie rushes into the hall.

"Ash! Martha told me you were in the cells. Thank His Mighty, you're—" She notices Sigur and fear flashes across her face.

He sweeps past Natalie without a second glance. I want to hug her, tell her everything is okay, but I can't in front of Sigur. I follow him outside. Fresh snow has carpeted the ground, and it glistens almost blue in the moonlight.

"Did they hurt you badly?" Sigur asks.

"I'll live. How did you know I was here?"

"My lieutenant has been tracking you. She contacted me when she saw what happened," he replies.

I knew someone was following me earlier!

He studies me for a moment.

"You look just like Annora," he says quietly.

I inhale sharply at the mention of my mother's name.

"Walk with me, Ash."

Sigur stretches out his hand, beckoning me.

I hesitate. Snow silently falls in the space between us, and a million thoughts run through my head, mostly ways I want to kill him. This is the man who tore my family apart. Even so, I'm curious to know what he wants. *Plus, he did just save your skin.* I sigh and reluctantly go with him.

We walk through the city streets, and I tell him briefly about my arrest and interrogation.

"I don't understand why she was so desperate to blame me for Chris's death. Or why the Emissary felt obliged to interrogate me herself," I say.

"The Emissary always has her motives, although why she wanted to blame *you* in particular is very worrying," he says. "I am just glad you were not hurt. When my lieutenant told me what had happened, I feared the worst."

"Why did you ask her to follow me?" I ask.

Sigur stops and turns to me. He hasn't replaced his gold

mask, so I can still see his face. His skin and hair are so white, he almost vanishes against the snow.

"You're Annora's son. Your safety is important to me."

I don't know what to make of that, so I carry on walking. We approach the town square, and Sigur stops beneath the three crosses, reminding me of the execution of Tom and Jana.

"Was the Darkling related to you?" I ask Sigur, remembering her name: Jana Marwick.

"My niece."

I gape at him. "And you allowed them to do that to her?"

"She made her choices. It's regrettable, but she knew the law. There's nothing I could have done; she was clearly guilty of her crime."

"You could've demanded they take her down. You could've ordered your guards to snatch her, you—"

"I cannot go breaking the law, not now that boundary negotiations have started with the Emissary. If there is even the slightest chance we can expand our territory, I have to take it. My people desperately need more space. We cannot stir up unnecessary trouble." Sigur touches the wooden cross. His hand smokes and burns, but he doesn't move it. "She understood."

This is exactly why I hate him so much! If it had been Natalie up there, I would have done anything to save her. My heart trembles just thinking about her. Sigur glances curiously at me. *Can he hear it?*

Across the square from us, the ancient clock in the school's tallest spire chimes a melancholy tune.

"I do not like having that school so close. It torments my guards," Sigur says.

"Because they're tempted to attack the students? I guess we must look pretty tasty," I say.

Sigur shakes his head. "I have ordered them not to. The Legion guards must obey my word, or the word of my kin, like you. It is our law," he says.

I raise a quizzical brow. "I'm not your kin."

"You are, according to Darkling law. Annora is my Blood Mate; you are her son. That makes you my Blood Son. The bond between us is just as close as if you were born of my own flesh and blood."

I give a noncommittal smile, not really sure how to feel about that. I already have a dad, but I have always wondered what it would be like to have a Darkling father, to have someone who understands me.

And while I should hate Sigur for splitting my family apart, he's making that hard to do. If he hadn't persuaded the Emissary to let me go, I'd be getting executed for Chris's death for sure. He saved my life. *Maybe I've misjudged him?*

Sigur goes to the gates, and the Legion guards stand at attention.

"One moment," he says to them, and turns to look at me with eyes like embers. "I hope you don't mind my asking, but how is your mother these days?"

"Is that meant to be a joke?"

"A joke? No, I don't think so, but I don't quite understand human humor."

Is he for real? Then it dawns on me. *He doesn't know.*

"Mom's got the Wrath," I say.

Sigur sways, and the Legion guards rush forward, but I grab him first and help him to a nearby bench.

"I don't understand. I thought that was why you banished her," I say.

Sigur shakes his head.

"Then why?" I say.

Sigur struggles to speak, his voice choked with emotion. "We had a fight."

"About what?"

"You." The words are barely a whisper. "I wanted you to come and live with us. She said she couldn't do that to your father—you were all he had left. So I made her choose. Him or me." He turns his glistening orange eyes on me. "She picked your father."

"So you banished her from the Legion?"

"I'm not proud of what I did." He sighs. "When she didn't get in touch with me these past weeks, I assumed she was still furious. I didn't know."

Mom chose us over Sigur? I run a hand through my hair. I've been wrong about her all this time. She does love me.

"How much longer does she have?" Sigur says.

"Not long."

Sigur stares off into the distance, his face blank as he tries to digest it all. He stands up and walks a few paces away.

"Sigur?" I say, following him.

He sinks to his knees, his purple robe splaying across the snow, and lets out a low, lamenting howl. His song is one of pain and loss. Grief spills over me as I listen to him. I finally have to face the truth: Mom's dying. The Legion guards watch us from the wall. The song isn't picked up by the other Darklings; they understand it's for us and us alone. When Sigur stops singing, he gets up and surprises me by gently placing his hands on either side of my face.

"I would like you to come to the Legion and visit your family."

"What? Now?" I ask, dumbfounded.

Sigur lowers his hands and nods. "What is the human expression? There is no time like the present?"

I hesitate. I want to see inside the Legion so much, my insides ache with it, but my dad must be worried sick, wondering where I am. I look longingly at the Boundary Wall.

I sigh. "I need to go home. My dad's probably having a total freak-out by now."

"Then you will come tomorrow instead for our Armistice Day celebrations. Yes?" Sigur says.

I grin. "Wild horses couldn't keep me away."

The metal gates open, and he slips inside. The gates shut behind him. I touch the rough stone wall with my fingertips.

Tomorrow I'll be on the other side.

20

NATALIE

"I CAN'T BELIEVE you did that to Ash! Since when did you start torturing people?" I say, following Mother into the laboratory.

Sebastian and Craven are already there, alongside several Sentry guards who stand watch outside the door with the silver marker above it. They're new; I haven't seen guards down here before. What's Craven hiding in there that's so important?

Mother narrows her cold blue eyes at me. "He's not a *person*. He's a soulless half-breed. Why do you care so much about him?"

"I don't care about him," I lie. "But he's innocent. He didn't kill Chris Thompson."

"Well, it hardly matters whether he did or not. Sigur Marwick's made sure of that," Mother replies, her eyes burning with fury.

The mention of Sigur's name reminds me of seeing him upstairs with Ash. What was Ash doing with the Darkling ambassador? Why didn't he tell me they knew each other?

"How dare Sigur just waltz in here making demands? This is

my house. If he wants to meet with me, he needs my permission first," Mother says to no one in particular, on a rant.

"That Dark needs to learn his place," Sebastian says to Mother. "We should revoke his diplomatic rights and ban him from leaving the Legion."

Mother laughs bitterly. "Oh, I'd love to do that, but I have to at least pretend Sigur has some authority. Otherwise, the Darklings will stop following his orders. I'm relying on him to keep control over those nippers."

"Don't call them that," I say, anger welling up inside me.

"Since when do you care what I call them?" Mother replies.

"Since when did you start thinking it was okay to torture innocent kids?" I say. "Seriously, what's wrong with you, Mother?"

"Don't you talk to me like this, young lady—"

"Or what?"

"I'll have you punished."

"For what? Pointing out it's wrong to hurt people?" I say incredulously. "If that's suddenly a crime, then go ahead, punish me."

Mother slaps me across the face. My skin burns where she hit me, but I don't react. I don't want to give her the satisfaction.

"Sebastian, take my daughter out of here. I have work to do," she snaps at him. "And make sure she doesn't leave her room. She's grounded."

I open my mouth to protest, but then let it go. Let her ground me—I don't care. Sebastian takes my arm and leads me back up the metal stairs. I peek over my shoulder at Mother as she talks to Craven.

"Open the door," she says to him, indicating the cell with the silver marker over it.

"Emissary, are you sure—"

"Just get the operating table prepared," she snaps.

"But it's not ready," he says meekly.

"I don't care. We're running out of time," she replies.

I tug on Sebastian's sleeve as we reach the platform over-looking the room.

"I want to see," I whisper, curious to know what's been hidden in that cell.

I can tell he's interested too. We lean over the steel barrier to get a better look. The three guards cautiously enter the pitch-black cell. Something roars. There's a struggle, then a loud wail, and one of the guards rushes out of the room, his face slashed to shreds. I clamp my hands over my mouth to stifle a scream.

Mother steps back as the remaining two guards emerge from the cell holding the struggling creature. They drag it to the operating table in the middle of the room and stand back. I gasp.

It's a boy. More accurately, it's a naked boy.

I shouldn't look, but my eyes are glued to him. He's the same age as me, short, with a tangled mane of chocolate-brown hair that surrounds his feline features. His skin is the color of honey, with brown spots like a leopard's down his flank and legs. My eyes widen when a long spotted tail coils around his leg.

The guards pin the cat-boy down, and Craven quickly injects him. He thrashes and snaps at Craven with his saber teeth, his eyes glimmering gold. His movements gradually became sluggish, and his arms fall to his sides; he's unconscious.

"Do it," Mother orders.

Craven clamps open the boy's mouth and jabs a syringe into the soft tissue behind one of his saber teeth. Honey-colored fluid fills the syringe.

"Neat," Sebastian whispers. "It's a Bastet. I've never seen a live one before."

Craven extracts the needle and places it on the tray beside him.

"What's Mother doing with a Bastet?" I whisper to Sebastian.

"They have natural defenses against Darklings, like toxic venom and this terrible-smelling musk that they spray from . . . well, you don't want to know where."

"Is that what was in that Go Away Wrath Spray?" I ask, remembering that horrific stench when Craven used it on the Wrath the first time I was down here.

Sebastian nods. "Probably. Come on, let's go."

I peer at the Bastet boy one last time. His eyelids flutter, like he's lost in a terrible nightmare. I wonder if he's dreaming of us.

The next day I pace around my bedroom, scheming up ways to get out of the house without being noticed by Sebastian or Mother. I called Ash earlier, letting him know I'd been grounded but that I wanted to see him . . . *somehow*. I need to make sure he's okay after last night. I'm also curious about why he left with Sigur Marwick.

There's a knock at my door, and Sebastian enters before being invited in. He's holding a letter and grinning from ear to ear.

"Everything okay?" I ask.

"I've been summoned to Centrum to spend a few days with Purian Rose," he says breathlessly, showing me the letter.

I scan the note. Sure enough, Sebastian has been invited to a spiritual retreat hosted by Purian Rose.

"Only a dozen other people are going—it's really exclusive," he says.

"Congratulations," I say flatly.

I wonder what Sebastian did that piqued Purian Rose's

interest. It must've been something big. I consider talking Sebastian out of going, but the thought of him not breathing down my neck for a few days is too good to pass up.

"Have a good time," I say.

"I've arranged for Kurt and Aaron to guard you while I'm away."

"Brilliant," I mumble. *Two* guards? Argh!

"I'm going to pack." Sebastian pecks me on the cheek and leaves, humming a happy tune.

At that moment, my heart tugs, and I rush onto the balcony, knowing what it means. Ash is leaning against the balustrade, an enticing smile on his beautiful lips.

"I figured since you couldn't come to me, I'd come to you," he says.

I throw my arms around him, and we embrace.

"How on earth did you get onto my balcony without being caught?" I say.

He indicates the flattop roof a few feet above us. "It's surprisingly easy to get up there if you know how."

I bite my lip. That's probably how the other Darkling managed to get into my room without being spotted. There are no guards on the roof.

"The view up there is amazing," he says. "Come on, I'll show you."

He hoists himself onto the roof and pulls me up after him. The motion makes us both fall over, and I land on top of him, giggling. We sit up and survey the burning ruins of the city. It really *is* amazing. Church bells ring out in a joyous chorus of music, celebrating the anniversary of Armistice Day, while ribbons of black smoke lace the skies. Below us, the streets are filled with families dressed in their finest clothes, all hurrying to get somewhere. Then I start to notice the less pleasant things: Sentry tanks patrolling the streets, barbed-wire blockades, the Boundary Wall.

Up above us, a crow soars through the gray skies, its long black wings cutting through the clouds of smoke and ash that continue to rain down on the city.

"Sometimes I wish I could fly away," I say.

Ash stands up and takes my hand.

"Where are we going?" I ask.

"Do you trust me?"

"Yes . . . I trust you," I say. "What are we doing?"

He grins. "Flying."

He starts to run, my hand still entwined in his. I have to sprint to keep up with him. The edge of the roof gets closer and closer. I start to panic.

"Ash!"

We're going to fall off, we're going to die, we're going to—

Ash leaps into the air, bringing me along with him. For a brief second, it feels like we're flying as we jump toward the building on the opposite side of the street. We land with a thud on its roof. I grin at him.

He lets go of my hand and bounds onto the next roof. The distance between the buildings isn't that far since the city is so crammed together, and it's surprisingly easy to get around. No wonder Ash managed to get on my roof without trouble. I chase after him, like a game of cat and mouse. The world around me blurs as we leap from rooftop to rooftop. Icy wind courses through my hair and stings my cheeks, and for a short time, I feel like a bird soaring through the sky.

I jump off another roof, and Ash catches me when I land. We fall down, wrapped in each other's arms. His body is hard underneath mine, his taut muscles easily carrying my weight. Every time he breathes, my body moves with him, like I'm bobbing up and down on the waves.

I trace my fingers over his lips, and he sighs, parting them slightly, showing a hint of fang. My heart quickens. The sight both scares and thrills me. I gently press my lips against his.

The jolt of electricity that passes between us is intense.

I laugh. "Did you feel that?"

"Feel what?" he mocks.

"That zap of electricity?"

He shakes his head, but I know he's lying.

"Maybe we should try again?" he suggests.

I roll my eyes. "For scientific purposes only."

We kiss again, and it's just like a bolt of lightning zinging through my body. He pulls me closer to him, and our kiss deepens. I can feel his fangs against my lips, but it's not an unpleasant sensation. After a few minutes, I grudgingly pull away, but I continue to lie on top of him, just listening to his heart. He plays with my hair, twirling a curl around his index finger.

"You should wear your hair down more often. It looks so beautiful," he murmurs.

I giggle. No one's ever called my hair beautiful before, not even Sebastian. But I don't think he actually likes me that much; he just wants to possess me. Ash sighs contentedly.

"Are you happy?" I ask.

"Yes."

I shift slightly on top of him, and his heart quickens. I still find the sound amazing. *I did that.*

"What was it like not having a heartbeat?" I say softly.

He's silent for a moment, and I wonder if I've put my foot in it.

"It was hell," he eventually says. "It was like being stuck between life and death; I could walk, talk, breathe, eat, but I never felt truly *alive*. I never felt part of this world."

"And now you do?"

"Yes. Because of you."

I snuggle closer to him.

"Do you only have one heart like a human, or two like a Darkling?" I barely know anything about twin-blood physiology, and I want to know everything about Ash.

"I only have one heart, like a human. When I met you, though, it activated just like a Darkling's second heart, so I guess whatever I have inside me, it's a combination of both species."

"Best of both worlds?" I say.

He chuckles. "I never really thought of it like that before; I always thought it was the worst."

We stay wrapped in each other's arms until the sun starts to set over the city. Overhead the clouds turn heavy and black, threatening to storm. In the distance I hear the eerie wail of Darklings calling to each other from within the Legion as they wake from their slumber. Ash quietly listens.

"Do you wish you were there with them?" I roll over onto my stomach to face him.

"Yeah. It's not easy being the only twin-blood in the city. It's . . ."

"Lonely?" I fill in for him.

He nods. "But I don't feel that way anymore."

He takes my hand and places it over his chest. His heart beats steadily under my fingertips.

"That's the beauty of having a Blood Mate. You're always with me. I'm never alone," he says.

"Don't you wish you could see your family again, though?"
I ask.

"I'm seeing them tonight."

He tells me about Sigur and how he's been invited to the
Legion. I don't know why, but I'm suddenly filled with an irrational fear. I don't want him to go, but I can't tell him not to
see his family.

"How do you know Sigur?" I ask.

"He and my mom are Blood Mates. Mom left my dad to be
with Sigur just as the war broke out."

"That must've been very tough on you and your father," I
say.

He sighs. "It's okay. I think I finally understand she didn't
have a choice. If she felt for Sigur what I feel for you, she had
no option but to be with him."

"How did they meet? You don't have to tell me," I add
quickly, realizing I'm being tactless again. I'm just so curious
about his life.

"Before the war broke out, Mom got involved with the Legion Liberation Front, back when they were civil rights activ-
ists rather than freedom fighters," he explains. "She really cared
about the cause. She even went to a sit-in at the Black City
University, demanding that Darklings be given the right to an
education."

"Wow, I can't believe she was involved in that," I say, remembering my father telling me about it.

He nods. "Sigur led the movement. She was infatuated with
him even before she met him. Dad used to tease her about it; he
thought it was just a silly celebrity crush. Guess he was wrong.
Thing is, I think Mom would've left my dad eventually anyway."

"What makes you think that?"

"They fought about me a lot. The deeper Mom got involved with the civil rights movement, the more she wanted to raise me as a Darkling."

"And your father didn't want that?"

"He thought it would be easier for me to integrate if I was more human. They never even asked what I wanted."

"And what did you want?"

"I wanted to be a Darkling. I wanted to live with my mom when the wall went up."

"Why didn't you?"

Ash looks off into the distance. "She never asked."

"I'm glad you stayed. We wouldn't have met otherwise," I say.

He kisses me then. Softly, slowly, and my body fills with sunshine, making every part of me bloom into life. When we eventually pull apart, he stands up and helps me to my feet.

"I should really go. They're expecting me," he says.

I lower my gaze. "You promise you'll come back to me?"

He lifts my chin and softly kisses my lips.

"Nothing will keep us apart," he says.

The storm clouds above us finally burst, and the first drops of rain splash against my cheek. A chill seeps through me. I hope he's right.

21

ASH

THERE'S A LOUD CLUNK as the metal gates slowly open. My stomach lurches, my nerves on edge. I'm finally going to step inside the Legion! I didn't tell Dad I was coming here; he doesn't even know I met Sigur last night or that I was arrested. It would just upset him, and he's got enough on his plate with Mom. He thinks I'm spending the evening with Beetle.

Two guards appear in the entranceway, silhouetted in the moonlight. They're over seven feet tall and broad like bears. Sigur stands between them, and although he isn't as tall as they are, he exudes more power. His pure white hair has been tied back with a bronze band, and he's dressed in an intricately embroidered orange robe that matches his glittering eyes. He's not wearing his gold mask, but then again, it's nighttime, so there's no sun to burn his skin.

He embraces me, and I tense up. I'm not prepared to play the role of the dutiful Blood Son just yet; we're a long way off from that. The guards usher us into the holding area and close the main gates. One of my escorts shouts a command to the gatekeepers at the second set of gates, and they open. The other

escort faces me and gives me a fangy grin. He's an Eloka Darkling like me, with black eyes and hair, although his face is sharp
and angular, with a pointed chin and long nose.

"After you," he says, bowing low.

I step over the threshold.

I'm inside!

The smell hits me first. Decay, sewage, sickness—all the
worst smells on Earth, and they're all shooting up my nose.
Sigur places a reassuring hand on my shoulder.

"You will get used to it soon enough," he says, then turns to
one of the guards. "Go ahead and prepare a feast for my guest."

The guard nods and rushes on ahead.

I breathe through my mouth, horror-struck at the sights
around me. We're in a colossal shantytown, filled with thousands of ramshackle huts. The ground is covered in ash and
mud and things I don't even want to think about. Outside every
hut, emaciated Darkling women hold their children up beseech-
ingly, calling to me in their native tongues.

Our escort leads us through a warren of passageways and
narrow streets. I try and keep track of where we're going, but
soon lose my way. I'll never get out of here on my own.

The escort looks me up and down. "Mmm. Not so different
from us. Just a little *pikko*."

"Pikko?" I ask.

"Small," Sigur explains.

The two men laugh, and my cheeks turn hot. I've never considered myself small before, but then again, I've been raised
around humans. Darkling children gather around me, curious.
I smile at them, trying my best to look friendly. They are, after
all, my extended family. They stare back at me with wide, black
eyes.

My escort nods toward them. "I wouldn't let them get too close, twin-blood."

"Why not?"

"You reek of human blood, and they're *hungry.*"

Fragg! I edge closer to my escort. The more I see, the more I realize how ravaged with hunger the Darklings are; many are little more than walking skeletons and teeth.

Sigur shoos them away. "Do not worry, Ash. You may smell human, but they can sense you are also part Darkling. We do not eat our own kind."

The escort slides him a guilty look. "Not unless all other options are exhausted."

This doesn't make me feel any better.

"Hang on. Doesn't the Sentry give you Synth-O-Blood?" I say.

"Rarely, and the blood they do send is tainted," Sigur says.

"Tainted with what?" I ask.

"Small amounts of acacia solution. It's just enough to make us sick and weaken us so we can't fight the humans. We eat it, as we have no other choice."

We approach a long rowboat like a gondola floating on the canal. Our escort takes the oar and quietly rows us through the Darkling city, away from the Boundary Wall and away from safety. The buildings are dilapidated, their roofs caved in, their walls crumbling. Shadows stir inside the windowless buildings, and I realize they're Darklings, hanging upside down from exposed rafters like bats, watching me with their sparkling, curious eyes. A thought pops into my head.

"Will I get to see my family?" I say, suddenly excited.

"We are all your family," Sigur says, indicating the Darklings around us.

"No, I meant my immediate family. Aunts, uncles, that sort of thing? I've never met them."

They stopped talking to Mom when she married Dad, disgusted at the notion of her being with a human. It devastated my mom, especially since she was so close to her youngest sister, Lucinda, who was ordered to cut off contact with Mom by my grandparents. Despite this, I want to see them; I'd love to know more about my Darkling heritage.

Sigur takes my hand, his face suddenly serious. "I am so sorry to be the one to tell you this, Ash, but they all perished in the Barren Lands at the start of the war."

I shake my head, grief and disappointment surging through me as it sinks in. *It's just Mom and me. We're all who's left. And soon it'll just be me.*

Sigur politely turns his head as I take a moment to compose myself. We spend the rest of the journey in silence. The boat drifts to a stop, and the escort guides us up a cobbled street to a set of wrought-iron gates leading into the Black City Zoo.

The zoo is unnaturally quiet and deserted. We pass empty animal enclosures, which are overgrown with eight years' worth of vines and weeds. Inside every cage are stone carvings of the animals that used to live inside them: bears, wolves, tigers. I'm guessing the real animals were eaten.

Our escort guides us to a man-made cave carved into a mound of granite. Above the entrance is a faded sign: NOCTURNAL ANIMALS. Inside, the cave is surprisingly hot and muggy. The narrow passageway is lit by rows of flaming torches, casting flickering shadows on the ground. We go deeper and deeper into the earth, until we suddenly emerge in a huge dome-roofed chamber.

Spiraling around the circumference of the room is a metal

walkway, which coils up three floors like a giant snake, leading off to a number of secondary chambers. In the center of the
room is a round banquet table, with strange grooves carved
into it. *What are they for?*

There's an echo of footsteps and voices from a passageway
to our right, and my heartbeat speeds up as they get closer and
closer. I swallow, nervous all of a sudden. Dozens of Darklings
enter the room, dressed in their finest robes. They all hurry to
greet me, bowing and introducing themselves. Eight of them
are part of the Darkling Assembly, the equivalent of the Sentry government. One very formal and serious-looking female
Darkling, with a long, narrow face, introduces herself as Logan
Henrikk. She seems less impressed than the others that I'm here
and goes over to talk to Sigur as I meet everyone else.

Soon the room is filled with a hundred Darklings, and the
party is in full swing, with music playing and Sanguis wine
flowing. Everyone wants to shake my hand. I turn to Sigur, my
arm aching, and give him a pleading look. He claps his hands,
and everyone instantly leaves me alone. The members of the
Assembly sit around the table, while the other Darklings make
themselves comfortable on the floor.

Sigur indicates for me to take a seat next to him at the table.

"So, what do you think of the Legion?" Sigur asks me when
we've settled down, pouring me a glass of Sanguis wine.

"I didn't realize things were so bad here," I say.

Sigur half smiles. "The Sentry government is good at propa-
ganda. If the humans knew how bad the conditions were, they
might be tempted to join Humans for Unity." Was that a sneer
in his voice?

I doubt people would join Humans for Unity if they saw
this place, but I keep my thoughts to myself. I've lived around

humans long enough to know they don't care as long as it doesn't affect their cozy lives.

I drink a few gulps of Sanguis wine, and my head starts to feel pleasantly fuzzy. I put the wine down on top of the unusual grooves carved into the table.

"What are these for?" I ask.

"You'll see," he replies.

I drum my fingers against the table. "I like what you've done with the place. Very Darkling chic."

Sigur smiles sadly. "It feels very empty without Annora."

I wince. Why did he have to bring Mom up?

He turns and studies me with his one good eye, which blazes orange in the firelight. There's a tenderness to his face I've not seen before.

"I'm so sorry, Ash. For everything. I never intended to hurt you or your father. It just . . ."

"Happened? Yeah, I understand." Once you find your Blood Mate, nothing can keep you apart, even if one of them is already married. I finally get that. My mom and Sigur didn't have a choice; fate threw them together. I drink some wine, glancing at Sigur occasionally. I've hated him for years, but maybe I was too quick to judge him. He clearly loved Mom, he saved me, and he never deliberately meant to hurt Dad. It just happened. *He let his niece die, though.* He can't be fully trusted. Music begins to play, the tune exotic and ancient, the sound of sitars and flutes echoing around the chamber. I sink back into my chair and take another gulp of the wine. I almost manage to forget the Darklings outside, shivering and starving while we're all in here having a feast.

The music changes to something slow and seductive, and everyone in the room begins to cheer. I sit up, alert, wondering what's going on. The candles flicker as a beautiful girl appears at the top of the spiral walkway, her inky-black hair twisting around her pale body, which is barely concealed beneath her flimsy halter-neck dress. A group of Darkling children surround her, their faces painted honey brown with spots on them. They're wearing cat ears and are crawling around on their hands and knees. The guests boo at the children in a jovial way, like they're at a pantomime. The kids hiss at them.

"What's going on?" I ask.

"A reenactment of the battle between the goddess Zanthina and the Bastet people," Sigur explains.

The girl gracefully dances down the stairs and leaps onto the banquet table.

"This is the goddess Zanthina," Sigur whispers to me. "Every night she dances across the sky to bring out the evening stars."

She begins to gyrate to the music, spinning and whirling, her footsteps sure and precise. I gulp, my cheeks glowing from more than just the wine. The children climb onto the table and dance around the girl, hissing at her, pawing at her skirt.

"These are the cat people," Sigur says. "They are envious of Zanthina's dancing and wish to kill her, so they can control the night."

The girl and the children begin an aggressive dance. She lashes out at the cat people. The children fall down one by one—Zanthina is victorious. Everyone claps and cheers. She bows. Her dark black eyes rest on me, and my heart falters. She's a twin-blood, like me.

"Ash, let me introduce you to Evangeline, the jewel in my collection."

Something suddenly clicks into place.

"You're the girl I saw at the execution the other day," I say.

Sigur pats Evangeline's cheek in an affectionate, fatherly way.

"Evangeline's my most trusted lieutenant," he says.

As Evangeline sits down, her leg presses against mine. The touch is so slight, and yet fire blazes across my skin where our legs have connected, roaring through my veins, awakening my senses, awakening the Darkling within me. *What the hell was that?* She smirks, like she knows the effect she's having on me. *It's just because she's a twin-blood, that's all. It's natural to have an attraction to her, right? Nothing to obsess about, no need to read too much into it. Right?*

She chats to Sigur in a very casual, mocking way, and after watching them for half an hour, I can see that their relationship runs deeper than just colleagues.

"You and Sigur seem very close," I say to Evangeline.

She nods. "He and Annora raised me."

Sharp pain stabs at my stomach at the mention of Mom's name. *She raised Evangeline?* All those years I was pining for my mom and wondering if she missed me, she was bringing up another child with Sigur.

"Evangeline worshipped Annora," Sigur says, not noticing how much these words cut me. "She used to follow her around like a little duckling."

Sigur ruffles Evangeline's hair, and she laughs, slapping his hand away.

"Don't make me hurt you, old man. This hairstyle took two hours to do," she teases.

He rolls his one good eye, shaking his head. "How things change. She was such a tomboy when she was little, not interested in her looks at all. I miss those days," he adds wistfully.

Jealousy twists like a knot inside me at how close they are. I wonder what it would've been like having a Darkling father, how much easier things would've been.

Sigur claps his hands, and everyone stops talking. "Bring in the guest."

There are excited murmurs, and I tear my eyes away from Evangeline as a teenage boy is led into the room. He looks slightly older than me—maybe eighteen or nineteen years old. His eyes are dilated, and he's dragging his feet, clearly drugged. Sigur waves a hand, and the room falls silent. He walks over to the boy and runs a claw down his fleshy cheek, drawing a fine line of blood. My stomach wrenches. The boy sways, intoxicated. Sigur gently lays him down on the banquet table, and I suddenly realize what the grooves in the wood are for. *Siphoning blood.* I stand up to protest, but Evangeline pulls me back into my seat.

"He's just a Hazer," she says. "I picked him up from one of the dens. He doesn't even know what's happening."

"Sigur allows you to go that far into the city?" I ask, surprised. It's one thing letting her stand on the Boundary Wall beside him during Jana's execution, protected by the Legion guards; it's altogether a different matter letting her wander the dangerous city streets alone.

She gives me a condescending look. "Sigur often sends me out on errands."

"Aren't you worried about getting caught?" I ask.

"Not really. Sigur's bribed a few of the Sentry guards, so whenever they're on duty, I'm free to come and go as I please. As long as I don't bump into a Tracker out in the streets, I'm safe."

Sigur drags his claw down the boy's chest, drawing gasps from the ravenous audience. He licks the wound with his black tongue, his eyes shut as he relishes the taste.

I swallow back my revulsion and desire. I know it's wrong, but I'm starving, and the idea of fresh blood is *so* tempting. The boy groans as Sigur slashes his neck, severing his jugular vein. Blood splashes across the table, and the Darklings moan. Sigur guzzles the liquid dripping from the open wound and the others watch hungrily . . . me included.

I chew down my hunger and try not to watch, although the smell of hot blood stings my nostrils and makes my insides squirm. I can only imagine how amazing it tastes, so fresh . . .

"Go on." Sigur steps back, blood on his lips.

I'm not sure if it's my hunger, peer pressure or the Sanguis wine, but suddenly it doesn't seem like such a big deal if I drink just a little. The Darklings move out of my way, giving me a proper view of the dying boy. His neck and chest are slick with blood; his breathing is shallow and ragged. I should be repulsed, but I'm not. The sight *excites* me, and for once, I'm not scared to admit it. I don't have to hide my true nature from anyone here; I can be the monster I truly am, and no one will judge me for it.

I plunge my fangs into the boy's neck and drink greedily, loving the sensation of being able to feed without people gasping or screaming, without worrying about getting caught. The boy lets out a final breath as the last of his life drains from his body.

I stagger back, the effects of the Haze in the boy's blood making me unsteady on my feet, and wipe my mouth, disgusted with myself. How can I be so reckless? It's this place, these creatures. They make me feel so irresponsible, so *inhuman*. But I am human—at least part of me is.

I sprint out of the cave into the open air. The stench of the city hits me again, and my stomach churns. I throw up until my stomach is empty.

"What's your problem?" Evangeline says, startling me. "It's rude to leave a feast. Sigur's really insulted."

"I don't care!"

"Why are you so upset? You were just feeding."

"On a *human*."

"So? That's what Darklings eat."

"I'm not a fragging Darkling, I'm—"

"Human?" She laughs. "Oh, Ash, you poor thing. You really think you're one of them."

"No I don't. I know I'm not human, but I'm not one of *them* either!" I say, pointing toward the cave.

I walk away, but Evangeline won't leave me alone.

"You've been around humans too long, Ash. It's good that you're here with your own kind. You'll come around to our way of thinking soon enough," she says.

"Will you just piss off?"

"Oh temper, temper," she teases. "You have to toughen up if you want to survive around here. Darklings don't have time for human emotions."

"How can you live with them? They're vile," I say, my voice choked.

They're not what I expected at all. They're nothing like my mom.

Evangeline's face stiffens. "Sigur's taken good care of me. He looks after all the twin-bloods."

"There are more of us here?" My curiosity is piqued.

She takes my hand. A different sort of hunger flares inside me, and my skin feels hot where our hands connect. An image of Natalie pops into my head, and shame crawls through me. Even so, I don't let go of Evangeline's hand.

She leads me into a crumbling building, which reeks of decay.

"What is this place?" I ask.

"The hospital," she says.

We go to a ward on the first floor. Evangeline silently waits by the door as I take in the scene. Rows of metal beds are crammed into the room, and nearly all of them are occupied by Darklings infected with Wrath. Each one is at a different stage of the disease. Some just have yellowed eyes and thinning hair, while others are at the end-stages, just like Mom. The cloying smell of rotting flesh hits my nostrils and bile rises up my throat.

"There used to be one hundred and forty-three of us," Evangeline explains. "The Wrath spread through the ghetto so quickly; first the Darklings got sick, then the twin-bloods. We hoped they'd be okay, because they're part human, but . . ." She shakes her head. "There wasn't much we could do. We're becoming extinct, Ash."

My throat chokes up. I knew twin-bloods were rare, but I never realized it was this bad. With no more twin-bloods being born in the USS due to segregation, it'll just be me and Evangeline left.

"Your mother took good care of us," Evangeline says. "She nursed the sick ones, despite the risks to herself. I helped out as best I could."

"Weren't you worried about getting infected?" I ask.

Evangeline gazes down at the ground. "I already am."

"You don't look sick."

"I have a natural immunity to the effects of the Wrath. We're not sure why I'm different from the other twin-bloods," she says. "I'm still a carrier, though, so I can pass it on."

She doesn't have to explain that any further. When Darklings mate, they often bite each other and blood share. Evangeline will never be able to do that; not with a Darkling, anyway.

"I'm sorry," I say.

"Maybe it's a good thing. Sigur thinks my blood might be the cure. We got close to finding a vaccine recently with the limited resources we have, then . . ." She shrugs. "We don't know. The Wrath's mutated. It's gotten worse somehow."

I leave the ward, unable to stand being surrounded by my sick brethren for another moment. We walk through the ghetto, passing burned-out, ruined buildings. Unlike the buildings on my side of the wall, these ones are covered in ivy and white flowers that are abundant with dark blue berries, giving the whole place an otherworldly beauty. Evangeline notices me looking at them.

"Some of the Darklings grew the flowers to make this place a little more bearable to live in," she says.

"How long have you been here?" I ask.

"Since I was eight years old. Sigur found me down an alley on Bleak Street, bleeding to death," she says. "He brought me back here. He's a great protector."

"He let his niece die the other day," I say.

"He can't save us all, even though he tries."

The thought of Jana on the cross with Tom, executed because of their forbidden relationship, reminds me of Natalie. My heart thuds *ba-boom ba-boom ba-boom*. I want to be with her so much right now. Being here just makes me feel more of an outcast than ever before. It's clear I'm not like the other Darklings. When I'm with her, I feel like I belong.

Evangeline surprises me by placing a hand over my chest. "How is this possible?"

"I found my Blood Mate," I say.

She looks surprised.

"You don't believe me?" I challenge.

"I believe you. It's just there aren't many Darklings over your side of the wall. I'm surprised you found your Blood Mate among them."

I wonder if I should tell her that my Blood Mate is a human. I barely know Evangeline, but an instinct deep inside me tells me I can trust her.

"She's human," I admit.

Evangeline drops her hand. "The connection only happens between Darklings. She can't be your Blood Mate."

"All the evidence proves otherwise."

"What's the human's name, then?" Her voice is hard.

I rub the back of my neck. What am I going to tell her, that my Blood Mate is the Sentry Emissary's daughter, Natalie Buchanan? I don't think so.

"Does it matter?" I say instead.

"You can't be with her. You can't turn your back on your own kind, Ash."

"I'm not turning my back on anyone. I'm half human, re-member—so why can't I be with a human girl? Why does everyone say I'm only allowed to have a relationship with a Darkling?"

"Because it's against the law," she says.

"That's not going to stop me from being with her."

We approach the canal. The Boundary Wall is just a strip on the horizon. Home is so far away.

"I need to go. Can you take me back to the gates?" I say.

She hesitates. "Will you come back? Sigur can arrange it."

I study Evangeline for a long moment, watching how her inky-black hair ripples like the surface of the oceans. I can't abandon her. There are so few of our kind left.

"I'll be back," I promise.

22

NATALIE

EVERYWHERE IS BLACK: the sky, the earth, the ash drifting all around us—the whole city is mourning for Chris. Even school's been canceled today, so students could attend his funeral. I tighten the black scarf around my neck, doing my best to block out the bitter cold.

Beetle plucks a cigarette from behind his ear and sparks up. I wouldn't say things are good between us after the argument on his birthday, but at least he's civil to me. I check my phone, hoping to see a message from Ash. He didn't ring me yesterday like I thought he would. I'm curious to know how it went at the Legion on Saturday. There's nothing.

"Have you heard from Ash?" I ask.

Beetle shakes his head.

We're standing at the back of the congregation, watching the funeral. Gregory stares blankly at the ebony coffin. He looks shrunken in an oversized black jacket that I vaguely recognize, and then it hits me: it's Chris's coat.

Day's up front with the rest of the mourners, including my mother, who is trying to look forlorn for the press, although her face is so pumped with toxins, I don't think she's capable of expressing any emotion other than mild surprise. I can't understand why she's taken such an interest in Chris's death; she paid for the funeral, then insisted on coming with twenty of her closest friends from the media to "pay her respects." Maybe it's because he went to my school? I know she's up to something.

She's flanked by Sentry guards, and there are more scattered around the cemetery keeping an eye on the proceedings. The upshot of all this added security is I don't need a personal guard with me today, which is a relief. Sebastian's still on his "spiritual retreat" in Centrum and isn't due back until later today, so I've got a few hours of relative freedom.

Juno Jones, the red-haired reporter for Black City News, stands nearby, doing a report on the service. She tells her cameraman to film Mother.

"It's such a tragic loss of a young life," Mother says to Chris and Gregory's parents, just loud enough for the journalists to hear. "Rest assured, the government is doing everything in its power to find whoever supplied this tainted Haze and bring them to justice. We suspect Darkling involvement."

Mrs. Thompson grasps my mother's hands, thanking her, and Mother's red-painted lips waver slightly, disgusted at being touched by a lowly Workboot.

"I hope we have your support for Rose's Law," Mother continues. "Keeping the Darklings permanently segregated is the first step toward a totally Haze-free society."

Mr. and Mrs. Thompson both nod enthusiastically, and I glower at my mother. So that's the reason she's here? To rally support for Rose's Law. What sort of person does that at a boy's funeral?

Gregory snatches a look at my mother, and I can see he's

thinking the same thing. Now isn't the time or place for Mother's political games; people are grieving.

"What's going on with you and Day?" I ask Beetle when she glances over at us.

He shrugs. "She's still punishing me for choosing Haze over her. I don't think she's ever going to forgive me."

"Maybe now that she knows Ash didn't get you hooked on Haze, she'll be a little nicer to him?" I say.

"I wouldn't count on it. She's stubborn."

I look at Day and feel a pang of sadness. There's so much I want to talk to her about. I miss my friend.

I check my phone again. Still no message from Ash.

Close by, Juno Jones starts talking quietly to the camera. "I'm here at the funeral of high school student Chris Thompson, the latest victim of Golden Haze, a deadly new strain of the drug being sold on the streets," she says, walking a little closer to the congregation. "Chris Thompson is the sixth teenager to die of the drug in the space of two weeks, sparking fear and concern in the city. Anyone with information about the source of Golden Haze is being urged to report it to the Sentry guard."

Chris is the sixth victim? I knew Linus and his friend died from it, but I didn't know there had been others. Beetle looks alarmed too.

"If the Darklings are blamed for all those deaths, people are bound to vote for Rose's Law," he says. "Then who knows what's going to happen to Ash—they'll probably force him to live in the ghetto with the other Darklings. They're already making him wear that ID bracelet."

My heart freezes. They can't take Ash away from me.

"We need to find out who really created the Golden Haze.

I can't let my mother blame the Darklings," I say. "That guy Linus must've got it from somewhere."

"That would've been his boss, Mr. Tubs," Beetle explains.

"Okay, we'll start there and do some investigating. Do you know where I can find him?" I ask.

Beetle's eyebrows shoot so far up his forehead, I think they're going to fly off. "You don't want to mess with him, my friend. He's dangerous."

"We'll take Ash for protection. We have to do something," I say.

Beetle scratches his head, messing up his already scruffy hair. "I can't go. I owe Mr. Tubs some money. Like, a *lot* of money . . ."

I let out an irritated sound. "Fine, Ash and I will go on our own."

Of course, I'll have to actually speak to Ash first. I check my phone again. Nothing.

"Well, if you go, let me know what you find out. We're all going to the Park tonight for an unofficial remembrance party for Chris. Meet me at the white mansion. Do you know it?" Beetle asks.

My heart clenches. "Yes, I know it."

The wind stirs, and a familiar tugging sensation pulls at my chest. Ash is lurking in the church ruins. Relief washes through me. I check to be sure no one is looking before sneaking off to join him.

The roof has collapsed, and the sky peeps through the bones of wooden rafters. Several crows are perched on them, their beady black eyes watching me intently as I carefully navigate the rubble.

We sit down on a pile of stones in the corner of the ruins,

hidden from view. I study Ash's profile, which is set like marble, so cold and emotionless apart from the little furrow between his brows, giving him away.

"You didn't call. I was worried," I say.

He turns to look at me, his eyes dark and haunted. His mouth twitches as if he wants to tell me something. Instead he rests his head on my shoulder. He smells amazing, like the earth after rain. We stay like this for a few minutes, not speaking.

"How was the Legion?" I ask.

"Natalie, I did something terrible . . ."

"What? You can tell me."

He presses his face against my neck. "I don't want to be like them. I don't want to be a Darkling. I'm not a monster, I'm not!"

What did they do to him?

"I don't know what happened, but one thing I'm sure of is you're a good person. You're not a monster." I press my hand against his heart. "I can feel it."

Ash pulls me toward him, and his lips find mine. The kiss is delicate and uncertain. My fingers twist through his hair, and I draw him closer, my body craving him more than oxygen. I moan with pleasure as he sinks deeper into the kiss, his lips opening, his tongue running across mine. Fireworks explode inside me, *pop, pop, pop!*

He pulls away. "This isn't right. Not here." He looks over my shoulder at the funeral.

I tell Ash my plan about visiting Mr. Tubs.

"We can snoop around and get some of the Golden Haze," I say. "If we work out what it's been blended with, then maybe we can trace it back to the original source. Whatever that gold stuff is, it can't be that commonplace."

Ash looks at me uncertainly.

"We have to at least try. I don't want my mother pinning this on the Darklings." I lace my fingers through his. "I can't lose you, Ash."

He nods. "Okay, it sounds like a plan."

"When should we go?" I ask.

Ash stands up, a new determination in his eyes. "Let's go now."

23
ASH

THE SIGN ABOVE Mr. Tubs's pawnshop hangs from a single screw, threatening to fall down at any second. I hold the door open for Natalie. We step inside the shop, which is brimming with tacky bric-a-brac like jewelry, weapons, hats, instruments, electrical equipment—basically anything someone could exchange for a few coins. It's hard to navigate through the piles of knickknacks. Mr. Tubs is nowhere in sight.

Fragg! I have to get my hands on that Golden Haze. It's our only hope of working out who's really responsible for Chris's and Linus's deaths. For the first time, I'm starting to worry about Rose's Law being passed. I hadn't fully considered the implications before. I could be forced to live in the Legion with those *creatures*. I'd never see Natalie again.

"I just had a thought. Won't Mr. Tubs find it odd that you're here?" Natalie asks me.

"Yeah, but don't worry, I've got a plan," I say, although the only plan I have is to get out of this shop without a stake through my heart. I squeeze her hand reassuringly, and she relaxes. We approach the glass counter at the front of the shop and ring the bell. A moment later, a short, tubby man from the Eastern territory emerges from the back room. An unlit cigarette hangs from the corner of his mouth. He instantly recognizes me.

I raise my hands as he reaches under the counter for a weapon.

"I brought you a client. Call it a peace offering," I say.

Natalie gives a nervous smile.

"Go on," Mr. Tubs says, his interest piqued.

"A Tracker took my poison sacs. I can't deal anymore," I say, the lies spilling off my tongue. "Now that Linus is dead, I figured you'd need a new guy, and I've got a bunch of clients lined up for you."

My pulse races as I wait for him to respond. He moves his hand from under the counter.

"I think about it," he says.

I exhale.

Mr. Tubs turns his attention to Natalie.

"So what does a pretty thing like you want?" His rheumy eyes drift toward Natalie's chest, and my fangs tingle, wanting to bite him.

"Well, I've got this big party coming up, you see," she says in a rush. "And I wanted to make it a really *fun* party."

"Tell me, pretty girl, how much 'fun' you want?"

"A lot. Around fifty mils?" Natalie says.

"You got money?" he asks.

Her cheeks turn pink. "Er, no." She turns to me, whispering, "My mother cut off my allowance the night I met you. Do you have any?"

Ha! As if. I shake my head. We really should've worked out these details, but I just assumed Natalie would have the money.

"You waste my time!" Mr. Tubs says, his round face getting red.

"No, wait." Natalie takes off her antique watch. "I'd like to pawn this. It's worth a lot."

I grab her wrist before she can pass the watch over. "You can't sell that; it was your dad's."

"We don't have a choice," she whispers back. "Besides, I know he'd understand why I did it."

She looks at me with determination, and I let her wrist go. I'm not going to boss her around; she can make up her own mind about things.

"Put a ten-day hold on it," I say to Mr. Tubs. "I'll work off the debt."

Natalie gives me a grateful smile, then hands the watch to Mr. Tubs, who inspects it with curiosity.

"Nice piece you got here. Watch face made from Bastet ivory, that very rare. I give you two phials of Golden Haze for it."

"I'll take it," she says.

"Follow me," he says.

He leads us into the backroom and down a flight of narrow stairs into the basement. Natalie gasps and grips my hand. The floor is writhing with humans, all lost in an ecstasy of Haze, kissing each other and pulling off their clothes, unaware or simply not caring that they have an audience. Languishing on several tatty sofas is a group of Darklings, who must've snuck over the Boundary Wall to visit the den. Darklings can get high by drinking the blood of a human who has taken Haze, and many think it's worth the risk of climbing over the wall to get a fix and some fresh blood. I try not to drink too much from my clients when I'm giving them a hit of Haze for this very reason; it's easy to get addicted.

They roll their dull eyes on me, the sparkle long gone from them. One Darkling has strange bite marks all over his face and neck, as if he's been attacked by an animal. Beside him are twin Darkling girls, both with a shock of white hair and gleaming orange eyes. Nordins. They have nubby stumps sticking out of their shoulder blades where their wings used to be. They're all feeding on a human—a woman in her thirties, her skeletal body ravaged by Haze. Her eyes are shut, and she looks blissful. My stomach churns as I picture the boy we feasted on at Sigur's place. They probably picked him up from here.

Mr. Tubs steps over the humans sprawled on the ground and goes into his tiny office at the back of the room. We follow. The room consists of an old desk covered in paperwork, a nudie calendar, a filthy fridge and several small TV screens showing CCTV footage of the Haze den. There's a bookshelf beside them filled with digital disks, with dates scrawled over them; I'm guessing these are recordings of the CCTV footage.

He notices me looking at them. "It for insurance. You report me to authorities, I have proof you come here too, and we both go to jail."

It's twisted, but it makes sense. He opens the filthy refrigerator at the back of the room. He takes out two green-capped phials of Golden Haze, just like the one Linus had, and hands them to Natalie.

"Listen, this very important," Mr. Tubs says to Natalie. "You take just a drop, okay? No more. It much stronger than regular Haze. Some kids, they didn't listen and they—" He waves a hand dismissively. "It their own fault."

My fangs throb again. He must be referring to Linus and

Chris. So that's the deal with Golden Haze? It's fine in small enough doses, but take too much, and it'll kill you? That's one heck of a risky game to play. How much is too much?

She pretends to inspect the venom before passing a phial to me. I pop the lid and sniff the liquid. My nostrils flare. It's Haze all right, although whatever it's been blended with smells rank.

"Do you know what the gold stuff is?" Natalie asks Mr. Tubs. *Way to be subtle.* "I hear it's meant to give you the best-ever high with no Haze Headache afterward."

Mr. Tubs gives a yellow-toothed grin. "That a *secret* ingredient."

"Are you sure you can't tell me? I mean, if it's not safe—" she says.

Mr. Tubs seizes the Golden Haze. "You don't like, you go elsewhere."

"No, no!" Natalie takes the Golden Haze and grabs my arm. "Let's go."

We exit his office and go back into the main den.

"Sorry, I totally messed that up," Natalie says.

"We got the drug. At least that's a start," I reply.

"Ash?" a familiar voice calls from the gloom.

A girl walks out of the shadows into the red light, her midnight-blue hair flowing down to her waist. *Evangeline.* Something stirs inside me at the sight of her, and I quickly force the feeling aside. In Evangeline's hands are several blood bags. A thunderous look crosses her face when she sees Natalie.

"What are you doing here?" I say.

"Getting some blood for Sigur. He doesn't eat that Synth-O-Blood crap. What are *you* doing here?"

I show her the phials of Haze, and she looks at me quizzically.

"Let's talk outside," I say.

It's begun to snow lightly, turning the once-black skies a hazy gray. We duck down an alley beside the pawnshop.

Natalie stretches a hand toward Evangeline. "Hi, I'm Natalie."

Evangeline doesn't shake her hand; there's a cold, hard look in her eyes.

"I know who you are. You're the Emissary's daughter," Evangeline replies. "What I don't understand is why you're here with Ash."

"She's the girl I was telling you about last night," I say. "Natalie's my Blood Mate."

"No!" Evangeline glowers at Natalie. "It can't be *her*."

"Why not me?" Natalie says defiantly.

Evangeline snarls and flashes her fangs.

"Whoa, easy there!" I say, getting between them. "Put your fangs away."

Evangeline steps back, taking a shaky breath.

"I know it's surprising, but I hope you can be happy for me," I say to Evangeline. "*I'm* happy."

Evangeline knows what it's like not to have a heartbeat. She must understand what it means to me to have found Natalie.

"Congratulations," she mutters.

I quickly explain to Natalie how I know Evangeline, which seems to relax her a little.

Evangeline points to the phials of Golden Haze in my hand. "Why are you buying Haze from Mr. Tubs?"

I tell her what happened with Linus and Chris.

"How come they died from it? Others must've taken Golden Haze and survived," Evangeline says.

"It's only lethal in high doses," I explain, remembering what Mr. Tubs told us. "If you take a small amount, it's okay."

"What do you think the Golden Haze has been blended with?" she asks.

"That's what we're hoping to find out," I say.

"I can run some tests back in the lab," Natalie says.

Evangeline flashes Natalie an angry look. "And *I'll* bring a sample back to the Legion. Our alchemists can study it too."

They both hold out their hands, waiting for me to choose who to go with. I know I should go with Natalie—she *is* my Blood Mate—but something is holding me back, telling me to go with Evangeline. I don't understand why I'm so confused when it's so clear-cut I'm meant to go with my girlfriend. Maybe it's because Evangeline is a twin-blood? I'm curious about her.

"If you want to go with Evangeline, that's fine," Natalie says quietly.

I smile, grateful that she's letting me off the hook.

"I'll catch up with you and Beetle tonight at the Park," I say, kissing her on the cheek.

She doesn't say anything as I leave with Evangeline.

24

NATALIE

I POP DOWN TO THE LAB, hoping to run some tests on the Golden Haze to find out what it's been blended with. Jealousy spikes inside me at the thought of Ash with Evangeline. How can I possibly compete with a twin-blood? They're so incredibly beautiful, and I'm just a plain human.

I think I'm in luck when I don't immediately see Craven in the laboratory, so I rush over to one of the microscopes. Then the door to the Biohazard lab opens and Craven exits, holding a thin black case. His wiry bronze-colored hair is unkempt, and there are dark rings under his green eyes, like he hasn't slept in days. He seems surprised to see me.

"Hello, pumpkin. What can I do for you?" he says.

"I . . . erm . . ." I quickly slip the Golden Haze into my pocket. "Do you know when Sebastian's getting back?" It's the only thing I can think of to say.

"He arrived home a few minutes ago. He's in his room."

"Great." I fake a smile.

I go upstairs, tiptoeing past Sebastian's room, not wanting

him to know I'm here, but a floorboard creaks underfoot. His door opens, and I gasp. Sebastian's gorgeous blond hair has been shaved off, and there's a raw-looking rose tattoo just above his left ear. The room behind him has been stripped bare. Even the silk sheets on his bed have been replaced with simple white cotton ones.

"You've shaved your hair," I say.

He runs a hand over his head and gives a cold smile. "Of course. Every follower of the Purity must remove their hair."

I'm too dumbfounded to speak. Instead I just head to my bedroom and put the phial of Golden Haze inside my jewelry box on my nightstand. Sebastian follows me a moment later and flops down on my plush bed.

"What are you doing?" I say.

"I wanted to hang out. I haven't seen you in a few days. I thought we could talk."

"I'm going out." I grab some clothes from the wardrobe.

"Where are you going?" he asks.

"None of your business."

"I'm your guard, so it is my business, especially after what happened to Malcolm."

My gut wrenches at the sound of his name. I keep having dreams about Malcolm and Truffles's dead, mutilated bodies, always followed by nightmares about the child in the cave. My eyes dart to the dark stain on my floor where Truffles's blood seeped into the carpet. I kick a rug over it.

I change in my bathroom, then hurry outside, Sebastian following me despite my protests. I'll work out a way to ditch him when we get to the Park.

In spite of its name, it's not an actual park with grass and swings. Nothing like that exists in Black City anymore. The

Park is short for Park Boulevard, an old street in the rich part of the city that was bombed during the blitz.

The gate creaks as I open it. The street looks like a photo negative; the white marble buildings have turned black with soot, while the dark ground is dusted with snow.

It's eerily quiet as Sebastian and I stroll down the center of the road. I study the houses on either side of us, their roofs long gone and their windows blown out by the bombs. Many of the structures have collapsed into piles of rubble. Even though the residents were evacuated a year ago, ghostly echoes of them still linger here.

"This brings back some memories," Sebastian says quietly.

Ones I'd rather forget.

We approach the mansion at the end of Park Boulevard. Sebastian reassuringly takes my hand. The once-elegant white building is now broken, derelict, and covered in ash. Thorny vines twist around the house, slowly dragging the building back into the earth.

"It's like something from a dream," I say quietly. "I know it was my house, but I don't recognize it at all."

I make a quick mental note to pick up a souvenir for Polly if I get the chance. I never got around to it the night I met Ash under the bridge two weeks ago.

Gregory sits on the stone steps by the front door of the mansion, alone, wrapped in his brother's coat. A sign on the front door reads: DANGER! UNSTABLE STRUCTURE. KEEP OUT. A large bonfire has been lit on the lawn, and several groups of people huddle around it toasting mallow-puffs, including Ash, Beetle and Day. She's standing slightly apart from the others, clearly not wanting to be with them, but not wanting to be on her own, either.

Ash's black eyes flicker in the firelight. The smile slips from his lips when he sees Sebastian holding my arm.

"Don't you dare make a scene," I warn Sebastian, shrugging my arm free. "If you care about me at all, you'll just play nice. Okay?"

Sebastian looks at Ash, then back at me. A dark emotion flickers across his face. My breath catches in my throat. He suspects something.

"Whatever makes you happy," he says.

We go over to the gang, and I stand opposite Ash, close enough so he knows I'm with him, but not so close that Sebastian has any more reason to be suspicious.

Ash's face is hard like stone.

"Sorry," I mouth.

He turns his attention back to the bonfire. I want to go over to him and take his hand, but I can't. Not with everyone looking.

"So, Fisher," Sebastian says coolly, "are you excited about your first hunt as a Tracker later this week?"

Ash's fist clenches.

"Don't taunt him," I snap at Sebastian.

I can't believe we have to go on a hunt. With everything that's been going on, I'd forgotten all about it. How can I hunt Darklings now that I'm in a relationship with one of them? I can't image how Ash is feeling about it.

Ash stares at the fire, acting like I don't exist. His skin takes on a warm blush from the flames, making him appear almost human. Part of me wishes he were human; everything would be so much simpler. We could hold hands in public, we could kiss, we could be together—*really* together, like a regular couple. *But then he wouldn't be Ash.*

"When did you convert to the Purity?" Day asks Sebastian, warily eyeing his shaved head.

"A few days ago. I had a moment of enlightenment," he explains, turning his gaze toward Ash. "Purian Rose showed me the error of my ways. I've been far too lenient on the Darklings. If I don't clamp down on the nipper threat, then before you know it, they'll be roaming the streets, attacking people and fragging our women."

My heart beats rapidly. Ash's mouth twitches.

"Of course, *you'd* never do that, would you, Fisher? Fragg a human girl, I mean?" Sebastian says.

"Seb, that's enough!" I say.

He gives me a malicious smile. "Sorry, sweetheart."

"Don't call me that," I retort.

"Why not? You loved it when we were together," he says.

"Don't push it, Sebastian. Remember who you're talking to. I'm your *boss,* not your girlfriend," I say.

Sebastian's green eyes darken with anger. "Yes, ma'am. My apologies."

Ash digs his hands deep into his pockets and walks down the pathway leading around to the back of the mansion. Gregory watches him leave.

I need an excuse to follow Ash.

"I'm going to the restroom. Stay here," I tell Sebastian, getting a small pleasure out of ordering him around.

"You're not going into that house. The structure isn't stable," he says.

"Where else do you suggest I go? In the bushes?" I reply angrily.

He grabs my wrist.

"Lay one more finger on me and I'll have you fired," I say.

He lets me go, muttering curses under his breath.

I follow Ash, hoping none of the other kids will risk coming into the house after me. Chunks of plaster fall from the ceiling with my every footstep as I cautiously navigate the loose floor-boards. I find Ash in the kitchen, running a finger through the thick dust on the countertop.

"I told Sebastian not to come. He wouldn't listen."

"You told me he wasn't your boyfriend."

"He isn't! We broke up months ago." I bite my lip. "Are you mad at me?"

"No." He walks out of the kitchen and heads into the study across the hallway.

I chase after him. "You're acting like you're mad at me."

"I'm not."

"Then why wouldn't you look at me earlier?"

Ash slams a hand against the wall, making a painting clatter to the ground. I flinch.

He turns his glistening eyes on me. "He smells like you."

I gasp. "What?"

"Your scent is all over him."

"He was on my bed earlier."

I instantly regret saying that when Ash grimaces.

"He's just a friend. Actually, he's not even that. He works for me."

There are two overturned chairs on the floor, and Ash picks one up and sits down. The scene brings flashes of memories back, images I've spent all year trying to forget.

"It's not fair. He gets to be on your bed. He gets to be with you in public, and I have to act like we barely know each other. I hate the fact I can't even look at you, in case someone realizes how I feel about you," Ash says.

"Sebastian's getting suspicious," I say.

Ash runs a hand through his hair. "Are you sure?"

"He doesn't have any proof, even if he does suspect something. It's not illegal to talk to you, and that's all he's seen us doing," I say.

Ash nods, then smiles faintly at me. "Did you find out anything about the Golden Haze?"

"No. How about you?"

"Evangeline's given it to their alchemists." He rubs his neck. "Look, I'm sorry I left with her earlier, but you understood, right? She's the only twin-blood I've ever met; I just wanted to spend some time with her."

Jealousy rages inside me, but I force a smile. "It's fine. You must be curious about her. It's only natural."

He looks down at his feet, and I swear his cheeks flush for a second. No, I'm letting my imagination get away with me. Ash cares for me. I'm his Blood Mate, after all. He gets up and retrieves the fallen painting from the floor. His eyes widen. He twists the painting toward me, and my parents' faces smile back.

"I grew up here," I say. "I lived here until my father was killed, just before the air raids last year. We were evacuated to Centrum shortly after the raids started; this is the first time I've been back since his death."

Ash leans the painting against the wall and takes in our surroundings. The study is vast, with wooden floors and dark green walls, both covered in dust and ash. A broken grandfather clock is by the door. On the clock face are twelve birds, representing the hours of the day. Time in my house was measured in birdsong.

Ash's black hair stirs as he walks around the room. He looks at me, startled.

"It's everywhere." He swipes a hand across the wall, removing a layer of dust to reveal a dark splash of dried blood.

I look away.

"What happened?" he asks.

The events of that night rush back to me, and I shut my eyes.

I wake to the sound of a nightingale singing. Eleven o'clock. Father's angry, urgent voice rings up through the floorboards. Who's he talking to so late at night? I sneak into Polly's room and find she's already awake. We tiptoe downstairs. Mother's hovering by the study door, her hair loose around her shoulders, talking quickly to a man hidden in shadows. Something stirs by his feet, and the smell of rotting flesh stings my nose.

Mother catches sight of us, and fear flashes across her face.

"Go upstairs!" she exclaims.

"No. Bring them in here," a soft, effete voice orders.

"No, don't!" Father yells from the study. "Run, girls! RUN!"

Polly starts to run, but I stay rooted to the ground, terrified for myself, scared for my father. I need to make sure he's all right.

"Come on!" Polly urges.

An adrenaline spike forces me into action. I rush into the study, and Polly follows. What I see makes me gasp. Father's tied down to a chair, beaten and bloodied. He stares at me, wide eyed.

"Father, what's going on?" I say.

"Go! Go!" he yells.

A snarl draws my attention toward the man in the shadows. By his feet is a Wrath, its yellowed eyes boring into mine, its fangs dripping with venom. I scream and fall back into Polly's arms. The Wrath puts the Sight on me, intending to eat me. It hungrily sniffs me, checking my scent to see what sort of food I am. It cocks its head, then backs away, disinterested.

"I think, Jonathan, you're not being totally forthcoming with me. Perhaps you need a little more persuasion?" the man says. I instantly recognize his refined, light voice. Purian Rose.

He raises a white-gloved hand and gestures toward the guards standing in the corner of the room—I hadn't even noticed them. They spring on me and Polly and stand us beside Father.

Purian Rose's wolfish eyes glower at us from the dark. "So which girl should it be?" He looks at my mother. "Emissary, why don't you choose?"

I kick and struggle against my captor as Mother looks between me and Polly.

"Don't make me choose. Don't . . . I can't," she says.

"Choose, or they both die," Purian Rose orders.

"Polly! Take Polly!" Mother says hurriedly, rushing over to me and pulling me into her arms . . .

"They tortured Polly until my father confessed to collaborating with the Legion Liberation Front," I say numbly. "Then when Purian Rose got everything he came for, he set the Wrath on my father. We were lucky to escape."

"I'm so sorry," Ash says.

"Sigur Marwick had promised to protect my father when he turned sides, but he didn't. He abandoned him. He abandoned all of us when we needed him the most."

Ash frowns. "Yeah, that sounds like Sigur, all right. He let his own niece die."

"I don't know why Rose let the rest of us live. Mother won't talk about it, other than to say we should count our blessings.

She's never let me forget that it's my fault Polly got hurt. If I'd run like Father told me to do . . ."

Ash pulls me into his arms.

"I never understood why my mother chose me over Polly. My sister was her favorite. Now she pretends like she doesn't even exist," I whisper.

Tears begin to well up in my eyes. I push Ash away and run out of the room. He catches up with me inside my old bedroom, which has been vandalized, the walls covered in graffiti and the furniture overturned and charred. My bed is still in one piece, although it looks like it's seen some action over the past year.

I lie down on top of the dirty bedcovers and don't protest when Ash joins me. It's reckless letting him hold me like this when there are people outside, but I'm gambling on the hope they won't come into the house. We lie like two spoons nestled against each other.

"I can't bear this world. It's so full of anger and hate. There's death everywhere you look." I turn to face Ash. "I want to stop feeling like this. Make me forget, Ash, please. Just for a short while, I want to live in a world where we're not meant to be enemies."

He looks at me, uncertain.

"Please, Ash . . ."

He kisses me hard, trying to force out the pain we're both feeling. His heart beats in unison with mine, and I'm flooded with his hurt, love, desire. He's all through me. Ash's hands run down my body, skimming over my breasts, stomach, sliding under the waistband of my jeans. I sigh and tug at his top, my fingers slipping under the cotton cloth and caressing his stomach. He tentatively presses his lips against my pulse and runs the tip of his tongue along my neck. I twist my fingers through his hair, and he groans, his senses exploding at my touch.

"Maybe . . . you . . . should . . . stop," he says between rapid breaths. "I'm . . . losing . . . it . . ."

I carry on massaging his hair, knowing what it's doing to him, knowing how sensitive his hair is to stimulation and loving the fact I can have this effect on someone as beautiful as him.

He trembles. "Natalie . . . stop . . ."

"No."

"*Stop* . . ."

I don't.

Ash plunges his fangs into my throat.

I scream, but the sound soon evaporates as the venom seeps into my blood, hot and tingly, making my skin numb where his fangs pierced my skin. The room starts to shimmer, and I blink once, twice, trying to focus, but there are so many colors, bright, beautiful rainbow colors swirling through the air. I swipe a hand through the rainbows and giggle when the colors burst and turn into butterflies! They dance and flutter around my hand. They're so pretty, I almost cry.

Bliss spills over me. I've never felt so happy. My hands grip Ash's hair, pull at his clothes, desperate to touch any part of his skin. I *need* to touch him—I crave him more than water, more than air.

Why was I so afraid to be bitten? It's not so bad. It's not like, when Father got attacked, his blood went *whooooosh* all over the floor—

A picture of his dead body bursts into my mind. It's as if he's here in the room with me, and it's happening all over again. Bliss turns to terror. My neck hurts. *Ow . . . ow . . .*

"OW! Get off me!" I say.

Ash leaps back, his cheeks flushed. His breathing is ragged, his whole body shaking. I manage to sit up, although my movements are sluggish, my body disconnected. I'm light-headed and dizzy, and desire still rages through me, but I use every last ounce of strength to push it aside. They're not real emotions. They're fake ones brought on by the Haze.

"You . . . drugged . . . me," I manage to say.

Ash puts his head in his hands.

"I'm so sorry," he mumbles through his fingers. "I warned you I was losing control, but you carried on. I thought you wanted this."

"I wanted you to kiss me, I wanted us to take things a step further, and I admit I got carried away, but I didn't want *that*. You know how my father died—you must know how much being bitten scares me," I say.

"I scare you?" he asks quietly.

I don't answer. We're only sitting a few feet apart, but I feel so distant from him. For the first time since we met, it's really sinking in what it means to be dating a twin-blood Darkling.

The bedroom door bangs open, and Gregory barges into the room, his lank hair plastered down the side of his gaunt face, his hazel eyes wild and crazed. He looks completely mad. He takes one look at Ash, and the blood dripping down my neck, and lunges for Ash.

"You rotten half-breed!" he yells.

Ash darts out of the way with lightning speed.

"You've got it wrong!" I say.

Ash shakes his head at me, fear in his eyes. I realize my mistake—what we've just been doing is infinitely worse than a Darkling taking a bite out of me. I grip Gregory's arm as he makes another attempt to punch Ash.

"He was giving me some Haze!" I say.

Gregory freezes and looks at me with utter contempt. Footsteps run up the stairs, no doubt drawn by our shouting.

"You're disgusting," Gregory sneers at me. "Letting a half-breed feed on you. I should tell your mother—"

"It's none of your business," I say.

"How can you let him do that? What are you? A race traitor?"

"Like Chris, you mean?" I zing back.

Gregory's eyes burn with fury, and he lashes out, hitting me across the face and knocking me to the floor. A loud growl fills the room. Ash bares his fangs at Gregory. There's nothing human about him now. He looks like a wild animal, full of anger and power.

Gregory edges back, his leg hitting the side of the bed.

"I'm okay," I say. *Don't do anything, Ash, please . . .*

Beetle and Day run into the bedroom, followed by Sebastian.

"Just you try it, mongrel. There's a bunch of witnesses. You won't get away with hurting me," Gregory says to Ash.

"What did Ash do to you?" Day says, spotting the blood oozing down my neck.

Ash takes another step toward Gregory, his fangs still bared.

"Ash, let it go. I'm fine," I plead.

"Arrest him!" Gregory orders Sebastian.

"Seb, if you arrest Ash, I'll get in trouble too," I say. "You owe me."

A meaningful look passes between us. He knows I'm refer-ring to his dark secret, the one I've been keeping for him all these months.

"I think you need to leave," Sebastian eventually says to Gregory. "And if one word about this gets back to the Emis-sary, I'll kick you out of the Trackers."

Gregory leaves the room, slamming the door behind him.

Ash reaches out for me. "Are you all right?"

I flinch, still angry at him for drugging me, even though I know I was partly to blame for giving him mixed signals.

Sebastian jabs a finger at Ash's chest. "If you *ever* touch her again, it'll be the last thing you do, nipper."

He takes my hand and hauls me out of the room.

Sebastian doesn't say a word to me until we're back in my bedroom.

He sits on the edge of my bed. "So you're into drugs now?"

"No."

"Then what were you doing with that half-breed?"

I flush at the memory of what we were doing on the bed be-fore he bit me. Sebastian puts two and two together.

"He's a twin-blood!"

"You're one to talk! You cheated on me with a Darkling," I snap back.

Sebastian painfully grabs my arms. "I only screwed her be-cause you weren't giving it up! If you'd slept with me, I wouldn't have needed to find it elsewhere."

"You're hurting me," I say.

Sebastian immediately releases me, running a hand over his shaved head.

"How can you choose him over me? I love you," Sebastian says.

"You don't love me. You never have—you just want to own me," I reply.

Anger flashes in his green eyes. "I'll have him arrested."

"If you arrest him, they'll execute me. Is that what you want?"

"No," he says quietly.

"Get out of my room," I say.

"Don't think I'm going to forget about this," he says before leaving.

I sit down on the bed, my whole body shaking. The phone on my nightstand rings. It's Day.

"I know we're not friends anymore, but I wanted to check to see if you were okay," she says.

I should be mad at her, but right now I need a friend. I start crying, tired and emotional after all the drama.

"Nat, don't cry. He's such a jerk, I can't believe he bit you—"

"I'm not crying about Ash," I say through my tears. "And he didn't attack me. We were kissing, and we got carried away." I figure there's no reason to lie about this; she already knows we're an item.

"Oh, I thought . . . Never mind," she says.

"What did you think? That Ash and I had split up?"

"Yes," she admits.

"So let me guess: you thought we could be friends again now that Ash was out of the picture. Was that it?" I snap, angry at her, angry at Sebastian, just angry at everyone.

"No, I thought you'd be upset and might need someone to

talk to who'd understand. I split up with the boy I loved, so I knew how heartbroken you'd be," she replies.

"Oh . . . ," I say.

"I'm trying to say I'm sorry, Natalie. I want us to be friends again."

I sigh. I do miss having a friend. "If we're going to be friends, you have to be nicer to Ash. He's got a kind heart, you know that deep down. He brings your family food, *and* he's been helping Beetle."

"He's still a dealer."

"He has no choice, Day. He needs the money."

There's a long pause on the other end of the line.

"Deal," she finally says.

We chat for a short while, the conversation light and easy. It's like we never fought. I hang up the phone, feeling a little better.

I lie back and lightly touch the two puncture wounds on my neck. I care so much for Ash, but today he scared me. If it weren't for our Blood Mate connection, would we even be together? For the first time since we first kissed, I don't know how to answer that question.

25
ASH

I RUMMAGE AROUND my pocket for my door keys. My hands are shaking from adrenaline, I'm still so wound up from everything that happened tonight. The keys slip out of my fingers and fall into a nearby bush.

"Fragg!" I yell, slamming my fist against the door.

Shame weighs on my shoulders as I think about Natalie and how she recoiled from me when I tried to touch her.

I scare her.

She's my Blood Mate, and I scare her! Why did I bite her? Of course she didn't want me to do that, what freak would? *She was after something else.* I could kick myself; I'm such a fragging idiot.

I find my keys and quietly enter the church, sneaking past Dad, who is asleep in the kitchen, keeping guard over the crypt. I head to my room in the bell tower. It's hexagonal in shape, with a tarnished brass bell hanging in the center of the room and tall glassless arches where windows should be. Most of the arches have been boarded up, but two have been left open. During the day I pin black plastic sheets over them to protect myself from the worst of the sunlight or bad weather, but at night I take them down to get a better view of the city. I don't have many possessions, just a few books and some sketches on the walls. Most of the drawings are of Black City, but there are a few of Natalie up there now too.

I stop dead. Studying one of the drawings is Evangeline, dressed in a blue robe that complements her inky-black hair. She traces her finger down the picture of Natalie.

"What are you doing here?" I ask.

She tears her eyes away from the picture. "I brought you something."

We sit down on my creaky bed. A waft of Calder lilies fills my nostrils as Evangeline pulls her hair to one side, smiling shyly up at me. Yearning unfurls in my stomach. I bet Evangeline wouldn't be scared if I bit her. In fact, I know she'd enjoy it; all Darklings do. I angrily shake the thought out of my head. I shouldn't be having these thoughts. Besides, if I did bite Evangeline, I could contract the Wrath. Sometimes I forget she's infected; she looks so healthy.

Evangeline hands me an ornamental wooden box.

"I found this in Annora's room. I thought you might like it," she says.

I open the box and slowly sift through the contents, studying each item carefully. I choke back the emotion as I realize what this box contains: all my mom's most treasured possessions.

There are three faded photos: one of me as a cub, one of my extended family, another of Mom and Dad on their wedding day. There are other mementos, like an old Legion Liberation Front pamphlet with Sigur's photo on it; a gold amulet shaped like a quarter-circle, with strange script written around the rim; and a lock of white hair tied with ribbon.

252

Evangeline lightly touches my leg as I look through Mom's belongings. It feels so natural, I don't think to move her hand.

The last things in the box are eight envelopes bound together with string. They're all addressed to me. I eagerly open them. In each envelope is a handmade birthday card, one for every year we were apart.

"She never forgot you, Ash," Evangeline says.

A solitary tear snakes down my face. I look away, embarrassed.

"It's okay," she whispers, wiping the tear from my cheek.

Her hand lingers on my face, and my skin tingles where she's touching me. Moonlight streams through the open window, making her pale skin look dewy and iridescent. My pulse races.

"Annora told me so many stories about you," Evangeline says. "I have to admit, I was a little jealous of you."

"Me? Why?" I ask.

"You have people who love you. Your mother, your father," she says. "I lost my parents during the war. I miss them so much. It gets—"

"Lonely," I fill in for her.

She nods, lacing her fingers through mine. "But I'm not lonely anymore, now that you're in my life."

Life would be so much simpler if Evangeline were my girlfriend. *But she's not, Natalie is.* I let go of her hand. Evangeline looks away, hurt.

"Can I see Annora?" she asks.

I nod.

We sneak down to the crypt, careful not to wake Dad. Mom is huddled in the corner of the room, shaking with pain. Her breath rattles, like there's fluid in her lungs. She's entered the final stages of the disease. Grief eats at me. I always dreamed that if she ever came back, this empty space she left inside me would disappear, but it's just gotten bigger.

Evangeline covers her mouth with her hand, stifling a sob.

I hang back, careful not to get too close, and study Mom, trying to find traces of the woman I remember from my childhood. I see glimpses: her reading to me when I was a cub; the fire in her eyes as she spoke about the Darkling civil rights movement; her and Dad dancing to a song on their anniversary, her cheek resting on his arm, her long dark hair in waves down her back.

Her hair is now lank ribbons falling out in clumps; her eyes are yellowed; her flesh, rotting. She's not my mother—she's a monster. I wish she hadn't come back. I don't want to remember her this way.

She lets out a moan and shudders as a wave of pain washes over her, then another, then another.

"Mom," I say, my voice choked.

I have to do something, but what can I do? There's no medicine to help her, no cure.

Evangeline rushes over to her, unafraid.

"Evangeline, no!" I say.

"I'm already infected, Ash," she reminds me.

Evangeline tenderly strokes Mom's limp hair, making soothing noises. I'm so grateful she's here and able to comfort my mom when I can't.

"Thank you," I say to Evangeline.

I kneel down beside them, keeping out of Mom's biting reach.

Another wave of pain grips Mom, and she wails. Evangeline holds her.

"Annora used to sing to the Wraths when she was nursing them in the ward," she says to me. "It distracts them. Sing to her, Ash."

My mind's blank. I can't think of any songs. Then one tune comes to mind, a lullaby Mom used to sing to me when I was little. The words to the song slowly come back to me, and I sing it softly to her.

"Hush, hush, don't you cry. Listen to my lullaby. Sleep, sleep, dream of me. I am always watching over thee. Love, love, I love you true. I will always be there for you."

Mom sighs, and the shuddering stops. It seems to have helped a little. She attempts a smile, but can't quite manage it.

"Ash . . . ," Mom whispers.

She stretches out a clawed hand toward me.

I hesitate.

She's your mom.

I cautiously reach out my own hand, and our fingers meet. I smile, but it's bittersweet, because we both know this might be the last time we touch.

26

ASH

USUALLY I'M NOT KEEN to get to school, but I'm desperate to see Natalie. I pick up Beetle on the way and hurry toward the town square, not taking my usual detour down City End to visit the Boundary Wall.

"How did it go with Mr. Tubs yesterday?" Beetle asks.

We didn't get a chance to talk about it last night, since Sebastian turned up with Natalie. I tell him what happened, about how Natalie and Evangeline are going to run some tests on the Golden Haze, feeling a bit useless that there's nothing more I can do to help.

"I hope they work it out soon, before they try to pin the deaths on any more Darklings," Beetle says, reminding me of my arrest last week.

"I'm sure Natalie will work it out," I say.

"Have you heard from her?" Beetle asks as we enter the town square.

"No."

"Well, maybe she went straight to bed after leaving the Park last night," Beetle says.

"Maybe," I say.

Nearly a thousand protesters have congregated in the plaza outside the school, holding placards high in the air, some supporting Rose's Law, others urging the Sentry government to free the Darklings. Beetle's aunt chants slogans into a megaphone, riling up the crowd, her long dreadlocks swaying with every word.

"Don't these people ever go home?" I snarl as we push our way through.

"At least they care," Beetle says defensively. "They're trying to get the Boundary Wall down, which is more than I can say for you."

I turn on him. "You know what? Go to hell. What exactly have *you* done to bring the wall down? All Humans for Unity does is paint placards and spout useless chants. I'm sure the Sentry government's quaking in their boots."

"We do more than that," he says.

"Oh, yeah? Like what?"

"You'll see. I have to go. Have fun at school." He goes over to his aunt.

What did he mean, *you'll see*?

I wait for Natalie on the school steps, passing the TV reporter Juno Jones and her camera crew along the way. Day waits by the entrance too, holding a pile of books. She opens her mouth to say something, then shuts it again.

"If you have something to say to me, just say it," I snap.

"I'm sorry," she blurts out.

"What?" Of all the things she could've said, I wasn't expecting that.

"I was wrong to accuse you of getting Beetle hooked on Haze."

"Yeah, you were," I say.

"I'm trying to apologize, you jerk."

I manage a faint smile. "Some apology."

Day smiles back. "Sorry. I mean it. Friends?"

I hesitate, then nod. It's what Natalie would want. "Friends."

We wait for Natalie in silence, things still awkward between us despite our truce. A minute later, the sound of horses' hooves echoes throughout the town square, and a familiar black carriage draws up outside the school. Sebastian emerges and offers his hand to Natalie, who refuses it. She steps out of the carriage, sweeping her beautiful blond curls away from her face, briefly revealing the two puncture marks on her neck. Guilt twists inside me. I can't judge from her expression if she's still mad at me or not.

A fight suddenly breaks out near the Boundary Wall, and Sebastian leaves to deal with it while Natalie walks up the school steps toward us. Juno Jones blocks the path and thrusts a microphone in Natalie's face.

"Ms. Buchanan! Can we have a second of your time? How are the students coping after the death of Chris Thompson?"

"We're coping as well as can be expected," Natalie says irritably.

"Why was your mother at his funeral yesterday? Did you know Chris well?"

Natalie shakes her head, trying to edge around Juno.

"Chris was the sixth teenager to die from Golden Haze, and a dozen more are now in critical condition in the hospital. Why do you think more people your age are turning to drugs?"

Natalie freezes. "More people are sick?"

"Yes, and those are the only ones we know about—"

BOOM!

A loud blast echoes around the town square. The shock waves knock me to my knees, and I cover my head as shards of glass rain down on us from the school's shattered windows. My ears ring like there are church bells chiming inside them. I move my head, and my ears pop; sounds assault my senses: panicked screams, fractured glass, heavy stones falling.

Part of the Boundary Wall has been destroyed, revealing the Legion ghetto on the other side. A thousand pale, famished Darklings stare back at us. Everything becomes deathly still, like the world is holding its breath. The Darklings don't move at first, perhaps from shock or fear of reprisal.

Then the scent of human blood hits them.

The Darklings howl.

They rush toward the hole in the wall, lured by freedom and smell of hot blood.

"Ash . . ." Natalie's voice is just a whisper, but it's like a siren's call spurring my body into action.

I rush down the steps and scoop her up in my arms.

"Are you hurt?" I ask.

"No. Where's Day?" she says.

"I'm here!" Day hurries toward us. Her usually immaculate black hair is matted with dust and blood, and her thin face is scratched, but otherwise she's okay.

"I need to find Beetle," I say to them. "Go inside."

Natalie shakes her head. "I have to make sure Sebastian's all right."

All three of us push our way through the crowd, heading toward the Boundary Wall where I last saw Beetle and Sebastian.

Pandemonium has broken out.

People push past us as they frantically try to get away from the Darklings pouring through the gap in the wall. Everywhere

I look, people are screaming as they're grabbed by the Dark-lings and fed upon. Terrified Sentry guards draw their swords and start slashing wildly, striking Darklings and people alike. Blood is everywhere, intoxicating, delicious. Hunger roars in me. I want to join the other Darklings. I want to *feed*.

"Ash, he's here!" Natalie yanks my arm, bringing me out of my bloodlust.

Beetle is lying unconscious on the ground, surrounded by dust and debris. His face is partially burned, and shrapnel sticks out of a gory wound on his stomach. He must've been close to the explosion to get shrapnel in him. *He probably planted the bomb.*

"He's not breathing!" Day says hysterically.

Natalie administers CPR, but it doesn't work; Beetle just continues to get paler. He needs oxygen and fast.

Day sobs uncontrollably. "Don't leave me, Matthias, please. I love you, please . . ."

"Ash, your blood!" Natalie says.

"What . . . ?" It suddenly dawns on me what she means. The *Trypanosoma vampirum* in my blood might resuscitate him—it feeds oxygen to my organs, after all. It might work for him too?

I sink my fangs into my wrist, tearing into the flesh until the blood pours freely from my veins. Natalie lifts up Beetle's shirt to reveal the open wound on his stomach.

"What are you doing?" Day gasps.

"Saving Beetle's life," I reply.

I hold my wrist over the wound on Beetle's stomach and allow my blood to seep into his body, aiming for the celiac ar-tery. I just pray this works. We wait with bated breath. After what seems like an eternity but can't be more than thirty sec-onds, color starts to return to Beetle's face. *It's working!* I keep my blood flowing through him, even when I start feeling weak and know I should stop.

All around us, people are still screaming and frantically pushing each other out of the way as another stampede of Darklings floods through the wall. If we don't get Beetle off the ground soon, we're at risk of getting trampled.

Beetle lets out a weak groan, his eyes flickering.

"He's alive!" Day says.

"Natalie, thank heavens, there you are!" Sebastian runs over to us.

He quickly takes in the scene.

"Seb, take Beetle into the school. He needs medical attention," Natalie says as she bandages my bleeding wrist. "I'll be right behind you."

"I'm not leaving you here," he says.

"We don't have time to argue! Beetle's hurt," she replies. "Please? He's my friend."

Sebastian relents and hoists Beetle into his arms, carrying him toward the school, Day following. They're soon lost in the sea of fleeing people. Natalie helps me to my feet, slinging my arm around her neck for support. I'm still feeling weak.

A Darkling lunges for a woman in front of us, and she shrieks as the creature sinks its fangs into her neck. The people around her panic and run back in our direction, toward the wall. We're immediately caught in a surge of bodies.

"Ash!" Natalie screams as we're separated.

The wave of bodies pushes her through the gap in the wall. Clawed, bony Darkling hands grab at her flesh and drag her deeper into the Legion territory.

"Natalie!" I force my way to the wall in pursuit of her.

She's surrounded by Darklings, their exposed skin crackling

and hissing in the sunlight, but they don't seem to care. They edge closer, their fangs dripping with venom.

"Get away from her!" I yell.

They turn to look at me for a brief moment, then glance away, disinterested. I'm part Darkling, after all, not food.

"Natalie, don't move," I say quietly.

The Darkling closest to her sticks out his snakelike tongue, tasting the air. He tilts his head to one side, and the other Darklings do the same. They don't move, just stand there watching her.

I sense someone looking at me and tear my eyes away from the Darklings. Evangeline stands twenty feet away, shadowed by derelict buildings. Her inky-black hair whips around her face in the wind. She steps into the hazy sunlight and lowers the hood of her blue robe, baring her fangs at Natalie.

"Leave her alone," I say to Evangeline.

She lets out a low, malicious laugh. "I don't think so, Ash. You may have forgiven this human for what her mother and the rest of the Sentry government did to us, but I haven't."

"Ash," Natalie whispers.

How can I protect Natalie? *Use the Sight!* I stop and fix my eyes on Natalie, focusing my mind on one thought:

Mine.

My vision turns deep red as the Sight takes effect, and the air around me fills with a potent pheromone that warns the other Darklings to leave my prey alone. It seems to work, as the Darklings slink back into their shacks, but Evangeline stays where she is.

Evangeline laughs. "Are you really trying to use the Sight on me again?"

What does she mean *again*?

Then it hits me.

"You were the Darkling at the museum," I say.

Evangeline looks spitefully at Natalie. "Did you like the little gifts I left for you?"

"What gifts?" Natalie says.

"That cat and bodyguard of yours," Evangeline replies.

"You killed Malcolm and Truffles? Why? What did I ever do to you?" Natalie says.

"You stole my heart!" Evangeline yells.

The world becomes still.

Natalie has Evangeline's heart?

"How is it even possible?" I say to Evangeline.

"A Tracker found my family during the war and killed them right in front of me," Evangeline says, slowly walking toward us. "He took me back to the laboratory in Sentry headquarters, where they stripped me naked, shaved my head and threw me into a cell like a dog. They experimented on me. They did *terrible* things, Ash."

"You're the child in my dreams," Natalie exclaims.

I can picture the scene. Evangeline as a young girl, terrified, alone, strapped to a gurney as she's experimented on by some sick, sadistic doctor.

"Then one day the Emissary came into the laboratory, wailing, sobbing, saying her younger daughter was dying. Natalie needed a heart transplant, but the rebels had taken over the hospital," Evangeline continues. "So they had to make do with what they had in the laboratory. They had *me*. As a twin-blood, my heart's compatible with a human's, and it's not like I needed it, right? A twin-blood doesn't need a heart to survive."

"It can't be true," I say quietly. "Natalie?"

"I didn't know the heart was hers. You have to believe me,

Ash," she says. She turns to Evangeline. "Is that why you killed Truffles and Malcolm? In revenge for my mother taking your heart?"

Evangeline nods. "I wanted you to experience the same fear I felt when they tore my heart out. I was conscious when they did it, you know?"

Natalie gasps. "No. I'm so sorry."

"Sorry?" Evangeline curls her lip. "You're *sorry*?"

"Yes. I never meant to hurt you," Natalie says meekly.

"Really?" Evangeline turns back to me, pain in her eyes. "Then imagine how I felt when we met at Mr. Tubs's shop and you told me Natalie, *the girl with my stolen heart,* was your Blood Mate."

A terrible thought sinks into my head.

Natalie's distraught expression reflects my own.

I look back at Evangeline.

"Natalie's not my Blood Mate," I say.

Evangeline shakes her head. "No. *I* am."

27

ASH

I SINK TO MY KNEES, unable to take this in. The damp earth soaks through my trousers, but I don't care.

Natalie's not my Blood Mate?

"I was waiting for the right time to tell you," Evangeline says. "I wasn't even sure if you'd believe me. I know you think you have feelings for her, but they're not real. You only feel connected to her because she has my heart."

"That's not true," Natalie says, walking over to me.

I look up at her.

"Please, tell her that's not true," Natalie repeats. "Ash?"

I don't say anything.

Part of me wonders if Evangeline is right. Do I only care for Natalie because she has a stolen heart? I look at Evangeline, and desire burns deep in my stomach. She's my real Blood Mate. All these years I've been alone, lost, thinking I was the only twin-blood in the city, and the whole time, she was there waiting for me. Is that why I was drawn to the Boundary Wall? Could I sense her on the other side?

Natalie's lip quivers. "Ash? Do you feel anything real for me at all?"

"I don't know," I admit.

She sucks in a pained breath.

Before I can stop her, Natalie climbs through the hole in the wall and sprints away. My heart cramps. What have I done? Evangeline grabs my arm as I attempt to run after her.

"Let her go," Evangeline says.

"Get off me," I say.

I chase after Natalie, and Evangeline follows. The city is still in an uproar, with people running through the streets, trying to escape the Darklings that are roaming free. I can't see Natalie anywhere. Fragg!

The roads are crawling with Sentry guards and tanks. There's a scatter of gunfire from one of the tanks, and a Darkling collapses to the ground, dead. We dart down an alley and climb onto the nearest roof to get away from the danger, using the rooftops to navigate the city. I head toward the Sentry HQ, the only place I can think of to find Natalie.

"Ash, where are you going?" Evangeline says.

"Where do you think?" I reply as we reach Bleak Street, just outside the Sentry headquarters.

We climb down the building and enter the alleyway beside the Sentry HQ. Evangeline takes my hand, stopping me. We're standing beside an overflowing yellow garbage bin.

"She's not worth it. You said so yourself, you don't even know if you have feelings for her—"

"Then why does my fragging heart feel like it's been ripped out of my chest?" I say.

She lets go of my hand, shaking her head.

"This is where Sigur found me, you know?" Evangeline says,

pointing toward the garbage bin. "After they tore out my heart, they threw me out here with the rest of the trash."

I shut my eyes. It's too horrific to imagine.

"I don't know what to do," I whisper. "I love Natalie, but she's not my Blood Mate. I'm so fragging confused."

Soft lips suddenly press against mine. Evangeline's lips. They feel . . . incredible. Her kiss is firmer, more intense, more desperate than Natalie's kisses. I pull away.

"What are you doing?" I ask, opening my eyes.

"Showing you what you're missing," she says, and kisses me again, deeper this time.

Desire rages through me, and I don't try and fight it. I pull Evangeline toward me and kiss her back, hard, searching for answers, needing to know if there's something genuine between us. If I'm going to throw away everything I have with Natalie, I need to be certain I'm making the right decision. Evangeline's lips part, and her tongue flicks across mine. It's intense, amazing—every part of my body is buzzing. Even so, only one name rings in my mind: Natalie.

I vaguely register a door behind us opening. There's a gasp. I break the kiss and turn to see Natalie in the alleyway, her eyes brimming with tears.

"Ten minutes! I wasn't even gone for ten minutes, and you've already replaced me with her," she says. "I can't believe I was coming to find you, so I could fight for you, for us, when it's clear you don't care about me at all."

"It didn't mean anything—I'm just confused right now," I say.

"Ash, don't say our kiss meant nothing," Evangeline says.

"Well, let me make this a lot less confusing for the both of you. I never, ever want to see you again!" Natalie says.

She slams the door in my face.

Evangeline walks up behind me. "She had to know. She was never meant to be with you."

She tries to take my hand, but I move it away.

"Leave me alone," I say.

"Ash . . ."

"You knew she was watching, didn't you?" I ask.

Evangeline's silence is answer enough.

"Just go!" I snap.

"No," she says.

I stomp away, but she chases after me. I can't believe how badly I've screwed everything up! I pinch the bridge of my nose, trying to push away the pain, but the pain isn't in my head. It's coiled like a snake inside my chest, and I can't stand it. I feel like I'm dying. There's only one place I can think to find any peace.

Half an hour later, I'm striding down Chantilly Lane on a mission, Evangeline still following me. We used the rooftops to cross the city, keeping out of sight of the Trackers. People below us are fighting, yelling, getting drunk. After the bomb earlier today, everyone's scared, excited, angry. Inside every house, families gather with their children, watching the news, trying to work out what's going on, while video footage of the event is being broadcast on all the giant digital monitors around the city. A news ticker continually streams updates at the bottom of the screen: *26 dead after city bombing . . . Government calls for people to vote for Rose's Law and crush the Darkling threat . . . Three Humans for Unity members arrested in connection with bombing . . . Emissary urges citizens to stay indoors until Darklings have been rounded up . . .*

I quickly phoned Beetle before coming to Chantilly Lane to make sure he was okay. His aunt Roach answered, giving me an update. The burns on his face will probably scar, and his stomach is being held together with a dozen stitches, but he's alive, thanks to my blood. It'll be out of his system in a few days, but it did its job: it kick-started his heart. I was relieved to hear that Day's parents had agreed to let her stay with Beetle overnight so she could take care of him.

Evangeline and I leap off the roof next to Mr. Tubs's shop and go inside. The best way to find peace is from a hit of Haze, and I need to feed on a human to get it.

The den is as smelly and claustrophobic as I remember. All I can see in the dim red light are shadows writhing around on the floor, lost in ecstasy. A voluptuous human woman makes kissing sounds at me and exposes her breasts.

"Only ten coins, and I can be yours," she says.

"No, thanks," I say.

We carefully climb over the bodies and find Mr. Tubs in his office. He gives me a yellow-toothed smile.

"You bring me another client?" he asks.

"I'm here for me. I want to feed," I say.

He flicks his hand, and someone stirs in the corner of the room. A spaced-out girl walks over to me, her deep blue eyes glazed over, her blond hair loose around her face. Her coloring reminds me a little of Natalie.

"She'll do," I say.

"How you pay? I still waiting for money for that watch," he says, referring to Natalie's wristwatch.

"Put it on Sigur's tab," Evangeline replies.

The Hazer girl takes my hand, and we find somewhere to sit on the sticky, slithering floor. Evangeline joins us. The girl tilts her head to one side, not even looking at me. Her neck is riddled with bite marks, her veins black where the blood's been drained from them. She doesn't look that appetizing, but right now I couldn't care less.

"Ladies first," I say to Evangeline.

She sinks her fangs into the girl's neck and begins to feed. I patiently wait for her to finish, itching to get a hit of the Haze now coursing through the girl's veins, so I can feel nothing except bliss, because right now I feel like I'm being ripped apart. How could I hurt Natalie like that?

The basement door opens, casting a shard of yellow light into the room, and several pairs of feet march down the stairs. Sebastian enters the den with a group of his Tracker friends, including Claw Neck and Gregory. They sit down on one of the sofas, and Mr. Tubs brings them a bottle of Shine without waiting to be asked.

I slink back into the shadows so they can't see me, grateful that the room is so dark.

Claw Neck is carrying a thin black case, and he heads straight for Mr. Tubs's office. He returns thirty seconds later and sits next to Gregory.

Sebastian pours everyone a shot of Shine.

"Shouldn't we be outside killing the nippers?" Gregory asks in his whiny voice.

"You'll get your chance tomorrow when we go on the hunt," Sebastian replies. "Aaron, Blake and Derek's squads are helping the Sentry guards. Everything's under control for now. We'll round up any stray Darks tomorrow."

"Just relax, boy. Have a drink," Claw Neck says to Gregory.

"Is this where the Trackers normally come to drink?" Gregory asks, looking a little anxious.

Claw Neck smacks Gregory's back jovially. "Of course! Mr. Tubs gives us free Shine, and in return, we don't tell anyone about his less legitimate business endeavors."

"He gives us information too," Sebastian adds. "Like where to find Darkling nests around the city. We've got a few good tips for tomorrow's hunt."

"Won't we be conspicuous, all in one big group?" Gregory asks.

Claw Neck chuckles. "We'll be splitting up. You'll be going with Aaron's troop to the Rise. Blake will take his cadets to the Chimney, and the rest will be coming with me and Sebastian on a hunt around the Hub."

"Does that nipper Ash Fisher have to come with us?" Gregory says.

"He might prove useful," Sebastian says. "Besides, I'm going to enjoy watching him squirm when I make him arrest his first Dark."

My fangs throb at the mention of my name. I'm not going on their stupid hunt; I don't care what they do to me. I don't care about anything anymore.

The woman who exposed herself to me earlier sidles over to them, and Sebastian pulls her onto his lap. She giggles and smears his cheek with slippery red kisses, running her hands over his shaved head. The rose tattoo on his face is still raw and sore looking.

"What was up with Natalie back at HQ? Why was she crying?" Gregory asks Sebastian.

"Who knows? Girl problems, probably," Sebastian says in a bored voice, idly playing with the hair of the woman sitting on his lap. "Maybe I'll go home and *console* her."

I don't like the way he emphasizes the word *console*.

"You two used to date, didn't you?" Gregory asks.

Sebastian nods. "For a while, but she got boring." He turns to the whore sitting on his lap. "You won't bore me, will you?"

She runs a provocative finger over his bottom lip, and he bites it really hard, drawing blood. The woman lets out a scream as he throws her to the floor, laughing as he lifts up her dress. The woman scratches his face and manages to scrabble away, warm blood on her hand.

"Natalie's pretty, though," Gregory continues as if nothing happened. "If you like that sort of thing."

Sebastian dabs at his scratched cheek with a handkerchief. "I suppose. Not as pretty as her sister, Polly, used to be. Now, *she* was something. Still, maybe I'll ask Natalie out again. She'll look good on my arm when I'm promoted."

"You're getting a promotion?" Gregory asks.

"Of course he is," Claw Neck chimes in.

"Purian Rose has entrusted me with an important mission," Sebastian boasts. "It's only a matter of time before I'm rewarded."

"What mission is that?" Gregory asks.

Sebastian and Claw Neck chuckle.

"When you've killed your first Dark and proved you're one of us, then *maybe* I'll tell you," Sebastian says. "Now, drink up, gentlemen."

They knock back their drinks and, after a few minutes, head upstairs. I let out a relieved sigh that they didn't see me. I wonder what Sebastian's "important mission" is. Whatever it is, it can't be good if Purian Rose is behind it.

Evangeline finishes drinking from the Hazer girl and passes her to me. The girl flops in my arms, barely breathing, her blond hair spilling over my fingers. White pearls of foam bubble out the corner of her mouth, reminding me of the Hazer girl from the night I first met Natalie.

"I'm going," I say to Evangeline.

She grabs my arm. "Don't you dare go back to her. You belong to me!"

"I don't belong to anyone. This was a mistake."

"If you leave now, that's it between us. I'll never be with you," Evangeline threatens.

I hesitate for a second, panicked at the idea of what I'm giving up. Evangeline's my true Blood Mate, the girl I was supposed to be with. Not just that, she's a twin-blood, the only one I know. If I leave now, I risk losing her forever and being on my own again. Except, it dawns on me, I wouldn't be alone, not really. I'd have Natalie. I never once felt alone when I was with her. I don't know if Natalie will ever forgive me, but I'm willing to risk losing it all to find out.

Without another word, I go upstairs into the pawnshop. I'm about to leave when I spot Natalie's watch in the glass counter by the till. I check no one is looking, then smash the glass, grab the watch and run out before anyone catches me.

The journey to Natalie's house doesn't take long, as I take my detour over the rooftops. I jump down onto her balcony and knock on the window, wait for a minute, then knock again, louder this time in case she didn't hear me. The curtain twitches, and Natalie's blue eyes peer at me through the tiny slit between the drapes.

"Natalie—"

She closes the curtains, shutting me out.

"Please let me explain," I say through the glass. "I'm sorry."

I wait on her balcony, praying she'll let me in, but after an hour, I know she's not going to come to the window. I place her watch on the balustrade, hoping she'll find it. It's not much of a peace offering, but I need her to know how sorry I am. How can I get a message to her? One name immediately springs to mind. As soon as I get home, I grab the phone and dial Beetle's number.

Day answers his phone, as I hoped she would.

"Do you know what time it is, Ash?" she says groggily.

"Yeah, yeah, sorry. How's Beetle?"

"He's alive. Did you need something?"

"Yeah. I need to ask you a favor."

I just hope this is going to work.

28
NATALIE

I HEAR ASH LEAVE, but I don't chase after him. I won't.

My pillow is wet with tears, but the pain won't wash away, no matter how much I cry. The image of Ash and Evangeline kissing haunts my every thought until I think I'm going mad. He broke my heart. Sorry, *her* heart. It wasn't ever mine to break. What really hurts is I still feel the same way about him. I love him more than ever; he's still the boy who ran across the rooftops with me, the boy I played in the snow with. Not that it matters now. I'm not his Blood Mate. He only ever wanted me because of some stolen heart.

My chest throbs, and I take one of my heart pills, although I know it won't help with this heartache. I roll onto my back and stare at the ceiling. The room starts to feel too small, claustrophobic, like the walls are closing in around me just like in my dream. I force myself out of bed and go over to the balcony window to let in some fresh air. I notice a small object sitting on my balustrade. My father's antique watch!

Ash must've got it back for me. I'm touched by the gesture, but I'm still furious with him.

I run my finger over the watch face, admiring how it shimmers in the moonlight. My finger halts. I look at the watch face more closely, turning it into the light. The ivory surface glimmers gold.

Horror and disbelief rise up inside me.

I remember seeing something glimmer like this before: the Bastet skull at the museum. What had Sebastian said? The Bastet's saber teeth were imbued with its venom? That's what makes the ivory shimmer gold.

I run to my nightstand and empty my jewelry box onto the bed. The phial of Golden Haze rolls across the sheets, sparkling with the same metallic sheen as the Bastet ivory.

I cover my mouth, muffling a scream as the truth hits me.

The Golden Haze has been mixed with Bastet venom.

And there's only one place in this city where you can get Bastet venom.

The Sentry HQ laboratory.

The Bastet boy is curled up in the corner of the cell, his tail wrapped around his naked body. His feet are chained to the wall. He's emaciated, and there are bruises all over his tanned, brown-spotted torso. *What have they been doing to him?*

They did this to Evangeline. She must have been so scared; she was only a little girl. As much as I want to hate her, I can't. They brutalized her and took away her only chance at love by giving me her heart. She has every right to be mad at them, at me. I hate them too for what they did, even though I know Mother did it to save me. But she didn't have to keep Evangeline awake when they cut out her heart; that was just cruel.

I cautiously enter the boy's cell. I found the key to his shackles in Craven's drawers. It makes me sick to think this is what Craven and my mother have really been working on these past weeks. It explains why they needed so many Darklings; they had to get the Haze from somewhere. The only question I have is, why? What could Mother possibly gain by contaminating the Haze? If the citizens find out their government has been knowingly poisoning children, there will be mutiny. It doesn't make sense. No wonder she was so keen to blame Chris's death on Ash—she wanted a scapegoat. She's been playing us all.

The boy lifts his head and looks at me with furious golden eyes. Only the tips of his curved saber teeth are showing; the rest have retracted back inside his skull.

"I'm going to let you go, but you have to promise not to hurt me," I say.

He gives a curt nod.

I know it's a big risk, but I don't care. I won't let Mother harm any more "specimens" the way she tortured Evangeline. I unlock the metal restraints around his ankles. The boy springs to his feet and grabs me around my throat, pushing me down on the hard cell floor. Panic spills over me in waves as he bares his saber teeth at me. I claw at his hands. *I don't want to die like this, please, not like this, not like Father.*

"You promised . . . ," I gasp as his viselike grip tightens around my neck.

The boy hesitates. He lets go of me, and I scramble to my feet.

"Take the back stairwell and go out through the kitchens. There are no guards there at this time of night," I say.

"I will remember your kindness," he says, and rushes out of the room.

I rub my neck and wait a few minutes to see if any alarms go off. When they don't, I know he's escaped. I curl up against the cell wall, trying to hold back the tears. How could Mother do this? Somehow I suspect Purian Rose is behind it all, but what proof do I have? My head spins just thinking about it. There's only one person I want to talk to right now, but he's the last person I want to see.

I go back to my room, hoping to go to bed and forget this day ever happened. I walk past Polly's door and notice it's open a crack. *That's odd.* I enter her room, wondering if she's awake.

I gasp.

Standing over Polly's sleeping body is Evangeline. The white curtains billowing in the wind.

"Get away from her," I say.

Evangeline turns to look at me, contempt written all over her face.

"I said, get away from her," I say more forcefully. I can't scream for help, not yet—Evangeline is too close to Polly. She'd kill her before anyone could reach us.

Polly stirs in her bed, unaware of the danger she's in. Her black hair pools over her pillow, and Evangeline lightly touches it.

"What do you want?" I say, panicked.

"I wanted to talk to you."

"So you broke into my house? Most people use a phone."

"Your sister is very pretty, even with her scars," she says.

"You leave her out of this," I say. "If you came here to punish someone for stealing your heart, then take it out on me— I'm the one who deserves it. She had nothing to do with this."

Evangeline takes a step toward me. I carry on talking, hoping to lure her away from Polly and gain enough time to call for help.

"You have every right to be angry at me. What my mother did to you was sadistic and cruel, and it's my fault that you got hurt," I say. "They took your heart, and not just that, they took Ash away from you. So I'm sorry, for everything."

She furrows her brow.

I take a deep breath. The next words are the hardest I've ever spoken. "If you want Ash, I won't put up a fight. He was never mine. He always belonged to you."

"You'd do that?" she asks.

I lower my eyes. "If that's what it takes."

She's silent for a long time.

"I don't want him to be with me because it's the only option he's got," she says. "I know, given the choice, he'd be with you. He showed me as much tonight."

"He kissed you," I point out.

"I kissed him."

"So where does that leave us?" I say.

"I'm not going to stop fighting for him. Ash is *my* Blood Mate, heart or no heart. But when he decides to be with me, it'll be because he wants to, not because you've given him no other choice," she says.

I nod.

Evangeline moves toward the balcony windows. "And, Natalie?"

"Yes?"

"Don't think this changes anything between us," she says. "I'm getting my heart back from you one day."

With that, she leaps onto the balcony and disappears into the night.

I hurry over to the windows and lock them tight.

• • •

I stay in bed until the following afternoon, the curtains drawn, the covers over my head, trying to block out the world. I had to pull a sickie, because it's Wednesday, a school day. Despite yesterday's bombing, Mother demanded the school be kept open and for everyone to go back to work, because the government "doesn't bow down to terrorism." It was surprisingly easy to act ill, given how I feel right now. When I eventually got to sleep last night, my dreams were filled with upsetting images of Ash and Evangeline kissing. At least I didn't have the nightmare about the child in the cave. I don't think I ever will again, now that I know the truth about Evangeline and my heart.

"Are you sure you won't come to the hunt later this afternoon?" Sebastian asks.

I fake a cough. "I really can't."

"I'll cover for you this time, but you *have* to come to the next one," he says, stomping out of the room. "If you change your mind, we'll be meeting at the Armistice Memorial at the cemetery."

There's no way I'm doing that. I won't hunt Darklings! I don't care what anyone says, I won't be a Tracker.

I hear Mother's screeching voice ringing through the floorboards. She's been screaming at her staff all day for allowing the Bastet boy to escape. Craven's been getting the brunt of her wrath. I'd feel bad for him, except he deserves everything he gets for creating that Golden Haze. At least the Bastet boy is gone; they won't be able to use his venom to make any more of it. It can't bring Chris back, but at least no one else will get hurt.

The door opens, and Martha brings in a tray of food.

"I don't want it," I mumble.

"You have to eat, dear."

"No I don't."

Martha pulls the covers back until my face is visible. "Come on, just one spoonful of soup. It will make you feel better."

"Nothing will ever make me feel better," I say, dragging the blanket over my head again.

She pats my leg and leaves, letting me wallow in self-pity. A few minutes later, the door opens again.

"I don't want to eat anything, Martha," I say.

"Don't worry, Nat. I think the anorexic look really suits you," Day says.

I sit up, and Day curls her lip at my appearance: matted hair, red-rimmed eyes and hollow cheeks. I check the clock. Has school finished already?

"What are you doing here?" I say.

"I heard what happened between you and Ash, and I thought you might need cheering up."

"I'm fine. I—" I burst into tears.

Day wipes my eyes with the frilled sleeve of her blouse.

"Come on," she says, dragging me out of bed, the way Polly used to do when I was a little girl and didn't want to get up.

I'm bundled into the shower as Day goes and gets me some fresh clothes. I let the water splat off my skin and glumly stare at the drain as it gurgles up soapsuds. I get dressed, then immediately crawl back into bed.

"Oh no you don't." She pulls me off the bed and ushers me out of the room.

We sneak down the corridor, past Sebastian's room. The door's open. He's getting changed into his Tracker uniform, readying for the hunt. The rose tattoo above his left ear still looks pink and sore. He turns, sensing me.

"Natalie?" he calls out.

I grab Day's hand, and we run down the stairs and out of the building before he can stop us.

"Where are we going?" I grumble as we walk down the city streets.

"You'll see."

Flakes of ash rain down on us like black snow as the Cinderstone buildings surrounding us continue to slowly burn, making the city smell like bonfires. There's a tension in the air; everyone is still shook up from yesterday's bombing. Tanks roll down the streets, while numerous Tracker squads assemble at various checkpoints throughout the city. It's unusual seeing so many of them out all at once, but I guess they need to be extra vigilant after the explosion.

The hairs on the back of my neck prickle. It's that feeling that someone is following us, but when I look, no one's there.

Farther down the road, we pass an attractive woman in her twenties, standing on a crate, handing out flyers to anyone who walks by.

"The Darklings are starving! The Sentry government has been lying to us," she says to a small group of people who have stopped to listen to her. "They told us the Darklings were being fed, taken care of, but yesterday we saw the truth with our own eyes. Humans for Unity was right all along. I say 'No to Rose's Law' and 'No to segregation.'"

There are a few murmurs of assent from the group.

She thrusts a flyer in my hand, and I quickly scan it. It's a picture of a burning black rose, with NO TO ROSE'S LAW written above the image and several slogans like NO BOUNDARIES and ONE CITY UNITED plastered over it. I fold it and put it in my pocket.

"How's Beetle?" I ask, feeling terrible it's taken me this long to ask.

Day gives me a worried smile. "His stomach is healing nicely, but his face is still sore. The doctor said he'll probably be scarred." She chokes on the last word.

I give her a quick hug.

"Are you two back together, then?" I ask.

"We're giving it a trial run. He's promised me he's quitting Haze for good."

"That's great," I say.

"We'll see," she replies.

We approach the city cemetery where Chris's funeral was held. Day pushes open the gate, and we go inside the graveyard. Kurt and a few of the cadets have congregated beside the Armistice Memorial, gearing up for their first hunt. We hurriedly rush past them, keeping our heads down so they don't spot us.

"You know, most girls take their friends to get ice cream when they're upset, not to the cemetery."

Day laughs. We head toward the church ruins where Ash and I once kissed. Why are we going there? I soon get my answer when I spot Ash anxiously pacing in front of the cracked stained-glass window. My heart tugs, drawing me toward him, but I won't be swayed. I turn to leave, furious, but Day takes my hand and pulls me into the ruins.

"You two need to talk," she says.

"We have nothing to talk about," I say to her, unable to look at him for fear my heart might shatter into a million pieces.

"Just give him a chance to apologize," she says quietly, looking at me with gentle brown eyes. "I'll see you later."

I take a deep breath and face Ash. We stare at each other

across the ruins. The void between us seems so vast. He looks tired, and I'm sure he hasn't slept all night. Even so, he's still devastatingly, heartbreakingly beautiful. His rippling black hair is getting long, and he rakes it back with his fingers.

"I'm sorry," he finally says.

"If that's all you've got to say, I'll go."

He's by my side in a flash. It hurts having him so close to me; he's so perfect, his scent so intoxicating. Bonfires, musk and rain. The scent of home. My eyes shimmer with fresh tears, and I angrily wipe them away.

He tilts my face up to look into his.

"I'm so sorry I hurt you, Natalie. I made a mistake, a really stupid, terrible mistake, and I don't expect you to ever forgive me. I don't deserve your forgiveness."

"Then why did you bring me here?"

"I just wanted to tell you something."

"What?" I whisper.

He runs a light finger over my lips, leaving a tingling trail across my skin.

"I love you," he says. "I love the way you bite your bottom lip when you're nervous. I love the annoying way you rattle mints against your teeth when you eat them. I love how brave you are. Those are the reasons I love you, Natalie, not because you have a Darkling heart."

"You really hurt me," I say.

"I know," he replies.

"If you really loved me, then why did you kiss her?" I challenge.

He sits on the dewy earth, and I kneel down next to him. He doesn't look at me.

"I kissed her because she's my Blood Mate, and that means

I'm drawn to her. I'm not going to lie. There's an attraction—not as strong as I feel for you, but it's there, and I was confused by what it meant," he says. "I needed to know how I felt about her. I wanted to know if what you and I had was real."

"And is it?" I ask in a whisper, my heart racing.

He tentatively touches my knee with his fingertips, and it sends tingles of pleasure through my skin. I don't move his hand away.

"Yes. It's real to me." He looks at me and in that moment he seems so broken, so vulnerable. "Was it ever real for you?"

I pluck a few strands of grass from the earth. "I don't know," I finally say, and he frowns. "Face it, Ash, we barely know anything about each other. I don't even know what your favorite color is!"

"Green," he says.

I let out a soft laugh. "See? I would've guessed black."

"How about you?"

"Silver," I reply.

"What else do you want to know?" he asks.

"What's your favorite book?"

"Easy. *The Wooden Boy.*"

I raise my eyebrow. "Seriously?"

"Yeah. He wanted to be a real boy—I could relate to that. All I ever wanted was to be a normal kid, to have a heartbeat like everyone else." He looks at me with eyes that glimmer like stars, a half smile on his lips, and my heart fumbles.

"It must have been really hard for you," I say.

He nods. "Ask me something else. Anything you want to know, I'll tell you."

"Tell me a secret," I say.

He studies me for a second, then looks at the ground,

uncertain. I'm not sure he's going to tell me anything. "My dad's hiding my mom in the crypt of our church," he says quickly.

I inhale sharply. Harboring a Darkling is a capital offense. To tell me—the Emissary's daughter—something like that proves he really trusts me. I lace my fingers through his.

"I won't tell a soul, I promise," I say.

He lightly squeezes my hand.

"Tell me one of your secrets," he says softly.

I bite my lip. Now is the perfect time to tell him about the Haze. *Trust him.*

"Ash, I found out something about the Haze. The Sentry—"

"What the fragg is going on here?" a furious voice booms behind us, making the crows in the rafters scatter.

Sebastian stands in the entranceway of the ruins, his face contorted with rage.

I snatch my hand away from Ash.

"Go away, Seb. This is none of your business," I say.

He stares daggers at Ash, then turns his eyes to me. There's nothing in them except hate.

"Why do you continue to humiliate me like this?" Sebastian says to me. "I loved you, I promised you the world, and yet you still choose that *thing* over me."

"Stop saying you love me. You don't!" I say.

"She who lies with the beast will be cast into the pits of hell," Sebastian says, quoting the Book of Creation. "For she who has tasted Sin will be forever drunk on its poison."

"Give the Purity crap a rest," I say. "If I'm a sinner, then so are you! You got that Darkling girl pregnant, or did you fail to mention that to Purian Rose?"

Ash looks at me, startled. "He has a twin-blood child?"

"He made her have an abortion," I reply.

Ash sucks in a breath.

"The creature was an abomination," Sebastian says.

"It was a baby, and you killed it to save your own skin," I say.

Sebastian's hand curls around the hilt of his sword. Ash steps protectively in front of me.

"Sebastian, are we hunting, or what?" Kurt calls out from the cemetery.

A cruel smile plays on Sebastian's lips. "Yes, we're hunting."

He draws his sword and points it threateningly at us. "You're coming with me."

29
ASH

SEBASTIAN MARCHES US OUT of the ruins, his sword at our backs. I slide a look at Natalie and try and get as much meaning into my eyes as possible, letting her know we'll be okay. She nods.

Claw Neck raises a dark brow at us as we join the other cadets, who are all dressed in their Tracker uniforms. We stand out like sore thumbs in our civilian clothes.

"I found a few strays," Sebastian explains, sheathing his sword.

Claw Neck doesn't push the matter. He addresses the cadets.

"Today will be a simple search-and-collect mission," he says. "We've had a tip-off that a Darkling is being hidden in a house on City End. We'll check the house and hopefully capture us a nipper."

One of the cadets makes a disgruntled sound.

"It may not be an exciting mission, but this type of hunt is a typical day's work, and you need to learn how to do it," Claw Neck continues. "And trust me when I say none of you maggots are ready to take on a nest of Wraths."

They usher us through the cemetery toward City End, which is brimming with people heading home from work. Sebastian stands behind me and Natalie, to be sure we can't make a run for it. We reach the house, an unassuming Cinderstone building with a yellow-painted door. Claw Neck kicks it down.

"Tracker inspection!" he says, then turns to us. "Never knock. It gives them time to run."

Sebastian points his sword at me.

"Go inside," he says.

I hesitate.

"Just do what he says," Natalie whispers.

We enter the house. It's small and shabby, with paint peeling off the walls and threadbare rugs. I try and think of a way to get out of this, but I can't. The cadets move to surround a husband and wife, who are huddled on the floor in the tiny living room. They look up in fright when they see Claw Neck and Sebastian.

"You have no right to be here!" the husband says, his voice breaking. "We've done nothing wrong."

"We've had a tip-off that you're harboring a Darkling, so shut it," Claw Neck says. "Search the property," he orders two of the cadets.

They break off from the group and start tearing the house apart, knocking over furniture, checking cupboards. One of the cadets tries opening the utility closet. The door is locked. The husband and wife flash a panicked look at each other.

"Open it," Sebastian orders the wife.

"No . . ."

He draws his sword.

"Just do it," the husband urges her.

The woman scrambles to her feet, gets the keys and opens

the door. Perched on the washing machine is a box of Synth-O-Blood.

"It fell off the back of a Sentry truck. We were going to sell it on Chantilly Lane," the husband says quickly. "I was laid off. We have bills to pay."

"Just take it," the wife says, sitting down beside her husband. "Please, that's everything. We have nothing else to hide."

The husband subconsciously glances at the rug by his feet.

The gesture doesn't go unnoticed by Claw Neck. He kicks the rug away to reveal a trapdoor.

A collective hush descends on the room.

"It's just an old storage room," the wife says.

Claw Neck opens the trapdoor and sticks his arm inside.

"There's nothing down there, I swear," she stammers.

Claw Neck grins.

The wife grasps her husband's hand. "It's empty, I promise!"

"Then what's this?" Claw Neck lifts a young boy from the hole like a rabbit from a magician's hat.

My heart stops.

The boy's a twin-blood, like me.

He's pale and skinny as a worm, with shoulder-length rippling hair. He stares at me, and for a fraction of a second, he smiles, and I know what he's thinking: *I'm not alone anymore.* Then that brief look of solidarity is replaced with betrayal. I want to tell him that I'm not really a Tracker, but that would be a lie. For the first time, I have to admit it to myself; I'm a traitor.

He's thrown on the wooden floor.

"What have we here?" Sebastian says, nudging the boy with his foot.

"Leave him alone!" I growl.

Sebastian looks at the husband and wife. "So which one of you is the cheating race traitor?"

The husband glances at his wife.

The boy whimpers.

Claw Neck grins maliciously at me, offering his sword. "Show us whose side you're really on, Fisher. Kill the nipper."

"No!" I say.

"Don't hurt him. He's just a little boy," the wife says.

The twin-blood boy peers up at me with sparkling eyes.

I step back. "I won't do it."

Claw Neck raises his sword.

"Mama!" the twin-blood boy cries.

"Please don't!" the wife begs.

With a swift movement, Claw Neck slices the woman's throat.

Several of the cadets scream. Natalie buries her head in my chest.

"Just take the damn nipper!" the husband says, his face stained with his wife's blood.

Claw Neck drags the boy outside, and we race after them.

"Let him go!" I lunge for Claw Neck.

Sebastian blocks me off and throws me to the ground. I hit the cobbles beside the boy.

"Leave them alone!" Natalie yells.

"I'm going to get you out of here," I say to the boy, taking his hand.

Sebastian presses his sword into the back of my neck.

Panic surges in me.

"Who should die?" he says to me.

He lifts his sword and points it at the twin-blood boy instead.

"Seb, don't!" Natalie cries out.

"Who's it going to be, Fisher? You or him?" he says.

The boy's hand tightens around mine. Sweat trickles down his brow, dripping into his sparkling black eyes. Eyes just like mine.

"Me," I say.

"No!" Natalie shouts.

Sebastian raises his sword and swings. I shut my eyes, waiting for the pain. There's the gruesome squelch of metal on flesh. Something hot and sticky splashes over my face and hair.

I open my eyes. The twin-blood boy's lifeless eyes stare back at me, asking just one question: Why me?

I smash my fists against the cobbles as grief rips through me. Sebastian never intended to let the boy live. Natalie rushes over and helps me to my feet.

"Why did you do it?" she says to Sebastian.

He gives her a cold, frightening smile. "Because I can."

I flash my fangs at Sebastian, wanting nothing more than to rip his fragging head off.

"Don't," she whispers to me.

"That's what happens to race traitors," he says to Natalie, then waves his men on.

One of the female cadets turns to her friend, her voice shaking. "Do you think the other cadets are doing this?"

The other cadets . . .

My heart stops beating.

My mind flashes back to Sebastian's conversation with Gregory at Mr. Tubs's and how he was being sent on a hunt in the Rise.

"Mom!" I say, terror rushing through me.

I grab Natalie's hand and break out into a sprint, dragging

her along with me. She struggles to keep up, stumbling more than once.

"Stop! Please . . . ," Natalie pants.

I don't have time to wait. I scoop her up in my arms and keep running. I don't stop until we reach my house.

"Dad!" I yell, running down to the crypt.

But Gregory is already standing in the center of the room, his sword drawn. Even in the dim light, I can see the line of blood oozing down the metal blade. Next to him is Dad, hunched over a skeletal figure on the floor. I don't move. I can't.

Dad stands up and walks toward me.

"Son," he whispers.

That's when I see her face, partially covered by a few limp strands of dark hair. I see past the rotting flesh, the thin black lips, and picture the woman she used to be. Her head is tilted to one side as if she's asleep.

Mom.

"How *could* you?" Natalie says to Gregory. "You monster!"

I charge at Gregory, slamming him against the wall. His feet kick at thin air as my hand clenches his skinny throat.

"Ash, let him go. You're not a killer. Your mother wouldn't want this," Dad says.

Gregory's fingers claw at my hands.

"You're killing him," Natalie says, trying to pull me off him.

"Why?" I scream at him.

"It's . . . your fault . . . Chris is dead," Gregory gasps.

"I didn't give him that Golden Haze, Linus did," I snarl.

"But he . . . asked you first, and you said no. If you'd given him the Haze . . . he wouldn't have . . . he wouldn't have gone to Linus. It's your fault he's dead," Gregory says, his eyes filled with pain.

"Ash." The word is just a whisper.

I drop Gregory and wheel around. Mom stirs on the ground. I thought she was dead!

Gregory runs out of the crypt before I can finish what I started.

Mom sucks in a raspy, painful breath as sticky blood oozes out of the wound in her chest. I kneel beside her and desperately cling to her hand. I don't see the Wrath in her anymore, just the woman she used to be. My mom.

"I'm sorry I left you . . . ," she says. "Forgive me, my sweet boy."

"I forgive you," I say.

She faintly squeezes my hand.

"Don't leave me, Mom. Please . . ."

I feel her slipping away.

"I love you," I say.

She exhales.

"Please don't die."

Her fingers slip through mine.

"Mom?" I whisper.

There's silence.

"Mom?"

Dad touches my shoulder. "She's gone, son."

Natalie wraps her arms around me, kissing my cheek, not saying anything. We stay like that for what seems like an eternity. I don't want to move. As soon as I do, then the world will start turning again and then it's real. Mom's dead. Somewhere in the distance, I hear singing. A mournful, heartbreaking lament. I know it's Sigur. His dual heart must've stopped beating.

"We need to get her ready for So'Kamor," I say, referring to the Darkling ritual for the dead.

Dad doesn't hear me at first. He holds Mom's hand in his, rubbing his thumb over her index finger where she used to wear her wedding ring. Darklings believe the index finger is directly linked to their dual heart. That's why they wear their rings there.

"Dad?"

"She should be with her own kind," he says quietly. "We'll bring her to the boundary gates after curfew. Sigur will let us in."

Natalie pulls me into a hug the instant we're alone in my bedroom.

"You don't need to be here," I say, my voice choked with emotion. "I know you're still mad at me."

She lightly kisses me. Even through my grief, I ache for her.

"I love you, Ash. Let me be here for you."

Taking my hand, she leads me to the bed. We climb under the covers. She places a hand over my heart, opening a channel between us. *Soul Sharing.* All my emotions instantly flood into her, my pain, my sorrow, my heartbreak. She absorbs it all, sharing it with me so I don't have to suffer it alone.

I stroke her skin, kiss her lips, run my hands over her legs, needing her. There's no embarrassment as our inquisitive fingers and lips explore each other's bodies. We silently remove our clothes, dropping them to the floor. I take a lingering look at her before lying down and pulling her toward me. Her body fits perfectly against mine, like we're two halves of the same whole.

"I love you, Ash," she says.

"I love you too," I say. "So begins my heart . . ."

"So begins our life," she whispers back, remembering the words I told her the night we first kissed on Beetle's barge.

"Everlasting," we say together.

The Blood Vow. We're now united under Darkling law.

I tilt my head to one side, offering my throat to her to consummate our union. Natalie runs a fingernail down my skin and tiny beads of blood bubble out of the wound. She gently licks the blood away.

Sitting up, Natalie scoops her hair to one side to reveal the two puncture wounds on her neck. I hesitate, remembering what happened before at the mansion.

"It's all right," she whispers. "I trust you."

I lightly scratch the scars with the tips of my fangs, opening the wound, and press my lips to her neck. Her hot blood spills over my tongue. It takes all my strength to only drink a few drops, sealing our bond.

She lies back down, and without another word, I maneuver myself on top of her, being as gentle as possible. She lets out a small gasp, then it's just bliss. All thought of nerves vanish as we kiss each other and let instinct guide our way.

Later, I hold Natalie as she dreams, her head resting on my chest. I can't sleep, although I wish I could. I know Dad will be knocking on my door soon, telling me it's time to leave.

Rain splashes through the open window, hitting the bell with a melodic *dong-dong-dong*. The air smells fresh, rinsed. Mom would've liked it. From the stories Dad told me, I know she loved the rain. Natalie stirs, and I kiss her head.

I get out of bed and walk to the window. The chilled night air prickles my skin, and I shiver, but I don't turn from the cold. I stare across the cityscape toward the Boundary Wall, which carves its way through the center of the city like a concrete spine.

The city is deathly still. Lights are out, streets are empty, the world is silent. I go over to the sink in the corner of my room and run some water through my hair, washing the dirt and blood out of it, thinking about the twin-blood boy. I wish I'd known he was in the city. I would've visited him and let him know he wasn't alone. In a small way, seeing him has given me hope that maybe there are more twin-bloods out there, not just me and Evangeline.

I return to the archway and tilt my face up to the moonlit sky. The Darkling in me awakens, lured by the night. I let out a lamenting howl, singing my sorrow for all my brethren to hear. In the distance, my song is picked up by another Darkling, then another, until the entire city is alive with their unearthly music. *"We are here. You are not alone, brother,"* they sing back. *"We love you."*

Natalie stirs.

"Sorry, I didn't mean to wake you," I say.

"It's okay," she replies sleepily.

There's a soft knock at my door.

Natalie pulls the covers around herself as Dad enters the room. He glances at her quickly, but doesn't say anything.

I'm surprised to see he's shaved off his beard, and he seems taller, like the weight of the world has lifted off his shoulders. He's wearing a smart gray robe, the one he saves for funerals.

"It's time," he says.

30
ASH

🌠 **WE WAIT BY THE IRON GATES** as the Legion guard goes to inform Sigur we're here. The part of the wall that was damaged in the bombing has been crudely reconstructed, and just a single squad of Sentry guards patrols it. We held back until they went on their rounds before approaching the gates.

Natalie peers up at the Legion guards patrolling the wall.

"Don't worry—they won't hurt you," I say softly. "They're not allowed to attack unless Sigur or his kin orders it."

The iron gates open, and we step inside the Legion. It's even worse than I remember. Debris from the bomb is scattered about the wet, stinking earth, and numerous shacks have collapsed. Hundreds of glittering black eyes peer at us from the buildings as I cradle Mom's body in my arms. She's wrapped in her Lupine-fur coat—the one Dad got her on their wedding day. He keeps resting his hand on her, muttering soothing words under his breath as if she can hear him. Natalie puts a hand over her mouth as the sights and smells of the compound assault her.

Evangeline is waiting for us, surrounded by two dozen

guards. She stares at my mom's body, her eyes watering. Natalie steps closer to me.

"Sorry about the cavalry. It's safer this way." Evangeline nods toward the emaciated Darklings who have come out of their homes, lured by our human scent.

Our escorts jab them with sticks, keeping them away from us. Dad murmurs a prayer.

"Stay close," I say to Natalie.

Something brushes past my leg. A young Darkling boy runs between us and lunges for Natalie, sinking its fangs into her leg. She screams, and one of the guards pulls the child off. Blood drips down Natalie's shin, and the Darklings howl.

"Move!" the lead escort says to us.

We run to the boat. I hold on to Mom as my feet slip and slide in the mud. I shouldn't have brought Natalie here; it was selfish. What was I thinking? Dad takes her hand and guards her. I give him a thankful smile.

Sigur approaches us, letting out a throaty growl. The Darklings back off immediately. They still respect the alpha, no matter how hungry they are. He glares at Natalie.

"What is she doing here?" he says.

"She's with me. You can trust her," I say.

Evangeline lets out a derisive snort.

"You should not have brought her here. You've put us all at great risk," Sigur says.

"Please, I need her. You of all people should understand," I reply.

Sigur glances briefly at my heart. So he *can* hear my heartbeat? He must understand how I feel about her, then.

"My father gave his life for you, Ambassador," Natalie says

to Sigur. "You trusted him—you can trust me. I'm not like my mother. I don't agree with anything she's doing."

"The first sign of trouble, and she must return immediately," he says to me.

I nod.

We climb into the rowboats and cross over to the zoo. Natalie dabs the Darkling bite on her leg with a tissue.

"I'm sorry about them," Sigur says, meaning the Darklings. "The Emissary cut off our food supply when the wall was bombed."

"My mother did that? Why?" Natalie says.

"The Sentry government thinks we collaborated with Humans for Unity to bomb the wall. It's just another thing to blame on us. Whatever helps them pass Rose's Law," he says.

At the zoo, Sigur leads us into a small chamber carved out of the rock. The room is lit by torchlight, casting long shadows around the circular room. There's a stone altar in the center of the chamber, with an enamel urn on top of it. Sigur places the urn on the floor, and I gently rest Mom on the altar. She looks so small and frail wrapped up in the fur coat.

Sigur tentatively peels back the blanket and looks at Mom. He starts to sob.

"She's at peace now," Dad says, his voice cracking.

Sigur embraces Dad. It's so bizarre, looking at them comforting each other, united in their grief.

Tears spill down Evangeline's cheeks. We both lost a mother tonight.

"You should go to her. She needs you," Natalie says.

I do and pull Evangeline into my arms. She cries silently against my chest.

A High Priest enters the room, dressed in floor-length green robes.

"I must prepare her for So'Kamor," he says.

I don't want to leave her here alone with all these strangers, except I realize now they're not strangers. She had a whole life here. She knew these people.

We all go outside. Sigur runs a tired hand over his brow. He looks utterly shattered. Evangeline catches me staring at him.

"Things have gotten worse since you visited last weekend," she says.

"So I've seen," I reply.

"That's not the worst of it," she says.

"What do you mean?" I ask.

Sigur wearily indicates for us to follow him. We head to the hospital that Evangeline took me to the first time I came here. The stench hits me first. Decay. Death. *Wrath*.

"The virus has mutated," Evangeline says as we enter the ward. "Three of the Darklings in here were perfectly healthy last week, and now they're in the last stages of the disease. Somehow the symptoms have been accelerated, and we don't know how."

She indicates the three Darklings that are lying in the metal beds nearest us. They stretch their hands, crying out, "Kill me," in their own language. Their eyes are yellowed, their skin beginning to rot. The first Darkling is a male, his bitten face a ghoulish green color. Beside him are twin Nordin girls with nubby stumps on their shoulder blades where their wings should be. Their once-flowing white hair is now lank, creating bald patches on their heads. I recognize all three victims; they were at Mr. Tubs's the first time I went there with Natalie.

I begin to shake as the truth crashes over me in waves.
"I know what's in the Golden Haze," I say, my voice quaking.
I look at Sigur.
"It's Wrath."

31
NATALIE

I LOOK AT THE SICK DARKLINGS on the gurney, my mind spinning.

"Bastet venom causes the Wrath?" I blurt out, disbelieving.

Everyone stares at me, even the Darklings lying in the hospital beds.

"What are you talking about?" Ash says.

"I think the Golden Haze is poisoned with Bastet venom," I admit.

"That doesn't make sense," Evangeline says. "Bastet venom is toxic to Darklings. It kills us instantly. We wouldn't live long enough to contract the Wrath virus from it."

"We would if the venom had been diluted with something. Like Haze or blood," Ash says darkly.

"It explains why Wraths suffer from necrosis," I add meekly, remembering what I read about Bastets at the museum. Their venom contains a flesh-eating bacteria, *Vibrio necrosis,* which causes tissue death.

A horrible thought occurs to me. The first Darklings to contract the Wrath virus were the ones sent to the concentration camps during the war. Had the Sentry been testing the effects of Bastet venom on Darklings even back then? Is that how they discovered the venom caused the Wrath virus in the first place?

Ash turns to me, alarm registering on his face. "How did you know the Golden Haze was poisoned with Bastet venom?"

I bite my lip.

"Tell me!" he demands.

"Ash, please . . ." My voice quivers.

"The Emissary did this, didn't she?" Sigur says. "She guessed we tested the Synth-O-Blood for poisons, so she had to find another way to infect us with the Wrath. So they created Golden Haze and supplied it to the drug dens—"

"The humans got infected and passed the virus on to the Darklings who fed off them," Evangeline finishes. "Except the Golden Haze has been killing the humans too. That's why the Emissary has been trying to blame their deaths on us."

Ash lets out a pained sound, like a wounded animal.

"Ash, I'm so sorry," I say.

"Why didn't you tell me?" he says.

"I tried to tell you earlier today, then Sebastian turned up and—"

"You should've tried harder!" he snaps.

Sigur snarls at me. "They deliberately poisoned us. They killed Annora."

I barely have time to react as Sigur grabs me by the throat, crushing the air out of my windpipe.

"I should throw you to the Wraths," he says.

"No, please!" I gasp, clawing at his hands.

"Let her go!" Ash demands.

"Have mercy, Sigur! She's just a child," Minister Fisher pleads.

"Her mother killed our children! What is it you say? An eye for an eye?" Sigur says to him.

The Darklings in the ward howl in unison, a bloodthirsty sound.

"If you kill her, I'll never forgive you. My mom would never let you do this, you know it," Ash says.

This seems to strike a chord with Sigur. He drops me, and I fall hard. Minister Fisher pulls me into his arms.

"You need to leave," Ash says to me, his voice flat, cold.

"Ash, I'm so sorry. Please forgive me," I say.

"Just go, before Sigur changes his mind," he replies.

Minister Fisher drags me out of the room.

"Let me go!" I protest. "I need to go back."

"Don't be stupid, child. They'll kill you," he says.

He looks so much like Ash right now. I hadn't noticed before because his face was obscured by a disheveled beard. They have the same shape eyes, the same high cheekbones, the same straight nose. It's hard not to listen to him when he reminds me so much of Ash.

We take the boat back to the shantytown by the entrance to the Boundary Wall. The guards escort us to the gates, holding on to my arms with more force than necessary. The news has already started to spread through the compound like a virus. I hear them muttering to each other. I don't understand what they're saying, but their fury is loud and clear. They spit at me as I pass. The iron gates swing open, and I'm tossed out like garbage. Minister Fisher stays inside.

I stare at the gates, praying that Ash will run out after me. *Please don't let this be over. Please, please, please.*

But the gates stay closed.

32

ASH

THE FUNERAL CHAMBER is near dark. Only the silvery outlines of the other Darklings are visible in the gloom as they stand around Mom's shrouded body. I hold Dad's hand, keeping him close—he won't be able to see as well as I can.

Evangeline gives me a wisp of a smile. My heart aches, wishing Natalie were here. I shouldn't have snapped at her earlier, but I was upset. Even so, it was wrong of me not to escort her to the boundary gates and let her know things are still okay between us, especially since we made love just a few hours ago. She must be so confused right now.

The High Priest begins to sing. I vaguely recognize the tune and sing the bits I know, which isn't much. I wish I'd spent more time learning about this side of my culture, but there never seemed much point.

The singing stops, and the High Priest ushers us forward.

"What are we supposed to do?" I ask Evangeline.

"We all need to say the thing we'll remember the most about Annora, to help keep her in our minds."

Sigur is first. "I will remember your kiss."

Evangeline can barely get her words out. "I will remember your kindness."

Dad is next. "I will remember your laughter."

Then the High Priest calls on me. I look at Mom's body, thinking of something to say. What will I remember the most about her? The way she sang me to sleep? How she read me *The Wooden Boy* each night, even though she must've been sick to death of it? How she wrote me a birthday card every year, even when she couldn't send it?

"I will remember that you are always with me," I say.

The High Priest picks up the urn I saw earlier, passing it to Sigur. Then he unsheathes a ceremonial knife from around his belt.

"What are they doing?" I whisper.

"You shouldn't look at this," Evangeline says.

The High Priest raises the knife over Mom's body.

"No!" I yell.

The priest plunges the dagger into Mom's chest.

"It's part of the ritual," Evangeline explains. "Her dual heart is harvested and given to her Blood Mate."

I bury my face in Dad's shoulder. Evangeline was right; I don't want to see this. He pats my back.

"It's done," Dad whispers to me a minute later.

I risk a look at Mom. She's been covered again. Sigur places the lid on the urn and offers it to Dad.

Dad shakes his head. "I have Ash. He's the best part of Annora. You keep her heart; it belongs to you. It always did."

Sigur gives a weak smile and clutches the urn to his chest.

The door opens, casting a sliver of light over the altar as

Evangeline slips out of the room. Dad and Sigur are busy talking to each other; they won't notice if I leave for a few minutes. I could do with some air anyway.

I find Evangeline outside beside the empty ape enclosure. We stroll through the zoo, passing the cages. At some point during the walk, Evangeline takes my hand, and I lace my fingers through hers, needing the comfort. Although it feels nice, natural, I still wish it were Natalie who was here with me now.

"It was a moving funeral. Annora would've been pleased with it." Evangeline wipes the tears from her eyes. "I can't believe she's gone."

I don't know what to say to comfort her.

"I was the one who brought your mother back to your house, you know?" she says.

"Thanks," I say.

"It was the least I could do. She looked after me for so long. I loved her."

"Why did you never tell Sigur that my mom was sick?" I say.

She lowers her lashes. "I was scared he'd blame me."

"Why? How did Mom get bitten?" I ask. I'd been wondering this for weeks.

"It was one of the Wraths in the hospital. I was working in the ward, and she came to say good-bye to me after her argument with Sigur. The Wrath attacked her—it was so quick. It's my fault. If she hadn't come to say good-bye . . ."

"It's not your fault. Besides, it's not what killed her in the end," I say, rage boiling inside me as I think about Gregory. "What will they do with her now?"

"They'll take her body outside just before dawn. The sun will cremate her remains."

I cringe at the thought.

"She's in the Elsewhere now, in a better place," Evangeline says.

"Do you really believe that?"

She nods.

A bird flies overhead, reminding me of the crow that flew over me and Natalie when we sat on the roof of Sentry HQ. My heart aches, thinking about that day, how it felt having her in my arms, how she kissed me.

"What are you going to do now?" Evangeline asks.

"What do you mean?" I say.

"Are you going back, or are you staying with us?"

I hadn't even considered staying with the Legion, but why shouldn't I? What's keeping me on the human side of the wall? My mom's gone, Dad would be safer without me, and Beetle would understand. There's only one reason to go back. *Natalie*.

"You're thinking about her, aren't you?" Evangeline says.

"Is it that obvious?"

"It is to me." Evangeline's eyes narrow into slits. "Don't you understand her betrayal? She knew about the Bastet venom, but she didn't tell you."

"Natalie said she didn't have the opportunity—"

"Don't be naive, Ash. She was clearly protecting her mother. Natalie's Sentry through and through, and don't you forget it," Evangeline replies.

"That's not true. She's not like the others."

"Don't be suckered in by her lies. She's played you for a fool."

"I don't believe that," I say.

"How can you still want to be with her?" Evangeline asks.

"Because I still love her," I say.

"You don't love her. You just think you do because she has my heart."

"She may have your heart, but that's not the reason I love her," I say. "It's not just a physical connection. It's something deeper. You may be my Blood Mate, but she's my Soul Mate. That's just as powerful."

Evangeline touches my chest. "We could have that connection, Ash, if you just give me a chance. I'd never lie to you or betray you. She can't be trusted—she's dangerous."

She looks at me with wide, expectant eyes. Her inky-black hair ripples around her pale, beautiful face.

I move her hand away. "And you're not dangerous? You killed a man, or did you forget? His name was Malcolm."

She lets out an irritated sound. "He was just a meat sack."

"You see, that's where you and Natalie differ. She'd never let a Darkling get hurt if she could prevent it, while you have no regard for human life at all."

"Maybe if they ripped your heart out like they did mine, you wouldn't feel so warm and fuzzy about humans either," she says.

I sigh. We sit down on a stone bench beside the abandoned lions' den. White flowers bloom around our feet, their petals the same color as Evangeline's iridescent skin.

"So, are you going to stay with us?" she says, her eyes sparkling with hope.

I look at the Boundary Wall in the distance, and for the first time ever, I'm yearning to be back on the other side.

"No," I say.

Evangeline turns her face from me, but I know she's crying.

"I'm sorry. I never meant to hurt you," I say.

She looks back at me. "Well, you have. I guess it's lucky I don't have a heart, because you would've broken it."

I reach out for her, but she pushes me away.

"I won't wait for you, Ash."

"I never asked you to," I say.

She sighs, her shoulders slumping, the fight gone out of her. Evangeline gazes up at the moon, her black eyes glistening in the silvery light. A single tear slides down her cheek, but she doesn't wipe it away.

"I just thought if you got to know me better, you'd want to be with me instead of her. But that's not going to happen, is it?" she says quietly.

"No. I don't think so."

She lets out a shuddering breath, and I feel terrible for hurting her like this, but I can't lie. Leading her on would be worse in the long run.

"Evangeline, do you even find me attractive?" I ask.

"Yes," she says. "You're very handsome—"

"No, I don't mean superficial stuff. Do you actually like *me*?"

She shrugs. "I don't know. I'm attracted to you, but it's . . . it's a physical thing. Like a craving. I barely know you, Ash."

I nod, understanding. There's definitely a physical attraction between me and Evangeline, but not an emotional connection like I have with Natalie.

"I think there's this real pressure on us to feel a certain way about each other, because we were meant to be Blood Mates. But you don't feel it for me, not really, and I don't feel it for you," I say.

She lets out a tiny sob. "Ash—"

I pull her into my arms and hold her as she cries. She's so small, so fragile. The zoo around us is deathly quiet, the cages bare and void of life. This is her world: silent, alone. It was my life, before Natalie. I am the lucky one. *How different things could have been* . . . I hate the fact I'm resigning her to this fate, but what can I do? The one thing Evangeline needs is the one thing I can't give her: my heart.

"You'll find someone else, someone better," I say as she pulls away from me.

"Who? We're the only twin-bloods left."

"No we're not. There's more of us out there. I've seen it with my own eyes," I reply. "We can search for them together."

Suddenly she stands up.

"There's no reason for me to wait. There's nothing for me here. Annora's gone, you've got Natalie, and Sigur doesn't really need me. It's time to go," she says.

"You can't go *now*," I say, getting to my feet.

"Why not? Give me one reason to stay."

I can't.

"Good-bye, Ash. Maybe we'll meet again someday."

She goes to the boat that will take her back to the Boundary Wall. Giving me one last, lingering look, she sails away. My heart tugs as it senses her leave.

I wonder if I'll ever see her again.

33
NATALIE

I BARGE INTO MOTHER'S OFFICE. She's surrounded by her cronies, who all stare at me in stunned silence as I pick up a glass paperweight and throw it across the room. It smashes against the portrait of Purian Rose hanging above the fireplace.

"Natalie!"

"How could you?" I scream. "You infected the Darklings with Wrath?"

The staff members scurry out the door, eager to get away, and I slam the door behind them.

Mother narrows her icy blue eyes at me. "I don't know where you heard that nonsense about the Wrath but—"

"Cut the crap! I know you did it. What I don't understand is why," I say.

Mother tenses, accentuating the sharp angles of her bony frame. She's about to protest, then sighs, relenting. "Because Darklings are vermin and need to be exterminated."

I knew she was involved, but to hear her admit it still knocks the wind out of me.

"What about Chris and those other kids? The ones who took your Golden Haze? Were they just vermin too?" I say.

"Their deaths were unfortunate, but I'm not going to lose any sleep over a couple of Hazers."

Anger flares up inside me. "Well, I'd start to worry if I were you. Sigur knows everything."

"How?" she asks.

"I told him."

Mother stands up, knocking back her green leather chair. It crashes to the floor.

"Do you realize the danger you've put us in?" she exclaims.

"I didn't put us in danger; you did with this insane plan! Why did you do it? I just don't understand," I say.

Mother turns slightly, so I can only see her profile, and stares into the fireplace. The orange flames flicker, and shadows dance over her pale skin. The effect makes her gaunt face look almost skeletal, and it hits me how sick she's looking, how tired.

"I had no choice, Natalie. After your father betrayed us, Purian Rose was going to have us all executed, to make an example of us." She doesn't sound like her normal confident self. She sounds . . . *scared.* "But I persuaded him to spare us."

"How?" I ask.

"I knew he wanted to pass Rose's Law—it was all he'd been talking about for months." She glances over her bony shoulder at me. "We had to find a way to persuade the citizens to vote for it. We knew there would be objections, especially from Humans for Unity."

I walk over to her. "I still don't see how this ties in with the Golden Haze. Why did you want to infect the Darklings with the Wrath virus?" I say.

Mother peers up at the portrait of Purian Rose like she's

worried he can hear us. His wolfish silver eyes glower down at us.

"Didn't you ever think it was odd that the Black City School was right next to the Boundary gates?" she says.

I nod. "Yes, actually, I did."

"It wasn't a mistake. The idea was to get the Darklings infected with the Wrath and then"—she licks her lips—"then we were going to open the gates and unleash them on the school. We were going to blame it on Humans for Unity and claim they let the nippers out. Those idiots have been playing into our hands this whole time with their protests."

I gasp. The horror of it is overwhelming. *Purian Rose ordered the deaths of hundreds of children?*

"Why?" I say.

"We'd win the ballot for sure. No one would be able to deny how dangerous Darklings were after that," Mother says. "I told Purian Rose I'd run the mission, and if it went wrong, I'd take the full blame. It was win-win for him."

I look her in the eyes, and for the first time ever, I see the frightened, vulnerable woman behind them.

"That was the deal I made with him to protect you and Polly. I had to do it. There was no other way," she says.

"But you sent me to that school." The truth finally dawns on me. "Rose *wanted* me to die so people wouldn't suspect he had anything to do with the Wrath attack. I mean, why would he allow the daughter of an Emissary to die?"

She grabs my hands and looks earnestly at me. "I pleaded with him to spare you, but he wouldn't listen. Why do you think I've had Sebastian watch you so closely? I wanted him there to protect you when the Wraths attacked. It was going to happen next Tuesday, the day after the boundary negotiations ended. We figured it would be the best time, as Humans for Unity would be furious when I refused to expand the Darkling territory."

"Sebastian knew about this?"

Mother doesn't need to answer. Of course he must have known about the plan. He's been helping Mother all along. That's why Sebastian was asked to attend the spiritual retreat. He was being rewarded.

I slip my hands free from Mother's grasp.

"Don't be mad at Sebastian. He was just following orders," she says. "It was his idea to orchestrate the Tracker trials. We hoped if some of the students had defensive training, it would minimize casualties."

"*You* ordered the Tracker trials? I thought that was Purian Rose's initiative."

"I convinced him it was a good idea to enlist more Trackers, but he didn't know my real reason for doing it," Mother says.

"Were you still going to go ahead with the plan, despite the fact Humans for Unity got there ahead of you and bombed the wall?" I ask.

She nods. "Purian Rose said it would be the final nail in the coffin for the Darklings and Humans for Unity. Citizens would have no choice but to vote for Rose's Law. In a way, the bombing worked in our favor; it proved Humans for Unity were extremists. People would believe us when we claimed they did it."

I shake my head, trying to take it all in. There's so much blood on Mother's hands it makes me sick to think about it.

On the floor by my feet are the shards of glass from the paperweight I threw at the wall. They sparkle in the firelight, just like Ash's eyes. My heart clenches when I think about him, think about how much I've lost because of my mother.

"I can't believe you went along with such an insane plan," I finally say. "I could've been killed. Don't you care about me at all?"

"Of course I care. You're my daughter."

"That's never mattered to you before. You let Purian Rose torture Polly. She's your daughter too."

"I had no choice!"

"You did. You could've stood up to Purian Rose that night. You could've tried something. Instead you just handed her over to him."

Mother's gaunt face hardens. "Don't forget, young lady, it was your fault Polly was even there."

I wince, stung by her words.

It wasn't your fault, Father's soft voice says inside my head. *You were just a child.*

My hands begin to shake as fury builds up inside me. I'm sick of Mother holding me solely responsible for what happened to Polly. It's not right; it's not fair.

"Don't you *dare* blame me," I say. "She was hurt because you didn't protect her. You're her mother. You should've done more to save her."

Mother blanches.

"Just answer me this one question: why did you choose me over her? I know she's your favorite, so don't even try to deny it," I say.

"I don't."

Even though I already knew, it still stings to hear.

"It's true I loved Polly more than you," Mother continues. "You were always your father's favorite, and for good reason."

"What good reason?"

Mother turns back to the fire and shuts her eyes. "John wasn't Polly's father."

I don't say anything for a minute as the news crashes over me. *Polly is my half sister?* But I suppose it explains why we don't look anything alike.

"Who's her father?" I ask, a horrible thought dawning on me.

Mother points a shaky finger at the portrait of the man with wolfish silver eyes hanging above the fireplace.

Purian Rose.

"No!" I scream, backing away from the painting.

"He has no idea Polly's his daughter," Mother says.

"You did it to hurt Rose, even though he had no idea Polly was his child?"

She nods. "I intended to tell him one day, but I was waiting for the right time."

"You mean when it benefited you?" I say, understanding.

"Politics is war, Natalie," she replies. "I needed an insurance policy. If anyone finds out Purian Rose has an illegitimate daughter, whom he *tortured,* it could end his career."

"So you were going to blackmail him?"

"Yes," she says.

"You're unbelievable. Aren't you worried he'd just kill Polly to stop the truth getting out?"

She laughs at this. "If he lays one finger on her, my associates in Centrum will release DNA reports confirming he's her father. The truth will still come out. This isn't the first time I've blackmailed someone—give me some credit."

I sit down in a red leather chair and bury my head in my hands, trying to process all this new information. Betrayal burns deep inside me. How could my parents keep a secret as big as that from me all these years?

Mother rests a thoughtful finger on her lips as she studies me.

I can tell she's trying to work out something. Her eyes narrow.

"Natalie, what were you doing with Sigur Marwick?"

"I don't have to answer that," I say, standing up.

She slams her hand against her mahogany desk, making me jump. Our mother-daughter bonding moment has ended. It's business as usual. I lift my chin and stare at her defiantly.

"I was attending a funeral," I say.

"*Whose* funeral?" she says slowly.

"Annora Fisher's."

Mother's red lips tighten. She recognizes the name. "Sigur's Blood Mate?"

"You knew her?" I ask.

"Oh, yes. She was high up in the Legion Liberation Front and caused us no end of trouble during the war. How did *you* know her?"

"She was my boyfriend's mother," I say.

Mother inhales sharply.

I smile coldly. I got the intended reaction. The only thing my mother hates more than Darklings is race traitors. I storm out of her office, ignoring her shouts for me to "come back right now, young lady!" and head straight for my bedroom. Taking out the suitcase from under my bed, I start to pile clothes into it. I tip my jewelry box on the bed and pick out the most expensive items, leaving my father's watch safe to one side. I'll pawn the rest. It won't be much, but it should be enough to get me a room in Centrum for a few weeks until I can arrange to have Polly sent down to me—my sister can't stay here with *her*. I still have friends in Centrum; they can help out. I just need to get away from here, away from these monsters.

My head swims all of a sudden, and I shut my eyes to stop

the dizziness. An image of Ash's face crosses my mind. He looked so betrayed. Please don't let it be over between us.

The door opens, and Sebastian staggers in without waiting to be asked. His Tracker jacket is open, revealing a white vest underneath. I can smell the alcohol from here. He must've been out drinking with the rest of the Trackers after his successful hunt with the cadets.

He notices the suitcase. "Where are you going?"

"Away."

"Don't go. I love you. I want you," he slurs.

"I think you should leave, Sebastian."

He lurches toward me, and I manage to turn my cheek just before he kisses me.

"Get out!" I shove him away.

He pushes me, and I fall back against the bed. My suitcase topples off, spilling its contents over the carpet. Sebastian rolls on top of me, and for a flash, I think of Ash and how we'd been like this earlier this evening. Except this time I'm pinned down by my wrists. My heart jackhammers inside my chest. There's no light in Sebastian's eyes. All that's there is darkness and hunger: the eyes of a predator. Sebastian shoves a cold hand up my top and cups my breast.

"No!" I scream.

He pushes his lips onto mine, forcing my mouth open with his tongue. He tastes of alcohol, fiery and bitter. I angrily bite his bottom lip, and he grunts, punching me hard in the face.

He flips me onto my belly, pushing my face into the pillow. I gasp for breath. My fingers find the jewelry box on my nightstand and I wildly strike out at Sebastian. *Crack!* The weight lifts off my back. I drop the box and the phial of Golden Haze rolls across the carpet. It smashes under my foot as I race out of the room. I don't look back. I just run. Away from Sebastian, away from my old life, as fast as I can.

It's started snowing, and the air is freezing cold, but I barely notice. I get half a mile down the road before I stop. I have no idea where I'm going, and I don't have any money. *Now where?*

There's only one person I know who can hide me.

34
NATALIE

BEETLE PUTS A BLANKET over my shoulders and hands me a cup of watery tea. I thank him, sipping it through my bruised lips. The flesh on his cheek where he was burned is still pink, and the skin is starting to look tight and shiny. He's going to be scarred for sure. His stomach is bandaged, and he struggles to move, but otherwise he seems all right. Better than I expected.

His barge is packed with Humans for Unity members. I told Beetle and his aunt everything I knew about my mother's plot to infect the Darklings with mutated Wrath, and within minutes, Roach was calling the other members.

Roach paces the length of the barge like a tiger in a cage, her long dreadlocks swaying behind her as she rants on the phone to her contact at Black City News.

"It was the government, I told you all along, man," she says. "They've been killing those kids, putting poison in the Haze. Yeah, yeah, yeah, we're getting proof. I'm not blowing hot air, Juno. This is the truth."

I put the teacup down on the table. The motion makes me wince. Every part of my body aches where Sebastian attacked me. I sob, the memory of it bubbling up before I can stop it. Beetle hugs me gingerly.

A few weeks ago, I never thought that I'd hug a Humans for Unity member, let alone help them to bring my mother down and stop Rose's Law. It's a risk, but I'm tired of being afraid of my mother, of Purian Rose. They need to be stopped. My father understood that, and I know Polly feels that way too. I'll find a way to protect her.

"Have you heard from Ash?" I ask Beetle.

"No, he's not gotten in touch. I sent a few messages, but I guess he's busy, with his Mom's funeral and all. Maybe he'll be at school tomorrow?" he suggests.

"Sure," I say, unconvinced.

"He'll come round soon enough. He's crazy about you," Beetle says.

I rub the bruises on my wrists where Sebastian pinned me down on the bed. How could I have ever loved him? He's nothing like Ash, who is kind, loyal and generous. I shut my eyes and think about Ash's lips as they kissed mine, the sensation of his fingers running over my skin, how it felt when we made love. It was the best moment of my life.

Beetle's aunt hangs up the phone, a huge smile on her face. "They'll run the story in the morning news if we can get them the evidence. The Sentry government isn't going to know what hit them!"

A skinny, blond-haired man enters the room, his face flushed. He looks elated. Roach sent him to Mr. Tubs's to get hold of some of the Golden Haze, since the phial I had broke when

Sebastian attacked me. The only other phials of Golden Haze are in the laboratory back in the Sentry HQ, and there's no way I'm going back there after what happened.

He takes off his rucksack and tips out the contents on the table. Over twenty phials of Haze roll out, along with a dozen digital disks, which I know are recordings of people who visited Mr. Tubs's Haze den.

"I didn't get a chance to see much of the CCTV footage, but this disk says it all." He pops it into the disk player and turns on the TV.

The footage is a little grainy, but it clearly shows Kurt giving Mr. Tubs a case of the Golden Haze.

"We've caught those bastards red-handed," the blond man says.

"Good work!" she says.

He grins. "I nearly didn't get it. The Sentry guard's crawling all over the city. They set Mr. Tubs's shop on fire, no doubt to destroy the evidence. It's just their bad luck I got there first."

Roach grins. "Excellent, we'll take this evidence to Juno. By this time tomorrow, the whole world's going to know what the Sentry government's been doing. We're going to bring that wall down once and for all! Humans for Unity!"

Everyone cheers. *Everyone apart from me.*

35
ASH

DAD, SIGUR AND I STAND around the Sun Altar on top of an old church overlooking the Legion ghetto, watching the hazy sun rise over the city. In the distance, on the Sentry side of the wall, I can already hear the din of factories starting up, of laborers heading to work.

Dad's face is tilted to the gray skies, his eyes shut in a quiet prayer. He looks both haunted and relieved, in hell and at peace. Everything I'm feeling. The cremation was quick; all that remains of Mom is dust and ash.

I look toward the Boundary Wall and hope Evangeline's all right. I wish I'd handled things better with her. *Where did she go?* I doubt she'll stay in Black City. Maybe she'll go to one of the other Darkling ghettos out west?

The Legion guards are back on the wall, although they're not at their usual posts. They've congregated around each other, talking animatedly. They're still angry; there are talks of an uprising.

"What's going to happen now?" I ask.

Sigur's gold mask turns to me. "We will go public with this

information. I hope it will be the ammunition we need to stop Rose's Law from passing. There are Darkling sympathizers out there, and this might just be what we need to spur them into action." He looks at the pale dawn sun. "I feel there is a change coming, Ash. This might've turned out to be a blessing in disguise. The Darklings will rise again."

"What will happen to the Emissary when the truth gets out?" I ask.

"Purian Rose will have her punished," Sigur says. "He will have no choice but to make an example of her in order to deflect attention away from himself. That is his way."

"Won't people work out that he was involved in the plot?" I say.

"They may have their suspicions, but they have no evidence. Not yet. I am determined to find it," Sigur says.

"Why doesn't the Emissary just tell the truth and say Rose put her up to it?" I say.

"Because she'll want to protect her daughters," Dad replies.

Panic suddenly surges in me. "But Natalie knows everything! What will happen to her if Rose finds out?"

"He'll execute her," Sigur says nonchalantly.

"*What?* Why didn't you tell me she was in danger?" I turn to Dad. "I've got to go."

He grabs my hand, holding me back, concern etched in his eyes.

"Dad, please. You know I have to protect her. You would've done the same thing for Mom."

He releases my hand. "Be careful."

I rush toward the boat that will take me back to the Boundary Wall, letting my heart guide me to the one thing it wants: *Natalie.*

36

NATALIE

BEETLE'S AUNT HAS GATHERED hundreds of Humans for Unity protesters in the town square. All I can see is an ocean of angry faces and countless placards being thrust into the air, with the slogans NO BOUNDARIES and ONE CITY UNITED written on them. Behind me, the school's ancient clock tower chimes nine o'clock, letting us know it's time to start class, but I'm in no hurry to get inside. To my left, the three crosses cast long shadows across the people in the town square, a stark reminder of Purian Rose's power. But this doesn't seem to be scaring anyone today. We're just too mad.

Above us, dark gray clouds roll in, threatening rain at any minute.

Roach is on her megaphone, commanding everyone's attention. All this is being filmed by Juno Jones and several other news crews who caught wind of the story. Even SBN news is here, watching with morbid curiosity. They're not reporting anything. How can you spin a story when your beloved government has been caught red-handed killing children with infected Haze?

This morning, Humans for Unity hacked into the digital screens across the city and leaked the CCTV footage of Kurt giving Mr. Tubs the Golden Haze. It was followed by a report by Juno, who revealed the plot to infect the Darklings with Wrath and unleash them on the school, as confirmed by an "anonymous inside source"—better known as Natalie Buchanan to her friends.

Ten minutes after the broadcast, Purian Rose was on SBN news denying he had anything to do with it and firmly putting the blame on my mother, calling her "a dangerously unstable woman with her own political agenda."

Shortly afterward, Kurt had "mysteriously disappeared," and my mother and Polly had gone into hiding with Craven.

I bite my lip, suddenly panicked, frightened that I've done the wrong thing. What's going to happen to Mother? To me and Polly? But it's too late to go back now. Whatever happens, I'll have to live with the consequences of it.

The Legion guards on the Boundary Wall are agitated. Occasionally they howl and beat their chests at the Sentry guardsman patrolling the damaged part of the wall. The tension makes the air thick like soup.

I wait on the school steps with Beetle and Day, handing out Humans for Unity flyers to the students. I idly scratch the wound on my leg, where the Darkling child bit me last night.

"I'm not sure I want to be an Emissary anymore. I don't want to end up like your mother," Day says to me as we pass a flyer to a boy walking into the school.

"You won't. You'd never allow yourself to become Purian Rose's puppet," I reply. "This country needs people like you. It's the only hope we have of things ever changing for the better."

Day smiles at me.

"Say 'No' to Rose's Law," Beetle says through burned lips, thrusting a flyer at a girl. She takes it with interest. Every day he gets a little better. He should really be in bed, but he insisted on coming today to support his aunt.

Since the wall was blown up two days ago, I've noticed a shift in people's mood. They're more willing to listen now that they've seen the truth for themselves.

Gregory heads up the stairs, wearing his full Tracker uniform, including the sword, and glowers at us. "It's illegal to hand out flyers on school property."

I look daggers at him, disgusted at how he can show his face around me after he killed Ash's mother. He yanks the flyers out of my hands and tosses them into the air before storming into the school. The flyers scatter to the ground in a rain of pink confetti. I bend over to pick them up, and that's when I feel it. The soft, rhythmic beat of another heart beside mine.

Ash is standing at the bottom of the steps, watching me. His black hair stirs in the breeze, whipping across his beautiful face. He smiles. It's such a small gesture, but it means so much. *I'm forgiven.* I fly down the stairs to meet him and almost fling my arms around his neck, when I remember the television cameras nearby. I can't hold him, not here, not now, when the whole country is watching. It's heartbreaking. We stand a respectful distance apart from each other, so we don't raise suspicion.

His eyes widen with alarm when he sees my face: the swollen lips, the bruised cheeks, the purpled eyes.

"What happened?" he demands.

"Sebastian," I say simply.

"He tried to rape her," Beetle says as he meets us at the bottom of the steps, followed by Day.

"I'm going to kill him." Ash's whole body is shaking with rage.

"Natalie, go inside," Day says suddenly.

"Why?" I ask. Then I see him.

Sebastian.

He climbs out of the black carriage that's just rolled into the town square. Sebastian's wearing his Tracker uniform, a gleaming sword strapped over his shoulder. There's a black-and-blue bruise around his right eye where I smashed him with the jewelry box. He looks hungover and squints against the sunlight. *Good. I hope he's been puking his guts up all night.* He barks some orders at the guards, then heads over to Beetle's aunt, seizing the megaphone from her. Her freckled face turns deep red with anger.

"Protests are now illegal! You are to leave the town square immediately," he orders.

"Since when did we lose the right to free speech?" Roach shouts, and the TV cameras turn on her. "Is that your plan? First muzzle the Darklings, then us? Are you planning on putting everyone behind that wall?"

"I won't ask you again. Leave the square immediately!" he says.

"Or what?"

He smashes the hilt of his sword into her face. Roach hits the ground, injured but not dead, her blood spilling over the cobbles just like the twin-blood boy's.

"Roach!" Beetle cries.

Fury crosses Ash's face, his nostrils flaring as he looks at the blood splashed on the ground.

Sebastian raises his sword, ready to strike her again.

"Get the fragg away from her, you son of a bitch!" Ash calls out to Sebastian. "You won't hurt anyone else ever!"

"Who's going to stop me?" Sebastian taunts. *"You?"*

The Legion guards on the wall begin to aggressively thump their chests, the sound like the beat of war drums, making everyone cower. Everyone except Sebastian.

The humans look at the guards and then at Ash.

My heart pauses, waiting.

A few wise people flee just before Ash gives a faint nod.

One by one, the Legion guards leap off the wall, black shadows against the stormy skies, their dark robes billowing like wings behind them. The protesters start to scream and scatter as the Darklings land in the square behind Ash.

"Guards!" Sebastian yells.

The Sentry guards hurriedly regroup around him.

The TV cameras continue to film it all.

Ash and Sebastian stare across the plaza at each other in a silent standoff, waiting for someone to strike first . . .

37

ASH

"HOW MUCH BLOOD has to be spilled before enough is enough?" I say.

Black storm clouds gather overhead, casting shadows across the square.

I think of Tom and Jana, the twin-blood boy, my mother. *Natalie.* How many more people have to suffer? I can't turn a blind eye anymore. It's time for action, even if it means war.

"I won't let you push us around anymore," I say, tearing off my copper ID bracelet and throwing it on the ground by Sebastian's feet. "This ends right here, right now."

Sebastian draws his sword, and the Legion guards bare their fangs.

"Ash, *please*. Don't do this," Natalie begs.

She looks desperately at me, her golden hair catching the wind, revealing the dark bruising on her face. My fangs flood with venom. I'll never let him harm her or anyone else ever again.

The first drops of rain begin to fall.

"Don't start a fight you're going to lose," Sebastian jeers.

Beetle comes to stand beside me, a hand over his injured stomach. He's never been afraid of a fight. Day takes his hand. Roach is the next to join our line, blood dripping down her face, along with several dozen people from Humans for Unity.

The raindrops start to fall faster, faster.

"You're still outnumbered," Sebastian says.

The school doors bang open, and there's a clamor of footsteps as hundreds of students and teachers file out into the plaza. Most stand beside me.

"One city united!" some chant.

"Down with the Sentry!" others yell.

The rest of the students join Sebastian. Gregory catches my eye as he moves past me. The image of him standing over my mom's bleeding body flashes in my head. He gives me a satisfied grin, his hand curling around his sword, clearly thinking the same thing.

Rage burns through me.

This ends today.

I won't be a victim anymore.

TV cameras pan between the two warring sides.

"What are you and your friends going to do, *nipper*?" Sebastian taunts.

There's a crack of thunder, and the rain clouds burst.

I charge.

Sebastian is caught off guard, not expecting me to finally take a stand. He doesn't have time to raise his sword before I'm on top of him. We crash to the ground, and the sword falls out of his hand, landing beside us.

It's the cue to fight that everyone has been waiting for. All hell breaks loose.

"Death to the Darklings!" Gregory yells.

"No boundaries!" Beetle shouts. "One city united!"

Others cry out, "Fight!" at the top of their lungs as the two sides surge toward each other. They clash in the middle of the square, in a cacophony of noise.

Sebastian and I roll across the cobbles, fists flying.

"I'm going to fragging kill you!" I yell.

Tom, Jana, Chris, Mom, Natalie. Their names keep ringing in my head, spurring me on.

I smash my fist into Sebastian's face, knocking out his front tooth. Startled, he momentarily loses his grip on me, and I manage to pin him down.

To our left, a Sentry guard takes a swing at Beetle, but Roach intercepts him and tackles the man to the ground.

"Don't mess with my kid!" she screams.

Sebastian spits blood in my face. "I'm going to make sure that whore Natalie suffers for what she's done," he says.

My poison sacs flood with venom, and I reveal my fangs.

Sebastian grasps for his abandoned sword beside us. I tilt back my head, ready to sink my fangs into his throat and—

"Ash!"

My head whips around at the sound of Natalie's voice.

Gregory has one arm around her waist, while the other is holding the blade of his sword up to her throat.

My heart stops.

"Get away from Sebastian, or I'll slit her throat," he says.

I release Sebastian, rolling off him. He clambers to his feet, staggering away like a coward.

"Let her go, Gregory," I say.

"Gladly," he says.

He thrusts her at me, and we tumble to the ground. Natalie lets out a shocked cry as her head smashes against the cobbles.

Intense, raw anger at Gregory bursts through me. My whole body shakes with it. First he killed my mother, and now he's threatening Natalie? I'm going to kill him.

Gregory raises his weapon, a murderous look in his eyes.

"This is for Chris!" he yells.

There's a clap of thunder.

Natalie and I reach out for Sebastian's discarded sword at the same time.

There's a glint of metal, a moment of resistance before a gruesome *pop!* as the blade of Sebastian's sword cuts through Gregory's flesh. The rusty smell of blood stings my nostrils.

I release my grip, and the sword clatters to the cobblestones.

Gregory stares down at the dark red stain that's started to form on his scarlet jacket. There's a look of confusion on his face, like he's trying to work out how the blood got there. He takes two rasping gasps of air before crashing to the ground, dead.

His lifeless body lies between me and Natalie, Sebastian's sword by my feet.

I look at Natalie, who is staring down at her hands in horror. They're covered in hot, sticky blood, as are mine.

The truth of the situation crashes over me.

Gregory is dead.

He's a Tracker.

Killing a Tracker is a capital crime, and the whole thing has just been caught on national TV.

38
NATALIE

🪶 **"WHAT DO YOU THINK** you're playing at?" Mother demands, slamming my signed confession on the metal table in front of me.

The interrogation room is narrow and cramped, the walls covered in sheets of aluminum, giving the impression I'm inside an anchovy tin. My wrists and ankles are shackled, and I've been dressed in a simple knee-length gray dress, the uniform of all female prisoners in Black City jail. My feet are bare and cold. The way the table's shadow falls over my feet reminds me of Gregory's blood, spilling across the ground. I swallow a dry lump in my throat. All my nightmares have been about him this past week, since Ash and I were arrested.

Mother's wearing the same style of gray dress, and it's strange seeing her out of her luxurious clothes. She was arrested and put on trial within forty-eight hours of the Golden Haze plot being exposed and is now awaiting her sentencing. Purian Rose isn't wasting any time over this; he wants the matter closed. She managed to bribe a guard to let her visit me today.

"What's happened to Polly?" I ask her.

"Don't change the subject," she says, but then relents. "She's fine. Martha has taken her to a safe house while I arrange to have her sent to Centrum to live with a few of my associates."

Polly. She must be so scared without me or Mother around.

In the corner of the room, a small CCTV camera watches us, the red light blinking. I chew on my bottom lip, drawing blood, frightened and trying desperately not to be. Outside the interrogation room, I can hear the din of the rest of the prison: the industrial sounds of the work rehabilitation rooms, the rattle of chains, the shouts of the male and female inmates.

Somewhere out there is Ash. The last I saw of him, he was being dragged into the men's wing by several Sentry guards, his face bloodied and bruised where they'd beaten him up.

"Why are you trying to protect him? He's a *nipper*," Mother says.

She looks even thinner than normal, like a stick insect, all sharp edges and bones.

"Don't call him that," I say.

She paces up and down the room, running a hand over her black hair. "I just don't understand, Natalie. After everything I've done to protect you, how you could just throw it all away for some Darkling boy?"

"I wasn't going to let him get punished for Gregory's death," I say.

Mother laughs coldly. "How very noble of you. You do understand that he confessed to the crime?"

"So did I." I indicate the sheet of paper on the table. "And I won't retract my confession, if that's what you're hoping I'll do. They can only charge one of us with Gregory's death, and that person's going to be me."

I sound a lot braver than I feel. The last thing I want is to go to court and be convicted, but I have to stay strong to protect Ash. I briefly wonder how they'll execute me. Will I be hanged? Crucified? Shot? My hands begin to shake, my resolve weakening. I think of Ash. He's who I'm doing this for. He has to live and continue the fight to free the Darklings. His life is more important than mine. Humans for Unity and the Darklings need him.

"Do you really think Purian Rose will let one of you go unpunished if you've both confessed to killing that boy?" Mother says. "He wants the pair of you dead."

"He has to. The law's the law—two people can't be convicted for the same crime," I say. The law of joint enterprise was abolished during the war to prevent military and government officials being charged with war crimes if another member of their group committed an atrocity. Until then, they would have all been held equally accountable. "So unless he intends to change the law, which won't go down well, considering how angry people are at the Sentry government right now, he'll have to play along," I finish.

I hope I'm right; otherwise, Ash and I will both die.

The guard bangs on the door.

"Time's up," he yells.

My stomach leaps into my mouth at the thought this might be the last time we meet.

"What's going to happen to you?" I ask her.

"Purian Rose will probably send me to his 'rehabilitation center' in Centrum," she says.

"What's that? Like a jail for rich people?"

"Something like that," she says. "It's where he sends people for a special sort of punishment."

A shudder runs down my spine. "Mother—"

"Don't worry about me, Natalie. I can take care of myself."

To my surprise, Mother takes my hand.

"Please retract your confession. I don't want you to die," she says, her normally cold blue eyes filled with worry. A strand of black hair has come loose from her tight bun. I fixate on that small imperfection, finding it oddly comforting.

"Natalie . . ."

I stare down at our hands.

"I'm sorry, Mother," I whisper. "I just can't. I love him. You must know how that feels."

"I loved your father very much. I wish I'd been able to save him. I'll never forgive myself for letting him die. You're just like your father, you know that?" she says, and there's real tenderness in her voice, like she's proud of this fact.

"Why did you cheat on Father if you loved him so much?" I ask. It's not an accusation, I'm just curious.

She sighs. "Because I'm an ambitious woman and a damned fool. I didn't deserve your father. He was too good for me."

The door opens, and a guard marches in. He hauls Mother to her feet.

"I love you, my darling girl," she cries as she's dragged out of the room, her pale skinny legs kicking at the guard, her hair unraveling in glorious waves around her face. She's never looked more beautiful or wild. That's the woman I'm going to remember as my mother.

The door slams behind her and tears spill down my cheeks.

"I love you too, Mom," I whisper.

It's the first time I've ever said those words out loud. I never truly felt it before, and now she's gone. At least she's going to live. I don't know what this "rehabilitation center" is, but it sounds better than my fate. That gives me some small comfort.

I look up at the red light flickering on the CCTV camera. Somewhere in the prison, another camera is watching Ash. I don't want him going to trial, but he'd never retract his confession.

All I can do is hope I'm convicted. That's the only way to save him.

39

ASH

THE COURTROOM IS HEAVING with people, and there are thousands more protesters waiting outside. Through the arched windows, placards bob up and down like jack-in-the-boxes. They all say one of two things: NATALIE BUCHANAN GUILTY! or ASH FISHER GUILTY! Opinion is really divided about which one of us should be punished for Gregory's death. Beetle, Roach and Day are sitting in the viewing gallery. They give me a thumbs-up.

I scan the room, in search of Natalie. It's been two agonizing weeks since our arrest, the longest fourteen days of my life. The only thing that's been keeping me going has been the thought of seeing her again. My heart yanks when I spot her sitting at a table to the right of the courtroom, looking pale and thin in a loose gray dress. Her hands and feet are shackled, like mine.

Our eyes lock across the room, and I exhale. It feels like I've been holding my breath for weeks. A slight smile plays on her lips. We mustn't look too happy to see each other: no one except our closest friends and family know our true relationship, and I intend to keep it that way. We don't want to add "race traitor" to our sentence; we'd both be executed for sure, then. At least at the moment, there's a fifty-fifty chance Natalie will walk free.

Please, Lord. Don't let her die. Not for me.

It hurts me to see that she has no one with her. Then again, I heard her mother had been sent to a rehabilitation center in Centrum. It just makes me more determined to clear Natalie's name and get her out of here so she can take care of Polly.

I lightly place a hand over my heart. It's a small gesture, but she knows what it means: I love you, I miss you, I'm with you.

The prison guard tugs my arm, dragging me toward my table on the left-hand side of the courtroom, opposite Natalie's. Dad is already waiting for me. He gives me a quick hug and tries to hide his shock at my bony frame.

"Where's Sigur?" I ask Dad.

"He wasn't allowed to come," Dad replies. "He tried—"

"It's okay. You're here. That's all that matters."

An usher enters the room. "All rise."

I suddenly feel sick with nerves. This is really happening. It's not some horrible nightmare. I'm actually on trial for Gregory Thompson's murder.

A side door opens, and the Quorum of Three enters, all dressed in their ceremonial red robes. The courtroom falls silent as the judges take their seats on the platform in the center of the room. The first judge is a female Darkling with a long, serious face. I vaguely recognize her from my first visit to the Legion. I think her name is Logan Henrikk. She's here because of me; since I'm a twin-blood, there has to be a Darkling on the Quorum to ensure a fair ruling.

The second judge is a willowy man with thinning hair, thick glasses and a hooked nose. He takes the seat on the right.

Finally, the third judge—a man in his late fifties, with immaculate dark brown hair and a strong chin—takes his seat between the two other judges, indicating his seniority over them. I've seen his face in the newspapers: his name's Benedict Knox. He was also lead judge at the Emissary's trial.

Natalie glances at me. She recognizes him too. My heart sinks. If he convicted the Emissary, he might be prejudiced against Natalie and vote to convict her.

"Be seated," the usher says.

I can't concentrate as he takes us through what's going to happen today, but that's okay. Dad's already explained it to me. The way it works is our Criminal Justice Bureau—the CJB—compiles a list of witnesses to bring to the Quorum of Three. The judges then call the witnesses in turn to hear their testimony. The Quorum of Three acts as both defense and prosecution to the accused, and they can ask questions to validate or discredit a witness's statement. After all the witnesses have spoken and all the evidence has been reviewed, the Quorum of Three cast their votes and make their verdict.

The system is rife with corruption, as it all boils down to the list of witnesses the CJB puts forward to the Quorum. Usually the witnesses go in favor of whoever paid them the most money: the victim's family or the accused. During any other circumstance, I'd be certain of being convicted, but given the fact that Natalie is the Emissary's daughter, and she's not the most popular person with Purian Rose right now, there's a chance he's gotten involved and swayed the witnesses in my favor. I just have to hope he wants to see me convicted of Gregory's murder more than her.

The lead judge, Benedict Knox, speaks, his deep voice commanding the courtroom.

"The Quorum wishes to hear the testimony of Natalie Buchanan."

Natalie steps up to the witness stand beside the judges' platform, her delicate hands balled into fists. She's shaking all over. I want to hold her, kiss her, tell her everything will be all right. All she has to do is tell them I killed Gregory, and she'll be free.

She sits down, her eyes flicking toward mine.

Say I did it, I silently plead.

"Please relate your version of the events," Logan Henrikk says. Her voice is surprisingly light and lyrical for such a serious-looking woman.

Natalie licks her lips. She briefly tells them about my fight with Sebastian, how he'd dropped his sword during the brawl, and how Gregory had held a blade to her throat.

"Then what happened?" Logan asks.

"Gregory threw me on the ground beside Ash. He raised his sword, and it was clear he intended to kill us. So I grabbed Sebastian's abandoned sword and thrust it into Gregory's chest." Natalie looks at me. "I did it. I killed Gregory Thompson."

There are excited murmurs from the viewing galley.

Day hides her face against Beetle's chest.

I shake my head. Natalie must know this isn't what I wanted.

Natalie steps down from the witness stand and returns to her table, not looking at me.

I'm called up next.

The judges turn their gaze on me as I take my seat. The courtroom is so silent, I can hear my heart beating. It's funny, when you consider a month ago I didn't even have a heartbeat. I glance at Dad. His eyes plead with me to tell them Natalie did it.

"In your own words, tell us what happened," the willowy male judge says.

I recount the events. The details are the same as Natalie's version of the incident, up until the bit where Gregory is killed.

"He lifted his sword over his head," I say. "I knew he was going to kill me—he hated me, and I hated him. He murdered my mother."

That gets a few gasps from the spectators.

"Go on," Benedict Knox says.

"I knew this was my best chance to get my revenge on Gregory for what he did," I say. "So I grabbed Sebastian's sword and stabbed Gregory Thompson."

Natalie shuts her eyes. A tear rolls down her cheek.

I'm dismissed. Logan Henrikk frowns at me as I pass her. I'm not doing the Darkling cause much good being on trial for murdering a Tracker, but I don't care. All that's important is saving Natalie.

Several other witnesses who were in the square that day are called to the stand. They tell their own versions of events. Some say I did it, the others say Natalie. It goes on like this all morning, until we're all exhausted listening to the testimonies. It's clear from their tense postures that the judges are starting to get frustrated. How can you determine someone's guilt when half the people must be lying?

So far it's fifty-fifty between me and Natalie.

"How many witnesses left?" Benedict Knox asks the usher.

"Two, your honor," he says.

I take a deep breath.

This is it. The end of the trial. Whatever the next two witnesses say will determine our fate.

"Bring in the next witness," Benedict Knox calls.

The room goes silent as Sebastian enters the room, dressed in his Tracker uniform. A shiny gold medal in the shape of a rose gleams on his chest. *So he got that promotion after all.*

He gives me an icy look as he walks by.

I smile, allowing myself the first flicker of hope that Natalie is going to be spared.

The people in the viewing gallery lean forward in their seats, eager to hear what he's going to say. The word of a high-ranking official, like a Head Tracker, holds a lot of sway in court. If it comes to deadlock with the witnesses' testimonies, what he says now could swing the Quorum's vote.

Sebastian sits down. The Quorum runs through a few preliminary questions before asking him to give his testimony. I don't dare breathe.

"This creature"—he points to me—"charged at me. We fought and during the struggle I was disarmed. Ash Fisher intended to kill me. I only got away because of Gregory Thompson. He saved my life. He was a hero."

"Did you see what happened next?" Logan Henrikk asks.

He wasn't even there! He ran away like a coward.

Sebastian turns to look at me. A dark emotion blazes across his face.

This is it, his chance to get his revenge on me.

A cold smile plays across his lips.

Sebastian looks back at the judges.

"I saw Natalie Buchanan pick up my sword and run it through Gregory Thompson's chest," he says.

"No!" I yell. "I did it, I did it!"

There are startled noises from the viewing gallery.

I look at Natalie. She seems almost . . . *happy.*

I bury my face in my hands. *No, no, no, no, no.*

Sebastian is dismissed.

He got his revenge, all right. He knew hurting Natalie was the only way to get back at me.

"Silence!" the usher calls out, and the courtroom falls silent once more.

"Call in the final witness," Benedict Knox says.

I sink down in my seat, knowing it's over. All the color seems to drain from the world. The girl I love is going to be executed.

Natalie, I'm sorry.

She smiles softly at me, holding my gaze across the courtroom. She places a hand over her heart, mirroring my earlier gesture.

I love you, she's saying to me.

I swallow a painful lump in my throat.

The door swings open, and Juno Jones walks in. Her expression is blank, although there are dark circles under her eyes like she hasn't slept in days. She doesn't look at either me or Natalie as she takes her seat in the witness stand. She's dressed in a tight, corseted blouse and leather trousers, her fiery red hair tied back into a slick ponytail. She's carrying a small black bag.

"Miss Jones, you were at the town square at the time of the riot?" Logan Henrikk asks.

"Yes, I was there filming a report for Black City News," she replies.

"Did you see the attack on Gregory Thompson?" Benedict says.

Juno shakes her head. "No, I was too far away. But we caught the incident on camera."

My heart starts to tremble.

Juno produces a digital disk from her bag and hands it to the usher, who sets up a screen and digital disk player. The lights are turned out as the screen flickers to life. All around me I can see the glimmering eyes of the audience, watching enraptured.

Footage of the riot bursts onto the screen. There are screams and shouts, and it's like I'm back there, smelling the blood, the fear. Caught in the middle of the fighting are me and Sebastian. We're on the ground, throwing punches at each other. Gregory holds a blade up to Natalie's throat.

My heart freezes as I watch the events unfold:

I release Sebastian, and he runs out of sight, leaving his sword.

Gregory throws Natalie to the ground.

He raises his weapon.

Natalie and I reach for Sebastian's sword at the same time.

The cameraman is knocked to the ground.

Gregory yells off screen, "This is for Chris!"

For a moment, all you can see are people's feet running in front of the lens.

There's a clap of thunder.

The camera is lifted to reveal—

Me.

Holding the bloodied sword.

I drop the weapon to the ground.

The room erupts into life as people talk excitedly to each other. The film is all the evidence they need. It's clear: I'm guilty.

Guilty.

The word rattles around my head.

Guilty.

Dad sinks his head into his hands.

Guilty.

Logan Henrikk can't look at me.

"I'm so sorry, Ash," Juno says to me as she's led out of the room.

"No, he didn't do it! It was me! I killed Gregory, please believe me!" Natalie screams, tears spilling down her cheeks.

I can't believe she's still trying to protect me when she knows it's over.

I catch her eye.

"It's okay," I mouth to her. "This is what I wanted." I hold her gaze for as long as I dare, trying to let her know that everything is going to be okay. I feel the echo of her heart beating in unison with mine.

I hear snippets of conversation from the people in the viewing gallery.

"Sebastian wasn't even there when it happened . . ."

"He ran away . . ."

"He was lying about Natalie . . ."

The Quorum of Three is quick to cast their votes.

"All rise," the usher says.

I get to my feet, feeling suddenly unsteady on my legs.

Benedict Knox turns to me.

"Ash Fisher, it is the belief of this court that you are guilty of the murder of Gregory Thompson. You are hereby sentenced to death by crucifixion."

40

NATALIE

"YOU HAVE TO COME OUT at some point," Day says from the other side of the bedroom door.

I'm lying on a small camp bed that's been crammed into Day's bedroom. After the trial, Michael and Sumrina kindly let me and Polly stay with them until we could sort out a new living arrangement, now that Mother has been sent to the rehabilitation center in Centrum and we've been kicked out of the Sentry HQ. Her contacts in Centrum said they'd take care of us, but there's no way I can leave Black City when it's my only connection to Ash. Martha's living with Roach and Beetle, as there's no room for her here.

The Darkling bite on my leg itches, and I scratch the scab, welcoming the pain. I want to feel something, anything, other than this grief.

Day enters our bedroom, dressed in an elegant black corset dress that I lent her for the occasion. Beetle lingers by the doorway. He's wearing a dark green suit. *Green.* Ash's favorite color.

"You have to come," Day says.

I hide my head under my pillow again so they can't see my

tears. I can't face what's about to happen. I've already witnessed the death of one person I love, the night my father was killed. I'm not going through that again. I just can't.

"He wants to see you," Day says softly, lifting the pillow off my head.

"I'm not going," I say.

"This is the last chance you'll get to see him. Do you really want to miss that?" Day says.

"I can't watch him die, I just can't. I love him so much, I—" My throat constricts with grief.

Day hugs me as I cry.

"I can't go, I just can't," I say after a moment.

The door quietly shuts behind them.

"Is Natalie coming?" I hear MJ ask Day.

"No," she says. "Come on, we'll be late."

The front door slams a minute later.

I sit up and throw the pillow across the room, letting out a loud yell, screaming until my lungs are raw.

Footsteps shuffle toward my room, and the door inches open. Polly enters, wearing her pink slippers and robe. She sits on the edge of my bed. She plays with the ends of her glossy black hair, and looks at me with wolfish eyes just like her father's, Purian Rose. Except her eyes are full of concern, not hate.

"I'm sorry. I didn't mean to disturb you," I say.

She gives me a look that asks, *Are you okay?*

My lip trembles as more tears threaten. "They're going to kill him."

She hesitates, then stretches out a pale hand and lays it on top of mine. I let the tears fall. After a few minutes, I wipe my eyes, my tears all spent, and Polly gives me something close to a smile.

I glance at the clock on the dresser. It's eleven thirty. Ash is being executed at noon. We go to the kitchen, and I turn on the portable TV, flicking through the channels, trying to find some news coverage. Polly squeezes my hand comfortingly.

I stop on Black City News, which is running a live feed of the execution. Juno stands in the center of the crowd, her face solemn. Thousands of people are in the town square, many thousands more filling the side streets. Juno speaks to the camera, but I don't hear what she's saying; I've turned the TV onto mute. I don't want to listen to them talking about Ash like they have any idea who he is. To some he's a traitor to the state for killing a Tracker, the worst kind of criminal. To others he's a martyr, a hero to all Darklings. *That's not who he is to me.* To me he's just the beautiful boy I met under the bridge. The boy who kissed me on the rooftops. The boy who loved me. The boy who's saving my life.

I shut my eyes.

Gregory holds a sword to my throat. The blade cuts into my skin.

"Let her go, Gregory," Ash says.

"Gladly," he replies.

He throws me to the ground beside Ash.

Gregory raises his sword, a murderous look in his hazel eyes. He's going to kill Ash—I know it. I have to stop him!

"This is for Chris!"

There's a crack of thunder.

I reach out for Sebastian's sword at the same time as Ash.

My hand reaches the weapon first. I thrust upward.

There's a flash of steel, a moment of resistance before the blade cuts through Gregory's flesh. Hot blood splashes over my hands. Oh, God . . . oh, God, what have I done?

I turn to Ash.

He grabs the sword from me.

It's dripping with Gregory's blood.

He drops the weapon to the ground.

That's what really happened the day of the riot. I killed Gregory to save the boy I love. Juno's film just missed that one crucial moment, because the cameraman fell to the ground.

And now Ash is going to be executed to save me. How can I let him die alone, when he's being crucified because of me? He needs me!

"I need to go!" I say to Polly.

I grab my coat and rush out of the house.

Please let there be time!

41
ASH

"RUMMY!" I SAY.

Dad lays his cards facedown on my prison bed. "Good game."

"I think you're letting me win," I say with forced cheer.

"Now, why would I do that?" he replies, equally forced.

They let Dad come into the cell to keep me company in my last hours. Sigur briefly met with me this morning, which was a pleasant surprise. He must've pulled a lot of strings and bribed even more guards to get to see me. I lean back against the wall. Harry, a lanky prison guard with short ginger hair, approaches my cell carrying a tray. There's a single pint glass of fresh blood on it. My last meal. He gives me a genuine smile.

"You have visitors," he says, placing the tray on my bed.

My stomach fills with butterflies at the tiny flicker of hope it's Natalie. I smooth down my unruly hair. It swirls and stubbornly sticks out at mad angles again.

Day and Beetle appear by the bars. They don't look me in the eye as I glance past them.

"Did they let her come?"

They don't say anything.

Dad takes my hand and gives it a squeeze. I wipe my eyes with my shirt sleeve; the prison-regulation material is thick and scratchy against my skin.

Beetle passes me a newspaper through the bars. I scan the headlines. It's mostly stories about the upcoming ballot for Rose's Law and how people are looking to vote against it, disgusted at the treatment of the Darklings in the Legion and angry at the Sentry government over the Golden Haze plot. People can't turn a blind eye anymore. Humans for Unity's membership has gone up fivefold since, and change is in the air. I just won't be there to see it.

I turn the page, and my own face stares back up at me. "Hey, I made page three."

No one laughs.

"Wow, why the long faces, everyone? It's like someone's died," I say.

"Ash," Dad says.

Day bursts into tears, and Beetle cradles her. I try not to look, jealousy burning through me. I wish Natalie were here.

"We should go to our seats," Beetles says quietly a minute later. "We'll be directly in front of you. You won't miss us, bro."

I hold Beetle's hand through the bars, and he clings to it for a long moment.

"I love you, man. You're my best friend," he whispers.

"Hey, you're gonna make Day jealous if you don't let go," I tease.

Day attempts a laugh, tears streaming down her caramel cheeks. She holds on to Beetle as they leave. He manages to make it halfway down the corridor before he starts to cry himself.

Dad kneels down on the hard concrete floor, and I join him

in prayer. I try to believe the words about walking with the Lord in the Eternal Garden, or at least make them sound convincing for my dad. I know he needs this, probably more than me. I don't think there's a place in his heaven for people like me, but I'm okay with that. Maybe I'll go to the Elsewhere, with Mom?

I'm so grateful Dad's here with me right now. For years I wondered what it would be like to have a Darkling father, someone who truly "understood me," but I realize now that man was with me the whole time. I couldn't have asked for a better dad. He took care of me, he loved me, and he never abandoned me no matter how tough life got. I'm proud to be his son.

I hear Harry's keys jangling against his leg before I see him. He hovers by the cell door.

"It's time, kid," he says solemnly.

Dad helps me to my feet. I lean on him a little. My shoulders feel heavy all of a sudden, my feet leaden. The sunlight shines through the small window of my cell. It prickles my skin, but it's a good sensation, reminding me I'm still alive.

"Nice day for it," I say to Harry.

He grimaces.

"You need to leave your clothes here," Harry says, looking at his feet.

I shrug off the shirt and trousers, grateful to get the itchy material off my skin. I don't mind it so much. There's a freedom to being so exposed. I like how the cool air feels against my bare skin. I sling the linen modesty cloth around my waist; there will be children watching, after all.

"Any messages?" I ask hopefully.

"Sorry, kid."

I have to accept she's not coming. I'm never going to see her again. I turn to Dad, who is busy picking up my discarded clothes and folding them into a neat pile on my bed, delaying the inevitable. A tear trickles down his craggy face.

"Dad?"

He hurriedly wipes his eyes. "Yes?"

"Take care of Natalie for me. I've asked Sigur to do the same. Make sure she's all right. Promise me."

"I promise," he says.

His sad eyes trace the contours of my face, and I know he's trying to commit me to memory. I can't believe how much he's suffered, first losing Mom and now me. This is worse for him in some ways. No one should have to see his kid die.

Harry holds out the shackles.

"Just a second." I turn over Dad's discarded playing cards on my bed, and I grin. So he *did* let me win!

Harry shackles my wrists and ankles and leads me down the long corridor to the awaiting transfer truck outside. Faceless prisoners poke their fingers between the bars of their cells as I pass, reminding me I'm not alone. Dad walks a few paces behind me, silent. The time for prayers is over.

42

NATALIE

I PUSH THROUGH the bustling streets, desperate to get to the town square nearly a mile away. It's already taken me ten minutes to get this far, and I'm barely around the corner from Day's house. I'm not going to make it, and panic starts to set in. There has to be a better way.

Ash's execution is being broadcast live on the large monitors on the rooftops. He's brought into the town square. He looks scared, although he's trying to hide it. His sparkling black eyes flick toward the camera, and it's like he's looking directly at me.

"Ash, I'm coming!" I cry out.

People around me turn and their eyes widen. They all start pointing and chattering.

"It's her—"

A shadow crosses the sky. People around me scream. A pair of iridescent wings sparkles in the sunlight above me, and I see it's Sigur. He swoops down into the crowd and people flee. I cower away from him.

"I am not going to hurt you," he says.

I laugh. "You tried to kill me."

"Yes, I did," he says. "But that's not why I'm here now."

"Why are you here?"

"My one regret in life is not having been with Annora when she passed into the Elsewhere. Ash needs you, now more than ever."

"How did you know where I was?" I ask.

"Ash requested I keep watch over you," he says. "When you were not at your home in the Rise, I came looking for you."

He stretches out a pale hand.

"Come, I will take you to him," he says.

I look at Sigur, then at the crowd blocking my path. I'll never get to Ash in time, not on foot. This could be my only chance. I take Sigur's hand, and he pulls me into his arms so we're chest-to-chest. His wings flap once, twice, then we're soaring above the city. The cold air whips against my face, and I wrap my legs around his long, lean torso, clinging on for dear life, adrenaline pumping through my veins as he goes higher and higher toward the clouds. I dig my fingernails into his icy-cold flesh. I've never flown Darkling Airways before, and it's terrifying. I keep thinking he's going to drop me, either by accident or deliberately.

My heart pulses erratically as we near the town square, but I soon realize it's not my heartbeat I'm feeling—it's Ash's.

43

ASH

THE ROAR OF THE CROWD is deafening as I step into the town square. I nearly throw up when I see the crosses, three of them, lined up near the wall. Which one will be mine?

Dad takes a seat beside Beetle and Day in the viewers' box next to the school, where the rest of the VIPs are watching. I know they don't want to watch this, but they're here for me. I check the faces in the crowd for Natalie, but she's not there, although I do spot her housemaid, Martha, swathed in black cloth, hiding toward the back. I give her a weak smile, although I doubt she can see it, grateful that she's taking such a risk to be here.

The Legion guards stand on the Boundary Wall, and I expect Sigur to be with them, but he's not. A figure in a blue cloak darts down one of the side streets, and for a second, I wonder if it was Evangeline, but I'm sure she's long gone from the city. It's probably a good thing; I don't want her watching me die and knowing there's one less twin-blood in the world, that our kind is one step closer to extinction.

A strong breeze stirs the ash on the charred buildings

surrounding us, scattering black flakes into the air. I feel like I'm inside a giant snow globe. It's really quite beautiful; why had I never noticed before?

Sebastian approaches the middle cross, dressed in his ceremonial Tracker uniform, complete with glistening medals. I notice the golden rose medal is gone. I'm guessing he was demoted after he was caught "lying" on the stand. That gives me a small amount of pleasure, especially since he was actually telling the truth. He looks older than his years, with his shaved head and rose tattoo and the harsh, stony expression on his face. Behind him a minister is dousing the cross with acacia solution. The fumes make my throat constrict. So I guess that's my cross.

Sebastian's green eyes flick up to mine and hold steady. "It'll make it much faster, nipper. Not that you deserve it," he explains.

By "it" he means my death. They obviously want it to be quick for the audience at home watching on TV—nothing's more boring than a slow execution.

"I'm going to relish watching you die," he says. "I hope you burn like the others."

I try to swallow, but my throat feels scratchy and dry. I remember Jana bursting into flames, and I just pray that doesn't happen to me. My allergy to acacia isn't quite as severe as full-blooded Darklings, although in these quantities, I'm not so certain. But maybe I'll get lucky. I laugh at the ridiculousness of that thought. *Lucky?* I'm about to be crucified.

Sebastian turns to the audience and reads from the scroll, his voice carrying across the town square.

"For the crime of killing the Tracker Gregory Thompson, Ash Fisher has been sentenced to death by crucifixion."

My knees feel like jelly, and it takes all my willpower to stay standing. I don't want to look scared, not with the whole country watching. I need to be brave. I can do this.

I wish Natalie were here.

The audience starts to murmur, getting agitated, reminding me of the last execution that took place here. I glance at the school's clock tower to my right. One minute until midday; the show's about to start. I peer over at the viewers' stand again. Dad's holding back the tears, trying to be brave for me. Beetle's hugging Day. Sigur still isn't here, and neither is Natalie, but I've given up hope she'll come.

The clock chimes.

One . . .

The crowd falls silent.

Two . . .

My shackles are removed.

Three . . .

The cross is lowered.

Four . . .

I'm bound to the cross with silver chains. They scorch my skin.

Five . . .

The acacia fumes fill my lungs, choking me.

Six . . .

The minister says a prayer over my body.

Seven . . .

The guards grab the ropes holding the cross.

Eight . . .

They winch the cross upright.

Nine . . .

My heart pounds loudly.

Ten . . .

Dad's sobs ring out across the square.

Eleven . . .

An image of Natalie flashes across my mind.

Twelve . . .

"Stop!"

44
NATALIE

SIGUR LANDS IN THE CENTER of the crowd, and sets me down.

"Stop!" I shout again.

"Natalie!" Ash calls out, his voice cracked.

The crowd parts as I run toward him. Sebastian cuts me off, grabbing hold of me, but Sigur growls at him, baring his long fangs. Sebastian lets me go.

I reach the cross and stare up at Ash. He's gasping for breath, his skin already blistering from the acacia wood. Tendrils of smoke start to caress his arms, turning them black.

"Ash, I love you!" I call up to him.

His skin crackles. The acrid smell of scorched flesh stings my nostrils as flames start to flicker out of his burned skin.

I stretch up a hand and touch his feet—it's the only part of him I can reach. My heartbeat speeds up as his gets weaker by the second.

"Fight, Ash! Please, I love you. Don't leave me."

The flames suddenly erupt, tearing down his arms, engulfing them in a raging ball of fire. Vivid yellows, oranges and reds melt into one another as the flames coil and twist into the sky, fanned by the wind. They blaze like wings, terrifying, beautiful. A phoenix rising from the ashes.

The crowd gasps.

Ash struggles for breath, his chest shuddering with the effort. His glittering black eyes flick down and catch mine. Flakes of ash float around him.

"I love you," I say again. "I—"

45

ASH

✦ **"–NEED YOU, PLEASE,** don't leave me, Ash," she says to me.

The molten heat along my arms is like a thousand daggers slashing my skin, making every nerve ending explode in agonizing pain. The sensation is almost unbearable as the flesh is scorched from my bones, but still I refuse to cry out.

"I love you!" she says again.

She shouldn't be saying this, not here, not in front of the cameras. She follows my gaze and glowers at the TV reporters.

"You heard me! I love him. I love a Darkling, and I'm not ashamed of it. We haven't done anything wrong."

"Natalie, no . . . ," I stammer.

Agitated murmurs spread across the crowd. This isn't the same crowd that watched Jana and Tom die. These people have seen too much over the past weeks; their eyes have been opened. One by one, they turn their backs to the stage, refusing to watch me die just like the Legion guards did during Jana and Tom's execution. *Purian Rose has the power to execute us, but he doesn't have the power to make us watch.* It's a small but significant protest against the Sentry. I know that somewhere in Centrum, Purian Rose is having a seizure.

Natalie touches my feet again, sending a jolt of electricity through my body, which sparks my heart. It beats more powerfully for a second, joining the rhythm of her own.

I take an unsteady breath. The air barely reaches the walls of my lungs. I can feel them closing up.

No, not yet. I'm not ready.

"It's all right, Ash," Natalie whispers. "I'm here. You're not alone."

Our hearts flutter in unison, and I focus on their comforting beat.

Then a sensation like winter's chill creeps up my legs and into my stomach as Death's grip takes hold.

It's happening.

"Ash, no," she sobs.

"It's okay," I say.

Ba-boom ba-boom ba-boom.

"Stay with me," she says.

Ba-boom ba-boom.

I rasp for air, but my lungs remain hollow.

"I love you, Ash."

Ice fills my heart.

Ba-boom . . .

46
NATALIE

I KNOW he's dead. His heart's stopped beating inside me. I lower my hand.

Sebastian indicates for the guards to douse the flames. He looks at me with cold, cruel eyes, a malicious grin on his lips. He got what he wanted. Ash is dead. The people in the crowd turn to face the stage once more, wanting to watch Ash being removed from the cross. I stare directly at the nearest television camera.

"This is a message for Purian Rose. I've realized something about you. You've terrorized us, turned families against each other, made us fear the Darklings, and why? Because without fear, you have no power," I say. "Well, I'm not afraid of you anymore. I will not live my life in fear. From this day on, you have no power over me or the people of this city."

Beetle stands up and pumps his fist in the air, shouting, "No fear, no power. No fear, no power!"

His protest call is picked up by the rest of Humans for Unity, then the crowd, before sweeping across the whole city like rolling thunder, thousands of voices chanting in unison, "NO FEAR, NO POWER! NO FEAR, NO POWER!"

I face the cross again. Ash is now lying on the ground, his arms and chest blackened and burned. Sebastian roughly peels the silver chains off Ash's wrists and ankles; the metal has seared into his skin, and I cover my mouth to stifle a sob.

Minister Fisher, Day, Beetle and Sigur join me. We all watch in silence as Minister Fisher cradles his son's body and lovingly strokes Ash's hair. I expect it to stir and coil around his father's fingers like it normally would, but it remains still. Everything about Ash is so still.

Day and Beetle hug me. I choke back the tears.

"We should get him ready for So'Kamor," Sigur says softly.

Ash's dad shakes his head. "He's having a human burial. It's how he was raised."

Sigur doesn't argue.

Sebastian hovers nearby. A wooden cart has been brought over to take Ash's body away.

"I want to say good-bye first," I say.

Minister Fisher gently lays the body back on the ground, and I kneel beside Ash. I move a strand of hair away from his closed eyes. He looks so peaceful, you'd almost think he was asleep.

"So begins my heart, so begins our life, everlasting," I whisper.

I press my lips against his.

A powerful jolt of electricity passes between us. It zings through my body, straight into my heart.

I gasp.

A second, faint heartbeat joins mine.

I grip Ash's hands, and the heartbeat gets stronger.

Please, please, please.

His eyes flicker open.

EPILOGUE
ASH

NATALIE SLINGS MY BANDAGED ARM around her shoulder and supports me as we leave the hospital. The burns will never fully heal, even with my Darkling regenerative abilities; I will always bear the scars of my execution. It's been a few days since my "miraculous resurrection," as the papers are calling it. Of course, Natalie and I know the truth. When my heart stopped beating, it triggered the dormant *Trypanosoma vampirum* in my blood, which kept enough oxygen circulating in my body to stop brain death. Then when Natalie kissed me, it reactivated my heart and . . . well, here I am.

Obviously, the truth isn't anywhere near as impressive as the idea of me being a messiah. "Black Phoenix," they're calling me. The boy who rose from the ashes.

I'm not comfortable being the poster boy for Humans for Unity's revolution, but at least I'm not doing it alone. After her televised outburst at my execution, Humans for Unity asked Natalie to be their ambassador. They've united with the Legion Liberation Front to defend the city, as we all know a reprisal is coming after the whole city cried out, "No fear, no power!"

I was worried Natalie would be arrested after admitting to everyone that she loved me, but that hasn't happened. The Sentry government must be afraid of what will happen if they arrest either of us; it could be the spark that ignites civil war.

We walk down City End toward my house, following the line of the Boundary Wall. I don't feel any desire to be on the other side. Everything I have, everything I need, is right beside me now.

Of course, I'd like to see the wall come down one day. There's still a division between the citizens about whether or not we should reintegrate the Darklings into society. Maybe in time it will happen, but it's going to take a lot of persuading. We can't go back to the way things were before the war, with Darklings feeding on humans and poisoning them with Haze. We have to come up with a new solution that satisfies everyone. Things won't happen overnight, as Roach keeps reminding me.

Until then, I'm going to spend as much time with Natalie as possible. It's not every day you get a second chance at life, and a second chance to be with the girl you love.

She smiles up at me, her beautiful blue eyes sparkling.

"I love you," I say to her.

"I love you too," she says, then kisses me.

We enter the Rise and find my house nestled between the two sleeping giants as always, except I know immediately something's wrong. The church looks like it's been shaken by an earthquake—pews are upturned, holy books are scattered across the floor, windows are smashed.

"What's going on?" I say.

Dad looks anxiously at the Sentry guards surrounding him.

"You have a visitor, in your room," he says.

It's only then that I notice one of the guards has a dagger

poised at Dad's neck. He shakes his head ever so slightly. I try to act casual, but panic is setting in. Natalie takes my hand, and we head to the bell tower.

"Who do you think it is?" she whispers.

I shrug. "Only one way to find out."

I push open the door.

Purian Rose stands by the arched window, sinking his teeth into a bloodred, heart-shaped apple from the trees in the cemetery. Golden juice drips down his bottom lip, and he wipes it away with his thumb, turning his cold gray eyes toward us.

"I hope you don't mind, but I helped myself to an apple from your orchard," he says to me in his strange, light voice.

"That's fine. They're all filled with maggots anyway," I say.

Purian Rose gives us a waxy smile. Up close, his skin has a very unpleasant, stretched look about it, and his hair is unnaturally black. He places the half-eaten apple carefully on the window ledge.

"What do you want?" I ask.

He sighs wearily. "I feel like I've been neglecting my spiritual duties as of late. It's time I started paying a little more attention to my flock."

His threat is clear: he's keeping tabs on me and my dad.

"If you do anything to hurt my father . . . ," I snarl.

Purian Rose gives me a chilling smile. "Well, that all depends on you now, doesn't it?"

"How so?"

"I must confess, even as a religious man, I was quite surprised to see you rise from the dead. Some would say it was a sign from His Mighty." He narrows his eyes at me. "I, of course, know better. Your resurrection was no miracle. You can die as easily as anyone else."

"What's your point? Other than you need to find a more effective way to execute me next time?" I say.

"My point, Mr. Fisher, is I don't like false prophets. Especially ones that threaten to unbalance the society I have spent the past fifteen years so carefully building."

"Then why don't you just arrest me or kill me?" I say. "I'm right here. Now's your chance."

"There is nothing I would love more than to slice your throat, but all that will do is make a martyr of you and give Humans for Unity more ammunition to rally support against me." He looks out the window at Black City. "And arresting you will just arouse anger. The people of this city seem to have taken you into their hearts. I hear they call you Black Phoenix? The 'boy who rose from the ashes.'"

My heart freezes.

Purian Rose turns his gaze back to us. "No, Mr. Fisher, I intend to break you down, piece by piece, until you're begging me to kill you."

He sweeps out of the room, and the door bangs shut behind him.

The instant he's gone, Natalie buries her face against my chest. She's trembling all over. I hold her until she's calmed down. "Why can't he just leave us alone?" she eventually says.

"He's trying to frighten us," I say, releasing her. "But threatening me isn't going to work. If it's a fight he wants, then that's what he's going to get."

I stride over to the arched window, where Purian Rose had been just moments before. I look out across the city, at the burned ruins of the houses bombed during the war, at the thousands of white crosses decorating the city cemetery, at the familiar black line on the horizon separating us from the Darklings.

The half-eaten apple rests on my window ledge, a dark reminder of his threats. I toss it out of the window.

Natalie takes my hand, and my heart squeezes.

"I thought the war was over," she says sadly.

I press my lips against hers in response. Her body is warm against mine, and I hold her like this for a while. I don't have the heart to tell her what I'm really thinking:

The war's only just begun.

ACKNOWLEDGMENTS

Writing a book is a very strange, solitary process. For endless months it's just you and your characters, and the real world around you becomes the fantasy. Then one miraculous day you look up from your computer, blink against the light, and realize you have a story ready to show to the world. However, getting the story from your laptop to the bookstores requires a whole team of extraordinary people, and while it's going to be hard saying "thank you" to all of you, I'm going to give it a try!

Firstly, I would like to acknowledge the two women who have made this dream possible: Ayesha Pande and Stacey Barney, my agent and editor. Ayesha, thank you for seeing past the vampires and taking a risk on my story. You are the best agent an author could ever ask for. Stacey, thank you for being my own personal cheerleader and for bringing the world "Nash"! You have made every step of this process an absolute joy and I am truly blessed to be working with you. My eternal gratitude must also go to Team Putnam: Cindy Howle, Ana Deboo, Linda McCarthy, Erin Dempsey, and Elyse K. Marshall. Thank you for your faith and hard work.

A big thank you also goes to my friends and extended family, Kate Richards, Vernon Richards, Edward Selley, Colin Brown, Angela Cranfield, Emma Cash, Robyn Bateman, Natalie Banyard, Emma Watkins, Lucy Paget, Faye Thomassen, Temi Lafinhan-Etti and Peter Gibb. You have offered me encouragement, support and wine in equal measure, all of which was desperately needed.

There are, of course, some very special people I must thank, for you have played a key role in every stage of this journey.

Mum and Pops, thank you for your love and guidance, I hope I've made you proud. Ruth Morris and Carol Armstrong, thank you for your unwavering faith in me. Genny Brown, you were my muse for Evangeline, I hope she does you justice. Amelia Vincent, thank you for the stunning author photo, your talents never cease to amaze me. Kirsty Morris Selley, thank you for your "very good" words of advice (ha ha), I owe you that holiday in Fiji. Tracy Buchanan, thank you for your friendship, brilliant insight, and for the endless hours you have dedicated to reading *Black City*. We did it, kiddo! And finally, a very special thank you to my Blood Mate, Rob Richards, for always believing in me, even in my darkest days, and for being so patient and understanding when I was lost in the burning streets of Black City. Without you there is nothing.